Wizardborn

BOOK 3 OF THE RUNELORDS

DAVID FARLAND

SIMON & SCHUSTER

London • New York • Sydney • Tokyo • Singapore • Toronto • Dublin

A VIACOM COMPANY

First published in Great Britain by Earthlight, 2001
This edition published by Earthlight, 2002
An imprint of Simon & Schuster UK Ltd
A Viacom Company

1 3 5 7 9 8 6 4 2

Simon & Schuster UK Ltd
Africa House
64–78 Kingsway
London WC2B 6AH

www.simonsays.co.uk

Simon & Schuster Australia
Sydney

A CIP catalogue record for this book is available
from the British Library

ISBN 0-671-02950-9

Typeset by Palimpsest Book Production Limited,
Polmont, Stirlingshire
Printed and bound in Great Britain by
Omnia Books Ltd, Glasgow

Beldinook
Lonnock
Brackston
Mystarria
Swamps of Callonbee
Castle Higham
Tal Rimmon
Aravelle
Twynhaven
Tal Dur
Isle of Thwinn
Blue Tower
Gorane
River Donnestgree
Balington
Courts of Tide
Aneuve
Carris
Borenson's Trail
Castle Crayden
Feldonshire
Village of Hay
Castle Fels
Old Ferecia
Alcair Mountains
Fenraven
Batenne
Indhopal
Keep Haberd
Inkarra

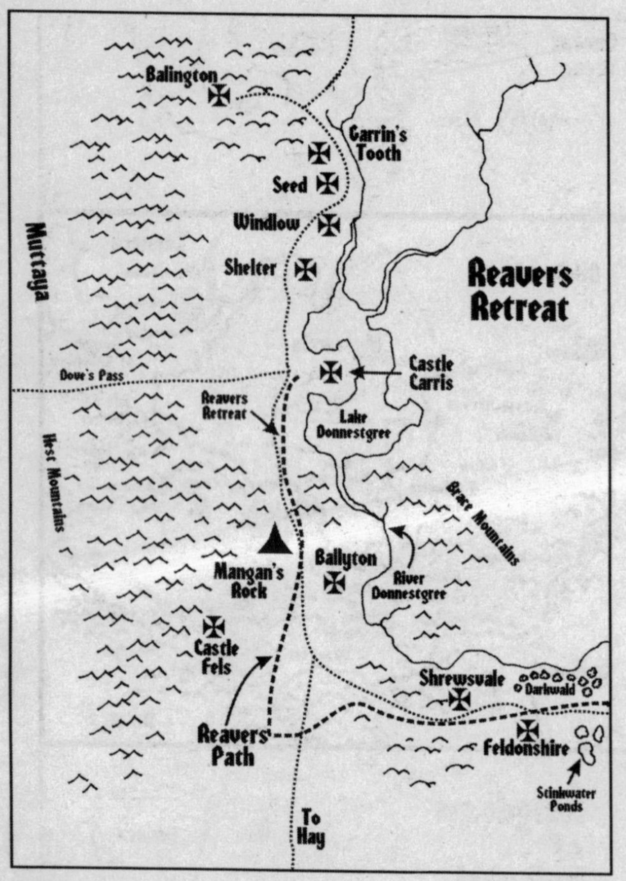
Balington
Garrin's
Tooth
Seed
Windlow
Shelter
Muttaya
Reavers
Retreat
Castle
Carris
Dove's Pass
Reavers
Retreat
Lake
Donnestgree
Hest Mountains
Brace Mountains
Mangan's
Rock
Ballyton
River
Donnestgree
Castle
Fels
Shrewsvale
Darkwald
Reavers
Path
Feldonshire
Stinkwater
Ponds
To
Hay

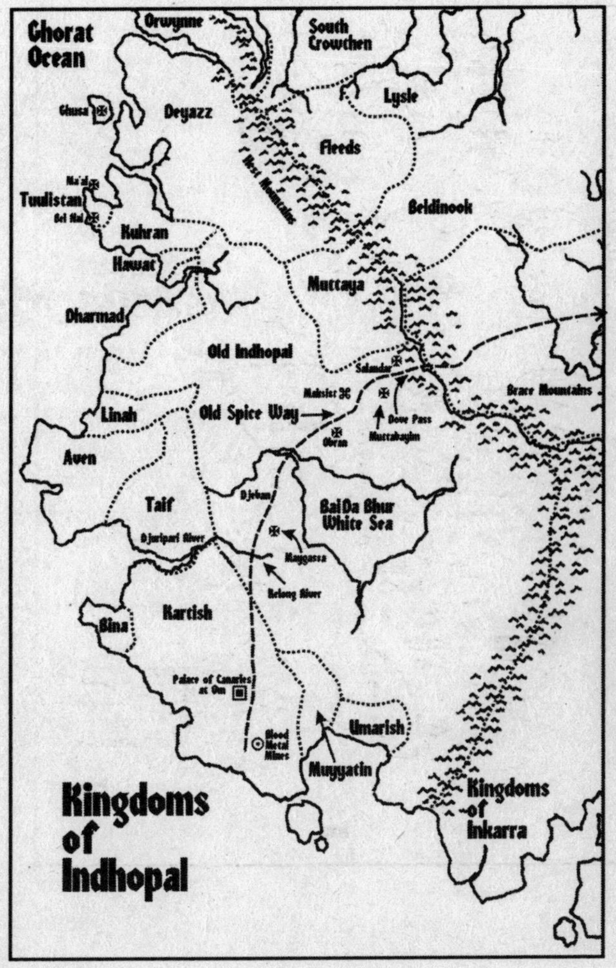

Ghorat Ocean
Orwynne
South Crowchen
Lysle
Deyazz
Ghusa
Fleeds
West Mountains
Ma'al
Tuulistan
Beldinook
Kuhran
Hawat
Muttaya
Dharmad
Old Indhopal
Salandar
Brace Mountains
Dove Pass
Linah
Old Spice Way
Aven
Taif
Djeban
Bai Da Bhur White Sea
Djuripari River
Maygassa
Belong River
Kartish
Bina
Palace of Canaries at Oun
Blood Metal Mines
Umarish
Muyyatin
Kingdoms of Inkarra
Kingdoms of Indhopal

Book 9:

Day 2 in the Month of Leaves
The Calm Between the Storms

PROLOGUE

King Croener of Toom bought dung for his fields
to make the grass grow deeper.
But found one day that warlords in gray
would sell their sons far cheaper.
– Nursery rhyme alluding to King Croenert, who hired cheap mercenaries from Internook to attack Lonnock

In South Crowthen, King Anders had been entertaining guests all night. Among them were a dozen fierce old warlords from Internook with their sealskin capes and horned helms. They'd sailed on ships painted like gray serpents, and the smell of sea salt clung to their beards. Their silver-gold hair was braided; the wind had burned their faces raw.

Any lord but Anders would have sought to buy their loyalty. The warlords of Internook were notoriously cheap. But Anders offered no money. He merely filled them with strong drink and tales of the treachery of Gaborn Val Orden. By midnight they were pounding the wooden tables with their silver mugs and shouting for the boy's head. To celebrate their decision, they killed a hog and dyed their braids in blood, then painted their faces with streaks of green, yellow, and blue. They'd take no pay for their services other than the spoils of war.

Thus Anders bought half a million berserkers for less than a steel eagle's worth of strong ale and a butchered sow.

Beside them the Lady Vars, counselor to the queen of Ashoven, watched how Anders worked the warlords of Internook with a reticent smile. She refused to touch even so much as a drop of his best wine. She was a stately woman, beautiful and cunning, with flashing gray eyes the color of slate.

As he urged the warlords to dispatch their ships to the Courts of Tide, the lady's lips drew tight. Though she tried to appear neutral, King Anders knew she stood against him. Too bad for her.

When the warlords were deep in their cups, she excused herself from the dining hall and fled to the docks, no doubt feeling lucky to escape his realm with her life.

But a storm was brewing in the northern sea, Anders knew. He went out into the night as Lady Vars sneaked away. From the door Anders could hear the wind singing over the whitecaps miles away, could smell ice in the salt air.

The beast within Anders stirred at the smell. It circled in his breast like a restless dog. It suggested a small spell that would insure that wind would fill the sails of the counselor's ship, and urge it onto the rocks. Ashoven's queen would no doubt find the wreckage on her own shores. She'd mourn her faithful servant's demise, never knowing what warning she might have borne. Perhaps the next counselor Ashoven sent would be more malleable.

Anders stood for a long moment in the doorway of his keep, listening to the receding hooves of Lady Vars's horse as it clattered over the cobblestone streets of the King's Way. Thick clouds above sealed out the starlight, and the fires in the Great Hall cast a ruddy glow over the cold ground that seemed to strain to reach beyond the courtyard. Somewhere down in the city below, a dog began howling. Soon, a dozen others joined their voices with its keen wail.

He whispered the spell that would end the lady's life, and sauntered back to the Great Hall.

A one-eyed warlord named Olmarg watched him knowingly as he returned. Olmarg stood at the table, leaning over the roast pig. He cut an ear off, chewed as he said in his thick accent, 'She bolted on us.'

'That she did,' Anders admitted. Several other lords looked up through bleary eyes, too far gone into their cups to bother speaking.

'Knew she would,' Olmarg said. 'The ladies of Ashoven have no taste for wine or war. Now that she's gone, we won't have to bridle our tongues.'

Anders smiled. Moments ago he'd have thought the man too drunk to think clearly. 'Agreed.'

Olmarg said, 'Our land is a cold one, and in the long winters our young men have naught to do but huddle in the keeps under the furs, warming the wenches. For as long as our old ones remember, we've sold our sons to the highest bidder. We need this war. We need the plunder. More than that, we need lands in the south. And there's none better to be had than Mystarria. Do you really think we can hold it?'

'With ease,' Anders assured him. 'Gaborn's forces are in disarray. There is far more than just the reavers for them to worry about. When Raj Ahten destroyed the Blue Tower, he killed the vast majority of Gaborn's Dedicates. Though there be many lords in Mystarria, few of them are Runelords.'

He let those last words settle in. Mystarria was the wealthiest land in all of Rofehavan. For centuries it had been well protected from attack – not because its castles were unassailable, but because of the number and power of its Runelords. With their wealth, the kings of Mystarria bought forcibles – magical branding irons – made from rare blood metal. They used those forcibles to draw attributes such as strength and wit from their subjects.

Now, without Runelords to protect it, the kingdom of Mystarria would not be able to stand for long.

'What's more,' Anders continued, 'to your advantage the

vast majority of Gaborn's troops have marched west to drive Raj Ahten from Mystarria's borders. They'll have a tough job of it, for Raj Ahten has leveled several castles, and his men hold the strongest that remain. Gaborn will have to spend his men to dislodge Raj Ahten. With any luck the two are already at one another's throats. That leaves Gaborn open to attack. Now it has turned his coastline into Gaborn's soft underbelly.'

'Soft, maybe,' Olmarg said, 'but soft enough? Mystarria's men outnumber mine twenty to one. Even with your help –'

'Not mine alone,' Anders assured him. 'Beldinook will sweep down from the north, joining us.'

'Beldinook?' Olmarg asked, as if he could not have hoped for such a boon. Beldinook was the second-largest kingdom in all of Rofehavan. 'You think old King Lowicker will bestir himself?'

'Lowicker is dead,' Anders said with finality.

At that, several warlords gasped. 'How?' 'When?' One fellow downed a mug in the old king's honor.

'I got word only hours ago,' Anders said. 'Lowicker was murdered today by Gaborn's own hand. His fat daughter is a surly creature. Surely she will demand vengeance.'

'Poor girl,' Olmarg said. 'I have a grandson who is not particular about his women. Perhaps I should send him to court her.'

'I was thinking of sending my own son,' Anders grinned.

Olmarg lifted a mug of ale in salute. 'May the better man win.'

At that, Anders's wife got up from her seat at the dinner table and shot Anders a glare. She'd been so quiet the past hour, he'd all but forgotten her. 'I'm going to bed,' she said. 'I can see that you gentlemen will be up all night trying to figure out how to carve up the world.' She lifted the skirts of her gown and walked stiffly upstairs to the tower loft.

There was a long silence. A burning log shifted in the hearth, as it steadily crumbled to ash.

'Carve up the world . . .' Olmarg intoned. 'I like the sound of that!' The unabashed greed that shone from his single eye gave Anders pause. There was a hardness to his jaw that Anders found chilling. Olmarg was a man without compunction. 'And Gaborn is still a pup. It will take little to strike off his head. If I can take a few key cities quickly – dispatch his remaining Dedicates . . . Gaborn would never be able to retaliate.'

Anders smiled. Olmarg saw things more clearly with one eye than most could with two. The world was turning upside down. It was true that Gaborn's forces vastly outnumbered them, but without Runelords to lead those forces . . .

'Carving up the world should not be so hard to do,' Anders said. 'I want very little of it. I'll take Heredon.' Olmarg raised a single white brow. Heredon was no small bit of land, but Olmarg would have no use for it. 'Lowicker's daughter will want western Mystarria, along with her vengeance. You'll want the coast –'

'Everything within two hundred miles of shore,' Olmarg said sternly.

'A hundred and fifty,' Anders suggested. 'We'll want to leave something for the others.'

'Others?'

'I've received missives from Alnick, Eyremoth, and Toom. Dignitaries should be arriving shortly.'

'A hundred and fifty,' Olmarg agreed. But he added thoughtfully, 'On the other hand, what if Gaborn is indeed the Earth King? Could we stand against him? Dare we stand against him?'

Anders laughed, a sound that reverberated through the quiet room and made the hounds sleeping before the hearth look up in anticipation. 'He's nothing but a fraud.'

But Anders tried to sound more self-assured than he felt.

The beast hidden within him lent him special powers. Anders could hear voices carried on the wind from far off. He could smell scents from miles away. But even the wind took time to travel.

He wished that he knew how Gaborn's battle with Raj Ahten had ended. But that news would not come until later.

At Anders's assertion, Olmarg sliced off the pig's other ear, and they celebrated.

With these affairs of state in hand, Anders climbed to the towers of his castle early in the night, found his wife brushing her hair in the bedchamber.

Her back was stiff with anger. As he crossed the room, she followed him with her eyes, raking her brush through her hair as if she were trying to rid it of burrs.

'You seem upset,' Anders said casually. He knew the source of her anger, sought to divert her attention. 'You should be overjoyed. The news was good today. I have done little but worry about the reavers rumored to be in North Crowthen, and now we hear that my cousin has driven them back.'

'A lucky shot with a ballista killed their fell mage,' his wife groused, 'and the sorceresses beneath her harvested her brain. There is nothing to rejoice about. They'll return in greater numbers.'

'Yes,' Anders said, as if to put a bright face on it. 'But next time, my cousin will be better prepared for them.'

His wife did not speak for a long moment. He let the tension build, until the words broke from her. 'Why do you lower yourself like this? We should have no dealings with barbarians from Internook. They stink of filth and whale blubber. And those tales you told –'

'Were all true,' King Anders countered.

'True?' she demanded. 'You accused Gaborn Val Orden of murdering King Lowicker?'

'Lowicker defied Gaborn today, denied him passage through

Beldinook, just as I said. For that, Gaborn slaughtered him as a man would slaughter a steer.'

'How do you know this? There have been no couriers!' she shouted. 'There could not have been: I'd have seen them.'

Years of neglecting his physical needs had left Anders thin and starved-looking, a rag of a man. He drew himself up, trying to appear authoritative. 'I received the message privately.' He did not want to argue the point. His wife knew full well that she had been at the table with him all afternoon. Had even a private messenger arrived, she'd have seen him.

Her mouth twisted in anger. He could tell that she was about to rail at him. He silently gathered a spell, reached out and touched her lips with his forefinger. 'Shhh . . .' he said. 'A message did come by word of mouth only. No doubt we will hear more details by morning.'

A confused expression slowly spread across her face. She said no more. He expected that she would be incapable of gathering her thoughts enough to speak for an hour, at least.

He opened the door to the balcony, stepped out. The stars blazed above the dark rooftops of the city. The night watchmen walked along the castle walls just below his keep. A cool wind whipped about, racing south. In the distance, he heard the shriek of a burrow owl. Otherwise the city was dead.

King Anders lifted his face, felt the wind glide through his hair, and basked in the sensation. In his breast, the beast stirred. He knew what the beast wanted. Anders whispered, 'Kill Gaborn's queen, lest her son become greater even than his father.'

He blew out softly, so that the sound of his words might drift to far lands, adding a little more force to the rising storm.

Chapter One: TONGUES OF LIGHTNING

Truth is stronger than many armies, and the wicked shall fall before it.

– A proverb of the Ah'kellah

Night had fallen in earnest while the Brotherhood of the Wolf rode south, but when the warriors reached Carris there was light to see by. An inferno blazed in a stone tower, its roof and inner chambers incandescent, as if it were a giant torch. Watch fires licked the city walls.

Lightning split the night on the southern horizon, like the flickering tongue of a serpent that spoke words of thunder.

The riders let their horses race the last two miles, harnesses and armor jangling. Of the forty lords in the retinue, only three had brought lances. They rode point, lest they should come upon a reaver in the darkness.

Ash mingled with rain so that mud pummeled them from the sky with the weight of mercury. It oozed through Myrrima's cloak.

As the riders crested the hill above the Barrens Wall, the men around Myrrima gasped in amazement. 'See there!' one cried. He pointed to the yawning pit from which the world worm had risen. It looked like a small volcano – a cone two hundred yards across and three hundred high. Steam billowed from its crown.

Only fires lit the scene. Yet with the endowments of sight, smell, and hearing that Myrrima had recently taken, everything seemed preternaturally clear.

Myrrima had taken endowments only yesterday. She could still almost hear the yelps of pain from the pups as they gave their sight and hearing to her.

Myrrima's heart pounded. She wondered if the worm might still be about, but saw no sign of a worm trail. It had retreated into the hole from which it had sprung.

It was hard to comprehend the devastation, to try to imagine the battle that had taken place here. Gaborn had driven his troops to Carris, heeding the Earth's summons, believing that he would find the city besieged by Raj Ahten's troops. Instead he'd found Raj Ahten surrounded by a ghastly horde of reavers, trapped.

He'd used his newfound powers as Earth King to summon a world worm – a beast of legend – from the Earth's core to dislodge the reavers.

The aftermath of that battle would be sung for a thousand years, Myrrima felt sure. The carnage took her breath away.

To the south lay a field of dead reavers, enormous and black in the darkness, their wet carapaces gleaming in the wan light as if they were a plague of dead frogs. Men and women swarmed among them, torches in hand. The plains were terribly broken and uneven, pocked with thousands of burrows. Squads of troops armed with spears and battle-axes were searching every nook for live reavers. But not all of the people out there were warriors. Some were coming from the city to cart off the dead and wounded – mothers looking for sons, children hunting for parents.

A reaver suddenly lunged from a burrow three quarters of a mile away, and out on the plain screams arose with the blaring of warhorns. The reaver charged straight for a knot of foot-men. Knights on chargers galloped to intercept the monster.

'By my father's honor,' shouted one lord of Orwynne, 'there's still reavers about! This battle's not won yet!'

The lords spurred their mounts down to what was left of the Barrens Wall. Beneath its arch, beside a bonfire, a dozen footmen huddled beneath muddy capes with hands wrapped around their longspears.

'Halt!' they called as the lords approached. A couple of guards struggled up. They wore mismatched armor, marking them as Knights Equitable.

Their bright eyes reflected the firelight. Jubilantly their leader shouted, 'Most of the reavers are in a rout – fleeing south the way that they came. Skalbairn asks that any man who can bear a lance give chase with him! But there's still a few of the damned things holed up in their burrows, if you've a mind to fight here.'

'Skalbairn is chasing the horde in the dark? In the rain?' Sir Hoswell shouted. 'Is he mad?'

'The Earth King is with us, and no one can stand against us!' the guard shouted. 'If you've ever had a fancy to slay a reaver and win some glory, tonight's the night for it. Some simpleton from Silverdale killed a dozen on the city walls today with nothing more than a pickax. True men like you should do as well – or better.' His tone was challenging.

The guard raised a wineskin in salute. Myrrima saw that the man's eyes gleamed from more than mere jubilation. He was half drunk, reveling in the victory. Obviously Skalbairn's men didn't know that Gaborn could no longer warn his Chosen warriors of danger.

Even though they'd been Chosen only a few hours ago, Myrrima could see how these men were already becoming complacent. Why should they keep a close guard so long as the Earth King would warn them of danger?

Obviously, Skalbairn's men hadn't heard the latest. Gaborn had used his abilities to dislodge the reavers from Carris, but in the aftermath of the battle, he'd sought to use his gift to kill Raj Ahten.

For misusing those protective powers, the Earth had withdrawn them – including the ability to warn Gaborn's Chosen warriors of danger.

These men, blithely celebrating their victory, had no idea how much trouble they were in. The Earth had charged Gaborn to help 'Save a seed of mankind through the dark times to come.' Full night was not yet upon them.

Myrrima glanced right and left at the lords of the Brotherhood of the Wolf – sober men with hard faces. They'd come to fight, but hadn't bargained for such madness.

'I'll warn Paldane's men,' Sir Giles of Heredon offered.

'Wait,' Myrrima said. 'Are you sure that's wise? Who knows where the rumors might fly, how the tale might grow in its travels?'

'The Earth King warned us that he has lost his powers in order to save our lives,' Baron Tewkes of Orwynne said. 'He can't hide the truth, and we can't hide it for him.'

If she were to tell Gaborn's secret, Myrrima feared she might betray a man who had never unjustly sought to harm another. Yet if she withheld the news, innocent men would die. To tell was the lesser evil.

Sir Giles took leave of them and galloped toward Carris.

'The rest of us will need to warn Skalbairn,' Tewkes said. He dismounted for a moment, cinched his saddle for a fast ride. Others drew weapons, and more than one man brought out a stone to sharpen a lance or a warhammer.

Myrrima licked her lips. She wouldn't be riding south with the others tonight. Gaborn had said that she would find her wounded husband a third of a mile north of the city, near the great mound. But reavers were still hiding out on the field. She tried not to worry.

'Do you want me to come with you, milady?' a voice asked, startling her. Sir Hoswell's horse had sidled up to her, and he was bending near. 'To find your husband? I told you that if you ever need me, I'll be at your back.'

She could barely make out his face beneath his hood. Hoswell leaned close, as if expecting her to fall into his arms at the first sight of blood.

Hah! she thought. Maybe when the stars have all burned down to ashes!

He had tried to seduce her once. When she resisted his advances, he'd tried to force her. He'd apologized, but she still didn't trust him, even though she had enough endowments now that she knew he would never try to force her again.

'No,' she said. 'I'll go alone. Why don't you find some reavers to kill?'

'Very well,' Hoswell said. He drew his steel greatbow from its pack, began carefully to unwrap the oiled canvas that protected it from the rain.

'You'll fight with that?' she asked.

Hoswell shrugged. 'It's what I use best. A shot to the "sweet triangle" . . .'

Myrrima spurred her own mount away from the other lords, rode under the arch toward the largest knot of dead reavers. Borenson would have fallen in the thick of battle. She imagined that he would be there.

In the distance, she could hear others searching the battlefield, calling for loved ones. They shouted different names, but all were the self-same cry: 'I am alive: are you?'

'Borenson? Borenson!' she called.

She had no way to know how severe his wounds might be. If he lay trapped beneath a fallen reaver, she'd make light of it. If he was disemboweled, she'd stuff his guts in and nurse him back to health. She tried to steel herself for whatever she would find.

She imagined what she would say when she found him,

rehearsed a hundred variations of, 'I love you. I'm a warrior now, and I'm coming with you to Inkarra.'

He would object – perhaps on good grounds. She had only gained a little skill with a bow.

She would persuade him.

As Myrrima drew close to the fell mage's final battleground, she smelled the remnants of the monster's curses. Residual odors clung like a mist to the low ground.

Even two hours after the mage's death, the curses' effects were astonishing. 'Be blind,' a curse still whispered, and her sight dimmed. 'Be dry as dust'; sweat oozed from her pores. 'Rot, O thou child of man'; her stomach knotted and every scratch felt as if it might pucker into a festering wound.

She rode in the shadows of reaver corpses that loomed on every side. She gazed in awe at crystalline teeth like scythes. She caught movement from the corner of her eye. Her heart leapt in her throat to see a reaver's maw open.

She yanked her mount's reins to turn it back, but realized that the reaver did not hiss or move.

It was dead. Its maw merely creaked open as the monster cooled. Its muscles were contracting like a clam's as it dries in the sun.

Myrrima looked around. All of the reavers' mouths were opening by slow degrees.

The air seemed heavy. No katydid buzzed in a thicket. No wind sighed through the leaves of any trees, for the reavers had uprooted every plant.

'Borenson!' she shouted. She scanned the ground, hoping the reflected firelight might reveal the form of her husband buried beneath a layer of soot.

A trio of gree whipped past her head, wings squeaking as if in torment.

Through the tangled legs of a dead reaver, she glimpsed a flickering light, and suddenly she had the wild hope that Borenson had lit the fire.

She spurred her mount. Around a bonfire had gathered a crowd of warriors from Indhopal. Myrrima felt unnerved by them, even though today they'd fought beside her people against the reavers.

These were no ordinary warriors. They were dark nomads who wore black robes over their armor, as some symbol of status. Their headgear bore steel plates that fell down over the ears to protect the shoulders.

Nine of Raj Ahten's dead Invincibles lay before the fire. The nomads seemed to be preparing to consign the deceased to a funeral pyre.

Among the dead Invincibles lay a girl with dark hair, practically a child. She rested upon a riding robe of fine red cotton, embroidered with exquisite gold threads to form curlicues like the tendrils of vines. On her temple rode a thin silver crown that accentuated her dark skin.

She wore a sheer dress of lavender silk, and in her hand someone had placed a silver dagger.

Myrrima had come upon Saffira, Raj Ahten's dead wife. Gaborn had sent Myrrima's husband to fetch Saffira from Indhopal so that she might plead with him to cease his attacks on Gaborn's people. Gaborn could have searched the world and found no one better to sue for peace. Rumor said that Saffira had taken hundreds of endowments of glamour and voice. She would have been more alluring than any woman alive, would have spoken more eloquently.

Obviously Borenson had found Saffira and brought her to the siege at Carris. Now she lay dead, among a few Invincibles. Myrrima imagined that the Invincibles had been her royal escort, and suspected that her husband would be nearby.

The leader of the Indhopalese was immediately recognizable. Every eye in the crowd rested on him, and many nomad warriors knelt before him – some on one knee, some on two.

He sat atop a gray Imperial warhorse, glaring down at the dead, talking in an even, dangerous tone. His dark eyes glowed in the firelight as if he struggled to hold back tears of rage. On the right breast of his black robe he wore the emblem of Raj Ahten, the three-headed wolf in red. Above the wolves were golden owl's wings, and above them flew three stars.

His insignia identified him as more than an Invincible or even a captain of Invincibles.

At his feet, several men in black burnooses knelt on hands and knees. One answered him in a frightened voice.

Myrrima seemed to have wandered into a confrontation. She didn't want to have anything to do with it.

A tall Invincible came up from the shadows behind her, a man with a forked beard and ivory beads woven into his black hair. The firelight reflected from his dark eyes and golden nose ring.

He grinned at her, and Myrrima could not tell if it was meant as a seductive grin or a friendly greeting. He jutted his chin toward the Indhopalese leader. He whispered, 'You see? He Wuqaz Faharaqin, warlord of the Ah'kellah.'

The news struck through Myrrima like a lance. Even in Heredon she had heard those names. Among Raj Ahten's warriors, Wuqaz Faharaqin was one of the most powerful. And of all the desert tribes, the Ah'kellah were the most respected. They were judges and lawgivers of the desert, hired to settle disputes among tribes.

The fact that Wuqaz Faharaqin was angry did not bode well for the object of his wrath.

The Invincible reached up a hand clumsily, as if he seldom greeted in this manner. 'I am Akem.'

'What has happened here?' Myrrima asked.

'His nephew, Pashtuk, murdered today,' Akem said. 'Now he question witnesses.'

'Faharaqin's nephew murdered someone?'

'No, Pashtuk Faharaqin was murdered.' He nodded toward an ugly dead Invincible who lay, as if in a place of honor, next to Saffira. 'He was a captain among Invincibles, a man of great renown, like the others here.'

'Who killed him?' Myrrima asked.

'Raj Ahten.'

'Oh!' Myrrima breathed softly.

'Yes,' Akem said. 'One of slain live long enough to bear witness. He say, "Raj Ahten call to Invincibles after battle, and try to murder Earth King" – a man who his own cousin by virtue of marriage to Iome Vanisalaam Sylvarresta. To fight a cousin, this is a great evil. To kill one's own men, this is also evil.' He did not say it, but Myrrima could hear in his tone that Raj Ahten would have to pay.

'These men,' Akem indicated the kneeling Invincibles, 'found the dying witness.'

Wuqaz Faharaqin questioned the witnesses one by one. As he did, his eyes blazed brighter and brighter.

Derisive shouts arose from the crowd. One lord strode forward, pointing at the witnesses. Myrrima did not need Akem to translate. 'This man say the witness no good. Need more than one witness. He say Raj Ahten would not seek to kill Earth King.'

Myrrima could hardly restrain her rage. 'I saw it!'

Wuqaz Faharaqin growled at her outburst, asked a question in his native tongue. Akem looked up at Myrrima and translated, 'Please, to tell name?'

'Myrrima,' she said. 'Myrrima Borenson.'

Akem's eyes widened. A hush fell over the crowd as men whispered her name to one another. 'Yes,' Akem said, 'I thought so – the northern woman with the bow. You slew the Darkling Glory. We have all heard! We are honored.'

Myrrima felt astonished. News traveled fast. 'It was a lucky shot.'

'No,' Akem said. 'There is not so great luck in all the world, I think. You must tell your story.'

Myrrima nudged her mount closer to the bonfire so that she could speak to Wuqaz face-to-face.

'I was thirty miles north of here when Raj Ahten caught up to Gaborn. There was murder in the Wolf Lord's eyes, and he'd have killed Gaborn sure, if Binnesman's wylde had not stopped him. I put an arrow in Raj Ahten's knee myself, but Gaborn forbade me or anyone else to kill him.'

Akem translated. Wuqaz tried to listen impassively, but his eyes continued to blaze. He spoke and Akem translated. 'Can you prove that you saw this?'

Myrrima reached into her quiver, drew out the arrow with which she'd shot Raj Ahten. His blood lay black upon its iron tip. 'Here's the arrow. Have your trackers smell it. They'll know Raj Ahten's scent.'

Akem carried the arrow to Wuqaz. The warlord sniffed it curiously. Myrrima saw that he, too, was a Wolf Lord. He growled low in his throat, spat a few words in his own tongue, and raised the arrow for all to see. Other lords rode close, sniffed at the shaft.

'The smell of Raj Ahten is indeed upon this arrow,' Akem translated. 'His hand pulled the shaft free, and his blood stains its tip.'

'Tell Faharaqin that I want my arrow back,' Myrrima said. 'Someday I intend to use it to finish the job.'

Akem relayed her message, retrieved Myrrima's arrow. Wuqaz and his men had more questions about her encounter. They seemed baffled as to why Gaborn had spared Raj Ahten, a man who proved to be his enemy. Myrrima looked at the stern faces among the Ah'kellah, and remembered something she'd once heard: in some places in Indhopal, there is no word for 'mercy.' She explained that Gaborn, as Earth King, could not slay one who was Chosen. The Ah'kellah listened intently. They asked what had happened after the fight, where Raj Ahten had gone. She pointed southwest toward Indhopal.

At that, Wuqaz drew his saber from the scabbard at his back, whipped its curved blade overhead, and began shouting. His warhorse grew excited, fought him for control as it danced forward. It reared and pawed the air. Myrrima had to fight her own mount as it backed away.

The Ah'kellah all began to shout, waving swords and warhammers overhead.

'What will happen?' Myrrima asked.

'Raj Ahten did great abomination to attack Earth King. Such deed cannot go unpunished. Wuqaz say, "Raj Ahten has sided with reavers against own cousin, against own tribe." He say, "Raise Atwaba!"'

'What is that?'

'In ancient time, when king do wrong, witnesses raise Atwaba, "Cry for Vengeance." If people get angry, they kill king – maybe.'

Wuqaz Faharaqin spoke encouragingly to his men.

'He warn, "Raise cry loud in markets,"' Akem translated. 'Let not your voice tremble. Retreat not from kaif who challenges, or from guards that threaten. If all Indhopal does not rise against Wolf Lord, they must know why Ah'kellah do so.'

With that pronouncement, Wuqaz Faharaqin leapt from his charger and rushed to his nephew's corpse. He raised his sword, stared down at the remains, and began shouting.

'He ask spirit to be appeased,' Akem said, whispering in respect for the dead. 'He ask it not to wander home or trouble family. Wuqaz Faharaqin promise justice.'

Wuqaz smote off the corpse's head with the clunk of metal piercing bone. Men cheered as he lifted his nephew's head in the air.

'Now he will carry head to tribe as testament.'

Wuqaz beckoned to the crowd. Tribesmen came forward,

Invincibles of the Ah'kellah. They were strong men, austere. Wuqaz Faharaqin took his nephew's head by the hair, held it high, and shouted. Akem said solemnly, 'He say, "There must be no king but Earth King."'

All around, the Ah'kellah repeated the words in chorus, chanting them over and over.

Myrrima's heart pounded as the Ah'kellah decapitated the other murder victims, bagged the heads. They began to toss the bodies into the funeral pyre. She didn't understand everything that was going on. She didn't understand desert justice, desert politics.

Myrrima asked, 'Will people really rise up against Raj Ahten?'

Akem shrugged. 'Maybe. Raj Ahten has much endowments of glamour. Wuqaz Faharaqin –'

'I don't understand. Raj Ahten has committed injustices against a hundred of your lords before this. Why should his people care if he commits one more?'

'Because,' Akem said forcefully, 'now there is *Earth King*.'

Everything fell into place. This wasn't about Raj Ahten. This was not just about a small injustice. It was about self-preservation: Raj Ahten had not been able to drive the reavers from Carris. But Gaborn had proven himself. So Wuqaz would seek to overthrow his lord.

She felt as if she had stepped into great events. Her testimony today, however small, would start a civil war.

Myrrima stayed for a moment longer, watched as the slender form of Saffira was consigned to the funeral pyre. She studied Saffira's lovely face, tried to imagine the girl in life, with a thousand endowments of glamour. Imagination failed her.

She turned her horse to leave. Akem folded his hands before his face and bowed low, out of respect. 'Peace be with you. May the Bright Ones protect you.'

'Thank you,' she said. 'And may the Glories guide your hand.'

She rode into the thick of the reaver bodies, into the darkness.

She found Borenson's horse, smashed like a melon. A search revealed only her husband's helm, a few bodies. But in the soft ground she found a man's handprints. Big hands, like her husband's.

He's crawled off, she thought. He might be making for the city even now, or maybe he crawled away and fainted.

Myrrima climbed from her saddle, retrieved Borenson's helm. She sniffed the ground for his scent, but the rain and stench from the reavers' curses confounded her. She could not track him. She considered where she might find the best vantage point from which to look for her husband. The mound around the worm's crater on Bone Hill seemed perfect.

She climbed to the lip of the crater. It was hard to imagine a living thing that could have bored such a hole.

Firelight reflecting from the clouds showed only a yawning pit. By inclining her ear, Myrrima could hear water churning somewhere in that void. The worm's course had cut through a subterranean river, forming a waterfall. But it was far below. If she stepped away from the hole, the sound faded.

Myrrima walked among the scree, sinking into loose soil with every step.

The ground was wet and unsettled. Bits of dirt cascaded into the crater. Myrrima's footing shifted as if the mound might suddenly slide beneath her, carrying her to her doom. Instinctively she eased back to safety.

The destruction of Carris was doubly apparent from atop the mound. But the view revealed nothing of her husband.

'Borenson!' cried Myrrima, as she scanned the plain in a circle. Wuqaz Faharaqin and his men left the bonfire, riding east toward Indhopal.

She glanced toward Carris. Her heart leapt. Guards had set watch fires against the return of any reavers. At the broken entrance of the city, she saw a warrior with red hair like her husband's, leaning upon the shoulder of a red-haired girl. He limped toward the city. Between the falling rain and lingering smoke, she could not be sure if it was him.

'Borenson?' she shouted.

If it was him, he could not hear her, so far off. He hobbled into the shadows thrown by the barbicans.

Carris was a bedlam as Myrrima rode beneath the broken barbicans, searching for her husband.

A week ago Myrrima had celebrated Hostenfest at Castle Sylvarresta. There, for the first time in two thousand years, an Earth King had arisen. The people of Heredon had hosted by far the finest celebration she'd ever witnessed.

As she had strolled through the concourses outside Castle Sylvarresta, brightly colored pavilions had covered the fields like gems in a copper bracelet, greened with age. The entrance to each pavilion was decorated with wheat stalks braided in intricate patterns, and wooden icons of the Earth King all arrayed in finery.

The smell of sweetmeats and fresh breads wafted through the air. Music swelled from a hundred sites around the city.

It had seemed a feast for the senses.

At the turn of each corner she met some new wonder: a jester in parti-colored clothes, carrying a wooden fool's head on a stick, came riding past her on a huge red sow. A young flameweaver out of Orwynne drew the flames of a fire until they rose up and burst into flowing shapes like golden lilies in bloom. A woman with five endowments of voice rendered an aria so beautiful that it left the heart aching for days afterward. She'd seen Runelords joust at rings on chargers caparisoned in colors so bright that they hurt the eyes and dancers from Deyazz wearing lionskins.

She'd tasted rare treats – eels kept alive in a pot and cooked fresh before her eyes; a dessert made of sweetened cream and rose petals cooled with ice; and confections stuffed with coconut and pistachios from Indhopal.

It had been a day to delight even the most downcast heart.

Now as she rode through Carris, her ride provided the dark antithesis of that day.

Instead of fair provender, her keen nose registered the stink of animals, spoiling vegetables, cloistered humanity, blood, urine, and war – all made more abominable by the lingering residue of the reavers' curses.

Instead of seductive music, she was haunted by the entreaties and sobbing of the wounded, mingled with the cries of those who mourned the dead and those who called out for loved ones.

Instead of celebration, there was horror. Myrrima rounded one corner to find half a dozen children, the youngest a girl of two, whispering words of encouragement to a mother that they thought was grievously wounded. A glance told Myrrima that the woman was dead.

A girl of twelve wandered in front of Myrrima's horse. She had gray eyes, dulled by shock, and her dirty face was cleaned only by the tracks of her tears.

That's how I looked at that age when my father died, Myrrima realized. Her stomach knotted in sympathetic pain.

She searched for Borenson among thousands of grisly wounded scattered throughout inns, private homes, stables, the duke's Great Hall, and blankets in the street.

Many wounded struggled near death. The reavers' curses set wounds to festering in unnatural ways. Gangrene set into abrasions that were only hours old.

The search was a foul chore. Nearly every private household had taken in one or two wounded. The stench of the place assaulted her senses. She could not pick up her husband's scent among so many competing odors.

'Borenson!' she shouted again and again as she rode through the streets, her throat going raw. She began to doubt her own senses, wondered if she'd only imagined that she'd seen her husband heading into the city.

He could be asleep, she thought. Perhaps that's why he doesn't answer.

Volunteers worked the battlefield, hauling the dead to the bailey outside the duke's palace. She worried that Borenson might be among them. Gaborn had said that her husband was wounded. Perhaps he'd died in the past few hours. Or perhaps someone had mistaken him for dead, and even now she might find him barely alive. She made her way toward it, and finally caught her husband's scent.

She rode with rising trepidation up to the bailey. Thousands of corpses were laid out. Whole families marched among them, carrying torches.

The blasted grass was a gray mat. The dead lay arrayed on blankets in rows. She could smell Borenson now.

Myrrima knew that dead loved ones never look quite as you expect them to. The faces of men that die in battle become pale, leached of blood, while the countenances of strangled men turn bluish-black. The eyes of the dead glaze over, so that it is difficult to tell whether a man had blue eyes or brown. A corpse's facial muscles can either contract horribly or relax in perfect repose.

Many a woman who has slept with a man for years doesn't recognize her own husband's corpse.

In the same way, when Myrrima found Sir Borenson, she did not know him by sight, only by scent.

He knelt over a dead man beneath the remains of a gnarled oak that had dropped all its leaves. His face was leached as pale as cream, and he stared down, his expression so twisted in pain that she would not have known him. Dirty rain matted his hair and covered him with grime, so that he looked like a squalid wild thing. Clotted blood from a groin wound stained his surcoat down the legs. His right hand gripped the handle of a horseman's battle-ax as if it were a crutch.

He looked as if he had been kneeling like this for hours, as if he might never move again. He had become a statue, a monument to pain.

Only his attire identified him. He wore the same clothes as he had two days past, including the yellow silk scarf that he'd chosen to sport into battle as a sign of her favor.

A little red-haired girl knelt above him, lantern in hand, weeping savagely. They stared down at a dead man who looked so much like Borenson that he might have been a brother.

'Borenson?' Myrrima called hesitantly. All the words of comfort that she'd imagined would come so easily suddenly caught in her throat. She could not imagine a wound that would cause the unadulterated agony she saw in his face. She asked softly, 'What's wrong?'

He did not look at her. Did not answer. She wasn't sure that he even heard. His left hand clutched at his belly, as if he'd just taken a blow to the stomach.

Acorns crunched under her horse's hooves as she approached. As she drew close, she realized that she'd thought that he was unmoving as he knelt. Now she saw that he was trembling all over.

She'd heard tales of men who had seen some great horror and retreated so far into themselves that they never spoke again. Borenson was a warrior. He'd been forced to butcher two thousand Dedicates at Castle Sylvarresta. The deed had so demoralized him that afterward he had quit his service to his king.

Before her knelt a man wounded both in body and spirit. He trembled, and his mind was blank. He was so far gone in pain that he could not weep.

'Myrrima,' he said in a stiffly formal voice as he gazed down on the dead man. 'I'd like you to meet my father.'

Chapter Two: COMMUNION

He who would walk the wizard's path must abandon roads that common men tread.

– Mystarrian Proverb

On the road north from Carris, Gaborn still smelled of war. The curses of the reavers' fell mage clung to him like the smoke of a cooking fire, and sweat soaked the padding beneath his ring mail.

The road was quiet, spooky. Night did not seem to fall from above so much as to rise up like vapors from the hollows of the fields. No birds chirped in the twilight. The hooves of the horses thudded dully on the muddy ground. Though seven people rode in the party, there was barely a creak of harness.

They came to a village. Once, Gaborn had known the name of every hamlet in his realm, but his memory had faded with the loss of his Dedicates in the Blue Tower.

It did not matter. The village was empty; not so much as one yellow dog roamed the streets, wagging its tail. He would offend no one by forgetting its name.

The village was old, cramped, with buildings made of cut stones. Some innkeeper in the distant past had built a hostel that nearly blocked the highway, perhaps imagining that riders were more likely to stop than try to forge their way around it. A few shops had sprung up next to the inn, and cottages next to the shops.

The horses' footsteps rang louder in the streets. Gaborn heard the ching of his ring mail thrown back from stone walls.

The village lay silent, accusing. No children played in the dirty streets. No washwomen railed at one another over a fence. No cattle bawled, calling the milkmaids to their stools. No one swung an ax, chopping wood for the evening fire. No smoke carried the mouthwatering scent of a roasting hen.

No hammers rang. No stars pierced the cloudy heavens. No children sang.

This is the way the world will look, Gaborn thought, when we are no more.

'We should have been for killing Raj Ahten,' Erin Connal said in her thick Fleeds accent, her voice weary.

'The Earth will not allow it,' Gaborn answered.

'Perhaps if we move against his Dedicates,' Prince Celinor offered. 'It would not be the same as attacking him personally.'

The thought of attacking Dedicates sickened Gaborn. The Dedicates were innocent, in most cases. Raj Ahten's beauty was as irresistible as lightning, his voice as overwhelming as thunder. In order for a Runelord to take an endowment from a vassal, the vassal had to offer it up freely. But no one could predict how he might react to Raj Ahten's sublime entreaties. It was said in Rofehavan that 'When you look upon the face of pure evil, it will be beautiful.' Truly, Raj Ahten was beautiful.

Some thought him so persuasive that he deluded himself with his own voice. Certainly he had gulled others often enough – even his own enemies. Women loved him on sight, men honored him. They offered their endowments and their lives in his service, for he told them that serving him would be to their benefit.

The world was heading toward a catastrophe, an all-out war with the reavers. Raj Ahten had already persuaded tens of thousands of people that mankind might survive the coming war only by pooling their attributes, their strength and stamina and wit, into one man who would be their champion. This one man would be immortal, the mythical Sum of All Men.

Of course, not all men were swayed by Raj Ahten's argument. So he waged war on Rofehavan, seeking to convert its people to his own use.

It was a vile act. Raj Ahten had grown so powerful that Gaborn despaired of whether he could be brought down. With such a rapacious lord, the best way to attack him was indirectly – as Erin said – by killing his Dedicates. For each time a Dedicate died, the lord lost the use of the attribute that the Dedicate provided.

Thus, by slaying a few thousand Dedicates, Raj Ahten could be weakened to the point that he might be defeated in battle.

But who could murder innocent Dedicates? Certainly not Gaborn. The men and women who gave themselves to Raj Ahten were simply too weak-minded to see beyond his exquisite mask. Others loaned Raj Ahten their endowments only through coercion. Yes, Raj Ahten managed to put the forcibles to them and take their attributes, but only because they feared him more than his forcibles.

'He took children as Dedicates at Castle Sylvarresta,' Gaborn chided. 'I'll not spill the blood of children.'

'He often did so as well in Indhopal,' Jureem said. 'Children and beautiful women – he knew that men of conscience would not easily strike them down.'

Gaborn felt sickened to the core.

Gaborn could bear no more talk of Raj Ahten. The Wolf

Lord's rapaciousness repulsed him. Gaborn thought, I should never have tried to turn him. I should never have hoped to make him an ally.

In the eerie streets, Gaborn stretched out his senses, used his Earth Sight to feel for any danger to his Chosen.

For the past day, he'd focused all his attention on Carris.

The Earth had charged Gaborn with Choosing people, selecting a seed of mankind to 'save through the dark times to come.' At the same time the Earth had bestowed upon him the power to sense the danger to his Chosen warriors.

Now, however, he had lost the power to warn them of danger, even though he could still sense it.

Thus weakened, in the event his people were assailed, he might be able to do little more than sense their danger before they died. But he hoped for more. His powers had dwindled, but he had to hope that if he could sense danger, he might be able to avert some disasters.

So he groped like a blind man, pushing the limits of his gift.

Danger seemed to be lurking everywhere. In Carris battles still raged. Skalbairn's Knights Equitable fought the reavers, driving them south. Within seconds of each other, two men died. Gaborn felt the loss keenly.

To the west, Raj Ahten fled through the wilderness, retreating toward Indhopal. Strangely, he seemed more dead than alive, and Gaborn could not help but wonder at the situation.

But to Gaborn's consternation, he sensed . . . dangers that were far more personal and far-reaching than any before. None were imminent. Instead, he could sense . . . layers beneath layers of impending doom. Close at hand, he sensed a threat to his wife, Iome. It would not come soon. Over the past few days, he had begun to learn how to gauge when threats would arise simply by the strength of the warning. He suspected that Iome would not face any danger until tomorrow. Yet he had to wonder at its source, for though he could sense peril, he could not always guess at its cause.

Beneath that lay larger portents. Tens of thousands of people at Carris seemed to be in jeopardy still. From a second attack? he wondered. But the trouble brewing in Carris was farther off than the danger facing Iome. He suspected that it would not strike until tomorrow night or the day after.

Beyond that, a cloud loomed over Heredon again. Gaborn imagined the dangers to be like peeling the layers of an onion. Iome's danger was great, and nearest at hand. Once it passed, there loomed a larger threat – the tens of thousands at Carris. Later in the week, hundreds of thousands in Heredon might die. . . .

Yet at the 'core of the onion,' at the kernel of the matter, he discerned one final catastrophe. It seemed to encompass every single man, woman and child that he had Chosen – a million people spread over half a dozen nations.

The Earth Spirit had warned Gaborn that the fate of mankind was upon him. Gaborn had accepted the role of becoming mankind's protector. He'd imagined that the threat would be years in the making. He'd imagined long wars and drawn-out sieges.

But the end of man was nigh. Five days? he wondered – certainly no more than a week. His mouth grew dry, and Gaborn could not catch his breath.

It can't be! he told himself. I'm imagining it.

But cold certainty began to creep into his bones.

In the streets, shuttered windows stared at him, like vacant eyes. He felt trapped in a hamlet of shadows.

Gaborn spurred his horse, taking a long lead. Iome, Celinor, Erin, Jureem, Binnesman, and the wylde all hurried to keep up. Thankfully, none of them drew near or spoke.

Just north of the village, Gaborn turned left on the track toward Balington. He remembered the village fondly from his youth, and had decided to spend the night there. He recalled its serenity, its lush gardens. It was a place strong in the Earth Powers, a place where he could commune with his master. The village lay only three miles off the road.

The horses made toward a pair of hills that stood like sentinels. The open fields gave way to a grove of majestic beech trees whose limbs soared high overhead.

As they reached the hills, Gaborn rounded a bend. An overturned cart blocked the highway. At the margin of the road, six swarthy figures huddled around a small fire, warming themselves in the cool night.

They leapt up as he approached. All six men were abnormally short, almost dwarfish. They bore an odd array of weapons – the spoke from a wagon wheel, a cleaver, a reaping hook, two axes for chopping wood and a makeshift spear. They wore leather work aprons instead of armor. Their leader had a grizzled beard and eyebrows like woolly black caterpillars.

'Hold,' he shouted. 'Hold where you are. There's a hundred archers in them trees. Make any false move, and you'll be leaking like a winepress.'

It took Gaborn a moment to realize that all six 'men' were not men at all. Most were boys in their teens – brothers by the look of them. Like their father, they were so short as to be dwarfish. They had their father's curly hair and strangely blunt nose. Yet they couldn't see beyond the light of their campfire; their threat was laughable.

'A hundred archers?' Gaborn asked as Iome and the others drew up at his back. 'I'd think you could turn your king into a pincushion with half as many.' He rode into the firelight.

The six men dropped to their knees, gaping at the lords before them. 'We saw your lordship riding south this morning!' one shouted. 'We thought looters might head this way. It's our homes, you see.'

'And we heard the earth groan, and saw the cloud rise up over Carris!' another added.

'Is it true?' a young man asked. 'Are you really the Earth King?' At that, all of the young men knelt and watched Gaborn expectantly.

Am I the Earth King? he wondered. How am I to answer that question now?

He knew what they wanted. Six small men without an endowment between them, come to hold the road against Raj Ahten's Invincibles. He'd seldom heard of such foolery – or such valor. They wanted his protection. They wanted him to Choose them.

He'd have done so if he could. In the past weeks, he'd had time to reflect on what he valued in mankind. His Days said that he valued men of insight, while others valued men of strength and cunning.

But Gaborn saw now that he valued most those who loved and lived well. He valued men of sound conscience and unwavering resolve, men who dared stand against the darkness when hope was slim. He felt honored to be in the presence of these good common folk.

'I'm no Earth King,' Gaborn admitted. 'I can't Choose you.'

The lads could not hide their disappointment, not by any act of will – even in the shadows thrown by the campfire. They let out hopeful breaths, and each of them seemed to collapse just a bit.

'Ah, well,' the father mused, 'not the Earth King maybe, but you're *our* king. Welcome to Balington, milord.'

'Thank you,' Gaborn said.

He spurred his mount ahead in the darkness, past the men and on beneath the beech trees. His friends rode behind. Silence followed at their backs. The night was growing cold. Warm air escaped his nostrils like fog.

He found himself breathing hard, afraid that at any moment a wracking sob would escape.

Another mile down the road, where soft hills flowed

together, he reined in his horse, and the others rode up behind. He'd had enough.

'It's time,' Gaborn said to the small group. 'I must speak with the Earth.'

'You'll try so soon?' Binnesman asked. 'Are you certain? The Earth withdrew its powers from you only two hours ago. You understand that the chances of a favorable response are slim?'

'I am certain,' Gaborn said.

There are ceremonies that wizards perform that common men do not attend. Gaborn looked back at his followers. 'Jureem, you'll care for the horses. Erin, Celinor, stay with him. The rest, come with me.'

He dismounted. Clouds were rushing in from the south, and only faint, broken starlight shone overhead.

Iome swung from her mount and took his hand hesitantly. 'Are you sure you want me there?'

'Yes,' Gaborn said. 'I'm sure.'

Binnesman took his staff and led the way, his wylde in tow. He ushered them up a narrow defile, following a stony path made by goats and cattle.

'One who approaches the Powers,' Binnesman counseled as they climbed the trail, 'one who seeks a boon, must do so in the proper frame of mind. It is not enough to merely seek a blessing. You must be pure of heart and single-minded in your purpose. You must set aside your anger at Raj Ahten, your fears for the future, and your selfish desires.'

'I'm trying,' Gaborn said. 'The Earth and I both want the same thing. We want to save my people.'

'If you could sublimate your desires wholly,' Binnesman said, 'you would be the most powerful wizard that this world has ever known. You would sense the Earth's needs and become a perfect tool for fulfilling them. Its protective powers would flow to you without restraint. But you have rejected the Earth's needs on multiple counts. The Earth bade you to save a seed of mankind, yet you seek to save them *all* – even those like Raj Ahten that you know are unworthy.'

'I'm sorry!' Gaborn whispered. But even as he did, he wondered, Who is worthy to live? Even if I regain my powers, who am I to decide?

'Far more serious than this first offense was the second. You were granted the ability to warn your charges of danger. But you tried to corrupt it, to turn the powers of preservation into a weapon.'

'Raj Ahten was attacking my men,' Gaborn objected.

'You should never have Chosen *that* one,' Binnesman said, 'no matter how great you thought the need. I warned you against it. But once you Chose him, you should not have sought to turn your powers against him. Your deed is the very root and essence of defilement.'

'Is there no hope?' Gaborn asked. 'Is that what you are telling me?'

Binnesman turned, starlight reflecting from his eyes, and planted his staff in the ground. He was huffing after the climb.

'Of course there's hope,' he said firmly. 'There is always hope. A man who lacks hope is a man who lacks wisdom.'

'But I've done great wrongs,' Gaborn said. 'I never should have relied on my own strength. I see that now.'

'Hmmm . . .' Binnesman said, with an appraising look. 'You see it, but have you truly learned? Do you really trust the Earth to protect you, or do you think like a Runelord – do you trust in your endowments?'

Gaborn answered slowly. 'I didn't take endowments for myself, but to better serve my people. I cannot bemoan the choice now. My endowments might still serve mankind.'

'Humph,' Binnesman said. He led them to a small clearing and scrutinized Gaborn from beneath his bushy brows. His eyes seemed to Gaborn to be cold pebbles.

Around him, the hills gave rise to dry grasses and a little

oak brush. Stones riddled the ground, but the soil smelled rich, delicious. It was the kind of place where Gaborn would have expected to hear the songs of crickets, or mice scurrying in the leaves, or the cries of night owls. But only a dull cold wind sighed over the hills.

Binnesman grumbled, 'This will do.'

The Earth Warden knelt and spat on the ground. 'With this libation from my own body, I give you drink, O Master,' Binnesman said. 'We seek your help in the hour of our need.' He nodded toward Gaborn and the others. Each spat in turn.

Binnesman raised his staff, whirled it overhead.

'Hail, Mother.
Hail, Protector.
The Tree of Life shades our home,
Come, Maker.
Come, Destroyer.
Come make us your own.'

He touched the ground with his staff and said softly, 'Open.'

A tearing sound arose as the roots of dry grass split apart. A slit appeared, spilling dark soil into mounds on each side of a pit.

Gaborn stared into the shallow grave. The rich ground was full of small white pebbles.

Gaborn let go of Iome's hand and began to disrobe. His eyes flicked toward the green woman to see her reaction, but the wylde, a warrior created by Binnesman from stones and wood, seemed unconcerned with notions of modesty, incurious about Gaborn's anatomy.

He gazed about, filled with anticipation. In Binnesman's garden the Earth had taken physical form, had come to speak to him in person.

But the hills here were bare, and he saw no shadowy figures lurking on their slopes.

With his clothes off, Gaborn climbed down into the soil. He tensed at the touch of the cold ground, but crossed his hands over his chest, took a deep breath, and closed his eyes. He whispered, 'Cover me.'

He lay expectantly for a moment, but nothing happened. The Earth did not fulfill even this small request.

'Cover him,' Binnesman said softly.

Iome felt unsure why Gaborn had asked her to come. She had no powers, could not help summon the Earth Spirit that he sought. She could give him only one thing: comfort.

He needed it sorely. She didn't know how to help him greet the future. They still faced a vast array of enemies: Raj Ahten might still badger him from the west, Lowicker's daughter and King Anders from the north. She'd encountered an assassin from Inkarra, while reavers boiled from the ground beneath their feet.

If we are all to die, Iome decided, then at least we should pass with dignity. She could give Gaborn that much.

But she feared that others would not.

She silently begged the Earth, 'Please, answer us.'

Soil coursed over Gaborn in a flow. Cool dirt intruded everywhere – beneath his fingernails, weighing between his toes, heavy on his chest, pressing against his lips and eyelids.

For several long seconds, he held his breath. As he did, he sent forth his thoughts, his longings.

'Forgive me. Forgive. I will not abuse the power you've loaned me again.'

He stretched out with his mind, listening for an answer. Most often the Earth spoke with the voices of mice or with the cry of a wild swan or with the sound of a twig snapping in the forest. But on rare occasions it spoke as if in the tongues of men.

'Forgive me,' Gaborn whispered. 'I'll bend to your will. Let me save the seeds of mankind. I ask no more of you. Let me be your servant again.'

He heard no answer.

He imagined the future as it might unfold before him if he did not regain his powers. He envisioned mankind running from reavers, holding out in wooded hills or hiding in caves, fighting as best they could.

He pictured himself using his one remaining power, his ability to recognize danger, to save those within range of his voice.

But in time he would fail. Perhaps he would end up alone, the last man on Earth, his one final gift seen for what it had become: a curse.

He held his breath until his lungs burned and his muscles ached.

Last night as he lay in the grave, the Earth had taken from him the need to breathe, had allowed him to relax every muscle, to slumber in perfect repose.

Tonight . . . he recalled the words that the Earth Spirit had first spoken to him. 'Once there were Toth upon the land. Once there were duskins. . . . At the end of this dark time, mankind, too, may become only a memory.'

The ground trembled faintly. Iome knew that Gaborn had summoned an earthquake at Carris. She thought that this was an aftershock.

But the earth continued shaking. The leaves of trees hissed, and a few boulders rumbled down the hillside. The soil beneath Iome's feet rattled, until Gaborn was thrust up from the dirt and suddenly sprawled on the surface.

All around, the dust began to mount in the air. Pieces of what looked like gray stone sifted up to the surface, until suddenly she realized that they were bones – the corrupted jaw of a cow, the skull of a horse, a shoulder blade that might have belonged to a wild bear. All of them rose to the surface along with Gaborn.

Gaborn desperately clawed dirt from his face, gasped for breath. He sat up, naked, spitting dust.

The rumbling stopped, and a boulder bounced downhill through the little knot of people.

Binnesman used his staff to point out the bits of bone that had risen. He frowned at them, squatted and stared. 'You have your answer.'

'But what does it mean?' Gaborn asked.

Binnesman scratched his chin. 'The Earth is speaking to *you*. What does it mean to you?'

'I'm not sure,' Gaborn said.

'Think about it,' Binnesman said. 'The answer will come to you. Trust what you feel. Trust the Earth.'

Without further ado, he took his wylde back down the hillside.

Gaborn crawled about, picking up fragments of bone, staring at them as if to read some message hidden there. Iome brought him his robe, draped it over his shoulders.

'Bones in the earth . . .' Gaborn was muttering. 'The Place of Bones beneath the earth. Search for the Place of Bones.'

Iome needed no wizard to translate for her. Surely Gaborn had to see it: the Earth had rejected him, rejected his plea. She whispered, 'The land will be covered in bones.'

Gaborn stopped, clutched the skull of a dog against his chest. 'No! That's not it at all!'

Iome put her arms around him, tried to hold him and give him comfort.

Gaborn had done his best to be Earth King. He was not a cold man, not a hard man. He was no warrior. If he had been any of those things, she never would have fallen in love with him.

Yet his mistakes were likely to get them all killed.

Am I strong enough to support him in spite of that? she wondered.

'What will we do now, my love?' she asked.

Gaborn merely squatted on the ground, naked but for the cloak thrown over him. 'First we must warn Skalbairn and the rest of my troops that I've lost my powers. After that, we will do what the Earth demands.'

Chapter Three:
A CONTRARY MAN

The gullible often mistake the pronouncements of cynics for true insight. Cynics will warn that all men are corrupt, and that existence is fruitless. But a wise man knows that not all men are corrupt, and that life brings joy as well as sorrow.

The cynics' pronouncements are merely half-truths, the dark side of wisdom.

– From the journal of King Jas Laren Sylvarresta

'The problem is,' High Marshal Skalbairn said, as he and Sir Chondler rode through the night woods in pursuit of the reavers, 'Gaborn loves his people too much, and Raj Ahten loves them too little.' Skalbairn had received a cryptic warning from Gaborn, who had taken refuge at Balington. Both Skalbairn and Chondler were still trying to make sense of it.

Marshal Chondler replied, 'Mark my words, nothing good will come of it. Men are never content to merely *plant* the seeds of their own destruction. They must first till and dung the ground, then nurture and water the tender sprout of it, until at last they're ready to reap the full harvest.'

High Marshal Skalbairn guffawed at the comment. 'No one would knowingly court disaster.' Chondler's mount forged through the trees ahead of Skalbairn's, and the marshal let a limb fly back and slap Skalbairn in the face. Obviously he did so in retribution for the rude noise.

'Ah, I'm wounded,' Skalbairn said.

'Sorry.'

'If that's the most significant wound I take this night, I'll be glad for it,' Skalbairn replied.

He was preparing another attack on the reavers soon. He wanted to reach a knoll where Sir Skerret, a far-seer, had lit a signal lantern in warning, but not a single damned trail seemed to lead to that knoll. The night was still overcast; and so high up in the Brace Mountains, the misting rain was turning to snow.

'Men do court disaster in a hundred ways,' Chondler affirmed. 'For example, have you ever noticed how easily a man can turn a virtue into a vice?'

'What do you mean?'

'Why, when I was a lad I knew a woman so charitable that everyone praised her. She baked bread for the poor, gave coins to the poor, gave her cow – and finally her house. At last she found herself begging on the streets outside of Broward, where she died one winter. Thus her virtue grew into a vice that consumed her.'

'I see,' Skalbairn said. 'And you think this happens often?'

'Ah,' Chondler said. 'But my story is not done: now, this very same woman had a son, who, when he saw that he had lost his inheritance, went about the countryside as a highwayman, robbing every man he chanced upon. No one could seem to catch him, and he thought himself to be a wondrously great robber, so that he was always bragging, "What a great highwayman I am!" And thus he was crowing to his cohorts at the very moment that I crept near to his camp and planted an arrow through his throat.'

'Hah, good move,' Skalbairn said.

'So, like the mother we either turn our virtues into a vice, or else like the son we convince ourselves that vice is virtue. But in either case we plant the seeds of our own destruction.

'Our grand Earth King Gaborn Val Orden thinks that his love of mankind is a merit – while it serves to destroy him, and us with him. Meanwhile Raj Ahten hopes to ride us all like mules till we drop.'

'Hah,' Skalbairn chuckled. 'What a circular argument!' He spoke the words as if in praise, but secretly he thought that Chondler was a contrary fellow who merely wished that he was a deep thinker.

'And we're stuck between the bastards! Well, damn all them kings and high lords, I say. It's every man for himself from here on out.' Sir Chondler reined in his horse and peered ahead. 'I can't see a path.'

Skalbairn had not known that the woods here in the Brace Mountains could be so murky. The pines didn't seem to branch overhead so much as press in his face; the wind-twisted limbs sometimes tangled like yarn.

After a moment, Sir Chondler blindly forged ahead.

Then he pronounced, as if he had just come to a momentous decision, 'I'm going to join this "Brotherhood of the Wolf." What say you?'

Skalbairn didn't know what to think. The rumors from Carris were so strange that he wanted to learn more before making a commitment.

Raj Ahten had attacked Gaborn. That was a baffling move. And in that attack Gaborn had somehow lost his Earth Powers.

This was perhaps the most discomfiting news Skalbairn had heard in his life. He'd not have believed it if Gaborn hadn't sent a warning, written in his own hand.

Skalbairn clutched the parchment in his fist even as he rode. In the warning, Gaborn told Skalbairn: 'Break off your attack until I join you tomorrow.'

Skalbairn didn't know what to think. But as High Marshal

of the Righteous Horde of Knights Equitable, many would watch to see whom he served.

'Me?' Skalbairn asked. He parried a limb with his ax. 'I've forsworn myself too often. I swore fealty first to Lord Brock of Toom when I was a lad, and then to the Knights Equitable, and now to the Earth King. I'm getting too old for this. I think I'll just let my allegiance lie where it's fallen.'

'But that's my point,' Chondler argued. 'It's not as if you haven't forsworn yourself before.'

'True. But you'd have me break oath with the Earth King after only three days. That's fickle even for a Knight Equitable! Besides, not all men are such fools as you think. Gaborn's story is not all told yet.'

Chondler laughed. 'You have more faith in the lad than I do.' He drew rein, peered ahead through the swirling flakes of snow. 'Pshaw!' he said in disgust. 'The path is gone. And we're in a fine spot for an ambush.'

'True enough,' Skalbairn answered, preparing to turn his horse around.

'Listen,' Chondler warned. 'We must be close.' He doffed his helm, cocked his head.

Skalbairn pulled off his own helm and relished the cold touch of ice crystals on his sweaty brow. The air was thick in his nostrils. He could easily discern the sound of reavers – tens of thousands of them just over the hill. The horde trampled trees in its passage, mashing them to pulp, and pounded large sandstone boulders to gravel. The ground rumbled, and reavers hissed, letting air vent from their bodies. They were stampeding south toward Keep Haberd, over the same path that they'd blazed on their way to Carris.

Distant lightning speared from the clouds and struck the jagged tooth of a mountaintop. By its light Skalbairn glimpsed an opening in the trees to their left, but waited a moment, counting. It was forty seconds until the thunder spoke, a distant murmur like an old man grumbling over some half-recalled grudge.

Forty seconds was too long for comfort, if the tales were true. Reavers feared lightning. But if it was more than forty seconds off, the reavers could endure it.

Well, I knew that this jig wouldn't last forever, Skalbairn thought.

For nearly four hours the lightning had held. The height of the storm at Carris brought an incessant groaning from the sky, and hail pellets plummeted like shot from a catapult. Even when the storm quieted, a few clouds wandered overhead, sending out flickering tongues from time to time. Not much of a storm, but good enough.

Skalbairn had seen reavers run headlong into rock walls to escape the lightning. He'd seen some fall insensate, like men who had endured too much pain. Thousands of the great beasts had merely stuck their eyeless heads into the sod and pushed, covering themselves with dirt in an effort to hide.

Easy targets all – blinded reavers, wounded reavers, fleeing reavers. Skalbairn's Knights Equitable chased the brutes down and made such a slaughter as he'd never dreamed. Nine thousand reavers in four hours, by last account. His knights were joined by various Runelords out of Mystarria, Fleeds, Heredon – even Invincibles out of Indhopal, men who had been his mortal enemies at dawn.

Skalbairn would earn a place in history. The bards would sing of Gaborn's victory at Carris, and forever now Skalbairn's own name would be linked to it. It would all sound very grand when sung to pipe and drums – the wild charge through the stormy night.

Of course the truth about his deeds wasn't half so exhilarating or dangerous as future bards might sing. The fact was that the reavers were fleeing on a course that paralleled a good road. Wagonmasters from Carris were rushing wains filled with lances and food to outposts to the south, so that his men could resupply. Skalbairn's men had ample time to pick their ground and set their charges.

Here in the mountains, of course, the terrain stifled him. But it stifled the reavers as much.

The reavers only ran in short bursts, making less than twenty miles per hour. And as they climbed higher into the cold mountains, they became lethargic, moving at perhaps half their normal pace.

Skalbairn said, 'There's a bit of a clearing off to our left.'

'I saw. But it leads to more of a cliff than a clearing.'

'I saw a meadow,' Skalbairn argued. Chondler was a contrary, stubborn man. 'I'll prove it.'

Chondler gave a heavy sigh that would have earned him a beating in any other army. But among the Knights Equitable insubordination was as ubiquitous as fleas in the bedrolls. Chondler turned his mount toward Skalbairn's 'meadow.'

Sure enough, it was a cliff. A quarter of a mile below spread a serpentine valley, and the reaver horde bolted through it like floodwaters through a chasm.

They were a seething mass. In Internook in the late fall the blue eels would swim to the headwaters of the Ort River. When Skalbairn was a boy he'd seen eels so thick that he couldn't spot a single pebble in the shallow riverbed. The reavers forging through the canyon below reminded him of those eels, at once loathsome and alluring.

Lightning flickered again, farther away. The reavers below did not miss a stride. The storm was blowing past.

But in the brief illumination he saw the reavers better. Blade-bearers fled by the thousands. At Carris the monsters had borne weapons – enormous blades twelve feet long, or glory hammers with heads that weighed as much as a horse, or knight gigs that the monsters could use to pull warriors from their chargers or from castle walls. But now, it looked as if half of the reavers had abandoned their weapons.

Among the blade-bearers were howlers, pale spidery creatures that even now stopped every few moments to send up their eerie cries.

Few glue mums remained alive. They moved slower than other breeds, and were less inclined to fight. Skalbairn's men had already dispatched most of them.

But among the reavers, the most fearsome were the scarlet sorceresses. They were easy to spot. The runes branded on their skulls and legs glowed dimly, like the light of warm coals in the midst of an ash-covered fire.

A scarlet sorceress below raced along and suddenly stuck its shovel-shaped head into the soil. It dug in with its feet, tossed its head, and thrust itself underground.

The whole thing happened so fast that Skalbairn could hardly credit his eyes. Yet he'd seen boars hide beneath the humus in the forest that way. The pulped trees and bottom soil on the canyon floor provided good cover – even for a monster that weighed twelve tons.

'Did you see?' Skalbairn asked. Even as he spoke, another scarlet sorceress went to ground, and another. The blade-bearers still seemed to be fleeing blindly.

'I see,' Marshal Chondler replied. 'They're setting an ambush.'

Just as boars in the forest did. They'd rise up out of the bushes at a man's feet and slash with their tusks.

Skalbairn looked north down the canyon course to where it wound out of sight. His lancers were still back a couple of miles, he suspected. Well out of harm's way, for now.

Up to the south, the canyon rim snaked higher. The sides of the canyon were steep, treacherous. A man on horseback could hardly hope to ride up those slopes.

South, the blade-bearers reached a widening in the valley, and would go no further. They burrowed into the steep sides of a cliff.

Sir Skerret stood atop a promontory three hundred yards

off with a lantern hooked atop his lance. By its light Skalbairn could see his regal profile, the silver tip of his beard jutting from beneath his helm, the golden light on his burnished plate.

'So that's why Sir Skerret summoned us. He's warning us off,' Marshal Chondler said.

Skalbairn couldn't let his men ride into the ambush, but the scarlet sorceresses tempted him. They were the prize, the heart of the reavers' forces. For centuries the lords of Rofehavan had offered a reward of five forcibles for any sorceress a man managed to kill.

More than the temptation, these reavers still presented a threat. They were marching south toward the wilderness. But it would not take much for the entire horde to veer east, into the cities along the river Donnestgree.

Skalbairn listened inside himself. Earlier today in the heat of the battle, he'd heard Gaborn's voice warn him of danger. A dozen times Gaborn had saved his life.

But inside he heard nothing now. Inside he felt only apprehension.

'Damn them,' he cursed the reavers. Without the lightning to chase them, the reavers would regroup, begin to fight in concert. Skalbairn was trying to avert a catastrophe. Why was Gaborn holed up in Balington? His message said that he could still sense danger. So why didn't he come and direct the attack personally?

Skalbairn crumpled Gaborn's warning and tossed it to the ground, then turned his horse back toward the road. 'Until tomorrow, then.'

Chapter Four:
A GATHERING OF WITS

The right use of power is the proper study of every Runelord.

– Inscription above the door to the Room of Arms in the House of Understanding

In rain and darkness they came to Balington well after midnight – seven sodden men riding between hills that bowed like bald heads in contemplation. To a man they wore the brown robes of scholars, their beards jutting from beneath peaked hoods.

Had you seen them, you might have taken them for wights, they rode so silently. Only the jangle of harnesses and the splash of a hoof in a puddle betrayed them as living beings. They did not speak. Most dared hardly to breathe. Fear lay naked upon some of their faces. Other countenances were thoughtful or pained. Some old men clutched swords and warhammers, straining to hear the rasping of reavers.

But the only sound around them was the patter of a cool rain. In the past few hours the storm had spread north. Water plummeted out of the heavens and drenched everything, turning the muddy road to a stream. The clouds above the hills sealed in the darkness like a lid. The sixty or so whitewashed stone cottages of Balington, with their thatch roofs, were only vague humped shapes in the night.

A red hound struggled from beneath a woodpile and trotted beside the little group, its tongue lolling.

At the crossroads ahead the only light shone from lanterns hung outside the inn.

Jerimas, the leader of the band, had never been to this inn. Yet he remembered it well. King Orden had thought it a restful place, a hideaway from the heat of summer. But Jerimas's nerves were frayed now. He took no joy in the sight.

He was still trying to cope with the aftermath of the battle at Carris. There were wounded to tend, people to feed, reavers to fight. A couple of hours ago, Gaborn had sent a message asking Jerimas and the other Wits who had served King Orden to come to Balington as soon as they handled their most urgent matters. But on the heels of this message, others had come, delineating the current state of the kingdom – the vanquishing of Raj Ahten, the threats of Lowicker and Anders to the north, and of Inkarran assassins to the south.

Most concerning of all was the warning that Gaborn's powers were severely weakened.

'So,' a scholar behind him said, 'Balington is spared once again.' He was referring to this hamlet's peculiar history. Though battles often raged around it, Balington always emerged unscathed. Two days past, Raj Ahten's army had ridden down the road not three miles west. His troops had been starving, in need of shelter and horses. Yet no one at Balington had bothered to flee. The mayor, merchants, and peasants of Balington had felt that their village was just a trifle too remote from the highway and a tad too small for invaders to bother with.

For the twentieth time in eight hundred years, the course of events proved the people of Balington right. Balington went unplundered.

'It's a fine run of luck,' another scholar said.

'Not luck,' Jerimas said. He inhaled deeply, smelled rain on the sod. He tasted an odd mineral tang, as if he were deep in a cave. The hills above him, the closed feeling, all added to the illusion. Though the ground here was relatively flat, for the past ten minutes he'd had a sense that he was traveling downward. 'This place is strong in Earth Powers. The people here live under its protection. I'd bet my best teeth on it.'

It was a fine place for the Earth King to come, Jerimas sensed. But he still had to wonder at Gaborn's purpose. The same messenger that had summoned Jerimas here also warned that Gaborn had lost some of his Earth Powers. Perhaps he was merely drained, and had come here to mend himself.

The scholars left their horses to the care of a boy who sprinted out of the stable as if he were dodging a hail of arrows rather than raindrops.

A track of mud before the door showed that men had been tramping in and out of the inn all night. At least one was the courier sent by Jerimas himself, warning Gaborn that he would not be able to make it until after midnight.

Jerimas gathered his thoughts. For over twenty years he had served as a King's Wit, a Dedicate to Gaborn's father. He'd seen the world through the eyes of King Orden, heard through his ears. The king's memories remained scattered through Jerimas's skull. He knew most of what Orden had thought, all that he'd hoped for.

Jerimas had *become* King Mendellas Draken Orden in every sense but title. For the first time since Orden had died, Jerimas would see his son.

For many men who had served as Wits, reuniting with the master's family proved painful. Widows felt unnerved by strangers who knew them intimately. Children resented men who too often seemed to be shades of their fathers.

Gaborn. My prize, my joy, Jerimas thought. He recalled the exultation he felt on first holding his son, and his hopes watching Gaborn grow. He remembered the terror of the day when assassins tore Gaborn's mother and siblings from him.

Jerimas was less than a father to Gaborn, more than a stranger.

Now, as ordered by long tradition, he suspected that he would have to report on the death of King Orden. Jerimas would be able to tell Gaborn more than the mere events that led to the king's demise. He could relate Gaborn's father's dying thoughts.

Bearing the Tale of the Dead was a ceremony that Wits routinely performed after the demise of a master. It was a solemn moment, a private occasion.

But more than that, Jerimas yearned to see where he stood. Would Gaborn accept the counsel that Jerimas and his fellow Wits so longed to give? Would Gaborn treat Jerimas and the others as friends? Or would he push them away?

Jerimas hesitated before knocking at the door, for he heard Gaborn's voice, raised in argument.

Prince Celinor said, 'My father already insists that you are no Earth King –'

'And now I have turned his lies to truth.' Gaborn forced a smile.

The fire in the common room had dwindled down to nothing but cherry-colored coals that brooded beneath an ashen quilt. Gaborn, Iome, Celinor, Erin, and Gaborn's Days, who had arrived less than an hour ago, all sat around it. The Days, a scholar who was charged with chronicling Gaborn's life, stood quietly at Gaborn's back. Jureem had left hours ago, to bear messages for Gaborn to the High Marshal and others. The wizard Binnesman was working on his wylde, a creature that looked like a woman with dark green hair, and skin of a paler green. She lay stretched out on a bar counter that was lit by a pair of tallow candles.

'Your Highness,' Celinor argued in a reasonable tone,

'when the world hears that you've suffered a setback, it will only lend credibility to my father's lies. I can already hear him crowing to his friends: "See, I told you he was a fraud. Now he claims to have 'lost' his powers. How convenient!"'

'Your father has worse problems than Gaborn to contend with,' Iome countered, 'with reavers surfacing in North Crowthen. If they march south, into your father's realm –'

'I'm not sure which he will see as a greater threat,' Celinor said. 'He fears your husband unreasonably. And now Gaborn is vulnerable to attack.'

'You're starting at shadows,' Iome said. 'Your father wouldn't dare move against the Earth King.'

Celinor looked to Gaborn for counsel, but with a glance Gaborn deferred to the wizard. Binnesman was hunched over his wylde. He held a stem with dainty pink flowers and dark serrated leaves. He used it to draw runes around each of the wylde's nostrils. The wylde held perfectly still, did not even breathe. It was unsettling, for she looked as if she had died. Nothing living could have kept so motionless. It added to the aura of mystery that Gaborn felt around the creature.

'Celinor is right,' Binnesman whispered without looking up. 'His father is a danger. There is sorcery at work here. The nature of his delusions and this business with King Lowicker both suggest that Anders suffers from no common madness.'

'Perhaps I can still reason with him,' Celinor said.

'If your father is one of the wind-driven,' Binnesman told Celinor, 'you can't reason with him. It would be dangerous to try. Mark my words: we are not battling reavers and men, but powers unseen.'

'Yet reason may still prevail,' Iome said hopefully, 'if not with Anders, then with those he seeks to deceive. Even if Anders clings to his madness, the world will not hear only his lies. Gaborn summoned a world worm today and drove the reavers from Carris. Men will hear of that, and true men will stand by him.'

'You mean that true men will *die* by him,' Celinor blurted, 'while false men circle like wolves. I swear, I'll not let my father be one of those false men.'

'Could you handle him alone?' Erin cut in.

'I believe so.'

'Even if it meant killing him?'

'It won't come to that,' Celinor said.

'But could you?' Erin asked fiercely. 'Or if sparks came to fire, would you be needing help to lop off his head?'

Celinor looked at her sharply. With his fine blond hair, lean build, and bright hazel eyes, Celinor had the appearance of a scholar or a healer, not a man capable of patricide.

Gaborn asked softly of Erin, 'Have we come to this? Would you have him fight his own father?'

'Not if we can avoid it. But I won't have him close his eyes to the risks he's taking.'

'Talk to your father then,' Gaborn told Celinor in exasperation. 'Tell him that I would like to open negotiations to renew old treaties. Perhaps that will assuage his fears.'

'I will, milord,' Celinor promised. 'May I take my leave now?'

Gaborn had never Chosen Celinor, and therefore could not know if he was in danger. Yet common sense dictated the answer. 'The roads are too wet tonight,' Gaborn warned. 'I think it best if you wait until morning.'

Gaborn turned to Erin Connal and asked, 'Will you go with him? If I sense that you are in jeopardy, I'll try to warn you. But take care not to lift your hand against any man, except to save your own lives.'

'As you wish, milord,' Erin said.

Someone opened the front door, and a cold wind blew into the room. Several men stood there. Gaborn could see only vague shadows. At first he thought them to be lords riding from Heredon or messengers from Skalbairn.

'Your Highness,' a scratchy male voice announced, 'the King's Wits. We come to bear the Tale of the Dead.'

For a moment, no one spoke. The only sound was the whisper of rain in the courtyard.

Erin Connal said, 'Milord, seeing as we've a long journey ahead, I'd best tend my horse.' She bustled from the room with Celinor in tow. Gaborn's Days followed, as if he had found urgent business outside.

Iome glanced at Gaborn, asking with her eyes if she should go. The bearing of the Tale of the Dead was a private affair. A man's dying thoughts could be as embarrassing as they were touching. 'Stay,' Gaborn said. Iome felt a warm flush. She wanted to be with him.

Binnesman was still working on the green woman. He asked, 'May I have half a moment? I'm drawing runes of protection with wood betony and must finish before the sap hardens.'

Gaborn knew that it would take time. With five endowments of metabolism, Gaborn could now amble faster than a commoner could run; and when others spoke, their words seemed to come laboriously.

But finishing the wylde was important. The creature was to be the Earth's warrior, but she could not fight until Binnesman *unbound* her, gave the wylde its free will. Yet he could not do that until he'd bound her with protective spells and taught her to fight on her own.

'Stay here and work,' Gaborn said softly. 'We need the wylde. Every moment counts.'

Iome and Gaborn stood hand in hand.

The Wits filed in. Most were elderly men. The youngest could not have been less than forty. Their hair was cropped short, and all wore simple brown robes common among the hearthmasters in the House of Understanding.

'Gaborn!' a tall graybeard called in greeting. The love that Gaborn's father had felt for him came thick in the old man's voice. Perhaps for Gaborn's entire life, this former Dedicate had been locked in the Blue Tower, an idiot who loaned the use of his mind to King Orden.

Gaborn reached out to clasp hands at the wrist, but after a moment's hesitation, he thought better of it and gave the man a hug. 'Hello, friend,' Gaborn said. 'You are . . . ?'

'Jerimas.' The old man spoke hesitantly, as if the name were a stranger's. He stared at Gaborn, searching his face. 'I . . . my name is Jerimas.'

Jerimas was thin, with wide-set eyes so dark they were almost black, and a triangle of a face. His hair had receded until he was left with only a narrow band of white along his ears and a sweeping beard of silver.

'Jerimas,' Gaborn repeated. He studied the Wits, saw how many of them held their head tilted to the left, just as Gaborn's father had.

'Are you ready to hear the Tale of the Dead?'

'It will have to wait for a more opportune time,' Gaborn answered. 'I didn't summon you here for that. I know the manner of my father's death too well.'

'His dying thoughts were of you,' one of the Wits blurted.

'I know that he loved me,' Gaborn said. 'And I am comforted by your presence here. But we have more important matters at hand.'

Gaborn took a deep breath. In the aftermath of Carris, he felt mentally overwhelmed and exhausted. For the past few hours he had considered a course of action. Now he needed these men's help.

'Right now, you men are in charge of Carris. You've seen to its defense, ministered to its people. But I require more of you – much more.

'For all purposes, each of you who served my father *is* my father. His every mannerism is imprinted upon you. I called you gentlemen here because I need your wisdom and counsel. I cannot manage the affairs of my kingdom alone.

'As Jureem should have reported to you and Skalbairn, I've lost some of my Earth Powers. I can still sense danger, and I sense it all around us. But I cannot warn my Chosen. I will need your help. I will need you to see to the defenses of Mystarria and Heredon.'

'You will stay close to advise us?' Jerimas asked. The look of hope in his eyes was hard to miss.

'I will do all that I can,' Gaborn said. 'But I make no promises. At dawn I will ride to Carris, to offer some brief comfort to the wounded. But I propose to spend some time with Skalbairn on the morrow, fighting reavers. We must punish them for their attack on Carris. We must make them fear us.'

At that, several graybeards nodded their heads thoughtfully in agreement.

'After that . . . I can't say. I sense that the Earth wishes me to fight elsewhere.'

'We could come with you,' Jerimas offered, 'stand at your side and offer counsel.'

'Perhaps,' Gaborn said. Now he came to the heart of the matter, to the question that troubled him most. 'Tell me, have any of you heard of the Place of Bones?'

The Wits all stared at him blankly. Some shook their heads.

'I . . .' Gaborn continued. 'It may not be the proper name of the place. It may be a description. The Earth has called me there to battle. I suspect that it may lie . . . underground. Perhaps it describes a mine, or a graveyard, or an ancient Duskin city.'

Again, the graybeards shook their heads. Gaborn had wondered about this for hours. Binnesman had been no help. The Earth Warden had been alive for centuries, knew much lore about faraway places, including Duskin ruins like Moltar and Vinhummin far belowground. But he could not tell him where the Place of Bones might be.

'Perhaps it is an ancient battlefield,' Jerimas said. 'Certainly, the caves at Warren might qualify as a "Place of Bones." Fallion spent four hundred thousand good men fighting the Toth.'

'I thought of that,' Gaborn said. 'And I've considered sailing for those ruins. But when I do, I cannot rest easy. That is not where the Earth is calling me.'

'Be patient,' Binnesman advised. 'The Earth will reveal its will in good time.'

Gaborn shook his head, tried to clear it. His thoughts kept circling back to his question.

'My lord,' Jerimas asked, 'Jureem said that you've lost some of your powers, but you can sense danger still? You worry about the reavers, and Inkarra, and Anders and Lowicker, but what of Raj Ahten? With his voice alone, he toppled the Blue Tower. Does he pose a threat? We've had no report on his whereabouts since nightfall.'

'I sense him. He's fleeing toward Indhopal,' Gaborn answered, 'over mountain trails that a man on a horse would not dare travel. I'm not worried about him for the moment. If he comes near Rofehavan again, I will sense his presence.'

'But you do know how our men fare in battle?' another lord asked.

'Many Chosen warriors have fallen in the past five hours,' Gaborn admitted. 'I sensed their danger, but could not warn them.'

Jerimas said, 'But Skalbairn's reports are phenomenal. His men are slaughtering reavers by the thousands. A few losses are acceptable.'

Gaborn nodded. 'So long as they remain but a few. I've ordered him to pull back until the morrow. I will lead the attacks myself.'

Another Wit, a heavy man with a goatee spoke up. 'We have seen wonders this day! And tomorrow will bring more.'

'Tomorrow will bring horrors as well,' Gaborn said. 'I will deal with the reavers as best I can. But in doing so, I must leave the matter of protecting our borders to you. You will need to put forward every effort at your disposal.'

'In the House of Understanding,' one Wit said, 'in the Room of Arms it is said that "A man's every asset can be a weapon." For a wise man, his cunning may be a shield. For a glib man, his tongue might serve as a dagger. For a strong man, his brute force might be a cudgel to break the backs of nations.'

'We must call our allies to our defense,' one Wit suggested, 'and turn our enemies against each other.'

Jerimas said, 'Milord, are you giving us free rein to do what we must?'

'Of course,' Gaborn said. 'I fear that war is coming, and we must fight brilliantly or perish.'

Jerimas offered cautiously, 'You've been loath to make hard choices in the past. You've taken few endowments yourself, and you sought to spare Raj Ahten's Dedicates. You have a good heart. But I fear that in war, a man's conscience must be the first casualty.'

Gaborn stared up at the Wits. Moments ago, he'd seen their faces full of love. Now he saw them taciturn, hard.

He knew his father's voice when he heard it.

'Without your full Earth Powers to guide you,' Jerimas said, 'we must act swiftly. There are bribes to pay, mercenaries to hire, endowments to take, assassins to assign, weapons to forge, borders to fortify.'

Gaborn gritted his teeth. He did not want to fight his neighbors, but he knew that he was being backed into a corner. He might not have a choice. 'What do you recommend?'

'You've already begun,' old King Orden answered through the mouth of Jerimas. 'You did well to send Celinor to his father.

'Now we must send messengers to Internook, and hire up all of the mercenaries we can, lest Anders or some other lord beat us to it. With the combined might of Mystarria and the warlords, Anders will not succeed in gaining any support for his cause.'

Gaborn liked that idea. It would give him men to bolster his own defenses.

'Next we must deal with the Storm King, Algyer col Zandaros,' Jerimas said. 'Your report says that he has already sent one assassin against you?'

'Yes,' Iome said. 'He carried a message case with a curse attached to it.'

'We've had no hostilities with the Storm Lord lately. So I can only conclude that he acted against you based on lies spread by Anders or Lowicker. You'll need to send a messenger to speak on your own behalf. Sue for peace, but prepare for the worst.'

'Agreed,' Gaborn said.

'Zandaros will feel slighted if you do not send a kinsman,' Jerimas warned. 'It is the Inkarran way. The closer the kin, the better. Paldane would have been your best choice.'

Gaborn felt uneasy. It was a risky thing for any man to go to Inkarra. The Storm King had an uneven temper. To Gaborn's consternation, Jerimas's gaze fixed on Iome.

'I could go,' Iome offered quickly.

Jerimas nodded, as if that would be best.

But Gaborn stiffened. He sensed danger around her. 'No, I dare not. I want you to stay beside me. We'll send someone else, perhaps my cousin.'

'It will have to do,' Jerimas said. 'I'll consider the matter.'

Gaborn felt emotionally and intellectually depleted, even with all of his endowments. His weariness went beyond physical pain. His mind had been racing now for hours, for days. He closed his eyes. 'I'll leave you men to it. Sue for peace and prepare our defenses. But send no assassins, make no preemptive strikes. Our battle –' He could not help but think of Binnesman's warnings. His battle was not with men or reavers, but with Powers unseen. What did that mean? How could he fight the Powers? How could one defeat Fire or Air?

'Our battles are not with men or reavers,' Gaborn said. 'I fear the battle cannot be won with sword or shield.'

At that, Binnesman looked up from his table where he'd been writing on the wylde. 'You're learning,' he said. 'You cannot win this battle any more than you can hope to stamp out the fires of the sun or draw the air from the sky.'

All eyes turned to the wizard, with his stooped back and greenish skin. Jerimas asked, 'What do you mean, we cannot win?'

'Simply that,' Binnesman said. 'Our goal is not to conquer, merely to survive.'

That was it. Gaborn hoped to save his people, nothing more. Gaborn stood and stretched as the Wits began to talk animatedly, speaking first of lords to contact, fences to mend. He left them to their work.

Binnesman bent back over his wylde, continuing his preparation of her. He placed a twisted root upon the green woman's forehead and began to chant.

Gaborn dared not disturb the incantation. Iome got up, and Gaborn went to the door. Iome followed behind him. Rain fell. As droplets blurred past the lighted doorway, they glowed briefly like golden ingots. Gaborn could hardly see the cottages hunched across the street.

A bead of sweat trickled down Gaborn's left temple.

Iome squeezed his hand, tried to comfort him.

'What's wrong?' Iome asked.

'I sense . . . a rising danger,' Gaborn said. 'I'd hoped my father's Wits might help, but I suspect that none of their plans, no matter how cunning they seem . . . can change much.'

'You're keeping me close on purpose,' Iome accused. 'Do you sense danger toward me?'

'Nothing immediate. But . . . stay close to me.'

Chapter Five: LOVE FOUND

Love well and die well. Compared to those two things, everything else you do in life pales to insignificance.
– A proverb of Fleeds

Erin brushed down her mount, fed it some rich miln. It would be a long ride tomorrow, heading north to Fleeds and beyond that to South Crowthen. The beast needed all the nourishment she could give it.

She looked forward to the journey, even if she feared that it would lead to an unhappy conclusion. Celinor's father sounded dangerous. King Anders was plotting against Gaborn, and had concocted some scheme to show that Erin was the rightful heir to Mystarria's crown. She suspected that she would have to confront the man.

Outside the stable, cool rain thundered out of the heavens. The scent of it hung heavy in the air and mingled with the sweet odor of horses.

After the battle at Carris, Erin found that she longed for the clean smell of rain and horses and the open field. The odor of battle, the decay at Carris, the images of men dying, thoughts of her father dead while Raj Ahten walked free – all preyed upon her mind.

She wanted to feel clean again. She wanted to stand in the autumn showers and let rain wash over her.

All evening in the inn, she'd been aware of Prince Celinor, watching her slyly every time she looked away. He'd done it on the ride north. He'd done it as she sat before the fire dwindling in the hearth.

He'd won her fair, she knew. Before the battle at Carris, he'd asked her to sleep with him if he saved her life. It was a clumsy attempt at courting. They were from different lands, with vastly different customs. He had no idea how to approach a woman of Fleeds. So she'd conceded to the spirit of his request.

He'd saved her life twice in battle, though he was too much a gentleman to remind her. Still, she could tell that he dwelt on those thoughts.

Celinor worked on his mount, replacing a shoe on its left front hoof. He did not speak to her.

She went up into the stable's loft. The straw there was warm, fragrant, and comforting. The roof didn't leak. It kept the straw dry.

The stableboy had brought the Wits' mounts in for the night. He finished feeding them and brushing them, then went home to sleep at last. She was alone with Celinor.

Celinor finished shoeing his charger. He went to the tack room to oil the leather of his saddle and bridle.

Erin crept up behind him, found a fine leather lead rope. She slipped her rope over Celinor's neck. He stiffened at its touch. She whispered, 'Come with me.'

'What?'

She said no more, simply pulled the rope tight and laid it over her shoulder, guiding him toward the loft.

'Where are we going?' he asked. 'What is the rope for?'

'In ancient times,' Erin said, 'the horsesisters would claim a husband in the same way they would claim a foal. They'd tie him up and take him to the corral. It's not often done that way anymore, but I'm a traditional girl.'

'You don't have to do this,' Celinor said. 'You don't

have to sleep with me. I mean . . . I saved your life twice today, but in case you weren't counting, you saved me at least as often.'

Erin turned toward him. 'So you're thinking that we're even? One deed erases another?'

Celinor nodded. Maybe he had accomplished all that he wanted just by getting her attention. Maybe he was just shy.

'The thing is,' Erin whispered, 'there are so many ways to save a person's life.' She couldn't quite express all that she felt. Her dismay at the events of the day, her pain at the loss of her father. 'I'm not doing this for you. I'm doing it for us.'

Celinor studied her thoughtfully. 'You would marry me? Now, in the middle of this war?'

'Wars are just things that happen to you,' Erin said.

Celinor stroked her hair, bent to kiss her. Erin leaned into him. 'If you don't want me,' she said, 'a fellow can always be slipping from the noose.'

'And what if I want to say yes with all my heart? How does a man marry a horsesister of Fleeds?'

She turned, took the lead rope, and guided him up to the loft where the straw was warm and dry.

Chapter Six:
LOVE LOST

Treasure the memory of good times, and cast away the bad.

– Adage from Heredon

'I'd like you to meet my father.' Borenson's words reverberated in Myrrima's mind, and she thought for a moment that he must be mad. 'Roland. Roland is his name.'

In the guttering light of the little girl's lantern, Myrrima peered at the corpse. Surely the dead man at their feet looked very much like Borenson, but he was younger by several years. The fellow lay on the ground, staring skyward. A gaping wound in his shoulder had been crudely bandaged, but blood blackened his tunic everywhere. The girl wiped tears off her face with her sleeve. A cool drizzle was falling.

'Your father?' Myrrima asked.

'He was a Dedicate,' Borenson said. 'He gave his metabolism to House Orden. For more than twenty years he slept in the Blue Tower. He woke only a week ago. I . . . have never met him before.'

Myrrima nodded, too shocked to speak. Borenson had never met his own father until now?

Borenson's voice was formal and strained, lacking inflection. 'It is interesting that you can grieve the death of someone you never met. When I was a child, I knew that my mother hated me. I used to dream that my father would waken, and he'd discover that he had a son. I used to dream that he would save me from my mother. Now, it appears that he did indeed come to see me. But I could not save him. Ah, well . . .'

The knights of Mystarria were said to be harder than stone. They were taught to make light of pain and death. It was said that in battle, Borenson's laugh unnerved even the strongest men. Now, though Borenson hardly acknowledged his torment, Myrrima knew it was ripping him apart.

Myrrima recalled her mother once telling her that when a strong person spoke honestly about his pain, it was often because he could not hold any more, and therefore sought to share the burden with others.

Every expression of consolation that came to Myrrima's mind seemed trite, inappropriate. Borenson looked up.

She'd never seen such pain in a man's eyes. They were bloodshot, and the lids were rimmed in red. The eyes themselves looked to be glazed with a yellow film. She realized that what she'd thought was rainwater on his face turned out to be beads of sweat standing out on his forehead. She remembered the words of an old rhyme that children in Heredon sometimes called out during games of hide-and-seek.

Let us go to Derra. Run away. Run away.
Let us frolic in pools at Derra,
Where the madmen play!

'Can I help?' Myrrima asked.

He turned away.

'You're not an easy one to leave behind,' Borenson said. His voice was tight with emotion.

'No,' Myrrima agreed. 'I won't be left behind. I came for you too.'

Myrrima climbed down off her horse, stood over her husband. The air between them was so charged that she somehow dared not put an arm around him.

'It would be better if you go,' Borenson said as if to the ground, still trembling. 'Go back to your home and your sisters and your mother.'

She knew how his deed this past week tormented him. He'd slain King Sylvarresta and two thousand Dedicates on the orders of Gaborn's father. For the murder of a friend, his mind was filled with torment.

She couldn't comprehend the anguish of someone who had been forced to slay idiots and children – people whose only crime was to love their lord so much that they were willing to share their finest attributes with him.

But now she saw something even darker in his eyes. There was a gulf of misery between them that words could not describe.

'What happened?' she asked as gently as she could.

'Ah, well,' he said solidly. 'Nothing much. My father's dead. I found Saffira, and now she's dead. Reavers got them both.'

'I know,' Myrrima answered. 'I saw her body.'

'You should have seen her,' Borenson offered, and his eyes suddenly blazed as if he beheld her glory in the distance. 'She shone like sunlight, and her voice was so . . . beautiful. I thought that surely Raj Ahten would listen.'

For a moment, he fell quiet. Then Borenson looked up at her again and said sharply, 'Go home! I'm not the man you married. Raj Ahten made sure of that.'

'What?' she asked. His eyes lowered, and Myrrima's gaze went to the oozing and crusted blood on his surcoat, there by his thighs. She imagined that he'd been stabbed, had taken a gut wound and was slowly dying. 'What?'

'I succeeded in the task Gaborn set for me,' Borenson

explained. 'I convinced Saffira to come here. I got her killed. I got us all killed.'

Borenson gripped the handle of his battle-ax and pulled himself to a standing position. He wavered for a moment, and Myrrima realized that he was on his last legs. Suddenly his complete dispassion made sense: she'd seen the wounded here in Carris, sometimes taking ill with gangrene from even the slightest scratch. The fell mage's curses made sure of that. Borenson had been down in the thick of the battlefield where the curses were strongest.

And now he stood trembling, with sweat beaded upon his brow and eyes covered in film.

He turned his back, began to hobble painfully away from them in the night, still using his battle-ax as a crutch. The rain had begun to fall more earnestly, and the cool drops hissed into the dead leaves all around. The little girl with the lantern let out a gasping sob. Borenson stumbled and fell in the muck there among the dead. He lay unmoving.

The child let out a shriek, and Myrrima said, 'Run and find a healer.'

The girl handed Myrrima a lamp, and Myrrima went to her husband, flipped his body over. With her endowments of brawn, it was easily done. Borenson's eyes were open to slits, rolled back in a faint. She touched his forehead, and it felt as if he were on fire.

The child didn't run for a healer. Instead, she watched as Myrrima pulled up Borenson's surcoat and ring mail, looking for the source of the blood and pus that oozed down his legs.

When she discovered the wound, it was far more horrifying than any that she'd imagined. Truly, Borenson was not the man she had married.

Raj Ahten had made sure that he was a man no more.

Chapter Seven: VOICES

When a storm sings through the trees, one often hears the voices of men far off. But those are the songs of the dead. Wise men do not listen.

– Proverb of Rofehavan

In Mystarria a cold wind sang above the village of Padwalton near the Courts of Tide an hour before dawn, shoving clouds through the sky. It stripped the brown leaves from the chestnut trees and let them drop on the hillsides to lie among the bones of leaves left from the preceding fall.

The wind moaned through barren branches, and a gust made the laundry hanging upon old lady Triptoe's clothesline dance and flutter as if it would come alive, while the bucket above her well swung slowly in the breeze.

A milkmaid felt the wind's prickly touch on her back. She squinted and turned to see if something had brushed against her. She drew her cloak tight and hurried her cow to the barn.

Then a finger of wind went skittering along the village street, dancing over the dark surface of puddles left from the night's rain.

It slapped against the door at the Red Stag, then slithered through a crack beneath.

The lady of the inn was just pulling a platter of savories

out of the oven – lightly toasted crusts stuffed with morel mushrooms in venison and red wine. She inhaled the scent as she carried them into the common room to cool, then noticed the chill.

The fire beneath the oven gave the only light in the room, and had kept it warm and cozy for the past hour.

The lady frowned at the draft, turned to see if the door was open.

In an upstairs room several Runelords lay abed after a hard ride. Word had reached them that trouble was brewing in Carris. They were racing from the western provinces to the far eastern borders.

One lord, Baron Beckhurst, lay sleeping soundly when the air brushed his neck.

'Kill the queen,' a voice whispered in his ear, 'lest Iome's son become greater than the father.'

Beckhurst rolled over and his eyes came open. He whispered, 'At once, milord.'

Without waking his companions, he got up. He briskly dressed in his ring mail, and went to the store of weapons that one of his fellow travelers had carried.

He selected a lance, well balanced and of a comfortable heft. Iron bands bound it in a dozen places. As he raised it to the sky, he pointed it high. Long ago, his mother had taught him a rune of the Air. He drew it with the lance tip, and a flickering blue bolt of lightning curled along its length. He grinned, rode from the inn.

The wind traveled on.

Chapter Eight: IGNITING HEAVEN

After the battle at Engfortd, asked I of gud Sir Gwyllium, 'How fared ye with yon forcibles?'

His demeanor became very thoughtful. Said he, 'No mytier weapon hath man devised! Forty-five strong knichts cleaved I twixt cock's crow and eventide, yet weary not. By my beard, such devices shall let courteous men put down every barbarity!'

Then said his wife, 'Nay, but with them methinks cruel men shall perfect *barbarity.'*

– On the discovery of forcibles, from the Chronicles of Sir Gwellium of Seward, *as recorded by his Days*

An hour before dawn, the stars above Raj Ahten blazed in a cold sky as if intent on igniting heaven. He raced over the Hest Mountains down toward the deserts of Indhopal, sweat drenching him, his blood crusting from wounds at his knee and chest. His shirt of black scale mail, torn from battle, rang like shackles with every step.

His serpentine trail twisted over the tortuous ridges and through the crevasses, curling among black pines that struggled up to bristle like spears through cracked rock and a thin crust of snow.

It was bitterly cold, and Raj Ahten clung to his warhammer. After the rout at Carris, reavers had fled blindly in every direction. Twice Raj Ahten had stumbled upon the monsters in the woods and brought them down.

Worse than reavers hunted in these woods. Gaborn had turned many of Raj Ahten's own Invincibles against him. A troop of them had ridden over the pass recently, leaving hoofprints in the fresh snow.

So Raj Ahten traveled over paths that horses could not follow, bypassing his armies in the mountains.

Wolves howled in the shadowed pines. They'd caught his blood-scent, and now loped behind, trying to match his pace. Raj Ahten could smell his own vital fluids, cloying amid the competing scents of snow, ice, stone, and pine.

He found himself breathing hard; the muscles in his chest were knotted. The air so high in the mountains was thin, pricking his lungs like needles.

His armor seemed suffocating; its metal leeched the warmth from his bones. He'd carried it all night, but finally he stripped off his torn shirt of mail and threw it down. Black scales broke off and scattered on the snow as if he'd tossed a carp against a rock.

Raj Ahten's stomach clenched from hunger.

With so many endowments of brawn and stamina to his credit, he should have felt vigorous, filled with endless energy.

He wondered at the strange illness that assailed him. Eleven hours past, Binnesman's wylde had attacked him, breaking the ribs in his chest. Perhaps they'd not healed properly. All night long, Raj Ahten had felt rising pain – in the wounds in his chest, in his muscles, as if he suffered from some wasting disease.

He feared that some Dedicates had died, causing him to lose stamina. But a Dedicate's death brought a sudden nausea and a wrenching sense of loss as the magical connection severed. He had not felt that.

Raj Ahten silently stalked over a small rise, and beheld an

oddity: half a mile ahead, in a shadowed valley, his spy balloon rested in a clearing, a great balloon shaped like a graak.

On the ground beneath it a fire burned, reflecting flames off the snow into the silk wings of the graak.

Some of his men huddled beside the fire brewing tea – his counselor Feykaald, along with his flameweavers: Rahjim, Chespot, and Az. The Days that chronicled Raj Ahten's life was also in the group.

Feykaald was old, his gray burnoose pulled up over his head, a black cloak wrapped around him like a blanket. The flameweavers wore nothing but loincloths, and luxuriated near the blaze. The flames of many fires had long ago licked the hair from their brown skins. Their eyes glowed like mirrors, perfectly reflecting light from the campfire.

Raj Ahten's most loyal followers sat quietly, as if awaiting him – or as if they were silently summoning him.

He thrust his warhammer into its scabbard, strode to the camp. '*Salaam*,' he said. Peace. The men acknowledged him, each mumbling '*Salaam*' in turn.

'Rahjim,' Raj Ahten asked the most powerful of the flameweavers, 'did you see a patrol pass by?'

'Riders came down the trail just as we landed, judges of the Ah'kellah, led by Wuqaz Faharaqin. He carried the head of his nephew, Pashtuk, in the bag. He will try to raise the Atwaba against you.'

'Troublemaker,' Raj Ahten said. 'I'm glad that not all of my men follow the Earth King.'

Rahjim shrugged. 'The Earth King could not Choose me any more than he could Choose a water buffalo.' Smoke puffed out from his mouth as he spoke.

Raj Ahten grunted, but merely stood gasping in the campfire's glow, warming his hands in its pale smoke. A log crackled; cinders shot into the sky.

The fire felt good. It burned away the cold and the pain. Flames fanned out along the ground, as if to lick him, though no wind blew. He suspected that the sorcerers manipulated the flames to his benefit.

All three flameweavers watched Raj Ahten curiously.

Rahjim ventured, 'O Great Light, do you feel . . . well?'

'I feel –' there was no word for it. Raj Ahten felt noticeably weak, frail, and disoriented. 'I am not myself. I may have lost some endowments.'

Rahjim studied him with that penetrating gaze. Flameweavers were often discerning healers, capable of diagnosing a man's most minor ailment.

'Yes,' Rahjim said. 'Your light is very dim. Please, breathe the smoke of the fire, and blow it out for me.'

Raj Ahten bent low to the fire, inhaled the pine smoke, blew it out slowly. The flameweavers studied the way that the smoke moved, traced its path through the sky.

Suddenly Rahjim's eyes widened. He looked to the others as if for confirmation, but dared not speak.

'What is it?' Raj Ahten asked. He wondered if he had contracted some illness due to the fell mage's curses.

'There are changes in you,' Rahjim admitted. 'This is no common illness. Wizardry is involved – Binnesman's curse. Remember Longmot?'

'Yes!' Az said, his own eyes wide. 'I see it too!'

'See what?' Raj Ahten demanded.

Rahjim said, 'The Earth Powers are withdrawing from you. That is causing . . . the changes.'

'What changes?' Raj Ahten demanded.

'You have lost stamina – a single endowment. And one of wit, one of brawn. . .'

'Only one? It feels like more.'

'You've lost your *key* endowments,' Rahjim said.

'Key endowments' was a term used by facilitators. It meant the endowments a man was born with. Like the keystones in an arch, they held a man together. The news was baffling.

'You are dying,' Chespot said plainly. 'In some sense, perhaps you are dead already.'

'What?' Raj Ahten demanded.

Raj Ahten had heard of dead men who still breathed, of course. As a child, he'd been raised on such tales. Just as a senile man can often mask his condition with endowments of wit – effectively remembering much even as his brain slowly withered inside his head – a slain Runelord with many endowments of stamina could sometimes survive for hours or days in a morbid state.

'What am I?' Raj Ahten asked, numb.

Rahjim said, 'You . . . are something that has never been before.'

Chespot eyed him critically. 'To live beyond your allotted hour is not a small thing. Your life is ended, but the endowments you've taken have not returned to those who gave them. You have taken a great step. I believe that you are the Sum of All Men. You are eternal.'

Am I? Raj Ahten wondered. For years he had gathered endowments, sought to become the Sum of All Men, that mythical creature that could become immortal. He'd hoarded the strength, stamina, and wit of thousands of men, and grown in might until he felt as if he were one of the Powers, like the Earth or Air.

Yet Raj Ahten felt diminished. This morbid state was not what he'd sought. Chespot was wrong. He did not feel like an eternal power. His senses warned that he was failing still – caught like a moth in a web somewhere between life and death.

Raj Ahten's Days asked, 'Your Highness, do you recall the precise moment that it happened?'

Raj Ahten scowled. Part of him had died with Saffira. She had been the most beautiful and the rarest of flowers.

And when he had called his Invincibles together and ordered them to help destroy Gaborn, they'd fought him instead. It was a grim struggle. He'd emerged from the battle only half alive.

'I don't recall,' Raj Ahten lied.

No one spoke for a long moment.

The flames from the bonfire spread out low to the ground, fanned toward him. Raj Ahten reached out until his right hand was nearly in them. The flame licked it, and in such piercing cold he felt no heat, only a warmth that seeped into his bones, easing the pain. Its golden curls were like sunlight shining through the trees, soft and glorious. The flameweavers nodded knowingly.

Az said, 'See how the Fire seeks him?'

Raj Ahten had imagined that the sorcerers moved the flames. Now he watched them curl toward him in awe.

Chespot reassured Raj Ahten, 'The Earth Powers withdraw from you. But not all who walk upon the face of the Earth need its sustenance. You have served our master well in the past. The forests of Aven are ash now, at your command. If you feel ill, if you continue to fade, my master will serve you. Step into the fire, and let it burn the dross from you. Give yourself to it, and it will sustain you.'

Naked desire showed in the flameweaver's face, as if he had craved this moment for years.

The flames of the bonfire crept out further, as if hungrily licking the snow.

Raj Ahten lurched away, stared at his right hand. It did feel better where the flames had touched him – as if he had applied a salve.

Binnesman had warned Raj Ahten that he was under the sway of flameweavers. It was true that they used him for their own ends, just as he used them.

In abject horror, Raj Ahten realized that a choice lay before him. He could continue as he was, wasting away until not even his endowments could save him. Or he could step into the fire and lose his humanity, become one of the flameweavers.

He staggered backward, retreated from the campfire out into the snowfield.

Feykaald and his Days got up and made as if to follow, but Raj Ahten waved them off. He wanted to be alone. His heart was racing.

Rahjim warned, 'The fire beckons. It may not always do so.'

Raj Ahten turned and jogged for several minutes, then stopped on a switchback and stood panting. He studied the road in the valleys below. It twisted among trees and a few miles ahead was lost beneath a thin blanket of clouds. Beyond, darkness reigned over the great desert.

A shadow flitted above the woods, an owl on the hunt. He followed it with his eyes until it winged into the stars. To the northeast, a few mountains loomed like islands of sand in a sea of mist. It was a beautiful sight.

The starlight struck the snow-covered ground around him. Trees were black streaks against the snow, the wan light draining all color from them.

Like a face drained of blood, he thought. All of his thoughts revolved around death. He closed his gritty eyes, blinking back the image of Saffira crushed on the battlefield of Carris, blood trickling down her forehead and from her nose.

She is dead, yet I live on.

He clenched his teeth, resolved not to mourn. But he could not turn aside his thoughts. She'd ridden down this road yesterday. With his endowments of scent, he could discern a trace of her jasmine perfume in the air, could smell the sweat of her horse. Saffira had died for her courage and compassion.

Saffira had died. Better if it had been Gaborn.

'Why?' Raj Ahten whispered to the Earth. 'You could have chosen me to be your king. Why not me?'

He listened, not because he expected an answer, but by habit. Wind sighed through the forests below. Nearby, mice rustled beneath a crust of snow in dry mountain grasses; the sound would have been inaudible to any other. Nothing more.

Raj Ahten had been raised on tales of men who had cheated death. Hassan the Headless was a king who'd lived eighty years ago, and had taken a hundred and fourteen endowments of stamina. In a battle, his enemy decapitated him. But just as a frog will live on after its head is removed, so did Hassan.

Hassan's body crawled about and even wrote a message in the sand, begging for a merciful death. But his enemy mocked him and put the undead corpse into a cage. Raj Ahten's mother said that Hassan had escaped, and at night on the desert one could still hear his fingers scratching in the sand as Hassan the Headless lurched about, seeking revenge.

It was a tale to horrify children.

But Raj Ahten had studied the matter, knew the full tale. Hassan had only lost part of his head – from the roof of the mouth up. His body had lived because part of the lower brain remained attached. So Hassan had survived for three weeks, tormented by hunger and thirst, until he burst with maggots.

Raj Ahten had performed a similar experiment with a highly endowed assassin named Sir Rober of Clythe. Raj Ahten felt convinced that his own endowments could keep him alive far longer than most would suspect.

Now a terrible choice lay before him, but in the end he feared he might not have any choice.

Raj Ahten clutched his fists. Blood raced through his veins. He vowed, 'Gaborn, the Earth *will* be mine.'

As Raj Ahten opened his eyes, downhill in the trees he spotted a silvery sheen that only his eyes could have detected – the color of heat from a living body. A moment of squinting revealed two huge bucks, antlers locked. One was already dead, worn from combat. But the living animal could not disengage.

It happened sometimes in the fall. The big bucks would fight, and their antlers would tangle hopelessly, leaving both animals locked in a death grip.

Even the victor looked only half alive.

I do not have to choose now, Raj Ahten told himself. I do not have to step into the fire and give away my humanity. Hassan had a small fraction of the stamina that I do.

From the misty canyons below, an Imperial stallion came galloping up the road. Raj Ahten studied the rider with keen eyes. A desert boy of nine or ten rode the huge mount, weaving from fatigue. He was dressed in a white burnoose, dark cape, and had his head wrapped in a turban. A message case was tied to the pommel of his saddle. The glint of gold embossing identified it as an Imperial message case. Raj Ahten knew that he bore ill tidings.

He stalked back to the fire, beneath the hovering spy balloon.

The boy whipped his horse as he neared. The stallion eyed the graak-shaped balloon, eyes rolling in terror. It danced about, thrusting its ears backward and flaring its nostrils. The beast was wet with sweat. Its breath came hard.

'O Great Light!' the boy cried when he recognized Raj Ahten. 'Yesterday at dawn, reavers took the blood-metal mines in Kartish! The very Lord of the Underworld led them.'

Feykaald gasped. 'If the attack was like the one in Carris . . .'

Raj Ahten had never fully comprehended how dangerous a reaver horde could be. His perfect memory replayed images of the fell mage crouched on Bone Hill, her citrine staff pulsing with light, issuing her incantations through scents while her minions huddled nearby. Her curses had blasted every living plant, had blinded and deafened his troops, had wrung the water from men's flesh.

The reavers in Kartish could do untold damage. The destruction of crops alone would lead to famines throughout all of Indhopal.

'Everyone went to battle,' the boy panted, 'except your servants at the Palace of Canaries in Om. They're taking your Dedicates north. They sent me –'

'You say the Lord of the Underworld led them?'

'Yes,' the boy said, eyes growing wide and panicked. 'A fell mage, very big. No one has ever heard of her like.'

Of course, Raj Ahten realized. The reavers would have sent their best troops to Indhopal. It was more populous than Rofehavan, more powerful. Only their most fearsome lord would have dared come against him.

Raj Ahten's course was decided. His people needed him desperately.

He yanked the boy from the horse, leapt onto its back. 'Follow me as you can,' Raj Ahten shouted at the flameweavers.

Feykaald looked up at him for orders. Raj Ahten thought swiftly. He felt ill, as if his very soul were waning. He needed to be strong. 'Go back to Carris,' he commanded. 'Find out what the Earth King has done with my forcibles. I'll need them.'

'He will not trust me,' Feykaald objected.

'He will if he believes that you are there against my will,' Raj Ahten said. He pulled out the gold message case, tossed it to Feykaald. 'Tell him of the reavers in Kartish. Tell him that the Lord of the Underworld leads them. Say that you came to beg him to come to the aid of Indhopal.'

'You think he will come?' Feykaald asked.

'He will entertain the notion.'

'As you command, O Light of the World,' Feykaald said.

Raj Ahten wheeled the stallion, raced for Kartish.

Chapter Nine:
WIZARDBORN

I don't have a father. Like all Earth Wardens, I was born of the Earth.

– The Wizard Binnesman

As the slow light descended from heaven, spreading across the blasted fields thirty miles north of Carris, Myrrima asked Averan, 'So, you know nothing more?'

'I've told you everything,' Averan said. She had told how she'd first met Roland Borenson, Myrrima's father-in-law, on the way to Carris, along with Baron Poll and the green woman. Averan had taken Myrrima up through the time that she'd left Roland and Baron Poll, only to be rescued by Myrrima's husband in company with Saffira. She told Myrrima how she'd helped Sir Borenson enter Carris to hunt for his father.

Averan could tell that her story hurt Myrrima.

In the back of the wagon, Sir Borenson slept deeply. A burning fever seemed ready to consume him. Myrrima had done all that she could for him last night. She'd applied balms from the healers, had poured libations of wine over him and whispered incantations to Water. They'd had to stay at Carris at night, for fear that they'd meet a reaver in the dark. But Myrrima had fled that foul place with her husband at the first crack of dawn, hoping that the king's wizard in Balington might heal him.

A force horse pulled the wagon, and the wheels nearly sang as they spun down the road through the deadlands.

Averan had secured a ride with Myrrima by claiming that she had an 'urgent message' for the king. But Averan had left out a few details in her story.

The sun had begun to rise far beyond the oak-covered hills, like a cold red eye. Averan squinted at it, then pulled her hooded robe over her face.

She didn't like the burning sensation that the sun caused. Her skin tingled at its touch. Her hands were itching, as if she'd handled poison ivy.

But she was glad that she wasn't Borenson. Myrrima had pulled up his tunic, looked beneath his armor, and Averan had glimpsed how he'd been wounded.

The wound would have been ghastly under any circumstances, even if it hadn't gotten infected. Averan had had no idea that people could do that to one another.

'Myrrima,' Averan asked, 'when you take the walnuts off a bull, he's called a "steer." And when you take them off a stallion, he's a "gelding." What do you call it when they take them off a man?'

'A eunuch,' Myrrima said. 'Raj Ahten made a eunuch out of my husband.'

'Oh,' Averan said. 'That means he can't have babies, right?'

Myrrima's dark eyes filled with water, and she bit at her lip. After a moment she said, 'That's right. We can't have babies.'

Averan didn't dare ask another question. It was too painful for Myrrima.

'I saw how you cried over Roland,' Myrrima said.

'He's dead,' Averan said. 'Everyone I know is dead: Roland and Brand and my mother.'

'I was at Longmot when the wight of Erden Geboren came,' Myrrima said. 'He blew his warhorn, and men who had died that day rose up and joined him on the hunt. They were happy, Averan. Death isn't an ending. It's a new beginning. I'm sure that Roland is happy, wherever he is.'

Averan said nothing. She couldn't be sure what the dead felt.

'You didn't know him long,' Myrrima said, as if she should feel better because of it.

Averan shook her head. 'He said –' She sniffled. 'He said he was going to petition the duke, so that he could become my father. I've never had a father.'

Myrrima reached out and took Averan's hand. She looked in Averan's eyes and said, 'If the duke had granted that petition, then I would have been your sister in-law.' Myrrima squeezed her hand. 'I could still use another sister.'

Averan clenched her jaw, and tried to put on a bold face.

She trembled. Her guts were still cramped and twisted in terror. She'd fed on reaver brains last night, but she didn't dare tell Myrrima what she'd done. She didn't dare tell a stranger how the reaver's memories now haunted her.

Averan crawled off the buckboard, into the wagon, and curled up in the hay. The new hay smelled of sweet clover, fescue, and oat straw. She buried her face in it, but it could not keep out the memories.

In her mind's eye, Averan beheld an enormous reaver mage, stalking uphill through a windy cave. The image and smells came preternaturally clear, like a waking dream, or as if the memory were more real than the life that she lived.

Averan did not see the scene as a person would. Reavers have no eyes; instead, their philia sense life in ways she couldn't understand. To a reaver, living animals glowed in the darkness the way that lightning glows.

Now, Averan recalled the reaver mage glowing, speaking to her in scents. 'Follow my trail.'

In memory, Averan had no choice but to follow. Yet she felt terrified, and knew that she was marching to a place where she didn't want to go. She detected scents in the air, the cries of reavers in supreme torment.

The philia near the One True Master's anus began excreting words, and Averan scuttled forward to taste them.

'Do not fear,' the One True Master said. 'You smell pain, but you shall not be subjected to it. The Blood of the Faithful will be sweet to you.'

The image faded. Averan realized that she'd blacked out.

She must have slept for a few minutes, because her eyes felt more rested. But her stomach still hurt from eating so much. She clutched it.

Averan fought a dull sense of panic. She remembered snatches of what had happened next. She recalled forcibles and an incantation.

The One True Master had given her servant an endowment. But Averan couldn't figure out exactly which. Averan hadn't been able to eat much of the monster's brains – not even a tenth of them. She didn't know all that the mage had known, couldn't make much sense of most of the reaver's thoughts and memories.

And it was the things that she didn't know that scared Averan most.

She tried not to fret, held an image of the reaver in her mind, wondered why the reavers saw living creatures as if they glowed like lightning. Averan supposed that it was because there is lightning inside of people. On warm summer nights when clouds used to roll low over the graak's aerie at Keep Haberd, she'd pull off her wool blanket and see small flashes of light against her skin. Beastmaster Brand had said that it was because there was lightning inside her.

Averan lay down next to Sir Borenson and rested her head on her hand. She noticed some pale green things – roots – woven into her robe.

She pulled a couple off, threw them into the hay. It had been raining all night, so her robe had been wet and then gotten covered in seeds.

Now the seeds were sprouting. They were everywhere in her robe, like little green worms. She decided to pick them out later.

The wagon passed under a tree, and Averan saw the shadows of leaves. She took a deep breath, inhaled the scent of fields and hills.

She sat up excitedly. They'd left the deadlands! Her head still ached. She squinted in the sunlight, pulled her robe close.

After a night of storm, the sun had surged into the sky, hurling splintered shafts of silver through broken clouds to dash against the emerald hillsides. The roosters at a nearby cottage celebrated by crowing as if it were the first sunrise in a month, and the whole land was filled with the cries of larks and the peeping of sparrows from under every bush.

To her left the round hills seemed to bow to the mountains. The night's rain had soaked into summer-dried grass and left the land smelling drenched and new. The leaves of maples and alders turning on the lower slopes made them shimmer in shades of scarlet, russet, and gold.

To the right, a silver stream wound through a stand of alders. White ducks gabbled as they fed along the stream banks downhill.

Ahead lay a village with thatch-roofed cottages squatting by the road. Honeysuckle and ivy trailed over the garden walls.

Everything here seemed so alive – everything but Sir Borenson. He had gone from pale to a feverish red. Sweat streamed from his forehead.

'Where are we?' Averan asked.

'Balington,' Myrrima said. 'You've been asleep for more than an hour.'

Averan looked at the cottages. Yesterday, she'd been able

to sense Gaborn's presence in battle. She'd seen the Earth King as a green flame that stood before her even when she closed her eyes. The Earth King was supposed to be here.

Now, she reached out with her feelings, tried to discern his location. But the flame had gone.

Still, there was something about Balington. She felt a power here, old and immense. She could not detect its center, could not tell if it meant her well or ill. She felt as if she were riding toward her destiny.

They drove into the village, past forty fine horses that stood all blanketed and barded outside the stables. Averan spotted a wagon there with several burly guards hovering nearby – keeping watch over the king's treasure. It looked as if the king were getting ready to ride.

A village boy in leather pants, green smock, and feathered cap led a milk cow along the road. Cream leaked from her swollen udders.

Myrrima stopped long enough to ask the lad, 'Where's the king's wizard?'

'Round the back,' he said, pointing toward the inn.

Myrrima drove the wagon to the back of the inn. She skirted a stone fence covered in jasmine and golden hop vines until she reached a wooden gate. She climbed down, unlatched it.

'Are you coming?' Myrrima asked. 'You said you had a message for the king's ears only.'

Now that she was here, Averan felt uneasy about the ruse. She feared that if she told Gaborn her story, he would think her mad. A dull pain throbbed at the base of her skull.

She summoned her courage. 'I'm coming.'

She hopped out of the wagon on stiff legs and entered the garden gate. Brown and white pigeons strutted atop the thatch of a dovecote, cooing softly. A gray squirrel went leaping up a nearby cherry tree, its tail floating behind.

Gaborn's Days stood at the top of the garden in a patch

of sunlight. The skeletal scholar, with his close-cut hair and rust-colored robes, stood quietly with his hands clasped behind his back, merely observing.

The king himself sat on a stone beneath an almond tree in the midst of the garden. He wore a shirt of ring mail, as if for battle. Sweat darkened the quilted tunic beneath his arms, as if he had been doing heavy labor. But he merely talked. At least thirty knights surrounded him, all sitting on the grass in their finely burnished armor, the young squires with their bowl haircuts and rougher clothes lounging in the shadows beyond. Most of the lords hailed from Mystarria, but she saw some blank shields, and even a pair of Invincibles who had ripped off their surcoats so that they no longer wore the gold and crimson of Raj Ahten.

Gaborn sat with his back straight and chin high, engaged in light conversation. The queen sat at his feet, in a robe as softly yellow as a rose.

Averan saw no sign of the wizard that Myrrima was seeking. Indeed, Myrrima whispered a question to a lord, and he nodded toward the inn.

Myrrima hurried back out of the garden, and Averan just stood a moment, too nervous to speak.

Some minor noble was saying, 'There's tales going around Carris that a certain commoner, a fellow named Waggit, killed nine reavers in battle.'

'Nine?' several men guffawed in disbelief.

'No man who survived Carris should ever be called common,' Gaborn said. 'And if the tales be true, I'm tempted to have this Waggit knighted and placed in my personal guard. What do you know of him?'

'He works in the mines at Silverdale,' the lord said. 'I hear he's somewhat . . . well, he's simple.'

'A fool killed nine reavers?' Gaborn asked in disbelief.

'With a pickax, no less,' Lord Bowen confirmed. 'The bards at Carris are already singing about it. I'd have brought the man to your attention sooner, but given his incapacity . . .'

'By the Powers, I would that all men were such fools!' Gaborn swore. 'I'll have him in my guard!'

The knights laughed, and Averan found herself smiling at the jest too. Gaborn could only make the man a guard if he cured him of his idiocy, and the only way to do that would be to have him take an endowment of Wit from someone who was whole. Surely Gaborn would not waste a forcible on a fool, for in curing one fool, it would only make another – and at great cost to the kingdom. For the forcibles used in the endowment ceremony were made of metal that was far rarer than gold.

She hadn't known what to expect of Gaborn. She normally dealt with old wrinkled dukes and barons. But Gaborn was not some pompous lord trying to impress people with his ten endowments of glamour. Instead he was a strong, lanky youth with dark hair and piercing blue eyes.

She'd expected that the Earth King would be grim and stern, full of himself. But Gaborn did his best to fit in, to cheer the men around him.

Averan decided that she liked him in spite of the fact that she knew that something was wrong.

An unlikely pair of warriors got off the ground. One of them she recognized from his tunic. He wore the colors of South Crowthen, and could only be Anders's son, Celinor. The other was a young horsesister from Fleeds.

'Milord,' Celinor said. 'We'll be leaving now, if we may.'

Gaborn looked thoughtful. 'I . . . sense no immediate danger.'

The queen blurted an old blessing out of Fleeds: 'Erin, Celinor – may the Glories ride before you while the Bright Ones blaze at your back.'

'And with you, My Queen,' the horsesister said.

Gaborn turned his gaze toward Averan's direction, caught

her eye. Everyone fell silent, watched her expectantly. She still wore the robe of a skyrider. Averan could tell by Gaborn's tone that he feared that she carried dire news.

'Well?' the king asked in a kindly tone. 'Do you have a message?'

Averan stammered, couldn't think how to start.

'Have . . . have you forgotten the message?' Gaborn asked kindly.

'I . . .' Averan didn't know what to say.

'Spit it out, child,' Gaborn's counselor said.

Averan found herself babbling, trying to explain all that she'd learned: 'A green woman fell from the sky, and her blood got on me, and ever since then, everything is so strange. I ate a reaver's brain. I can remember things – the way a reaver sees and smells and thinks. I know what they know. In the Underworld, there's a fell mage. She's called the One True Master. She's the one who sent the reavers to Carris. You didn't beat her –'

Around Gaborn, knights and lords stared at Averan, dumbfounded. One lord blurted, 'Where did this child come from? I didn't see a graak fly in. What is she saying?'

Averan knew that she wasn't making much sense.

Another knight said, 'She's gone mad.' He got up and started to walk toward her.

Averan shouted, 'No!'

Gaborn raised his hands, warning the lords back. He looked at her sharply. 'You say you *ate* a reaver's brain and learned what it knew?'

'Yes,' Averan said. 'I ate the brain from the fell mage you slew. I know what it knows. She came to destroy all the blood metal beneath Carris, so that she could hurt us. But – in my visions I remember the screams of reavers. They've learned how to take endowments, too.'

Gaborn hesitated a moment. He seemed pensive, thoughtful. Ages ago, mankind had developed their rune lore in an effort to mimic the way that reavers gained strength by eating the glands of their dead, or learned by eating the brains of their dead. But this was the first time anyone had discovered that reavers had learned to take endowments from their own.

'Tell me,' Gaborn asked. 'Do you know anything about the Place of Bones?'

'Yes!' Averan shouted. 'That's what the reavers call the throne where the One True Master rules, among the bones of the enemies she's eaten! It's in the Underworld, near the burning stones.'

The queen let out a yelp of surprise and alarm, and climbed to her feet.

'Can you tell me the way?' Gaborn asked.

Averan stood dumbfounded. She recalled bits of the journey, flashes of images of reavers marching up through twisting caverns in the Underworld. But they were just snatches of images – a long march through dangerous territory where the great worms lived, the hot vents near caves of fire. There were cliffs and ledges that no man could scale, and the trail went past tunnels that led to the wilds. She couldn't describe it.

'There is a trail,' Averan said. 'I . . . don't know how to get there. The trail is long and twisted, and no commoner could ever make it. Even for a reaver, the trail was terribly har—'

'But there is a trail, one that a bold man might follow?' Gaborn urged hopefully.

'Yes,' Averan said. 'But there are millions of tunnels down there. There are hundreds of reaver hives, each with a thousand passages. You – you could waste a lifetime looking for the hive of the One True Master. Even if you found it, finding her would be another matter!'

Gaborn's eyes seemed to bore right into her. She knew what he was thinking. He wanted to go into the Underworld. But Averan didn't know the way.

'What's going on here?' someone demanded.

She turned. A wizard stood at the head of the garden

in russet robes. He seemed to be a kindly looking man, with a weathered face and skin that was just a tad too green. His eyes were as clear blue as a summer's day. His hair might have once been the color of chestnuts, but now gray streaked through it. His cheeks were as ruddy as sandstone, and the hair of his beard grew thicker at the base than at the tips. His strange robe looked to be woven of reddish roots.

Averan had never seen anyone like the wizard before. Yet everything about him seemed familiar. She had never met her father. By all accounts, reavers ate him while she was an infant. But she looked upon the wizard and wondered if perhaps everyone had lied. Perhaps this man was her father.

The wizard stared at her with a gaze so intense that it could have bored holes through a millstone. She sensed power in him, a power older than the hills, stronger than iron.

Behind him stood Myrrima and the green woman who had fallen from the sky.

'Averan!' the green woman called.

The wizard strode forward, his robes swishing in the silence that suddenly seemed to descend upon the garden. The green woman followed.

He stopped a moment, glanced down at the pale roots sprouting in Averan's coat. 'Here, child,' Binnesman said gently, 'show me your hands.'

Averan held out her hands, opened them wide. Her palms itched more than before. Yesterday shapeless green blobs showed on her palms. The green woman's blood had seemed to be seeping below her skin.

Now, to her surprise, each palm bore a dark-green image that had enlarged overnight. For the all world, on each hand, it looked as if she had tattoos of oak leaves.

Binnesman smiled, then touched each palm. Immediately

the itching eased, and the dull ache at the base of her skull went away.

One of the king's counselors, an old fellow with silver hair, gaped at her hands and said in astonishment, 'She's wizardborn!'

Chapter Ten:
STRANGE TIDINGS

If you listen closely, you'll learn as much from your child as it does from you.

– Adage from Heredon

Iome stared at Averan, heart pounding. Such a small, frail-looking girl, Iome thought. Yet she appeared like a portent of doom.

Iome had thought her husband mistaken. She'd suspected that the Place of Bones existed only in his imagination, that he'd been unable to accept the Earth's rejection.

Now she feared that he would coerce this innocent child into leading him into the Underworld to battle this One True Master.

Binnesman leaned over the girl. *Wizardborn.* Jerimas's pronouncement hung in the air.

'Not merely wizardborn,' Binnesman said. 'She's an Earth Warden – the apprentice I've long awaited.'

Binnesman held the girl's hands and smiled at her gently. His soft voice, his warm touch, all were meant to comfort her. But Iome sensed by his rigid stance and the way that he refused to meet the child's eyes that the wizard was at war with himself.

'Let us not speak in the open daylight,' Binnesman said. 'Come inside with me.'

He took the girl's hand and led her to the common room of the inn. Every lord in the place followed, until there was no room around the bar where Averan sat, and men crowded the doorway.

Once he had her sitting on the bar, Binnesman asked easily, 'Tell me, child, is Averan your name?'

The girl nodded.

'How did my wylde know?'

'I was riding my graak and I saw her fall from the sky. I landed, and tried to help, and her blood got on me. She came north with me to Carris –'

'Hmmm . . .' Binnesman muttered. 'A strange coincidence, don't you think, that I lose a wylde and that you should find it?'

Averan shrugged.

'It's more than a coincidence,' Binnesman said. 'Tell me, what were you thinking about when it happened?'

'I don't remember exactly,' Averan said. 'I guess . . . I was hoping that someone would come help me.'

'Hmmm . . . You're a skyrider? You're good with animals, I suspect. Do you like animals?'

'Yes,' Averan admitted.

'Are you good with graaks?'

'Master Brand said that he thought I was the best that he'd ever seen. He was going to make me beast master someday.'

'Hmmm . . .' Binnesman said thoughtfully. 'Do you have a favorite animal?'

Averan shook her head no. 'I like them all.'

Binnesman mused for a long moment. 'Do you like plants better than animals, or rocks?'

'How could you like a rock more than an animal?' Averan asked.

'Some people do,' Binnesman said. 'As for myself, I like plants about as much as I do people. When I was a boy, I used to love to walk in the meadows and count buttercups, or the number of seeds on a sheaf of wheat. For hours I used to study how ivy curls its way up a tree. Sometimes I felt as if I were waiting for a revelation. I used to . . . I would sit and listen for the dry summer grasses all tangled with weeds to whisper some cosmic truth.

'I used to try to think like an oak, and imagine how far the tangled roots of an aspen traveled, and wonder what dreams the willow dreamed.

'Tell me, do you ever do that?'

'You sound crazy!' Averan blurted.

Jerimas barked out in laughter, and said, 'Now there's a child who speaks her mind!'

'I suppose I do sound crazy,' Binnesman admitted. 'But everyone has a touch of madness, and those who can't admit it are usually farther gone than the rest of us. Wizards are, as anyone can tell you, quite demented.'

Averan nodded, as if that sounded reasonable.

'I love the Earth,' Binnesman explained. 'And what's more, I know that you must love it, too, in your own way. Loving it so much is not bad, or shameful. You'll find great power in moving outside yourself. There is power in studying the ways of plants and animals and stones. It lies at the heart of the Earth Powers.

'The green in your hands comes because Earth Blood flows through your veins.'

'But . . .' Averan said. 'I . . . it was an accident. I got the green woman's blood on me.'

Binnesman shook his head. 'No, Earth Blood was inside you all along. It has always been a part of you, ever since you were born. You are wizardborn. But among us creatures of the Earth, blood calls to blood. That's why I came to the garden just a moment ago. I felt you here. What's more, I suspect that you summoned my wylde from the sky. And when you touched the green woman's blood, you couldn't get it off because it flowed to you. Like was seeking like.'

'I've felt so strange ever since,' Averan argued. 'I've had . . . queer new powers.'

'You would have developed those powers in time,' Binnesman assured her. 'The extra Earth Blood just speeded the process, heightened your awareness. But I assure you, if you had not already been a creature of the Earth, the blood would have washed off your hands.'

Iome listened in fascination. She stared hard at the girl. Averan had red hair and freckles, and in every way other than the odd tattoos of green on her hand seemed a normal child. But she had an intensity to her gaze, a fierceness of spirit, and a maturity that Iome would have found surprising in a woman twice Averan's age.

Gaborn ventured a question. 'You say that you've developed strange powers. Tell me about them.'

Averan glanced up at the men in the inn, as if afraid to speak openly, as if afraid that no one would believe her.

'Go ahead,' Binnesman urged.

'Well, for one thing,' Averan said, 'I can't sleep very well unless . . .'

'You're buried underground?' Binnesman asked.

Averan nodded bravely. 'And the sun hurts me now. Even when it barely touches me, I feel like I'm getting a sunburn.'

'I can fix that,' Binnesman said. 'There are runes of protection from such things – spells so potent that they'll almost let you walk through fire. I'll teach them to you.'

'And I can feel where food is – like carrots underground, and nuts hidden in the grass.'

'That's also a common gift for Earth Wardens,' Binnesman said. 'The "Fruits of the Forest and of the Field" are all yours to eat. The Earth gives them to you freely.'

'And I used to be able to see the Earth King,' Averan

said. 'I could close my eyes, and see a green flame, and imagine precisely where he was. But . . . that doesn't work anymore.'

She looked at Gaborn doubtfully. There was no condemnation in her eyes, no accusation. But Iome knew that she knew for certain that he had lost his powers.

'Well,' Binnesman said in surprise, 'that's one for the books! I've never heard of any such power before. But every wizard has his own gifts, to suit his own needs. I'm sure that you'll discover more as you grow. Is there anything else?'

'Just the reavers' brains,' Averan admitted.

All the time that this strange little girl had been speaking, several lords leaned close, drawn by her peculiar tale. Iome did not notice it consciously until one of the lords guffawed, as if unable to believe her.

'Where did you get the reaver brains?' Binnesman asked.

Averan pointed up to the green woman. 'Spring killed one on the road and started eating it, and it smelled so good, I couldn't help myself. Afterward, I had strange dreams – dreams that let me see what it was like to be a reaver, to think like a reaver and talk like one and see like one.'

'What did you learn?' Jerimas asked.

'I learned that reavers talk by making smells,' Averan said. 'The philia on their faces let them "listen" to each other, and the ones above their bungholes make smells.'

A skeptical lord crowed, 'So you're telling us that they talk out their asses?'

'Yes,' Averan said. 'In that way, they're not too different from some people.'

Jerimas laughed aloud, and said to the lord, 'She got you, Dullins.'

But the mocking affected the child. Averan withdrew, and she began to tremble just a bit, staring from person to person. 'I'm not making this up!' she said. 'I couldn't make this stuff up.'

Iome knew that she was right about the smells. There had long been a debate among lords as to whether reavers emitted any odors at all. Most swore that you couldn't smell a reaver. Others believed that they disguised their scent. But yesterday, at Carris, the fell mage had sent waves of reeking odors over Gaborn's armies, causing terrible damage.

'I'm not lying,' Averan said. 'And I'm not crazy. You can't think I'm crazy. I don't want to be locked up in a cage, like Corman the Crow.'

'We believe you,' Iome said, smiling gently. She'd never heard of Corman the Crow. But sometimes there was nothing that could be done with a madman, and such unfortunate souls had to be locked away for their own good, in the hope that time would cure their minds.

'I know you're not crazy,' Gaborn said. He seemed to want to draw her back out of her shell. 'So reavers can talk in smells?'

'And read and write too.'

Iome felt perplexed. She'd never suspected such a thing.

'How come we've never seen their writing?' Gaborn said.

'Because they write with smells. They leave smells written on stones along every trail. That's the way that they like to talk best. In fact, it's easier for a reaver to write a message than to talk face-to-face.'

'Why?' Gaborn asked.

Averan struggled to explain. 'For a reaver, a word is a smell. Your name and your smell are the same thing, so that all a reaver has to do to say "Gaborn" is to make your smell.'

'That sounds simple enough,' Gaborn said.

'It is, and it isn't. Imagine that we are talking, and you said to me, "Averan, that's a beautiful pair of rabbitskin boots you're wearing. Where did you get them?" And I said, "Thank you, I found them by the roadside, and no one claimed them. So now they're mine."

'When we talk like that, every word goes out of our mouths and stays in the air for a moment. Then it fades all by itself. So our words are a line of sounds, coming out of us.

'But with reavers, words don't disappear on their own. All those smells, all those words, simply hang in the air – until you erase them.'

'And how is that done?' Binnesman asked. Everyone in Gaborn's retinue crowded round Averan, as if she were some great scholar in the House of Understanding. They hung on her every word.

'After I create each scent, I have to make its opposite, the unscent that erases it.'

'What . . . ?' Binnesman asked. 'You say "I." But you mean the reavers?'

'Yeah, I mean the reavers make the unscent.'

'The scent's negative?' Gaborn asked.

'Yes,' Averan said, uncertainly, as if she'd never heard the word *negative* before.

'So when I say the word "Gaborn," I have to create a scent that says "not-Gaborn," before I speak again. I have to take the word "Gaborn" from the air.

'And that can be very hard to do,' Averan said. 'If I scream the word, if I make the scent strongly, I must unscream it, too. And the farther away you are, the longer it takes for you to get my message. So reavers learn to speak when they're close together, to talk softly, to make scents that are so faint, other animals can't even smell them. They're just whispers that float in the air.'

'Wait a minute,' one lord said. 'You say you have to make this word disappear. But why couldn't you just make all the scents anyway? You can walk into a room and smell carrots and beef and turnips all boiling at the same time.'

'You can,' Averan said, 'but it doesn't mean anything. To a reaver, it would just be a jumble of words. Imagine if you took all the words I've said in the last two minutes and said them all at once. Could anyone make sense of it?'

'The reavers must talk slowly, then,' Gaborn mused.

'Not much slower than how you and I are speaking now,' Averan said, 'at least when they're close together. But it's hard to understand each other across great distances.

'So reavers do write,' Averan continued, 'all the time. If a scout passes down a trail, he'll leave messages behind, telling what he sensed on side journeys, where he last saw enemies.'

This news astonished Iome and everyone else in the room. For ages men had wondered how reavers communicated. Most men assumed that they did it by waving their philia about. But Averan's words would profoundly change the way that men perceived reavers. The girl knew this, and now seemed to have lost her inhibitions.

'And another thing,' Averan said. 'Reavers don't see like we do. They can only see close by, and they see the world all in one color, but it isn't a color. I can't explain it, but it's the color of lightning. Lightning blinds them. When it flashes, they feel the way you would if you were staring into the sun. It's very painful.'

'You're a brave little girl,' Gaborn said. As if she had been waiting for his reassurance, Averan's resolve broke. Tears suddenly filled her eyes, and she began to sob. 'Your tale brings certain questions to mind.'

'What?' Averan asked.

'For example, can you tell me about the nature and disposition of the reavers' troops?'

Averan stared at him blankly. 'Nature?'

'The reaver armies,' Gaborn clarified. 'Do you know how many reavers there are?'

Averan shook her head. 'I . . . one of the reavers I ate was a scout. The other a mage. I don't know about numbers.'

Gaborn turned back to Averan. 'Let me pose it another

way. You don't have any idea how many reavers there are in the Underworld?'

Averan seemed to gather herself. She closed her eyes for a long moment and said, 'The Underworld is full, but the reavers – they can't live just anywhere. Food is scarce.'

And we're food, Iome thought. Gaborn glanced back at his counselors. The Wits showed little emotion.

'Your Highness,' Averan continued, 'I'm scared.'

'Of what?' Gaborn asked softly.

'The One True Master has unraveled much of the Master Rune. Yesterday, you destroyed the Seal of Desolation that her apprentice laid on Carris.'

Gaborn nodded. Gaborn had killed the most powerful reaver mage ever mentioned in the tomes. Some small part of Iome had been clinging to the hope that Gaborn had already slain the most powerful of all reavers. But this child described it as being a mere 'apprentice' to a far more powerful master.

'Tell me about her,' Gaborn demanded.

Iome's glance flicked up to Binnesman. The mage, with his perpetual stoop, looked suddenly pale. He leaned on his staff, as if seeking support.

'In the Underworld,' Averan said, 'the One True Master is taking endowments. And she's giving them to her leaders.'

'Reavers have always been able to eat one another and grow that way,' Gaborn said. 'Are you sure it isn't the same?'

'This is different,' Averan said. 'Reavers can eat each other's brains to learn. And they can eat the musk glands under their arms to grow. But now they've discovered rune lore. She's already deciphered the runes of grace, scent, and brawn. Now she's trying to perfect metabolism.'

There was a moment of silence as warriors looked at one another meaningfully. Facing reavers was bad enough. Facing one that had endowments of metabolism was terrifying.

'But there's something more,' Averan said. 'I don't understand it all. The Seal of Desolation that you destroyed, that was part of something bigger. She plans to bind a Seal of Desolation to the Seal of Heaven and the Seal of the Inferno.'

Binnesman drew back, leaned on his staff for support. 'That . . . that's not possible! No one could decipher so much of the Master Rune!'

'It is possible,' Averan said. 'I saw the runes taking shape at the Place of Bones! You saw the Seal of Desolation –'

'But,' Jerimas blurted, 'it has taken mankind thousands of years to decipher the shapes of even the smallest of runes – brawn and wit! How could one reaver learn so much?'

'She divines them by looking into the fire,' Averan said.

Binnesman backed away. 'By the Tree!' he swore. His face was hard. He looked bewildered, as if someone had just bludgeoned him for no apparent reason. 'By the Tree . . .' He knew something that Iome didn't, she felt sure. Or perhaps he merely suspected something. 'You're sure that this One True Master is a reaver, not some other creature?'

'I've seen her,' Averan said. 'She's enormous, but she's just a reaver.'

Binnesman shook his head, as if he could not believe it. 'Not just a reaver.'

'You say that she's binding these seals,' Gaborn asked Binnesman. 'What will that do?'

'She plans to bind the Powers of Fire and Air against us,' Binnesman said. 'Earth and Water would diminish. Life would . . . change in ways so fundamental, I cannot even begin to guess at the repercussions.'

Jerimas concluded, 'She'll destroy the world!'

'No!' Averan said. 'She doesn't want to destroy the world – just . . . *change* it into the kind of place where we can't live anymore.'

'Is that even possible?' Gaborn asked Binnesman.

Binnesman frowned, stroked his beard. 'If she comprehends so many pieces of the Master Rune, the world has not seen a creature with such power. . . .'

'Averan,' Gaborn said. 'This is imperative. I need to find this One True Master. I need to kill her, and I must do it quickly. How can I get to her? You say that you can't draw me a map. But you also say that you learn by eating reavers. Is there a certain kind of reaver that you need to eat, one who would know the way – another scout perhaps, or a howler?'

Averan looked up at him. Her eyes were filled with an unnamable expression. Iome could see a mixture of loathing and embarrassment and a pure desire to help. 'Maybe!' she said, as if the idea had not occurred to her. 'There are markings in the Underworld – directions.'

'Directions?' Gaborn said. 'So you need to understand their language better? Can't you get that from any reaver?'

Averan shook her head, said in a confused tone, 'No. Not all reavers speak the same language.'

'What?' Gaborn asked. 'Like Rofehavanish and Taifan?'

Averan tried to explain. 'Not like that,' Averan said. 'But a carpenter doesn't speak like a warrior, does he? He has his own words for tools and the things he does with them, his own language. Reavers are the same way. They each have different jobs. If you're ever going to reach the One True Master, there's a certain reaver you need. The reaver . . . there's no name for it. There's just a smell.'

'Does it have any special markings?' Gaborn asked.

Averan wrinkled her brow. 'It's a Waykeeper,' she said slowly, as if searching for the right description. 'It's a Waymaker. It knows where the trails in the Underworld lead, and which doors are locked, and how they are guarded.'

'How many of these monsters are traveling with the horde?'

'One.'

'Just one?'

'Yes!' Averan said. A fierce light came into her eyes. 'Just one – a big male, with thirty-six philia, and huge paws, and runes on his arms. I – I might know him if I could see him, and could smell him!'

Gaborn stepped backward, looked at Iome. His eyes were haunted, his expression that of a trapped animal. Iome knew that he was leaving, going someplace that she dared not follow.

'Gentlemen,' Gaborn told the knights there in the inn, 'prepare your mounts. We'll ride for Carris within the hour.'

Chapter Eleven: A SMALL THING

Miracles are as common as soapwort seeds and spiderwebs. People tend to forget that, until they hear a newborn baby cry.

– *The wizard Binnesman*

Binnesman pulled up the gray blanket that covered Sir Borenson, looked beneath his tunic, and glanced away, frowning. 'He's infected. We'll have to bring that fever down.'

He covered Borenson quickly, so passersby would not see, but it was too late. Myrrima had come out of the inn to find a couple of squires in the wagonbed, already gawking at the wound. She'd shooed them away. But now a number of knights that knew Borenson either in person or by reputation had begun to gather around the wain, and Myrrima was rapidly finding that nothing attracts a crowd like a crowd.

Borenson lay unconscious amid the sweet-smelling hay. Myrrima felt anxious for his welfare. She had seen people die before. She believed that in his current state, her husband ought to be able to hang on for another day or two. But she still felt nervous. Sometimes, the sick could fool you, die just when you thought them recovered.

Sweat glistened on his face. All around, the lords and

squires who had come to ride in Gaborn's retinue were preparing for the journey south. Those with ready mounts stood in their armor, elbows on the wagon, gazing in. Binnesman had Averan and his wylde at his side.

Binnesman turned to Averan. 'Do you know what sweet woodruff looks like?'

'White flowers?' Averan asked. 'Beastmaster Brand used to put the leaves in his wine.'

'Good girl,' Binnesman said. 'I saw some growing under the hedge round back. Go and pluck a dozen leaves for me.'

Averan raced off around the inn, while Binnesman went back inside for a moment. By now twenty men were standing around the wagon.

A knight of Mystarria came up, a fellow with a long black moustache that flowed over his chin guard. He glanced in the wagon. 'Sir Borenson? Wounded?'

'Aye,' a bystander said. 'He took the worst of them.'

'Head wound?'

'Worse – got his walnuts cracked.'

The fellow squirmed, reached over to look under Borenson's tunic.

'If you want to look,' Myrrima said, reaching out to grab his wrist, 'it will cost you!'

'Cost me?' the knight asked. He smiled disarmingly. 'How much?'

'An eye,' Myrrima said. Around her the crowd erupted into laughter.

Binnesman came back out of the inn with a bit of creamed honey in a bowl. As soon as Averan returned with the small, pale spade-shaped leaves of the sweet woodruff, he said, 'Now, bruise the leaves by rolling them between your hands.'

Averan rolled the leaves.

'Put them in the honey.'

She dropped them in.

Binnesman reached into the pocket of his robe, pulled out a bit of dark dried plant stem. 'Hyssop,' he told Averan. 'Always pick it two days after it rains, and make sure you use the moldy leaves, down near the roots.'

He crushed the dried leaf, put it in the honey, stirred it with his finger. He added a dried leaf of agrimony, the herb that soldiers most often took to staunch wounds on the battlefield.

At that moment, some fellow came up to the back of the crowd and blurted, 'What's going on?'

'Borenson has lost his walnuts,' a knight said, 'and Binnesman's going to grow him some new ones.'

Several men snorted in derisive laughter. It was a bad joke, and Myrrima didn't laugh.

'Really, how soon until he can ride again?' the knight teased.

Binnesman whirled on the crowd. 'Is this what we've come to?' he shouted. 'Do the children of Earth stand here upon sacred ground and mock the Earth?'

Myrrima felt sure that the knights had meant no disrespect, but Binnesman seemed furious. He drew himself to his full height, glowered at the knights, so that to the man they began to back away from his challenge. More importantly, they all began to back away from the knight who had made the jest, Sir Prenholm of Heredon.

'How dare you!' Binnesman said. 'Have you learned nothing in these past few days?

'You could not have withstood the Darkling Glory, but Myrrima here, a woman who at the time did not have a single one of the greater endowments of brawn or grace or stamina, slew it single-handedly.

'You with all of your endowments could not stand against the reavers at Carris – but Gaborn called a worm, a single worm, and routed the whole of the reaver horde!

'How can you doubt the Power I serve? There is nothing broken that cannot be mended. There are none who are sick that cannot be healed.

'The Earth created you. It gives you life from moment to moment. And in this hallowed valley, Sir Prenholm, I could plant a stick in the ground and by dawn it would grow into a better man than you!'

Myrrima drew backward, afraid. A green fog had begun to coalesce at the wizard's feet, and he radiated power. The air carried a copper tang mingled with a scent of moss and old roots.

Sir Prenholm grew pale, and now stood alone, shaking. 'I meant no disrespect. It was only a jest.'

Binnesman shouted and pointed at Borenson. 'By the Power I serve, I tell you that this eunuch can father children still!'

Myrrima didn't expect such a boon. She didn't even believe it could be done. But Prenholm had goaded Binnesman into boasting. Even if Binnesman *could* restore her husband, there was one thing that Myrrima knew: magic carried a price. Binnesman's deed would cost.

The knights and lords stood like scolded children, none daring to speak.

Binnesman took his bowl of honey and herbs, and swirled it through the green fog around his feet, then knelt and mixed a pinch of dirt.

He glanced at the growing crowd, handed the bowl to Myrrima. 'Take this down to the river. Kneel and make the rune of healing in the water seven times. Then cup your hand in the water and mix it with this concoction. Wash your husband. He'll be ready to ride within the hour.'

Then he leaned close and whispered, 'But such a grievous wound will take longer to heal – if it can be healed at all.'

'Thank you,' Myrrima said, her heart hammering. She took

the bowl carefully, afraid that she might spill it, and laid it on the buckboard.

She drove the wagon around the corner, along the stone wall of the inn's garden, down to where the stream rushed beneath the alders. Their leaves flashed gold, and sunlight struck the tree trunks, blazing them silver.

She stopped in the shadows of the trees. A pair of mallards came up in the water, gabbling, begging for a crust of bread.

Myrrima pulled off Borenson's blanket.

She climbed out of the wagon, stood by the water's edge. After the rain last night, the golden leaves of the alders lay plastered to the ground. The stream flowed freely, gurgling through the rocks. The mallards climbed up on the bank near her feet.

She knelt over the water and made the rune of healing seven times.

It was peaceful, such a serene setting for a disturbing day. She felt as she made the runes that she should speak some incantation, but knew none. A song came to mind, a senseless ditty that she'd composed as a girl when she used to scrub her clothes on the washing stones beside the river Dwindell.

I love water, for water like me –
whether in rain, pools, or puddles –,
all runs to the sea.

Tumbling, splashing, foaming through hills,
giving drink to dry valleys,
where deep water stills.

I love the water, and water loves me.
I'll drift down the slow river,
till it joins with the sea.

She watched the river, the deep pools, hoping that perhaps she'd see the dark back of a great sturgeon, swimming in mystic configurations.

But none came. She cupped the water in her palm, mixed it with the wizard's concoction.

She daubed her fingers with the balm of honey, herbs, dirt and water, then carried it to Borenson and reached beneath his tunic.

She gently took his organ in her hand, tried to work the mixture over the ragged wound where his walnuts had been. She was painfully aware that she had never touched him there before, even on her wedding night.

In his sleep, Borenson winced in pain. He grimaced and pounded his hand into the hay.

'I'm sorry,' Myrrima said, but she did not spare him the medicine. Nothing good comes without a price, even healing.

When she finished, he groaned deeply, and called out, 'Saffira?' He raised one hand in the air, like a claw, as if to grasp her.

Myrrima found herself shaking. Binnesman's concoction might heal a wound of the flesh, she realized, but can it heal wounds of the heart?

Sweat was pouring off Borenson, and his face was flushed. Regardless of Binnesman's promise, she suspected that it would take hours until he regained consciousness.

She turned, knelt by the water. The morning sun winked through the leaves. It seemed pleasantly warm. She decided to keep a vigil throughout the day.

She stood silently grieving for what seemed like long minutes. With her endowments of metabolism, it was easy to lose track of time, to have it stretch out of all proportion.

The riders in town were mounting their horses when she heard her husband gasp. She climbed up, looked over the wagon. He'd wakened.

Outwardly there was little change in his appearance. Beads of sweat had sprung up on his brow, and the armpits in his tunic were drenched. His eyes still looked yellow and filmed, and his face was pallid. His lips were blistered from fever. He gazed up at the trees, at the sky.

'You're looking a little better,' Myrrima lied. 'Do you feel better?'

'I've never felt worse,' he said with a dry throat. She unslung her waterskin, forced a dribble down his throat. He drank weakly, pushed it away. 'What are you doing?'

'Trying to save you,' Myrrima said. 'You're lucky you didn't take sick and die.'

He closed his eyes painfully, shook his head. The tiny gesture spoke volumes. He didn't want to live.

Myrrima held silent for a moment. She felt as if she were trying to pound through his armor, get at the soft flesh underneath. She let him sit, and asked in a softer voice, 'Why? You knew you were infected, and you merely walked away. Why?'

'You don't want to know,' Borenson said.

'I do.'

He opened his eyes to slits, studied her dispassionately. 'I don't love you. I . . . can't love you.'

Myrrima felt stung by the words. Her heart suddenly pounded, and she fought to control her tone. She knew vaguely what he'd been through. She'd seen the light in his eyes when he spoke of Saffira. She'd seen him call for her in his sleep. She knew that with her endowments of glamour, Saffira would have been irresistible to a man. And Raj Ahten had castrated her husband. 'Did you bed her?' Myrrima tried to keep the pain and anger from her voice. 'Is that why Raj Ahten took your walnuts?'

'What is it to you?' Borenson demanded.

'I'm your wife.'

'Not –' he began to say. Borenson shook his head. 'I never

touched her. No man could have touched her. She was too beautiful . . .'

'You don't know what love is,' Myrrima said with finality.

For a moment, neither of them spoke. 'I knew it would hurt if you found out,' Borenson said.

Myrrima could think of nothing to say for a long moment. 'I'm your wife, still,' Myrrima said. She could see his torment but felt incapable of reaching him. Raj Ahten had done so much to hurt him. 'Why didn't he just kill you?'

Borenson groaned, pushed himself up in the straw. 'I don't know. Raj Ahten doesn't usually make strategic mistakes.'

There was anger in his tone, suppressed rage. Myrrima liked that. If he was angry, at least it gave him something to live for.

Myrrima heard the scuffing of a footstep, looked up.

Gaborn strode down the road, his face clouded with concern. Iome followed at his side, and appeared more shocked at Borenson's injury than anything else.

Gaborn came straight to the wain. 'How are you feeling?'

Borenson responded in a tired voice, 'Fine, milord. And you?' The tone of sarcasm was impossible to miss.

Gaborn reached down, touched Borenson's forehead. 'Your fever has broken.'

'I'm glad that's all that is broken,' Borenson said.

Gaborn said, 'I . . . came to thank you, for all of your efforts. You've given much for Mystarria.'

'Only my conscience, the lives of my Dedicates, and my walnuts,' Borenson said. He was still unaware of the spell that the wizard had cast on him, the hope of regeneration. He spoke from his pain. 'Is there anything else you'd like, sire?'

'Peace and health for you and your kin,' Gaborn said, 'and a land without war, where men have never heard of Raj Ahten or reavers or the Darkling Glory.'

'May you have your wishes,' Borenson said.

Gaborn sighed. 'There are forcibles to help speed your recovery, if you want them.'

A look of pain clouded Borenson's eyes. He looked hurt, broken. 'How many can you spare me?'

'How many will you want?'

'Enough to kill Raj Ahten,' Borenson said. 'It's true that he's still alive?'

Gaborn did not hesitate. 'I can't give you so many.' Now there was pain in Gaborn's eyes. He wanted to give in to rage, he wanted Borenson to get his vengeance. If any man deserved it, Borenson did. He'd been forced to kill children that Raj Ahten seduced to be his Dedicates. He'd been forced to slay even men that he called friends. Raj Ahten had ripped away his manhood.

Borenson painfully pulled himself up to the side of the wagon, as if to prove his resolve. 'I was the best guardsman in your father's service. If there is any man alive who can take him –'

'I can't,' Gaborn said. 'You can't. The Earth Spirit forbids it. For the sake of us all –'

'Yet you came here to seek a favor of me,' Borenson said. 'I can tell by that look on your face. And you're offering forcibles. . . .'

'A hundred of them,' Gaborn said. 'No more.'

That was a lot of forcibles, more than twice the number of endowments that Borenson had had before.

Iome took Myrrima's arm, drew her away so that the two men could barter alone.

'What's happening?' Myrrima asked.

'Gaborn needs your husband to deliver a message to King

Zandaros, suing for peace. It's a great deal to ask on the heels of what has happened.'

'I see,' Myrrima said. She knew that Borenson would carry the message. Eight days ago he had vowed to go to Inkarra to search for the legendary Daylan Hammer, the Sum of All Men, in hopes of learning how to defeat the reavers and Raj Ahten. He'd planned to go in secret, sneaking into the land, for the borders of Inkarra had been closed to the men of Rofehavan for decades.

But Myrrima could immediately see how carrying the message might work to their benefit. If Borenson could persuade Zandaros that it was in his best interest to ally himself with Mystarria, Zandaros might even help them find Daylan Hammer. Even if he couldn't persuade Zandaros, at least delivering the message would give Borenson a pretext for crossing the border.

'Where will he get the Dedicates?' Myrrima asked as they strolled to the banks of the river.

'There is a facilitator at Carris,' Iome said. 'Your husband can take endowments there.'

'The city is in ruins,' Myrrima objected. 'Are you sure it would be safe? The reaver mage's curses are so thick in the air that illnesses are breaking out everywhere!'

'He'll have to forgo taking stamina for a bit, but Batenne is along the way. Gaborn assures me that your husband can get endowments there.'

Myrrima paused. She'd never seen a map of Mystarria, had no idea where Batenne lay, though the name was familiar. It was a sprawling city in the far south, in the wine country along the borders of the Alcairs. Wealthy lords and ladies often wintered there.

Iome asked, 'Will you be going with him?'

'If he'll have me. I guess . . . even if he won't.'

'Of course he'll want you at his side,' Iome said. She had such childlike confidence that he would.

Myrrima squeezed Iome's hands, said nothing for a long moment. She asked, 'How do you do it? How do you love so easily?'

The question seemed to catch Iome by surprise.

'I see it in your eyes,' Myrrima said. 'I saw it when you looked at your servants. I see it when you look at me. There is nothing feigned about it. Yet I am married to a man who says that he does not love me, and I believe him. He will not even try to feign it.'

'I don't know,' Iome said. 'Love isn't something that you feel. It's something you give.'

'Doesn't it tear you apart, to give yourself away like that?'

'Sometimes,' Iome admitted. 'But if someone loves you in return, it makes the occasional hurt all worthwhile.'

Myrrima wondered at the conversation. Everywhere she looked, wars were breaking out. Yet she worried about love. She felt guilty even talking to Iome about it. But life without love would be so cold and empty it would be a kind of death all its own.

'I guess,' Iome continued, 'I learned to love from my father. He cared for all of his people equally. If he thought a man to be lazy or vile, he didn't hate the man or condemn him. He thought that men could cure their every vice, if they just sought to change. And he was sure that if you showed a man enough kindness, he'd desire to change.'

Myrrima laughed. 'If only the differences between men could be settled so easily.'

'But you see my point? If you want love, you must first give it.'

'I don't think that my husband knows how to love.'

'You'll have to teach him,' Iome said. Her face was full of concern. 'Always, you have to set the clear example. Not everyone learns how to give love easily. I've heard that for some, learning to love can be all but impossible. They keep their feelings hidden away beneath a coat of armor.'

Only moments ago, Myrrima had been thinking the same thing – that she felt as if she were trying to pierce her husband's armor. Myrrima shook her head. 'He's so full of self-loathing. How do you prove your love to a man who refuses to see it, or to believe it?'

'You married him,' Iome said. 'That should give him some hint.'

'The marriage was all but arranged.'

'You're going with him to Inkarra. He can't fail to see that.'

Myrrima shook her head in bafflement.

'Maybe he'll learn to love you when he can love himself,' Iome said. 'He's making great changes, great strides. He's given up his position in life, lost his endowments. Locked inside the warrior's coat of mail, a fine man is struggling to get out. Help him discover that.'

Suddenly Borenson made sense to Myrrima. Iome was telling her that he did not know how to love because he'd never been truly loved.

She'd heard much about him, about his reputation for being a man who grimly faced the worst challenges, who laughed in battle. Of course he would laugh in battle. Death meant little to him. It would only bring a release from pain.

Up on the road, Gaborn's troops were mounted and preparing to leave. Gaborn called out to Iome, 'Ready?'

Iome clenched Myrrima's hands, then strode swiftly uphill to join her husband.

Myrrima headed back toward the wagon, to check on Borenson.

'He wants me to take a message to King Zandaros,' Borenson said as she approached. 'When I'm ready to ride.'

'Will you?'

'When I can ride.' He winced in pain at the very thought.

'There's something I must say,' Myrrima offered. 'I know that you say you don't love me. But I'm still your wife, and perhaps it is enough that I love you.'

He lay silently for a long time, and Myrrima simply touched his hand.

After a while, he reached down under his tunic, felt his groin wound. A mystified expression crossed his face.

'What's the matter?' Myrrima asked. 'Are you less of a man than you thought you were, or more?' He kept prodding himself, unable to comprehend what had happened. 'Binnesman treated you,' Myrrima explained. 'He says that you'll be ready to ride within the hour. In time, you may recover completely.'

The look of wonder and relief on his face warmed her heart. For a moment, he seemed at a loss for words, unwilling to trust his good fortune. At last Borenson teased in a guarded voice, 'If that wizard can grow new walnuts on me, I'll drag him to the nearest inn and buy him a pint of ale.'

Myrrima smiled warmly and shot back, 'A pint of ale? Is that all that they're worth to you?'

Chapter Twelve:
THE FACE OF THE EARTH KING

Every man is born with ten thousand faces, but he reveals them to the world only one at a time.
– Torin Belassi, on the 'Art of Mimicry'

Gaborn and Iome went to their mounts in the stables, and Iome held silent for a long moment. She could tell that Borenson's bitter words had upset Gaborn. Borenson had always been open with Gaborn, and Iome thought them to be as close as brothers.

'He will heal,' Iome said as they strolled into the stable. 'Binnesman promised.'

Gaborn shook his head. 'No, I think not. Not really. We've used him badly. He's angry at Raj Ahten, angry at me. And he's suspicious. Zandaros is not likely to offer any concessions just because I send a friend as an ambassador. I might well be sending Borenson to his death.'

Iome bit her lower lip, troubled by what Gaborn said. Zandaros had cut off contact with Mystarria before Gaborn was ever born, and he'd sent an assassin to kill Gaborn. Zandaros sounded dangerous, but Iome knew that Inkarra was a strange land, with customs all its own.

'Are you sure you want Borenson to speak to King Zandaros?' Iome asked. 'Zandaros's nephew seemed to think that the Storm King would favor me – and I am your closest relation.'

Iome tried to make the offer sound as casual as possible. She did not want to go. It would be a long, hard journey to an unforeseeable end, and she would be risking her life as well as that of the son growing in her womb.

Gaborn shook his head. 'No. Not you.'

She glanced up at his face. His gaze was directed inward.

They entered the stable, found their mounts to be well fed. The horses' manes and tails were plaited, and the beasts had been washed and combed. Gaborn's horse wore barding that had been brought from Carris during the night. The beast's armor gleamed like silver. The chaffron on its head had a twisted horn that spiraled up, and the platemail on the horse's chest and flanks was burnished. Beneath its armor was a quilt covered in white silk. It looked like some marvelous beast that had walked out of the clouds.

The lords in Carris wanted Gaborn to make a grand entrance, a triumphal entry to lift the spirits of his people. Iome and his Wits thought it expedient. Paldane's old chancellor, Gallentine, had sent a message warning that rumors in Carris had begun to spread, to the effect that Gaborn had been slain in battle. 'It would ease the people's minds,' he said, 'if Gaborn would come.'

So Gaborn would parade once around the city, but only because he needed to pass by on his way to battle.

The reavers would be racing south over the open plains today, and he planned to lead his men against them. He needed Averan's help in finding the Waymaker.

All through the night, he had huddled with his counselors, plotting the deed. Reports from Skalbairn came in hourly. The reavers had dug into burrows once it got cold, and by dawn they had still not stirred.

The night's storm had similarly delayed Gaborn's departure from Balington. He dared not send warriors racing on force horses in the dark, over roads that had turned to mud.

Thus, though the weather slowed Gaborn, it had stymied the reavers completely. The reavers had traveled only forty miles in the length of the night. This gave Gaborn a great advantage.

He'd sent to castles in his lands south of the Brace Mountains and ordered lances, ballistas, and food delivered close to the reavers' trail.

In the early hours of the morning, messengers brought more good news: the rain had almost completely bypassed everything south of the Brace Mountains.

The fields would be dry – perfect for a cavalry charge.

Once Gaborn had felt as ready as he could be to face the reavers, he'd consulted with his counselors and drawn up missives to send to kings throughout Rofehavan.

Long through the night, he'd acted on matters both monumental and mundane. He'd drafted plans for the evacuation of Carris, and for sending the Indhopalese troops to help defend his castles to the north. He'd sent bribes to various lords, including an offer to hire mercenaries out of Internook to protect his coast.

Another messenger, one from Heredon, had brought astonishing information. Gaborn had offered aid in putting down the reaver horde that had arisen there. But the Iron King sent back a curt missive declining his offer. The courier himself had heard news that the Iron King had easily defeated the reaver horde. The reavers had surfaced on the northern coast and marched south along the seashore. A lucky ballista shot from a ship slew the fell mage that led the horde. Her followers immediately retreated.

Now Gaborn was ready to ride for Carris.

Gaborn and Iome mounted their chargers, rode out of the stable. Six young heralds, all dressed in the blue of House Orden with the symbol of the green man upon their surcoats, rode before the entourage. All six heralds had long blond hair, and bore golden trumpets.

Following them, a seventh young man would bear the king's standard.

A wain had pulled up outside, and the knights in Gaborn's retinue each took a long white lance from it, and held it high, so that the lances bristled overhead like spines.

The knights themselves were a mixed bunch, wearing colors from half a dozen kingdoms, to signify that Gaborn was not the lord of one land only, but of the whole Earth.

Jureem, Binnesman, the wylde, and now young Averan would ride with the king's counselors near the van of the troop. Near the end of the train followed an inconspicuous wagon that bore Gaborn's forcibles.

As Gaborn rode out of the stables, his men gave a cheer. Binnesman spurred his mount forward and handed Gaborn the branch of an oak tree to bear, as if it were a scepter, though a bit of ivy still clung to it.

So Gaborn began his ride to Carris looking like an Earth King out of the old tales.

Yet to Iome he seemed preoccupied.

They had ridden six miles down the road when the heralds in the vanguard topped a woody knoll, turned their mounts, and shouted, 'Milord, there are giants ahead!'

They needn't have yelled the warning, for at that very moment, a frowth giant topped the hill and stood peering at Gaborn.

A huge red stallion, hanging limp with a broken neck, was clearly visible upon the giant's hunched back. The giant's golden fur looked dirty and matted in the morning light. He was an old frowth, with streaks of white in his hair, and his silver eyes were as huge as bowls. He had iron studs in his ears, and one through his nose. Lockets of hair beneath his long snout were braided in warrior's knots.

'Wahoot!' the giant cried, raising his snout in the air.

Pigeons in the nearby oaks flew up in alarm and began to circle. Iome knew nothing of the tongue of frowth giants, and had no idea what the creature had said, although he'd sounded victorious. Soon other giants came running uphill, their thick mail rattling like the chains to a drawbridge.

The first giant reached up with one hand, hurled the dead horse into the road. Other giants came and did the same – twenty-two giants in all. They left a grisly pile of dead horses before Gaborn's retinue.

They're like cats that way, Iome realized, leaving headless mice on their master's doorstep. The leader of the giants bowed his head and closed his eyes, his enormous front arms extended before him and crossed at the wrists. 'Wahoot!' the frowth shouted again.

Gaborn sat in his saddle, looking perplexed. Most of his men were gaping in awe at the monsters.

It was an eerie moment. Until a hundred and twenty years ago, no one had ever seen a frowth. Then, during a brutal winter, a tribe of four hundred of the huge creatures migrated over the northern ice. Many of them were wounded and scarred, and apparently fled some unknown enemy.

The frowth could not communicate well in any human tongue, had never been able tell what fearful creatures hounded them across the ice. Yet with a few gestures and words, some giants had learned to work beside men – lugging huge boulders in quarries or trees for foresters, or fighting as mercenaries.

But the frowth rarely frequented Rofehavan. They lived in the wilds along the mountain ranges.

These giants had come in company with Raj Ahten's army, and had eaten people in Iome's kingdom. They were the first that Iome had ever seen. She was simultaneously terrified of the creatures and fascinated.

'Can anyone talk to them?' Gaborn asked among his retinue. 'What do they want?'

'Wahoot!' the giant cried again and began nodding his head up and down rapidly. He pointed at Gaborn. 'Wahoot!'

'He speak Indhopalese,' one knight said, a handsome Invincible out of Indhopal with dark skin and a Dharmadish accent. He rode up to Gaborn's side. 'He say you *mahout*, an elephant rider. Very grand. Very powerful.'

'Wahoot!' the giant shouted again, pointing at the dead horses.

'I think he likes you!' one lord jested to Gaborn.

'No,' the translator said. 'He cross hands. He give self. He serve.'

The giant opened his mouth and rapidly made hissing and clicking noises with the back of his tongue. He raised his snout in the air and sniffed. He was no longer trying to speak in his pidgin dialect of Indhopalese. Instead, he was speaking in pure frowth now.

'What's he saying?' Gaborn asked.

But no man had ever deciphered the tongue of frowth giants well. Not even the translator from Indhopal ventured a guess.

'Will you fight for me?' Gaborn asked the creature. The giants had fought well in Carris yesterday.

The giant grunted, making a deep sound from his belly. He raised up his huge iron-bound staff, which was still stained dark from reavers' gore.

'Maybe,' the translator said. 'He is offering to work.'

Gaborn looked quizzically at his men. 'Does anyone have a good use for a giant?'

'I do,' one knight shouted jovially. 'His hide would make a fair rug!'

The other knights laughed uproariously, but Gaborn studied the creature. He raised his staff to the sky, and roared, 'Wahoot?' then spread his arms wide, as if to embrace the whole world.

'He say, you great mahout,' the Indhopalese Invincible

offered. 'Great rider of the world.'

But Iome wondered. 'No,' she realized. 'He's asking a question. He wants to know . . . if Gaborn is the Earth King!'

Before anyone else could move, Iome pointed at Gaborn, and shouted, 'Yes. He's the great rider. *Rajah mahout.*'

The giant gazed at her, as if contemplating. His silver eyes were wide and knowing.

The other giants began to grumble rapidly. Each of the frowth peered at Gaborn and blinked their eyes nearly closed. They began stooping and letting their jaws go slack as they did, so that they displayed their teeth in a nonthreatening way. They held the pose for several long seconds, then a dozen of them began to lope off to the west, toward the Hest Mountains.

'Hey, where are they going?' Gaborn asked.

Iome could think of only one answer. It was said that wild frowth roamed the Hest. Perhaps these frowth were going home. The other ten merely stood and watched Gaborn attentively, the way that a dog watches its master as he leaves the room. It was clear that they intended to follow him.

Gaborn asked his men, 'All of Carris is waiting. Do we dare let these giants come with us?'

Binnesman said, 'Well, since we have no dancing bears in our retinue, I suppose they'll have to do.'

The men all laughed at his jest, and the troops rode on, skirting the pile of dead horses. The ten giants that were left fell in line at the end of the retinue, behind the wagonload of forcibles.

Gaborn rode on in silence for a few minutes. Iome saw the worry lines in his brow.

'You did me no favor to lie,' Gaborn whispered, 'even if it was only to a frowth giant.'

'Lie?' Iome asked in surprise.

'Whatever I am, I am no Earth King anymore. I'll not betray their hopes, their trust.'

She saw how his failures haunted him. She realized how hard he was trying now to hold up under the rigors of this day. She loved Gaborn for his virtue, for his sense of decency and honor.

'You are the Earth King still,' she said. 'The Earth asked you to perform one task. Your powers may be diminished . . . but that task remains: save your people.'

Iome considered telling him about the son that she carried inside her. She wanted him to be strong, and wondered if this news would help. But at the moment, guilt and useless self-recrimination tore at him. She didn't dare burden him with the knowledge that she carried his child.

'You're right,' Gaborn said softly. 'My people need a king. Even if the Earth will not sanctify my calling, the people still need a king.'

Gaborn closed his eyes. His face went slack as he relaxd every muscle.

He raised his chin high, and when he glanced at her, there was determination and strength in his eyes. His nostrils flared, and his look was one that held her, saw through her, accepted her, and dominated her all at once. It was a look that intimated endless power.

'Milord!' Iome said, trying to catch her breath. She knew that he had studied mimicry in the Room of Faces. Yet the transformation that had come over Gaborn in that instant was astonishing to behold.

For in that moment, despite every doubt that Gaborn had expressed, and despite the fact that he felt bereft of his powers, she recognized for the first time that she looked upon the face of the Earth King.

Chapter Thirteen:
A CHILD'S LESSON IN WIZARDRY

Men name the four powers Earth, Air, Water, and Fire. Such appellations are good enough for common folk, but only wizards ever learn their true names. We call upon them only in our hour of greatest need, and sometimes at our own peril.

– *Excerpt from* The Child's Book of Wizardry, *by Hearthmaster Col*

Averan clung tightly to the pommel of the saddle as the cool wind whipped her face. The force horses galloped south across hills as green as emerald, beneath a blue sky marbled by high cirrus clouds.

Binnesman had her riding in front of him, her back snug against his warm riding cloak, his big left hand wrapped around her protectively. He did not trust her on such a fast horse alone.

She thought it laughable, for at the age of five she'd once ridden a graak through a wild storm where the wind blasted her while lightning sizzled under the clouds below. The graak fought the air currents so hard that its wings would sometimes buckle. It was an experience that only another skyrider could sympathize with, and it was one that would have loosened the bowels of many a brave knight.

Still, she was glad to have the wizard ride with her. Averan had never traveled with so many people before, and with the dangers of the road the journey felt much safer for the company. There were advance guards ahead of her, stern Runelords armed with lances at her back, and fierce giants as the rearguard.

Averan was especially glad to have Spring in the retinue, for Averan had been the first to find the green woman. A small part of her still felt responsible toward her, even if she knew now that Spring was a wylde. And Averan was also happy to have Iome as part of the company. With Averan being a skyrider, she seldom got much contact with other women.

The force horse raced, its hooves pounding a rhythm against the road, its barding and the king's armor jangling like music.

Averan suspected that riding a kingly force horse was as close as she'd ever again come to riding a graak.

Binnesman remained silent for a while, and his grip on her was loose. He seemed weary.

'Will Borenson truly be healed?' Averan asked.

'I hope so,' the wizard answered. 'Healing a flesh wound is a small matter. Restoring a body part is a greater magic, and carries a hard price. But for a true healing such as he requires, a healing of the heart, the afflicted must also desire to recover.'

'Is it hard work – healing such a wound?'

'Very hard,' Binnesman said. 'Nearly impossible. But we were in a place of Power, with a wylde at our back. On another day, in another setting, I would not have tried it at all.' He fell silent for a while.

They swept like a gale through villages that Averan had only seen distantly from the air. Garrin's Tooth she'd always thought of as merely a lord's estate with odd-shaped fields and some clustered buildings just north of the Solace Mountains.

But on the ground, with the full sun shining on it in the early autumn, it was a riot of life. The buildings turned out to comprise a fine tall inn, with whitewashed sides and green trim, and flower baskets hanging from every window. The odd-shaped fields were vineyards and hayfields cut from the rolling hills, where a blue stream threaded and pooled, reflecting the sky and the black swans that swam upon its surface. The lordly manor there was such a fine estate that it took her breath away.

Then she was out of the hills completely, galloping past villages with names like Seed, and Windlow, and Shelter – each an oasis of life among rolling autumn fields where huge black-eyed Susans grew taller than a child. Averan loved the way the yellow flowers bobbed in the wind, with their dark faces.

The retinue was making as much as thirty miles per hour, traveling so fast that the giants at the end of the train could hardly keep up. They panted and grunted, sometimes emitting barking roars as they loped. They fell behind, but caught up whenever the horses rested.

During one of these rests, Averan began to pick at the seeds that had sprouted on the cuff of her robe.

Binnesman playfully slapped her hand. 'Stop that.'

'Why?'

'You're growing your wizard's robe,' he said. 'It will protect you from sun and from fire, from wind and cold. And whether you are walking in the woods or out among the open fields, whether in daylight or darkness, it will shelter you.'

Averan glanced at the sleeve of Binnesman's robe. The rootlike fibers in the robe were a reddish tan, the color of maple leaves in autumn. She couldn't see if there had ever been any cloth beneath those fibers. Nor could she imagine it offering much shelter from prying eyes.

'Beastmaster Brand said I'm growing fast. What happens when I get too big for my robe?'

'You'll never get too big for your robe,' Binnesman said. 'It grows to fit you just right.'

'I hope my rôbe looks better than yours,' Averan said. 'No offense, but it's kind of baggy. I'd rather have something pretty.'

Binnesman laughed. 'I'm sure yours will grow to be the envy of Earth Wardens everywhere.'

'So,' Averan asked, 'when are you going to teach me how to do spells and stuff?'

'Well, there's no time like the present,' he said. 'This will protect you against Fire.' Binnesman drew a rune on her hand. Immediately the sun that had seemed blinding over the past few days dimmed. Its rays no longer burned her. 'And this will protect you against Air.' He drew a second rune. Averan had not even noticed in the past few days how chafing the wind had become, as if it carried winter upon it. But suddenly there seemed to be a lull. Averan traced each of the shapes again herself.

'Those should help for the moment,' Binnesman said. 'I'll teach you more rune lore and spells later.'

Not long after they resumed their ride, they approached the deadlands that surrounded Carris. A dark ugly line lay on the horizon, and intuitively Averan wanted to stay away. Something vital had been leached from the soil there. On the ridges ahead stones now somehow seemed revealed to be the misshapen bones of a dying Earth, much in the way that the white knuckles of a leper are displayed as his skin sloughs off in decay.

Averan had hoped that she would never again have to visit Carris, even in her nightmares, but here she was riding toward it.

Binnesman called out to Gaborn, 'Your Highness, may we stop for a moment?'

Gaborn did not ask why. He could see the ugly line ahead,

and knew that the animals would need to forage. 'Troops, halt!' he shouted.

The horses immediately began to forage for grass, and the giants all stopped and dropped to the ground, panting.

Binnesman rode away from the troops, toward a hill half a mile to the west. The wylde rode at his side. At the base of the hill, Binnesman halted beside a stream, let the horses graze and drink.

'You can stay here, if you like,' he told Averan and the wylde.

He climbed the hill and stood beneath a great oak tree. He bowed toward the desolation, and raised his staff overhead in both hands. Averan heard him chanting, but the wind carried his words away.

For long minutes, it seemed as if nothing happened. Then she saw a thin green mist that seemed to seep from his staff, blowing on the wind as if it were seeds or pollen.

The green woman had gone to the creek. She knelt in the water and picked up a crayfish, held it up and stared at it curiously. Someone had dressed her since last they'd met, and the green woman now wore a tunic of brown, with green leggings and some new leather boots. But she wore Roland's big black bearskin cloak over it all. The attire made her look more human.

But Averan knew that it was all an illusion. She was a wylde. Binnesman had made her, as a woodcarver might make a doll. He'd made her from stones and bark and Earth blood. He'd given her a life of some sort, made her to be his warrior.

'What's Binnesman doing?' Averan asked Spring.

Spring looked up at Averan, followed her gaze, saw the wizard standing there, and squinted. 'Don't . . . know.'

Averan studied the wylde. She was learning fast. A few days ago, she could only repeat a few words. Now she could answer some basic questions.

'Spring,' Averan said. 'Are you scared?'

'Scared?' the wylde asked, cocking her head to the side. She dropped her crayfish back into the water, studied Averan.

'Scared,' Averan said. 'It's a feeling. Your heart starts to pound, and sometimes you shake when you're really scared. It's a feeling that comes when you know that something bad is going to happen.'

'No,' Spring said. 'Not scared.'

'You don't get scared even when you fight reavers?'

Spring shook her head with an expression that said she was utterly baffled.

Maybe she doesn't have feelings, Averan thought. She'd never seen Spring cry or laugh.

'Do you feel anything?' Averan asked. 'Do you dream when you sleep?'

'Dream?'

'Do you see things when you close your eyes?'

The green woman closed her eyes. 'No. Not see.'

Averan gave up. She wanted to be friends with the wylde, but the creature could hardly talk.

Absently, Averan began to teach her a few more words.

When Binnesman finished, he bowed again toward the deadlands, then climbed downhill.

Nothing had changed. The lands to the south were as desolate as ever.

But the transformation that had taken place in Binnesman over those few minutes was astonishing. Beads of sweat stood out on his forehead, and he trembled from exhaustion. He fell down at the edge of the stream and drank deeply for a long minute. He shook so badly that Averan worried that he would not be able to climb to his feet by himself.

'What did you do?' Averan asked.

'The land is sorely cursed,' Binnesman said, 'with plagues and sickness, rot and despair. It needed a blessing.'

'Did you fail?'

'Fail? Not at all!' Binnesman said. 'Some magic works slowly. The effects of this spell may not be fully seen for a century or more.'

He patted her head.

'Binnesman,' Averan said. 'Can your wylde dream?'

The wizard frowned. 'Dream? No, I think not. Perhaps she'll dream of feeding, or of hunting. But nothing more.'

'Oh,' Averan said, disappointed.

'You mustn't think of her as a person.'

'I was hoping we could be friends.'

'That . . . would be dangerous.'

'You mean she'd hurt me?'

'No,' the wizard said. 'Not on purpose. But she's not human. She'll protect you, but she has no emotions – Oh, look what you've done. You've got me calling "*it*" a "*she.*" The wylde could have taken any form. It could have looked like a walking tree, or taken the shape of a snake. But I was called to protect mankind, and so I guess it is only fitting that my wylde take the shape of a human.'

'So she can't feel anything?' Averan asked.

'Pain, hunger,' Binnesman said. 'Perhaps some other simple things. But the creature will never be your friend. It's like a salmon, swimming upriver. It will serve its purpose – if we are lucky – and then it will expire. You must get used to that notion. She won't be having you over for tea.'

'Oh,' Averan said. She didn't tell him that she thought that Spring was being cheated, that it wasn't fair.

They mounted their horses, joined Gaborn's retinue, and soon were off.

'No more spells today,' Binnesman said as they rode. 'I'll talk instead. The path to wizardry,' he offered in a lecturing tone, 'is a path to Power. But it is not an easy path. Do you truly wish to walk it?'

Averan asked, 'How should I know?'

'Spoken without guile,' Binnesman said. 'I should have

expected as much from a silly child.' He thought for a moment. Averan could tell that he'd never really considered how to teach this subject. 'Let me put it another way: your path, I suspect, will be hard, full of perils. Will you undertake the journey?'

'Are you talking about the Underworld?' Averan asked. 'Do you want me to go with you and Gaborn?' Averan didn't want to go there, to that darkest of dark places.

'Perhaps,' Binnesman said. 'My wylde will need to feed, and that's where her food is.'

'I know,' Averan replied. 'I can feel the hunger for blood too. I was full last night, but I'm already craving it again. I feel . . . no food that I eat satisfies. I mean, I can eat meat, I can eat grass, and nothing fills me. It's like I'm just eating air. I can't imagine what it would be like to go on this way for very long.'

Spring was riding a gray stallion nearby, lounging in the saddle as if she'd been born on one. She heard Averan talking about food, and she said, 'Blood, yes!'

Binnesman listened thoughtfully. She liked that about him. 'It's very strange that among your powers you should hunger for reavers. You can resist the cravings, you know. You do not have to eat reavers or anything else. The Earth will not force you into service. If you resist the cravings, they will go away. But of course, you will lose the power that comes from obeying that urge.'

'Like Gaborn?'

'Like Gaborn.'

'And the cravings will never bother me again?' Averan asked.

Binnesman shook his head, and his beard brushed her neck. 'I . . . can't say. They'll diminish certainly, but they'll bother you from time to time. They will bother you till the day you die, I think. You may always crave reaver blood a little, and you'll try to imagine how it would have been to walk that path to power. And you'll perhaps wonder what could have been. But then that is the way with life. In choosing one path, we must ignore others.'

'Brand used to say that life should be a journey, not a destination,' Averan said. 'And you should take joy in the journey.'

'Hmmm . . .' Binnesman said, 'many among the wise would agree with that, but I don't think that we have to settle for one or the other, a journey or a destination. Life can be both.'

'So what do I have to do to be a wizard?' Averan asked.

'It's simple, really,' Binnesman said, 'though we tend to make it seem more complex than it needs to be: we gain power through service. I serve the Earth, and it serves me in return.'

'That sounds easy,' Averan said.

'Does it?' Binnesman asked. 'It's impossible for most, and extremely difficult for those who can manage it at all. That's why there are so few wizards of any merit. However, it may very well be easy for you. That's why you've got green oak leaves appearing on your palms, and roots sprouting in your cloak, and you're already gaining powers that others will never master.'

'But what have I done for the Earth?' Averan asked.

'I have no idea,' Binnesman said. 'You took care of graaks. Could that be a service? And you tried to save my wylde as it fell from the sky.'

Averan didn't think either of those sounded very important.

'Let me ask, have you ever seen wrongs in the Earth, and sought to make them right?'

Averan's head bobbed up and down.

'Tell me about the first time,' Binnesman said.

'I was little –'

'How old?'

'I don't know, maybe two or three?'

'Go on.'

'My mother had taken me down to the river to help with her washing, and I saw a bush. I don't know what kind it is. I've never seen another like it, either before or since. But there were these icky fat green caterpillars all over, eating it. So I killed them.'

'All of them?'

'Every one I could find. I got most of them the first day. My mother caught me, and made me go home. But I snuck back later and got every one.'

'And how did your bush do?'

'Very well, thank you,' Averan said. 'It got big, and when the red berries came out, I planted some. Now there are more like it growing all around Keep Haberd.'

'I suspect that in doing this,' Binnesman said, 'you performed a great service for the Earth. Now, tell me about the reavers. What do you see when you see them?'

'I see . . . that same wrongness,' Averan said. 'When they came boiling over the hills toward Keep Haberd, and the skies were filled with gree, and their feet made the earth thunder – it was wrong. They were out of place.'

'Did you want to kill them?' Binnesman asked.

'I knew that they'd kill Brand, and my friend Heather, and everyone else that I knew. I didn't want to kill them really. I just wanted them to go back where they belong.'

'I think,' Binnesman said, 'that that could be your destiny, if you choose it – to help drive them back. Perhaps it already *is* your destiny and there is no avoiding it.'

Averan felt nervous. 'But I'm just a little girl.'

'With an unnatural taste for reaver brains,' Binnesman argued, 'and the potential to become an Earth Warden.'

'And what does that mean, to be an Earth Warden?'

'You can become the Earth's protector. *Life* will become

your occupation, to protect and nurture the small and helpless things of the world.'

'Like mice and plants?' Averan asked.

'Or humans,' Binnesman said.

'I never thought of humans as being small and helpless,' Averan said.

'Children seldom see them so,' Binnesman answered. 'But now that you've seen a reaver, you know better. There was a time, ages and ages ago, when men lived in packs, and ran about to and fro, hiding from the reavers. We lived in the forests like deer, always terrified, always huddled and shaking. Even now, terror comes easily to us, and men still know better how to flee than to fight.

'But in time, mankind discovered how to dig for metal to forge weapons of brass and iron, and how to raise fortresses, and how to wage war in cooperation. The blood metal and endowments made men equal to any predator, and raised them to the status of Lords of the Overworld.

'So it is easy for you to look at a Runelord and imagine that nothing could be so powerful, so masterful as a man.

'Yet nothing is farther from the truth.'

Averan was quiet, thoughtful for a long moment. 'How long have you known that mankind is in trouble?'

Binnesman stroked his beard. 'I've known that dark times were coming for ages, now. Mankind needed no protector, needed no Earth Warden to watch over them, for many thousands of years.

'But when I heard the Earth whisper my name, when I first felt the urge to protect and nurture mankind, I knew that dark times were upon us. Until I saw the ruins at Carris, I had no idea how dark they might become.'

'Is that how it happens?' Averan asks. 'You hear the Earth calling? Is that how you learn what to do?'

'It's not a sound heard by human ears,' Binnesman said. 'It's more like a trembling, a knowledge that strikes to the core of you. Suddenly you just know . . . everything: why you exist, and how you are connected to the Earth, and what you must do.'

Binnesman could not hide how he felt. The moment he first understood his purpose in life, felt his connection to the Earth, must have been powerful indeed. He sounded rapturous. . . .

It filled Averan with longing.

'So you will be called to protect the beasts, I think. You love them more than plants or minerals, it seems. You've heard of Alwyn Toadmaster, haven't you?'

Averan laughed. The antics of Alwyn Toadmaster had made some of her favorite bedtime stories as a child.

'Well, he was real,' Binnesman said. 'He really did live in the swamps of Callonbee. And when the marshes dried up for six years, he collected all of the frogs' eggs he could and stored them in the wells at Brachston, which of course drove the townspeople mad. Imagine having to fish a hundred pollywogs out of your cup every time you took a drink!'

Averan giggled, but a part of her felt horrified. What if the Earth called her to take care of something nasty, like frogs? 'Did he really hop around like a frog, and catch flies on his tongue?'

'What do you think?' Binnesman asked.

'I think they made that part up.'

'I suspect you're right,' Binnesman said.

'So,' she asked nervously, 'you just know? You just wake up one day and know what you're here to save?'

'It's not always so easy,' Binnesman said. 'Everything is interlinked. Sometimes, in order to save one thing, you have to let another go. For example . . . people,' Binnesman said pointedly, glancing toward Gaborn. 'Gaborn was given a gift, the ability to Choose people, and to save a seed of mankind through the dark times to come. But he wasn't commanded to save all of the people. So he has tried to Choose the best.

'In the same way, the time may come when you have to choose to save something while letting another thing go.'

'I hope I can take care of the graaks,' Averan said wistfully. 'Or maybe deer.'

'Ah, now a graak,' Binnesman said playfully, 'is in my opinion a thoroughly unpleasant animal. So I'm glad you're here to save them, if they need saving.'

'I guess if everyone got to choose what animals to save,' Averan said, 'we'd probably all save bunny rabbits.'

Binnesman nodded sagely. 'Or kittens.' The old wizard wrapped a huge arm around her, gave her a hug, but neither of them spoke for a while. They had entered the deadlands.

She thought about Roland, lying there in Carris, and wondered if she'd see Baron Poll.

Chapter Fourteen: TRIUMPHAL ENTRY

A cunning *man considers him a fool who acts against his own best interests. An* upright *man considers him a fool who acts against the interests of the whole of mankind.*

Therefore, all men are fools.

And since I must live in the company of fools, I'll stake my lot then with upright fools.

Throw that damned cunning *fool to the bears!*

– Duke Braithen of North Crowthen, excerpted from the sentencing of Chamberlain Whyte upon numerous charges of larceny

The throng outside Duke Paldane's keep in Carris was thick with the denizens of Rofehavan – lords and merchants in their smelly woolen garments, all of them nattering loudly, or so it seemed to Feykaald.

He stood alone with his back to the stone wall, the sun shining brightly upon him. As he did, he closed his eyes and listened.

The tide of voices overwhelmed him. With a dozen endowments of hearing and only half as many endowments of stamina, the noise swelling around him set his ears to throbbing and caused a painful buzz at the base of his skull. Even the opium he had smoked earlier did little except to leave him feeling disjointed, disconnected, and slightly out of control. The bitter taste of it clung to his teeth. He frowned in concentration as he picked voices from the crowd.

'. . . "Not even the Earth King can fix that," I told him. Them apricot trees won't be growing back for twenty years . . .' said one tall peasant loudly.

'. . . without so much as a by-your-leave . . .' cried a woman deeper into the crowd.

'Pardon me. Good day. Pardon. I beg your pardon,' a young girl apologized as she nimbly weaved through the crowds.

'Mark him with the black robes. If I was king, I'd bull his kind out of the city. Who does he think he is?' some old washwoman whispered about Feykaald, while her companion grunted assent.

Soon the fanfare blared in the far hills, and Feykaald looked across the black horizon to see the king's retinue riding forward.

He leaned back and closed his eyes, like a reptile sunning himself, as he waited.

Gaborn was deeply troubled as he rode for Carris.

He felt abundantly aware of his weaknesses as he listened to Binnesman begin training Averan.

The Earth Powers were great indeed. But those powers could only be controlled and handled by those who gave themselves fully into the Earth's service.

So Gaborn acted as the Earth King, though he felt that he was something less.

His mind seethed. The end of the world drew near. He could feel it like an ache in the bones. His counsel with his fathers' Wits last night, the messages he sent, the small battles he won – all of them were insignificant.

He suspected that the key to saving his people lay in confronting the One True Master.

A mad plan had begun to assume shape in his mind.

All of it hinged upon Averan. The key to finding the One True Master was for Averan to consume the brain of the Waymaker. Vainly he tried to consider other plans. Binnesman's wylde consumed the brains of reavers too, but the creature could hardly speak. It could rarely understand questions, much less answer them.

So Averan would have to eat. Afterward . . . Gaborn dared not think about what he had to do.

In the more frivolous days of his youth Gaborn had dared dream that he might act upon the stages of Mystarria. To that end, he'd studied the art of mimicry in detail in the House of Understanding, in the Room of Faces.

In the city of Aneuve, the Room of Faces was unlike any other. Many 'rooms' throughout the city were located at alehouses or in open squares. Thus, for example, the Room of Feet, where one learned the arts of traveling, was not a room at all, but a series of hostels and stables all about the countryside, where one had to travel in order to learn his lessons.

Other rooms were more secretive. Classes were taught in stark dormitories or dim halls. Some hearthmasters jealously guarded their intellectual properties, like Hearthmaster Vangreve in the Room of Dreams, and thus they taught in vaulted chambers underground, far away from the listening ears of any spies.

But the Room of Faces was built in the open, a place to be visited and admired, on an island in a magnificent castle, the Castle Rue.

A merchant had built Castle Rue eight centuries ago – not as a place of retreat during war, but simply for its elegance and beauty. Thus its stonework was all covered in plaster that stained it rose at dawn and at sunset, as it lay against the emerald sea. Its lofty towers and minarets soared far into the air, and its expansive gardens grew lush, watered by reflecting pools where white water lilies bloomed year round and frogs peeped in the evening. Elegant bridges spanned its numerous water concourses.

It was a perfect place for rest and reflection. At nights, one could wander the grounds of the castle, meander through its streets and purchase extravagant foods of every kind: blue crab claws boiled in saltwater, smoked swan legs, pork seasoned with coriander and cooked in quinces, fresh pastries filled with figs and cinnamon, mugs of hot rum sweetened with goat butter and nutmeg.

The lavish Great Room at Castle Rue housed the oldest and one of the most impressive theaters in all of Mystarria. And everyone who studied there hoped someday to play the lead in some great play, such as Tanandeer's *This Cage of Iron*, or Bombray's *The Simpleton's Tale.*

In one of his more embarrassing periods, Gaborn had dared dream of that, of being one of the great actors.

But the House of Understanding was more than just an elegant façade, or cobbled streets rich with the scent of delicacies, or ornate theaters where mimics plied their art.

It was a place of study and practice. It had dozens of training halls scattered all about, and various nooks and crannies.

The great mimic Torrin Belassi had made it his life's work to study faces – the way that the eyes crinkled in joy, or the lips parted in lust. And while he was alive, artists had made subtle impressions of his face showing those expressions.

Now, the ten thousand faces of Torrin Belassi hung on the walls throughout Castle Rue. Each mask was cast in hardened clay at the center of a plaque perhaps three feet in diameter. In honor of the kings of Mystarria, the borders of each mask were adorned with oak leaves, and the whole mask was fired from earthenware that made it look as if it were cut from sandstone.

One could wander an alcove for hours studying masks with names such as 'Recognition of an Old Friend,' or

'Challenging a Thief in a Darkened Room,' or 'A Father Contemplates His Firstborn Son.'

Thus it was that in the Room of Faces, Gaborn had once studied a plaque entitled 'How I Imagine the Earth King Will Look.'

It was the expression of a wise conqueror, benevolent and strong and above reproach. It was a look that held love for all men, and promised salvation to children and beggars and fools.

As he rode to Carris on the second day of the month of Leaves, Gaborn wore that face.

He knew that he would never play in the Great Room at Castle Rue. He'd never act in *This Cage of Iron*, playing Sir Goutfeet.

Gaborn regretted that. It was a part that spoke to him. Sir Goutfeet was a man whose role as a knight left him feeling as if he were somehow entombed in his own armor. Meanwhile, the good sir's squire always tried to make him feel valiant by directing him toward battles that he could win, until the enfeebled knight finally was reduced to bludgeoning whores and barmaids in an effort to settle their petty squabbles.

But Gaborn knew that he would never play on a stage.

Instead, as he rode for Carris he settled into his role as Earth King. All of Carris would be his audience, and never had Gaborn acted in a more prominent part.

Doubts and concerns clouded his mind. He passed through the deadlands as if through a dream, and all along he wondered about this girl Averan and her strange gifts, wondered where she might lead him, and if he dared follow.

All too soon, his heralds began blowing golden horns, so that by the time he topped the rise overlooking the Barrens Wall, half of the population of Carris had issued from the city gates or mounted towers or the city walls.

Even at a mile and half, the volume of the cheers that greeted him was astonishing. At the noise, crows and gulls and pigeons that had been roosting in the city all flew up and circled the city's towers like confetti.

Riding beside Gaborn, Iome gasped in horror as she saw the ruins of Carris. Words could not have described it for her – the toppled walls, the great wormhole, the field of dead reavers lying on the barren lands, their mouths all opened hideously wide as their jaws contracted.

Then Gaborn rode down to Carris to thunderous applause. Horns blew, men cheered and raised their fists and shouted in triumph. Women wept in gratitude, and many a mother raised her infant up over the crowd to show their child. 'There, there is the Earth King! Remember this moment. Remember it all of your life!'

He was their savior, after all. He had summoned the world worm and destroyed the reavers' fell mage. He had scattered the reaver horde single-handedly.

And in a moment of foolishness, he had forgotten who he was supposed to be.

As they rode over the causeway, they halted. The dead reavers from yesterday's battle had all been dragged from the entrance to the city – all but one.

There, in the gray dust of ruin, sat the head of a single reaver, its mouth propped wide: the fell mage. The monster was incredible. Iome gasped at the size of it, for its mouth opened wide enough that it could have swallowed a hay wagon. Along the rim of its jaw and along the back of its head were the long, snakelike philia, the sensory organs of the eyeless creature. Each philium on this beast was three to five feet long, and as thick as Gaborn's leg at the base – nearly three times the size of the philia he'd seen on other reavers. The mage's gray head shimmered from a multitude of tattooed runes that glimmered like fire, and in the morning sunlight, its enormous crystalline teeth glittered like quartz.

Iome gasped at the trophy in awe. 'I've never heard of one so large!'

Gaborn said, 'Rumor has it there's a bigger one.'

A messenger stood just outside the city gates. As Gaborn passed, the messenger shouted, 'Milord, news from Skalbairn. The reavers have left their holes within the past hour, and are on the move south!'

Gaborn nodded at the messenger, said, 'Tell him that I'm coming.'

Then he smiled and waved as he entered the city, holding his pose. Stern, regal, wise, indomitable. The mask of the Earth King.

His people cheered.

He could not stay long at Carris. He needed to reach the Place of Bones, confront the One True Master. But first he'd have to join Skalbairn, begin his campaign against the reavers. He needed to find the Waymaker, and learn the paths of the Underworld. The urge was becoming a compulsion. He felt driven.

He rode through the streets inspecting the damage. The odors of despair and rot – the residue of the fell mage's curses – still clung to the city. He wondered how the people here could endure it.

He halted only once, when Lord Bowen shouted and pointed into the crowd. 'There he is: that one's Waggit!'

Gaborn reined in his charger and stared down at the grinning idiot. Waggit had straw for hair, and eyes so pale that they looked like holes that opened into a vast sky. But by the powers, was he big! He was cheering wildly, a pickax raised in his hands, bits of reaver gore still clinging to it.

So, he had indeed killed at least one reaver, perhaps even more. Gaborn frankly doubted the tale. Certainly the number of kills was exaggerated. No matter. Waggit was a hero now in the eyes of Carris, and the world needed heroes.

The fool did not notice that Gaborn had stopped and was staring, until Gaborn pointed at him. Then Waggit stopped, and to the delight of those around him seemed perfectly dumbfounded that the Earth King had taken notice of him.

Gaborn's heart went out to the young man. In a world where the cruel and the cunning gained status by riding upon the backs of the poor, men like Waggit were too often unjustly scorned. Yet his stupidity was something that a single endowment of wit could cure. And in granting an endowment of wit from a weak and cowardly man to someone like Waggit, one might thus create a warrior of great worth.

Unfortunately, endowments of wit remained beyond the grasp of such simple folk. Gaborn would gladly have given any ten Merchant Princes of Lysle for such a man.

'Waggit of Silverdale, on your knees!' Gaborn shouted.

The man had no courtly graces. He clumsily squatted down on his knees and bowed his head, frowning terribly, as if he knew that he had committed some offense but could not remember what it was. Gaborn rode near, saw bits of oat straw in the big man's blond hair. He'd obviously slept in a stable last night. Perhaps he did so every night.

Gaborn could heal him with a single forcible. By ancient law, any man who killed a reaver earned a forcible from his king. If the rumors were true, Waggit had earned nine. Yet Gaborn wondered if the man might not be happier if he remained an idiot.

Gaborn drew his sword and touched each of the man's shoulder blades. '*Baron* Waggit of Silverdale, arise!'

The people of Carris erupted into a wild cheer as the idiot got up from his knees. To their greater astonishment, Gaborn reached down a hand and urged the young man to ride with him, aback his charger.

Then Gaborn put on the face of the Earth King once again.

It was not a perfect performance. Some of his subjects had obviously heard rumors that he'd lost his powers. He saw frightened faces in the crowd, and one man shouted, 'Milord, is it true?'

For a moment he let his expression slip. People saw. A young peasant boy, perhaps four years old, sitting with his mother atop a pile of barrels asked, 'Why does he look so sad?'

Gaborn set Baron Waggit down as he left the city, and was gone.

Feykaald watched Gaborn parade by the Ducal Palace in mild consternation. He searched for signs of weakness in Gaborn, but the young king looked regal, confident – *almost* everything these peasants expected from an Earth King.

But Feykaald saw through the façade. For years now Feykaald had served Raj Ahten. He'd been faithful, prudent, as a servant should be. He'd watched Raj Ahten grow from an ungainly child into the most sublime and powerful lord the world had ever known.

In great part, Raj Ahten was becoming the Sum of All Men because of Feykaald's faithful service. Now, even though some of his master's key endowments were gone, he lived and looked as glorious as ever.

The boy who paraded through the streets of this broken city was not even a faded shadow of Raj Ahten.

Gaborn rode by on a horse that Raj Ahten would not have fed to his dogs, with a jubilant idiot from the crowd on the saddle behind him. Gaborn's armor was dirty from the road, as was his mount.

The retinue passed, ragged knights from half a dozen realms, some filthy frowth giants in ragged chainmail that Raj Ahten had outfitted himself.

In no way could Gaborn best Raj Ahten – except . . . in the matter of the world worm.

Gaborn had indeed summoned a worm and saved Carris when Raj Ahten could not. One could almost imagine that he purposely kept his power veiled beneath a plain exterior.

Feykaald envied the boy such power. If only his master could somehow gain the Earth King's crown.

As Gaborn paraded by, Feykaald watched the faces in the throng: the jubilant children, the hopeful mothers, the old men with worried frowns.

He did not feel a part of this crowd. Carris hoped for the Earth King's favor, but Feykaald did not. The world was large, and Gaborn could not hope to protect all of it. At this very moment, reavers invaded Kartish.

While Gaborn paraded, Feykaald's people died.

And that is the way it will remain, he told himself. The world is huge, and Gaborn is small. He cannot protect Rofehavan and Indhopal too.

Feykaald put his hopes in his own king.

So Gaborn paraded past.

But Feykaald's presence in the crowd did not go unnoticed. A single rider peeled off from the king's retinue, circled behind the giants, and brought his horse through the crowd.

'Greetings, Kaifba,' Jureem said in Indhopalese, bending close so that he could look down on the kaifba from his tall horse. 'The smell of opium hangs heavy on you today.'

Feykaald opened his eyes and cocked his 'good' right ear toward Jureem, 'Eh?' he asked, maintaining by long habit his pretense of being nearly deaf.

'The opium –' Jureem said loudly.

'Ah –' Feykaald nodded, and finished his sentence. 'Is a pleasant reminder of home.'

'It can also hide deceit in a man,' Jureem accused.

Petty criminals in Indhopal often smoked opium to keep the nerves sedated and the pupils dilated. This could help them conceal their duplicity even during a rigorous examination by torture.

'Or it can ease an old man's painful joints,' Feykaald said softly.

'What is your business here?' Jureem demanded.

'I came to speak with your king on an urgent matter,' Feykaald said. 'I wish to seek his counsel.'

'Yet you let him pass by?'

'Surely he will stay and hold court? His triumph was great. Will he not remain and accept the applause of his people?'

'You were seen leaving the city in company with the flameweavers last night,' Jureem argued.

'I returned only moments ago.'

'I wonder why you are even here,' Jureem said.

Feykaald smiled kindly. 'I flew last night in the balloon because I hoped to view the reavers' movements. I saw little of import.

'But in the mountains, I intercepted a messenger who brought ill news. Reavers have attacked Kartish. The very Lord of the Underworld leads them. I have come to beg the Earth King for his aid.'

'Raj Ahten seeks Gaborn's support?' Jureem asked, incredulous.

'No,' Feykaald said. 'He would never ask the Earth King for succor. But after the battle yesterday, I have to ask myself, where else can our people turn?'

'You're lying, or hiding something,' Jureem said. 'I will warn Gaborn against meeting with you.'

'He will do so anyway.'

'Remove your rings,' Jureem commanded in a dangerous tone.

'Eh?' Feykaald asked.

'The rings!'

Feykaald felt reluctant, but he was an old man, not naturally disposed to open battle, and Jureem's tone warned that if he did not give up the rings, Jureem would take them. He pulled five rings off his scrawny fingers, then placed them in Jureem's plump palm.

Jureem pulled open the secret compartment of one ring. The needle inside dripped with green poison from a bush called 'malefactor' in Feykaald's tongue.

'What is this?' Jureem demanded.

'A little protection for an old man,' Feykaald said innocently. Jureem grunted, opened the compartment on a second ring. 'One can never be too safe,' Feykaald added.

Jureem pocketed the rings. 'I fear that there is treachery in you.'

'What?' Feykaald asked, cocking his ear as if he hadn't quite heard. Feykaald had learned long ago the tools of manipulation. He knew that feigning anger would serve him well now. 'You insult me with such accusations! You broke oath with one master, and now you want to school me in fidelity?'

Jureem held silent, but his eyes raged.

Good, Feykaald thought. He feels guilty for mistrusting me. Now is the time to strike, to offer the hand of friendship.

Feykaald shook his head. 'Forgive my outburst, my brother. But both of us have led a wayward past. Now, we both hope to live only by the tender mercy of the Earth King. You do not trust me, I know. But I assure you that I am no different from you.'

Feykaald sighed heavily and glanced off to the east, out over the darkened battle plain to the Hest Mountains rising blue in the distance, and beyond them to Indhopal. 'I only hope, my old friend, that for the sake of all of us, we do the right thing in supporting this Earth King.

Do you think Gaborn will send aid to Indhopal?'

'I do,' Jureem said with finality. 'Speak with him. Watch him closely, and you will see. The time may come when you wish to serve him with your whole heart.'

Feykaald looked him in the eye, his face a mask of hope. 'Indeed, I well may, my brother,' Feykaald said. He reached up and squeezed Jureem's bicep, as was the custom among his people.

Feykaald retrieved his horse. The magnificent gray Imperial charger had been through much over the past few days. The gelding had its endowments, but the endless ride had left it lean, almost to the point of being gaunt.

He found himself growing curious. Could Jureem be right? Would Gaborn really come to Indhopal's aid? What powers might he have hidden inside him still?

If Feykaald could convince the boy to come, then dispatching him afterward would be that much easier.

By the time Feykaald got his horse saddled, the king and his retinue were issuing out over the plain. Feykaald raced to catch up.

Chapter Fifteen:
SUBVERSIVE INFLUENCES

Thoughts are the threads that bind us to deeds. Deeds are the ropes that bind us to habits. Habits are the chains that bind us to destiny.

To escape your destiny, sever yourself from evil thought.

– Inscription carved upon the West Wall at the Palace of the Elephant at Maygassa

Raj Ahten raced for Kartish filled with dread and a sense of purpose.

All of his years of work – all of his efforts to become the Sum of All Men, all of his training in war – were about to reach their climax.

He envisioned the reavers at Kartish gathered as they had been at Carris, with the Lord of the Underworld crouched upon a Rune of Desolation while legions of warriors guarded her. The image filled him with apprehension.

Yet many of Raj Ahten's finest troops were also in Kartish. He envisioned knights charging across the plains, warriors clad in saffron surcoats, crimson capes flapping in the wind, lances slamming into reavers.

It would be a battle that children would hear of for centuries, as their fathers told the tales around the hearth at night.

So it was that dawn found him racing down from the Hest Mountains while the morning sun crept up behind him, filling the desert of Muttaya with light as if it were a winnower's basket. The desert sands were the color of rose in the dawn, streaked in places with a faint hue of palest amethyst where streams boasted their lush vegetation. To the north stood the Hills of the Elephant Dream – ochre-colored stones heaped in blocks that looked like a herd of elephants from the distance.

Fifty miles off in the desert below he spotted a knot of riders spread out on the highway, men in dark robes – Wuqaz Faharaqin and the Ah'kellah racing before him. At this distance, the shimmering air currents and dust of the road clouded his vision.

His mount was weary. Even this great stallion could not catch them easily. He needed a fresh horse.

Wuqaz and his men rode for Salandar, and from there would race to the heart of Indhopal. There Wuqaz would seek out any lord who might oppose Raj Ahten, any who harbored resentment or a treacherous nature, and try to inflame such men against him.

Raj Ahten knew that he could get a fresh mount there, but wondered how safe it might be. If these men suspected that he was on their trail, they might try to ambush him. Salandar would be the place for it.

In the morning light he also saw the balloon of his flameweavers, a bright speck like a blue graak high in the air. He'd bade them follow as best they could, but they rode the air currents faster than his force horse could manage.

At their speed, they'd reach Kartish before him.

From the mountains the desert appeared barren, lifeless. But as he rode down into the valleys, life revealed itself everywhere. Nightjars flitted among the shadowed trees in the hills, their gray wings fluttering languidly, catching moths that flew in the morning. Mountain sheep ran from his path, leaping over brown rocks. Fire-tailed weaver birds rose up from a streambed in raucous clouds.

Though he was at the border of the desert, the rains came often in winter to the pass, and trees grew in thickets in every fold of the mountains.

Raj Ahten had always loved the deserts of Indhopal.

As he passed the village of Hariq, he stopped at a well long enough to let some women, all dressed in white muslin with green shawls on their heads, draw water from the well for him and his mount. He'd ridden in upon a borrowed horse, without his armor, with his hooded cloak pulled over his face. To a casual observer, he seemed only an anonymous lord. With the murderous Ah'kellah ahead, he preferred it that way.

It was not until the women saw his face beneath the hood that they recognized him, and began to fawn over him.

The village was nearly empty, for at this time of year many of the mountain folk migrated south for the winter, following the Old Spice Way down into Indhopal.

Yet for those who stayed, it was a time of celebration. The harvests were in, and life seemed good.

He soon reached Salandar, with its white adobe walls baked as hard as stones over the centuries. He reached for his warhammer and rode with one hand on it, peering from beneath his hooded robe for sign of an ambush.

The markets were filled with vendors: men with woven baskets stuffed with pistachios, almonds, dried fava beans, pine nuts, chickpeas, lentils, rice, and groundnuts. Others hawked spices: cumin and za'tar, sumac and coriander, allspice and saffron. Old women carried pots filled with boiled eggs or turnip pickles on their heads, or baskets loaded with olives, eggplants, or limes. In the meat markets animals hung by strings from their feet: pigeons, ground squirrels, and succulent young lambs.

The streets were filled with people. Nomad women in

bright woven shawls in from the desert bartered for goods. Camel traders hawked their wares. Children raced about. Young men and women huddled in the shadows of vendors' stalls to shyly hold hands. Qat dealers bundled their herbs and sold them in a dazed stupor. Old men played chess by the roadside, fanning themselves with palm leaves. Wealthy men with jewels pinned in their turbans took breakfast on their verandas overlooking the avenues, served by beautiful wives.

Red chickens strutted through the streets, while white rock doves swirled like snow over the gardens at every manor.

Nothing seemed amiss in Salandar.

He saw no sign of the Ah'kellah, and managed to negotiate the streets without drawing attention.

Raj Ahten stopped to trade his horse at the fortress and announce himself. He questioned the warlord in charge, a wiry man from Indhopal named Bhopanastrat, about the Invincibles. Bhopanastrat was a competent man who had served Raj Ahten well – from a distance.

'Some Invincibles did pass through an hour ago, and took fresh horses. Wuqaz Faharaqin led them.'

'Did he name their errand?'

Bhopanastrat shook his head. 'He said that they were going to Maygassa.' Bhopanastrat bent near and whispered as if afraid to speak of a secret aloud. 'It is said that there is trouble in Kartish. I thought . . .' He winked his left eye, to show that he knew how to keep a secret.

Raj Ahten seemed to be gaining on Wuqaz, but the man was still an hour ahead of him. He could not yet guess Wuqaz's mission. He might well have lied to Bhopanastrat. Wuqaz was a portentous name. It meant 'Breaker of Necks.' Among the Ah'kellah it was a title as much as a name. He would be a formidable adversary.

Raj Ahten doubted that he could stop the Ah'kellah. If he tried to catch the men, they would fan out like grouse fleeing the falconer. He might get one or two, but the rest would elude him.

He suspected that their report could have dire consequences. Raj Ahten had conquered all the nations of Indhopal, but some of them had been under his dominion for less than a year. They were like spirited colts that had not yet been broken. They bucked and bit at him while he gouged with his spurs.

They would be eager to throw off his rule, and Wuqaz Faharaqin was the type of man to lead them.

Yet Raj Ahten also had to wonder at the 'trouble in Kartish.' If a lord at this distant outpost had heard of misfortune, how bad might the situation there be?

He impatiently took breakfast as he waited for Bhopanastrat and a dozen force soldiers to prepare for the journey. He dined on a rich pigeon stew made with onions, and flavored with plums, saffron and ginger.

Raj Ahten sat for a moment, began rubbing his left wrist. He felt a numbing pain in the arm. He wondered at it, could not think how it might have been injured.

He was, he suspected, alive now only because of the vast number of endowments he'd taken.

He thought of the flameweavers in their balloon, riding the east wind faster than his horse. They'd invited him to join them, to become one of them.

In company with Bhopanastrat and a dozen men, Raj Ahten forged north across the desert borders, racing through encampments and villages named only after the clans that settled them – Isgul, Qanaat, Zelfar.

The desert came alive at this time of year. Small flowers took the opportunity to bloom after every spat of rain, and it had rained three days before. Bouquets of salmon-colored flowers blossomed on the greasewood, while the ground was strewn with a carpet of white.

Birds were everywhere. Bright yellow bee-eaters streaked

across the land like fiery arrows, skimming among the flowers. Lapwings raced away from him on stilted legs, feigning broken wings to draw him from their nests, and filled the morning with their mournful *peewit, peewit.* Sand grouse by the thousands perched on the banks of streams, looking like round speckled brown rocks until they erupted into the sky.

Everywhere that Raj Ahten rode, the illusion that he'd seen from afar – that the deserts of Muttaya were barren and lifeless – was dispelled.

He stopped once again at a fortress in Maksist to trade his horses for camels. He asked the warlord in charge about Wuqaz.

The warlord said warily, 'I did see the men you seek. The Ah'kellah left the village only half an hour ago. Some took camels south, others took horses to the north and west.'

'How many men went south?' Raj Ahten asked.

'Twelve men, O Light of the Universe.'

Raj Ahten bit his lip. He was only half an hour behind them now. If he hurried, he would catch them.

'Give me your best force camels.'

'My lord,' the man said hesitantly, a worried expression on his brow. 'Salaam.'

'Peace,' Raj Ahten assured him.

'The camels I have are not worthy of you. The riders you seek – they took my best animals and kept spares for palfreys.'

Raj Ahten began to seethe. 'Is there a merchant in this city who will have the camels I seek?'

'I will gather the best animals in the city,' the man said. 'Meanwhile, sit at my table, eat your fill. Rest.'

The warlord took a horse and raced from the fortress. True to his word, he came back shortly with thirteen force camels.

'Forgive me,' he said as he leapt from his horse. 'These are the best I could find.' He got on his hands and knees, then bowed deeply, so that his white turban swept the ground.

It was the pose of one who offered his life to atone for an indiscretion.

He is a wise man, Raj Ahten realized. If I were angry, I might order him tortured to death. This way, he tempts me to take him quickly.

'You serve me well,' Raj Ahten said. He took the beasts gratefully.

He ordered the captain to get eighty men on horses and take them west and north, to hunt for the Invincibles in that band.

He wished that he knew which direction Wuqaz Faharaqin had gone. Raj Ahten went to the road at the edge of town, and for long moments he tried to catch Wuqaz's scent. He rode now atop a camel with a dozen other men, and Raj Ahten could not tell from the faint traces in the air which party he rode with.

Raj Ahten could not let him live. Nor could he afford to take the time to hunt the man down.

South, he decided at last. Wuqaz would go south into Taif, or Aven, where the Ah'kellah were most revered.

Raj Ahten led a dozen of his best men south into the desert, heading through old Indhopal toward Kartish.

The first leg of the journey was easy. The ground lay flat and hard.

Baobab trees grew on the verge of the desert, rising up in twisted majesty. During certain seasons, wildebeests and gazelles migrated through the region in vast herds, but this late in the fall only a few dry bones garnished the prairie. Ostriches and jackals loped away as his men approached.

After they forded the muddy Deloon River, all of the watercourses went dry. It had not rained this far south.

The wells at Kazir and Makarang were both dry. It was not until he saw camels tied by a bright red pavilion pitched beneath a baobab tree half a mile from the caravan way that they found water.

The baobab had a trunk thirty feet wide, and an enterprising trader had hollowed it out. The hollow held clay cisterns of precious water.

Upon seeing the thirteen men riding out of the desert, the trader grew uneasy. Only the worst kind of marauders would dare steal a man's water, but the worst kind of marauders sometimes traveled this road.

He rested his hand upon his khivar as Raj Ahten approached, and stared at him from eyes as brown as ripe almonds. He was an elderly man, with a beard trimmed impeccably. The old man bowed.

Raj Ahten hailed him, tried to put him at ease. 'Salaam. The trail is dry, and I feel weighed down by too much money.'

'Let me lighten your load, O Great One,' the trader said with a satisfied grin, 'while you drink your fill.'

With that, Raj Ahten dismounted and found a place to sit under the shade of the baobab. Raj Ahten took out a silver flask he'd brought from Salandar. It was filled with lemongrass tea flavored with honey made from morning primrose.

As a preamble to conversation, the two men shared introductions, and Raj Ahten offered a drink to the old man, for as the old proverb went, 'In the desert, drink must come before trust, trust before friendship.'

For a moment they talked cordially of poetry, weather, and the health of the old man's sister. The man recognized Raj Ahten and showed by his cordial demeanor that he, too, was of good breeding.

'Twelve men came riding from the north, did they not?' Raj Ahten finally asked.

'Yes, men of the Ah'kellah, in a great hurry,' the man said. 'They were rude.'

'Ah,' Raj Ahten said, fearing that he'd asked his question

too soon, had given offense. 'Men on the run are seldom polite. Did they speak of their destination?'

'They are going south to raise the Atwaba,' the old man said. 'They are angry with our beloved lord.'

'Indeed?' Raj Ahten asked, feeling mirthful. The trader was being extraordinarily polite by pretending that he did not recognize Raj Ahten. 'What did they say?'

'May my tongue be cut from me if I ever repeat such tales!' the old man intoned.

'It is a secret safe with me.'

'They say that Raj Ahten, bless his name, broke a truce and sought to kill the Earth King, his cousin by marriage.'

Raj Ahten grinned. 'I am sure that it is all a misunderstanding. When I meet these men, I will clear it up.'

'May the wind speed you,' the old trader intoned.

'Tell me, was Wuqaz Faharaqin among them?'

'I could not say,' the trader answered. 'The name I know, but these men did not offer me their names.'

Raj Ahten nodded thoughtfully. He could imagine how the Ah'kellah would tell his tale. They would describe the Earth King as a strong leader, vying for Raj Ahten's rule. If things went ill for Raj Ahten in this battle at Kartish, it would only justify that view.

Among the simpleminded, the charges of injustice would cause trouble. But here so close to Deyazz, men would ridicule such charges. A second cousin by marriage was still considered a stranger in this country.

But elsewhere . . . 'See here,' the kaifs would say. 'Our lord fights for the reavers in Mystarria, while reavers tear apart Kartish. Raj Ahten fights his own cousin! What is he, a man or a reaver?'

This would be a serious accusation in the minds of the young and simple. At the very least, certain kaifs would use it as a pretext to demand apologies – bribes of gold and forcibles and spices.

But for those who hungered to throw off his reign, no apology could ever suffice.

Bhopanastrat and the other Invincibles finished watering the camels. Raj Ahten realized that he did not actually have any money. Normally, Feykaald handled such things.

Raj Ahten went to mount his camel, and said to Bhopanastrat, 'Pay the man.'

'As you wish,' the warlord said.

What happened next came so fast that Raj Ahten did not have time to stop it. The old man got up from his seat and dusted off the back of his burnoose, ready to take his coin. Bhopanastrat drew his khivar and quickly slashed the old man's throat.

He staggered back three steps, turned toward the baobab, and sank to his knees. He slumped forward against the tree trunk, facefirst, blood gushing from his neck.

'What?' Raj Ahten demanded. 'Why did you do that?'

'He was rude, Great One,' Bhopanastrat answered. 'He demanded money. He should have felt honored to give water to his king.'

'Is that the kind of man you think I am, killing harmless old men in the desert?' Raj Ahten asked. Bhopanastrat dared not speak. 'We are not in Rofehavan,' Raj Ahten shouted. 'These are my people!'

'Salaam,' Bhopanastrat begged, bowing his head low. 'Forgive me. I did not know you could care so much for one worthless old man.'

Chapter Sixteen: TWYNHAVEN

The women of Fleeds are coarse and barbaric. That's why the men of Fleeds love them so fiercely.

– From the journal of Duke Paldane

The rain and darkness held Erin and Celinor at Balington. Several times in the night, messengers had come and gone for Gaborn. They left their force horses down in the stalls, fed them rich miln, but no one climbed into the loft where the lovers lay wrapped in one another's arms.

Celinor promised his undying love a dozen times during the night, until at last Erin realized that it must be some odd custom among his folk. She had worried that if he kept it up, she'd not hear the next time a messenger opened the door.

'Why talk about love when you could be making love?' she finally whispered. That kept him quiet, except for the panting and kisses.

But the few moments of stolen bliss could not last, and when an owl swooped into the rafters of the stable, Erin had known that it was time to go.

Early morning found Erin and Celinor far north of the village, riding the king's highway through patches of fog that shrouded the dales between the green hills. Crows flew up, cawing in the distance. Their jagged path through the sky intersected sprawling oak trees where they might roost.

Erin and Celinor did not talk much on the ride north. The strange wizard child and her warnings of danger lay heavily on Erin's mind.

For miles around, the homes and inns were still abandoned. Raj Ahten's army had passed by here yesterday, and the people had fled his presence. There was no food along the highway, and only once did they stop at a small cottage to pick some pears from a tree.

As Erin gathered the fruit, Celinor wandered to the side of the house and picked a peach-colored rose. He brought it back, held it up for her to admire, and sniffed its delicate scent. Then he offered it to her.

'And what are you thinking I'll do with that?' Erin asked. She'd eaten rose apples in the winter of course. But picking the rose violated her people's custom. Fleeds was a poor land, especially in the southeast. Every blade of grass was a valuable commodity among the horseclans.

'It's to admire,' he said lamely.

'Oh,' she said. Belatedly, she recalled that in some countries men gave roses as cheap gifts. She sniffed it, admired it for all of thirty seconds, and then – not wanting it to go to waste – tried to feed it to her fine black mare. The mare would have none of it.

Celinor came to her rescue. 'You can wear it,' he said. 'In my country, women pin roses inside their robes. It's like perfume, but doesn't have the cost.' He took the rose, and pinned it to the back of the silver brooch that Erin wore on her cloak. She could barely taste the sweet fragrance.

'Cuts down on the smell of horse sweat, I imagine,' Erin said. She wondered at his gesture. Did her odor offend him? Or was he just trying to be nice?

'They say that if you bruise the petals,' Celinor offered, 'they smell even sweeter.'

He pulled her close and hugged her fiercely. She decided he was trying to be nice. Different lands, different customs.

In fact, he was more than nice. She thought briefly about kicking in the cottage door and looking for a bed. He'd shown himself to be more than an adequate lover last night.

At that moment, a pair of young horsesisters came riding south from Fleeds. They crested a nearby hill and sent the crows flapping up from a field.

As they drew nearer, Erin studied them. Both girls looked to be from poor families, and could not be accounted as knights at all. Their boiled-leather armor was painted with symbols in green and yellow that identified their clans. Each sported a sash of horsehair, dyed red and braided for luck. Their helms were of leather with iron plates sewn into them, with horsetails flowing out the back. Instead of heavy lances, they bore only spears.

They looked flushed with energy, as people who have recently taken endowments often do. Erin suspected that the girls had put the forcibles that Gaborn had given her people to good use.

One girl had bloodstains from a side wound. She reeked of whiskey, which she'd used to clean the wound.

'You coming or going?' the wounded girl said as they drew near.

'Coming,' Erin said.

'The road's a hard one ahead. Lowicker's brat, Constance, is after blocking every byway. She's salted the roads with caltrops. And if you ride off into the trees, her archers will be using your hide for target practice. We barely made it.'

Erin had expected as much.

'Is it war, then?' Celinor asked.

'Who can tell?' the other girl answered. 'We didn't see any troops taking the field, if that's what you mean. She's not hankering to throw against the Earth King, but she doesn't want his horses pissing on her roads. I'd say she's waging a *tantrum* instead of a war.'

Celinor laughed aloud at the notion and wished the young

women well. His laugh rang false, though. Erin knew that he had to be worried. 'Maybe we should veer into the mountains, and circle Beldinook,' he suggested.

'We could be for cutting across Lowicker's fields,' Erin offered. 'It would save time, and it would be like spitting in their faces.'

'An arrow loosed in a fit of tantrum will kill you as easily as one loosed in war. We've got more important things to do than spit in the faces of Lowicker's men.'

Erin wasn't so sure. Fleeds and Beldinook had gone to war dozens of times in the past, and the news today raised her ire.

Still, she fought down her anger enough so that she followed when they neared the border and Celinor veered west on a side lane that led to Twynhaven.

They reached the remains of the village a dozen miles down the lane. There was nothing left. Fire had taken the place.

It was not a normal fire, Erin could see. For one thing, flames had engulfed the whole village, circling just inside the city wall. Within that circle, the inferno had consumed every piece of wood – every wain, every timber in every home, every tree.

Rocks still stood in some places where cottages had been. Chimneys thrust up like blackened bones, and stone fences parceled out the squares of ash. At the very center of town, even the stones had melted to slag.

No one had escaped.

Erin and Celinor rode through the streets, saw cracked and burned corpses. Here was a mother carrying her child. There was a horse that died in its panic. Beyond that, a family lay in ruins.

In a daze, Erin realized that flameweavers had destroyed this town. She knew that Raj Ahten's sorcerers had summoned the Darkling Glory somewhere in Mystarria. They'd burned people alive as part of their sacrifice. This had to be the village. Twynhaven.

In the three days since, only one pair of footprints showed that anyone had ventured into town. The footprints criss-crossed the street, from burned-out hovel to burned-out hovel. Obviously, it was a looter, probably looking for lumps of gold or silver among the ashes.

There were other villages up the road. But the peasants nearby most likely wouldn't brave this place. Some thought it dangerous to tread ground where people had been murdered.

Erin and Celinor rode in silence. We should have killed Raj Ahten for this alone, Erin thought. We should have killed him.

They were riding reverently, studying the destruction, when Celinor suddenly reined in his mount, and pointed. 'Look at that!'

Erin didn't realize what he was talking about for a moment. She stopped, studied the ground.

In the midst of a nearby building, in the shadows thrown by the morning sun, she could just make out a faint green flickering. It was as if a low flame eeled along the ground. If the sun had been shining full, she would not have seen it.

The green flames shimmered over the cold ashes like a fog. They seemed to form a circle, perhaps fifteen feet across, and within it gleamed a fiery rune. Footprints in the ashes showed where a flameweaver had walked out of that circle, in company with the Darkling Glory.

More importantly, another pair of footprints in the ashes showed where the looter had stepped into that circle – and vanished.

The hair rose on the nape of Erin's neck, and goosepimples stood up on her arms.

Her glance flicked toward Celinor. 'Is that what I think it is?'

His face was hard. His nostrils flared with each breath. 'A door,' he said in awe, 'to the netherworld.'

Raj Ahten's flameweaver had opened that door in his summoning. Erin would have expected him to close it when he was done. But she was no sorceress. Perhaps closing the door was harder than opening it.

Her mouth felt dry, and her heart began to hammer. She had a curious notion, a thought that suddenly burned bright in her consciousness.

'If Raj Ahten can summon a Darkling Glory through that door,' she said, 'perhaps we can summon a Glory of our own.'

Celinor reined his mount back a few steps. 'It would be madness to try!'

'Would it?' Erin asked. 'You know the lore as well as I do. Erden Geboren had Bright Ones and Glories to fight for him. Someone had to summon them.'

Celinor asked, 'How do you even know anything can get through?'

'There's a way to find out.'

She climbed down from her mount. The ashes on the ground were cold and wet. None stirred beneath her feet, but the moisture intensified their bitter scent.

Erin drew near the rune, pulled a dagger from her sheath, and tossed it into the circle.

The dagger never reached the ash-covered ground. Instead the green flames whirled toward it, circled in a vortex, and took it.

Then the green fire went flickering over the ashes again. So near to it, she could feel a dry heat. It was intense, but perhaps not enough to burn her.

I could do this, she thought. I could step into another world. Her heart was hammering and her throat was dry. She edged closer to the circle until she stood on the very brink.

She glanced over her shoulder at Celinor. 'Don't!' he

warned. 'Even if you made it through, how do you know you can come back?'

He's right, she realized. She imagined stepping into flames, with salamanders and Darkling Glories all around. Legend said that men had first come from the netherworld. So there had to be land and food.

She glanced out over the fields of Mystarria, the distant oaks standing burnished golden in the morning sunlight, crows flapping over their path in the sky. Leaving it all was a wild notion.

She had promised that she would accompany Celinor to his father. Heart still hammering, Erin drew back from the circle, and rode north.

Chapter Seventeen: WARRIORS

In Indhopal, Sky Lords are represented as men with the heads and wings of birds. I traveled there one time to see the bones of a Sky Lord, and found that it was only a child's skeleton fit with the wing bones of a graak.

In Inkarra, enormous sea graaks are often swept inland with onrushing storms, and legends there say that these are the descendants of the Sky Lords.

North of Mystarria, folktales say that powerful wizards of the Air can transform themselves into birds at will – with ravens, owls, and vultures being the most likely forms.

– *From* Accounts of the Sky Lords *by Sir Garion Gundell*

By noon Baron Beckhurst had traveled far west beyond the Red Stag inn. He rode as if in a dream, neither awake nor asleep. Though he rode a mount, if he closed his eyes he could almost sense that he was flying. He knew what it would feel like to have wings, to feel the air yielding beneath the sweep of his pinions.

As a child it had been his favorite fantasy, one that kept him awake long into the night. Now, he felt as if his dreams were on the verge of becoming reality.

Everywhere, if he listened, he could hear the voice of the

wind. It rustled the dry grasses in the field, and whispered among dying leaves. It spoke eloquently in the flapping of a crow's wing, or in a pennant snapping above an inn.

'One deed,' the voice whispered. 'Kill Queen Sylvarresta, and you shall fly.'

At a crossroads two hundred miles south of Carris, he stopped in the shadows of some old silver birches that leaned precariously in the sandy soil by a river.

A flock of starlings zigzagged down the river in a cloud, and filled a dead tree so close by that Beckhurst thought almost that he could ride up and touch them. In one moment, the tree was naked and dead, and in the next moment the birds clothed every limb as if they were leaves. They kept up a raucous chorus, flitted up from the tree, circled and returned.

A single starling burst from the flock, flew up and settled on the point of Beckhurst's lance. It cocked its head to the side and gazed down at him. It blinked, its dark eyes looking wiser than an animal's should.

'Bless my lance, Great Lord,' Beckhurst murmured.

Beckhurst let his horse dip its head for a drink of water. The starling winged away.

The dry leaves above him rustled like paper as they struck one another. A dazzling golden light played over the fields to the north.

Presently, two knights rode up from the south and joined him. A driving wind came with them, scattering leaves in their wake, raising dust beneath the hooves of their mounts, whipping their capes and the manes of their terrified horses.

Both were big men, like Beckhurst himself. Both bore shields and lances. Both had stormy gray eyes. None of them spoke when they met. They all just sat on their mounts, letting them drink, as if awaiting a signal. A gust circled them like an invisible beast, stopping to pace this way and that.

Suddenly, Beckhurst raised his nose. He tasted a delicate perfume, as if a fine lady had just passed by in a closed room.

'The queen can't be far now,' one knight said. 'A couple of hours more.'

'Come the draught, come the storm,' Beckhurst whispered, as if in prayer.

A blast shuddered around them, stripping leaves from the birches and roaring like a wounded bear. The horses staggered back, eyes showing white and ears thrust forward in alarm.

As one, the knights spurred their chargers northward, following the scent.

Chapter Eighteen:
RAJ AHTEN'S SPIDER

Beware the traders of Indhopal. They will sell their own mothers quicker than they will sell you a good horse.
– Adage taught in the Room of Gold

Gaborn left Carris with a heavy heart. He could sense danger to tens of thousands of the people in the city. So he ordered his father's Wits to remain there with Paldane's Chamberlain, Lord Gallentine, to aid in evacuating the city, and asked them to bolster its defenses as best they could. He kept only one of the Wits at his side, the faithful old Jerimas.

After Gaborn left Carris, scouts fanned out, searching among the dead reavers. It was entirely possible that the Waymaker that Gaborn sought had met its fate during the night, along with so many other reavers. Finding it might not be hard, if it was dead. Few reavers had thirty-six philia on their heads. It was a rare trait – perhaps one in five hundred. Fewer still would be large males with large forepaws.

The scouts inspected the field but found no reavers at all that matched Averan's description.

A mile south of Carris, Gaborn halted his troops to investigate a strange circumstance. The reavers had dug some wide trenches here that wove about in a braided design. Water from Lake Donnestgree had flooded the muddy banks of the concourse, and the waterway extended inland in a broad bow for nearly a mile. The trenches themselves looked to be four feet deep – rather shallow by reaver standards.

The curious thing was the smell. The water gave off a horrible stink, like that he'd smelled at some geysers, and any fish that had swum into the concourse from the lake now floated belly-up in the reeking trench.

Iome took a perfumed handkerchief from her riding cloak, held it over her nose.

'What is this?' Gaborn asked as he gazed down into the water. 'Is this a reaver's version of the jacks?'

'I think not,' Jerimas said. 'It smells of sulfur.'

Gaborn was not surprised when the answer came from Averan. 'It's not the jacks. It's their drinking water.'

Gaborn glanced at the child, who was mounted double with Binnesman, to see if she was joking.

'Reavers drink?' Jerimas asked. 'Popular wisdom has held for centuries that reavers, like desert mice, do not need water, but take all their fluid from their prey.'

'Of course they drink.' Averan scrunched her eyebrows. 'The fell mage was terribly thirsty when she died. Look in the water. You'll find big yellow stones. The reavers carried them here and threw them in, so that they would melt. There is no fresh water down where they come from, just water like this.'

Gaborn had seldom considered what the conditions in the Underworld might be like, down so deep where the reavers lived. Few men had ever dared make that perilous journey. But he could see one of the yellow stones now. He made a mental note: I'll need to take fresh water.

'What more can you tell us?' Gaborn said. 'What were the reavers going to do with that tower?'

He pointed out a huge section of tower, twisted like a narwhale's horn. But Averan only shook her head. 'I think its part of a building. I don't know everything.'

As they were thus occupied, Jureem rode up in company

with a fellow countryman of obvious importance. He was an elderly man, with a back that looked to be permanently stooped from years of bowing to his master. His face was leathery and tough as camel hide, with the exception of the baggy folds beneath his eyes. His long hair was still black with streaks of silver. He had his head cocked slightly, listening with his right ear.

He rode proudly on a gray force horse. Across the pommel of his saddle was a staff of sandalwood, carved in the shape of a cobra. As he neared, even at a distance of twenty feet, the kaifba smelled strongly of garlic and olive oil.

'Milord,' Jureem said as he drew close. 'I present Kaifba Feykaald, High Chancellor to Raj Ahten, Lord of Indhopal.'

'At your service,' Feykaald said. He spoke with only a hint of accent. With his straggling teeth, the gnarly bones of his knuckles, and his intense gaze, he seemed to Gaborn to be a spidery thing, the very embodiment of evil. His pupils were dilated widely, and Gaborn could detect the bitter scent of opium poppies.

'You honor us,' Gaborn said. 'What brings you to me?'

'Eh?' Feykaald asked, cocking his head. Gaborn repeated the question.

'I have come to beg your aid,' Feykaald said. He handed a gilded message case to Gaborn. 'In the mountains this morning, Raj Ahten received this warning. Reavers have attacked the blood-metal mines in Kartish. By now they are well entrenched. An enormous reaver leads them – the very Lord of the Underworld.'

The news made Gaborn's heart hammer. Could it be possible? No man had ever seen the legendary Lord of the Underworld, and thus no one could say with certainty what she would look like. Would the Lord of the Underworld herself march against Kartish? He doubted it. He'd sought communion with the Earth, and felt drawn to the Place of Bones, and Averan had confirmed his suspicions that he would find the reaver lord there.

Gaborn studied Feykaald's movements. He spoke almost casually of the problem, as if it were a small matter. He was like a trader who sought to lure a buyer into a poor bargain. Gaborn immediately sensed a trap.

'I warned Raj Ahten of this myself. He did not believe me. Does he really dare hope that I would help him now?'

Feykaald's lower lip trembled, as if he'd held great hopes, and feared that Gaborn would dash them. 'He . . . does not know that I have come to you. The situation is very grave. Raj Ahten rides to Kartish, but I suspect he will arrive too late. More than that, I fear that he will not be able to dislodge our enemy.'

'You speak of what *you* think. What does Raj Ahten think?'

Feykaald looked down. 'He thinks . . . that the sun and moon revolve around him. He thinks that all men are less than dust beneath his feet. He imagines that he can defeat the reavers himself. But I know he is mistaken. He does not have your powers.'

'I can offer no support,' Gaborn said, 'without your master's agreement.'

'Please,' Feykaald said. 'I do not ask for Raj Ahten, or even for myself. I ask for my people.'

Gaborn countered, 'I will not take an army into a realm where they are not invited, to fight beside a lord who will not assure me a truce. Raj Ahten has broken faith with me before. He would do so again.'

'There are children in Indhopal, O Great One,' Feykaald said. He spoke too loudly. He bowed his head and folded his hands before his eyes, in an attitude of supplication. 'They are brown, but otherwise they are children like your children. They laugh like your children. They weep like your children. They hunger and bleed like your children. And like your children, they too dream that an Earth King will appear in their most desperate hour. If you will not show mercy to our men and women, at least you must show mercy to our children.'

Gaborn shook his head. He suspected that Feykaald stood against him despite his protestations. His Earth senses warned of danger should he go. Yet he also knew what he'd witnessed through Binnesman's Seer Stones two days past. He'd seen the reavers rising in Kartish. The situation there would be grimmer even than what he'd found in Carris.

Feykaald sought to lure him to Kartish for reasons of his own. Gaborn doubted that Feykaald could guess how deeply he wished to help.

But the Earth had bade him find the Place of Bones.

'I cannot send my army,' Gaborn said.

Feykaald glanced toward Jureem as if seeking his intercession. He begged, 'Salaam,' peace, and bowed deeply.

By asking for peace, he suggested that Gaborn might take offense at his next words, and begged him to remain calm.

'Peace,' Gaborn answered.

'Hear me: one small favor I beg. It should not displease you.'

'What is it?'

'There are Invincibles in your camp, men who rode from Indhopal. Three or four hundred survive. I beg you: if you will not send your own men, at least send these.'

Gaborn considered, felt a sense of foreboding. The Earth warned him that if he did send these men, they would die. Whether death would come at the hands of the reavers or of Raj Ahten himself, Gaborn could not know. 'No. I cannot allow it.'

'It is a small thing that I ask,' Feykaald persisted. 'These men are of limited worth to you. They have endowments *now*, but you must ask yourself how long this will be true. Four hundred Invincibles is not a force that Raj Ahten takes lightly.

He will order the deaths of their Dedicates, lest his own men come against him. They will die – innocent Dedicates – men, women, children. They will die, and to what purpose? So that you can parade a few Invincibles as trophies of war?'

Gaborn studied Feykaald with growing dislike. 'Are you begging a favor, or seeking to extort me?'

'Extort? Never!' Feykaald said. 'I do not speak of what I would do. But I know my master's mind.'

Gaborn did not doubt that Raj Ahten would do as Feykaald warned.

'You are right,' Gaborn said. 'Indhopal is their homeland, and I will allow any Invincible who wishes to protect his people to return to Kartish.'

Jureem beamed, as if he had not expected such a boon.

'Thank you, O King of all the Earth,' Feykaald said with a bow.

'But – ,' Gaborn added, 'my Earth Powers also warn that there is great danger in Indhopal, and none of the men who go there will survive. I must warn them of this.'

Feykaald's eyes grew steely. He nodded acquiescence, but his face was unreadable. 'One more small favor, I beg you.'

'Another?' Gaborn asked.

'Forcibles. If you could spare even a few hundred, they might be of incalculable value.'

Now the man was asking too much. 'I have none to spare.'

Feykaald bowed his head in acceptance. 'Very well. One more thing I ask of you, then.'

Gaborn felt as if he were in a market, haggling with one of Feykaald's countrymen. Feykaald was asking for much, giving up nothing. Gaborn warned him, 'One more thing you may ask of me, but I weary of your requests.'

'Peace. I beg of you: ride to Kartish yourself. If you fear Raj Ahten, you can Choose his armies, and thus be assured that they will protect you.'

'I cannot.'

'I beseech you by all that you hold dear, by your love of the land, by your honor and virtue,' Feykaald begged. 'Without the Earth King to guide us, our men are as dross in the fire. If you could but see my people, you would Choose them as you Chose the people of Carris.'

Gaborn shook his head. Words could not express how much he wanted to comply with this last request, but his power of Choosing was gone. And he had another path to tread. 'I have battles of my own to fight, on other fronts. Your master will have to make do without me.'

Feykaald lowered his eyes. He shook his head. 'Forgive me. I took it upon myself to come here, to beg your aid. I cannot go back to Indhopal – not now. Raj Ahten will see my deed as treason. I am willing to accept this, to be named a traitor, if I can do some small good for my country. Therefore, I throw myself on your mercy, and beg asylum. I offer my services, as Jureem has done. I will serve you well, so long as you do not ask me to betray my own people.'

The man sounded sincere. His hands were trembling, and his eyes pleaded for this boon. Yet Gaborn could not trust him. Nor did he sense any danger to Feykaald.

'Go back to Raj Ahten,' Gaborn said. 'He will not harm you.'

'By the Powers, by the Earth, I beg of you!' Feykaald whined. 'Have mercy. Have mercy on an old man! You cannot guess the fate he would devise for me.'

Gaborn wondered. Perhaps in Feykaald's twisted mind, these threats were real. Or perhaps he feigned fear to achieve some greater end.

There was something in this man . . . a blackness at the core of him. Gaborn felt no immediate threat. Feykaald would not draw a knife on him now. Yet he did not doubt that Feykaald would cause great mischief if given the opportunity.

Or is that my own fear talking? Gaborn wondered.

In the House of Understanding, in the Room of Faces, Gaborn had learned to spot deceit in a man. But he could not be sure of Feykaald. A lying man will often avert his eyes, or blink when trying to assert his falsehood. The pupils of the eye may become constricted. But Kaifba Feykaald watched Gaborn steadily, without blinking. And the opium he had smoked obscured the true size of his pupils.

A lying man may tremble, but Feykaald held calm. A lying man will often have muscles tighten in his neck, and so he may toss his head, trying to appear aloof.

Feykaald showed none of those signs. Yet, there was a message in his body language. He hunched forward, possibly from a stooped back. But Gaborn suspected that it was more than that. His manner was not that of a liar, but of a merchant, intensely interested in making a sale.

Feykaald was trying to sell him a story. Gaborn did not buy it.

He considered possible motives. Perhaps Feykaald truly wanted to milk Gaborn for aid. Perhaps he sought to paralyze him into inactivity, or to divide his forces.

Or perhaps . . . Raj Ahten wanted Feykaald to remain nearby.

As Gaborn considered that, a cold certainty grew. Of course Feykaald was a spy. That's why Gaborn felt so uncomfortable in his presence, felt a lingering sense of danger.

I could easily send Feykaald away, Gaborn thought.

He looked to his counselors, considered what his Wits had told him the night before. 'You must turn your enemies against one another.' It was possible that he could turn Feykaald against his master, by feeding him false information.

At the very least, there was one advantage to keeping Feykaald close by. He had served Raj Ahten long and well. By keeping the old man here, under any pretense, he would be denying Raj Ahten the use of a counselor.

It seemed a prudent thing to do. He could put Feykaald up someplace where he would do no harm, have him watched. There were residences built for that very purpose at the Courts of Tide.

But all such plans were swept away by one other thought: perhaps I can truly turn him.

'I thank you, Kaifba Feykaald,' Gaborn said. 'You have given me much to think about. I will consider taking you into my service, but my mind must be clear on the matter. Will you ride with me today?'

'Tell me only how I can better serve you,' Feykaald said, bowing so low that Gaborn feared he would fall from his horse.

Chapter Nineteen:
BARON WAGGIT

In exchange for his numerous worthy entitlements, the duties of a baron are these:

To prudently oversee the lands with which he has been entrusted.

To uphold the king's laws, offer up the king's taxes, and to maintain highways and other edifices of public benefit.

To offer up his own life, or the life of a son or suitable tenant, in the king's service during times of war.

– From the Book of Common Law

'Did you hear that, boys! My Waggit's a baron now!' Scallon laughed. The big man slapped Waggit on the back and forced another mug of rum into his hand. All around, men in the inn at Carris grinned at Waggit and congratulated him.

Waggit remembered riding the king's horse. Waggit remembered being knighted. It was better than a dream.

He closed his eyes and promised himself that he would remember those things. But it was hard to remember. He always forgot everything. He'd promised himself last night that he'd try to remember killing the reavers, but already the memories were fading. He could only remember killing two or three. He only knew that he'd killed nine of them because everyone told him so.

'Don't just sit there squintin' at it – drink it down, now,' Scallon shouted. 'If you're going to be a baron, you'll have to learn to hold your liquor in something more watertight than your hand.'

Everyone laughed and pounded Waggit on the back. They leaned in so close that he could smell their breath, and he took a huge swallow. The rum burned his throat. Waggit didn't like the feel of it, but he liked to get drunk. The only problem was that whenever he got drunk, he'd always wake up and find that his money was gone.

And the only way to keep it safe was to give it to Scallon. He'd keep it hidden good.

'Can you believe it?' Scallon shouted to the crowd. 'Waggit's a baron! He'll be having a house and lands, and money-bags so heavy that even he won't be able to lug them around.'

Lugby, a friend who worked the mines in Silverdale with Waggit and Scallon, said, 'And I suppose you'll be there to help him?'

Scallon laughed. He was a big man with a beard, and when he laughed, spittle flew everywhere. 'Who else but his best friend? He'll be needing a chamberlain now. Who better than me?'

'Just about anyone,' Lugby blurted.

Scallon glared at Lugby, who was old and going crippled in the back from long hours bent double in the mine. Waggit had never seen Scallon so mad. 'You'll be eating your words, now,' Scallon said in a dangerous tone. 'You'll eat them or choke on them.'

Scallon reached down with a beefy fist, gripped the long knife slung in his belt. Lugby lurched backward, terror in his pale eyes.

The room went quiet, and men retreated from the two.

Waggit wondered what was going on. Why was Scallon mad enough to kill? He'd seen the big man beat others senseless before, but he'd never seen him kill.

'I –' Lugby said, his eyes flickering through the common room. 'I meant no disrespect. I was only thinking that if you're to be his chamberlain, you might be needing a good man to work the kitchens.'

Silence hung in the room for a moment as everyone waited to see how Scallon would react.

Scallon laughed heartily. 'Aye, we'll need help in the kitchens.'

Lugby began to grin at his good fortunes.

'Can he cook?' Waggit asked.

'Can he cook?' Scallon roared. 'Why, he can boil you up the finest mess of beans you've ever tasted!'

That was good enough for Waggit.

He grinned and drank some more, until he could not feel the rum burn his throat raw any longer and the room began to spin. Waggit lost all sense of time. He stared at the spit dog treading around in its circle as a young hog roasted over the fire. He wanted to pet the dog, but he knew that the innkeeper would just slap his hands with a ladle. Innkeepers were firm about that: no stopping the dogs from their work. That's what life was all about, after all. Work.

Waggit worked all day long, swinging his pick in the mines. Work made money. Work and beans had made him strong – strong as a bear.

Waggit roared like a bear, and everyone around him stared and laughed. So Waggit roared again and stood up, raking the air with his fingers. It was a good joke.

Scallon was talking to another fellow, a man in a greasy leather apron. After a moment, Scallon jabbed Waggit with an elbow and said, 'Did you hear that? The king owes you some forcibles for killing the reavers. Nine forcibles. You're going to be a rich man.'

'Oh, he doesn't . . . owe me nothin',' Waggit said, the words coming thick to his mouth. 'He let me . . . he let me ride his horse.'

'Well, he does owe it, see,' Scallon said. 'It's the law. It's an old law, written before he was born, written before we were all born. If a man kills a reaver, he can go to the king and get a forcible. That way, a brave man like you, even if he's lowborn, can become a knight.'

'Oh,' Waggit said. The room was really spinning now, and Waggit sat and laid his head down in his hands.

'And you'll be needing those forcibles, see.' Scallon leaned close. His face was covered with layers of sweat. Dirt from the mines had worked into the creases around his eyes. 'See, you'll be needing them to sell. You're going to have a house and lands, and you'll be needing some money to get things going. Like, you'll want to buy a fine horse, and some carriages. Maybe now that you're going to be rich, you'll be wanting to marry Andella even.'

Once Scallon said that, Waggit could think of nothing else. Andella sold ale at the inn at Silverdale. She was the most beautiful woman ever. All the men told her so.

'You think she'd marry me?' Waggit said.

'My friend,' Scallon said in a reassuring tone. 'There's one thing in this world that I'm sure of: that trollop would sleep with a hog for enough money.'

Waggit grinned and tried to imagine Andella lying sound asleep beside a pig. His head was spinning so badly, he couldn't manage the feat.

'So come on,' Scallon said. 'Let's you and me go raise your fortunes.'

'I can't,' Waggit said. 'I'm too drunk to walk.'

'That's okay,' Scallon said. 'I'll help you.'

'But . . . I don't want to lose nothin'.'

'You won't lose nothing,' Scallon promised. 'I'll hide the

forcibles for you, along with all the other coins you've given me over the years.'

Waggit looked up through bleary eyes. 'Are you . . . you sure you won't lose 'em? You lost my money once!'

'Oh, that was long ago,' Scallon said. 'I found it all again, remember? I brought it to you all shiny and new. You bought those boots with it.'

That was the problem. Waggit couldn't remember. He couldn't remember Scallon ever finding his money. He couldn't recall ever having new boots. He forgot everything. He'd even forgotten his real name. People hadn't always called him Waggit, but he forgot what his real name was.

'Oh,' Waggit said, as Scallon lifted him to his feet.

They walked out of the inn, into the broad light of day, and for a long time, Scallon kept urging, 'Come on, lad. Keep your feet moving.'

Waggit had to stop once to throw up, and it took forever to reach the duke's keep.

The guards at the door seemed to recognize him, for they saluted with their swords.

He'd never seen such opulence in his life. He'd never been in a fine house. The duke had rich panels on his walls, and beautiful tapestries. The audience hall had the largest hearth he'd ever seen. When a wealthy man appeared, Waggit was all flustered. 'Duke Paldane,' he blurted in awe.

But the small fellow with the pointed beard looked at him with crafty eyes, and said, 'No, the duke is dead. I'm Chamberlain Gallentine, acting in his stead. I understand that you've come to demand forcibles?'

'Er, yes, your lordship!' Scallon said. 'That's what he's after – just that what's rightfully his.'

Chamberlain Gallentine had fierce dark eyes.

'So you want your endowments now?' Gallentine asked.

'Uh, not the endowments,' Scallon said. 'He just wants the forcibles for now.'

Gallentine smiled. 'Is that so?'

Scallon shoved Waggit in the back, and Waggit nodded enthusiastically.

'I suppose that your friend here will sell them for you, to buy you ale?' the chamberlain asked.

Waggit shook his head. 'No, he'll hide them good, so no one steals them. He's a good hider.'

Scallon shoved Waggit in the back again, and Waggit felt sure that it was a signal for him to say something. But he didn't know what.

Gallentine smiled even more coldly. 'Sir,' he said to Scallon, 'I trust you can find the door by yourself? Or do I need the guards to . . . take your hand?'

A low growling noise came from Scallon's throat. 'I don't need no guards.' He gave Waggit another angry shove in the back and stalked from the room.

Waggit felt alone and scared. He could tell that Scallon was mad, really mad. Sometimes when Scallon got mad enough, he'd punch Waggit real hard. Waggit figured that as soon as he got out the door, Scallon would be waiting to hit him. The worry drove all other thoughts from his mind.

'Now,' Gallentine said. 'What shall we do with you?'

Waggit shook his head. He knew that something had gone wrong. He'd been bad. He wasn't going to get his forcibles or his lands. But he couldn't figure out what he'd done bad.

Gallentine walked around him, studying him as if he were a calf in the market. 'You've got big bones. That's good. And you did kill nine reavers. That means you can move fast. How, exactly, did you dispatch those reavers?'

'I just jumped at 'em and whopped in the soft spot!' Waggit said.

'Who showed you the soft spot on a reaver?' Gallentine asked.

To his own surprise, Waggit remembered that. 'Lugby

did! He drew a picture on the ground, and showed me over and over.'

'No doubt when the reavers came, your friend Lugby let you take the first swing,' Gallentine said.

Waggit couldn't remember for sure. But now that he thought about it, he didn't have to push anyone out of the way to get at them.

'Tell me, Waggit,' Gallentine said. 'Do you know what death is?'

'That's where . . . you go to sleep, and don't wake up.'

'Very good. Did you know that the reavers could have killed you?'

Waggit didn't answer. Gallentine sounded angry, and Waggit didn't know what the right answer was. He shook his head in bafflement.

'So your friends shoved you in front of the reavers, and didn't tell you that they might kill you?'

Waggit didn't remember anyone mentioning that.

'Let me ask you this, Baron Waggit: do you think you could do it again?'

'Kill reavers? I guess.'

Gallentine studied him for a long moment, nodded his head. Waggit had got the right answer!

'Let me ask you another question. Have you ever . . . dreamed of being like other men? Have you ever wondered what it would be like to remember things, to know things that other men know?'

Waggit nodded.

'Wouldn't that be worth more to you than gold?'

Waggit wasn't sure. 'Scallon said I should ask for the forcibles.'

'You've earned the forcibles,' Gallentine said, 'and you may have them. But the law only allows it if you use them in the service of your king. In other words, if you take them, you must do what he says.'

Waggit got confused. It must have showed on his face, because Gallentine added, 'He'll want you to kill reavers.'

'Oh,' Waggit said.

'The king left no certain orders as to how I should handle you. Obviously, he wants to reward you, and he did leave some forcibles in my care to use as I saw fit. Rarely do our lords ever grant forcibles to fools. How about if I make you an offer? I'll give you one forcible now, one endowment of wit, so that you have the capacity of a common man.

'After that, I'll give you a horse and let you ride after the king. You can take your time, make your own decision. If you wish to become a knight and enter our lord's service, you may take more endowments.'

Waggit wasn't exactly sure what Gallentine offered. He used too many big words, like 'capacity.' 'Will I remember things?'

'Yes,' Gallentine said. 'From now on, you'll be able to hide your own coins, and find them when you want them.'

'Will I remember . . . about riding on the horse with the king?'

'Do you remember it now?'

Waggit closed his eyes, pictured it. 'Yeah.'

'Then you will remember it for as long as you live,' the chamberlain promised.

Waggit got so excited, he couldn't speak. He nodded his head real hard, and Gallentine smiled.

'Very well, sir,' Gallentine said, with a tone of genuine respect in his voice.

Gallentine led him to the facilitator. He climbed the tower to the Dedicates' Keep and waited for the facilitator to prepare. Peeking east out the archery slot was like standing on a mountain. Lake Donnestgree shimmered in the morning sunlight.

Boats bobbed on the water by the thousands – riverboats with high prows used for hauling goods, and makeshift rafts formed by lashing barrels together and laying planks on top. Waggit waved at the people, but no one waved back. 'Someday I want to ride on a boat,' Waggit said.

'Not with those unlucky souls,' Gallentine said. 'Those are the sickest of the sick. The king's evacuating them downstream to safety. It's the air here – the fell mage's curses. Too many people died of the rot last night.'

Waggit peered harder and saw that indeed the rafts and boats were loaded with wounded men and women, people who had been mauled by reavers or crushed by falling stones. They lay on the rafts with bloody bandages wrapped around them, or blankets laid over. He saw the tiny forms of children, and the gray heads of old men. He felt sorry for them. But he still wanted to ride a boat.

Soon the facilitator returned up the tower stairs with a Dedicate and a forcible.

The facilitator took the forcible, a thin branding iron about a foot long, made of metal, and put it to the young man who offered himself as Waggit's Dedicate.

The facilitator sang in a birdlike voice as he placed the iron to the Dedicate. Waggit was lost in the song for a long time, until he smelled charred flesh and heard the Dedicate wail in pain.

Then the facilitator waved the forcible around the room. It left a trail of light that hung in the air, glowing like a fiery snake. The facilitator continued to sing in his piping voice as he pressed the forcible to Waggit's arm.

Waggit felt good then, better than he'd ever felt before. The forcible burned him, and as it did, he felt as if his head exploded, and the light itself filled him. At the same moment, he saw the eyes of his Dedicate go dim, and the young man stared at him, with a mouth like an open door that led to vacant rooms.

Waggit did, indeed, remember it for as long as he lived.

Chapter Twenty:
REMARKABLE GEMS

Since the days of King Harill, reaver bones have been a favorite trophy of warriors in Rofehavan, and thus gave rise to the trade in what is called 'reaver crystal.' Many a lord delights in displaying long teeth or even whole skulls above the doors in his keep, while bits of reaver knuckles have been used for rings, bracelets, and necklaces.

New bones and teeth are nearly as clear as quartz, usually with a bluish or aqua tint. Impurities in the bone can sometimes make it almost opalescent, and some bones even seem to have images of animals or trees inside them. Unlike quartz, after a few dozen years, the colors in the bone mellow to a ruddy gold, and after two or three centuries they take on a richer reddish hue. The older bones are highly valued in Indhopal.

Artisans may engrave the bones, but the cost is prohibitive, since the only tools strong enough to shape the bone must have edges of diamond.

– Hearthmaster Thornish, from the Room of Stones

Myrrima insisted that Sir Borenson eat a quick meal in the inn at Balington. His wound was healing quickly, and his fever was gone, but he no longer had his endowments. He was a common man, and needed food and rest like any other.

She still had some of Binnesman's salve, and Myrrima applied it again to him before the meal, dipping her hands in the water and making the healing runes. Borenson took her ministrations patiently.

The wizard's restoration was incomplete. Borenson's flesh had healed without a scar, but he didn't have his walnuts. His scrotum hung empty except for a bit of fluid.

Myrrima secured a small container from the mistress of the inn and carefully stored the rest of the wizards' balm.

Afterward they ate in silence. It was a goosey affair. The serving girl gawked at her husband, while passersby peered in through the doors or glass window. After the king had departed, the inn was astir. The mistress of the inn and the various cooks and stable hands all gathered around and gabbled like geese. 'Oh, did you see our new queen?' the mistress said. 'I didn't know the Sylvarresta girl would be so dark of skin.'

'It's the Taifan blood,' the stablemaster said.

'Well, I'm not one to judge,' the mistress said. 'There will be many tongues a-wagging about his choice. You can see that she's Indhopalese, but if you ask me, it makes her look exotic.'

'The very word,' the stablemaster said. 'Exotic – that's what she is. That Iome Sylvarresta is not an ugly girl, not in the least.'

The mistress of the inn, who had strawberry-blond hair, said, 'Still, it makes you wonder. Will creamy skin go out of style?'

Every word that Gaborn and Iome had said was repeated, and the greater the secret, the more certain it was to be bandied about. It seemed that the mistress of the inn had her bedroom right against the common room wall.

Soon, the inn filled with people – a good half of the village. Myrrima heard some peasant ask loudly, 'I heard they brought a wounded knight into town, and the king's wizard turned him from a steer into a bull!'

Immediately the room went silent. There was tittered laughter and a good deal of nudging, and everyone looked Borenson's way. He pretended not to notice, but with his pale complexion, his face turned crimson.

Word of Binnesman's alleged healing had spread too fast. Everyone kept looking his way, then pretending they hadn't. Myrrima felt as if people were waiting for her husband to grow a new set of walnuts as they watched.

When the lady of the inn came and asked, 'Would Sir and Madam . . . er, uh, like the use of a room?' Borenson could take it no more.

He shouted, 'Why? If I wanted to rut, I'd just as well rut in the street like a dog, for all the privacy I'd get.' The patrons of the inn fell silent. Most of them flinched or stepped closer to the bar, as if afraid he'd pull out a warhammer and start swinging.

Borenson threw down his mug and stormed out of the inn, red in the face and blinking in embarrassment. Myrrima whispered an apology to the lady, set a coin on the table, and rushed out on her husband's heel.

She felt . . . very strange.

She was relieved to end the meal. Her husband walked quickly, as if he fought the urge to run as he made his way to the stables. He saddled up his charger. It was a huge animal, bred to carry a knight in full armor along with its barding. 'Damned fools,' he kept muttering as he cinched the saddle tight.

'Yelling at the innkeeper was uncalled for,' Myrrima said. 'She meant no harm. It's a small town. Having the Earth King sleep here is probably the biggest thing that's happened since . . . well forever. People will talk.'

Borenson's face burned with embarrassment. He muttered, 'Uh-oh, Diddly-O! Ain't it funny how his walnuts grow.'

'I don't understand.'

'My . . . predicament will be on the mouth of every minstrel for miles,' he said. 'They've been singing this damned ballad about me and Baron Poll for years.'

He was right. Everywhere he went from now on, he'd draw attention. He couldn't escape the notoriety. All he hoped for now was that he not be thought of as half a man.

'Well . . .' Myrrima said, her voice full of sincerity and conviction, 'if anyone asks, I'll tell them the truth: your walnuts grew back larger than before. They've got to be the hairiest and most astonishingly perfect walnuts ever to grace a man.'

Borenson was still for a moment. Then he smiled. 'That's it!' he said. 'Tell them just like that.' He grinned mischievously, and Myrrima couldn't really define the expression. There was real fear and embarrassment all mingled with his desire to burst out laughing.

She climbed into the saddle on the big horse. He leapt behind, and they rode out of Balington.

For a long time, neither of them spoke. The silence felt clumsy. Borenson held her lightly, one arm around her taut stomach, just beneath her breasts. His chin rested above her shoulder.

She knew that he could smell her hair, feel her skin through the fabric of her blouse. She wished that he would kiss her, or hold her tenderly. But too many things held them apart. They were still more strangers than husband and wife.

She needed more than that.

'If we're going to ride together,' Myrrima said as they entered the blasted lands, 'we ought to be on better speaking terms at least.'

'Agreed,' Borenson said. His tone remained noncommittal.

'Tell me something about yourself that I don't know,' Myrrima said.

'I don't like puddings or custard,' Borenson answered. 'I can't abide them in any form. It's the damned texture.'

'All right,' she said. 'Then I'll be sure to bake tarts. Now tell me something important.'

He had to know what she wanted. She wanted him to open his soul to her, talk about all of his deepest feelings.

'There's nothing important about me.'

'Tell me about Saffira, then,' Myrrima said, broaching the subject that she knew he'd least want to discuss. 'What was she like?'

'Smug,' Borenson said.

'What makes you think she was smug?'

He sighed heavily. 'She asked about you. She wanted to know if you were pretty. She knew that you couldn't compare.'

'What did you tell her?'

'You don't want to hear,' he said. She knew it was not flattering. 'I couldn't look at her, couldn't hear her Voice, without feeling . . . enslaved. But I'll tell you what she was. I think that she was mostly an empty shell of a girl. She doted on Raj Ahten, and knew little of the world. I thought that she might even betray us.

'But she surprised me in the battle. She showed some courage, and some compassion. If she'd been a little smarter, she might have managed to stay alive.

'Mostly, she was just a girl with too much glamour.'

'You're just saying that to comfort me,' Myrrima protested. 'A couple of hours ago, you thought you loved her.'

He fumbled for an answer. 'Now I'm telling you what I think about her. What I think and what I feel are entirely different. Both are equally true. Maybe you're right. Maybe I don't know what love is.'

'My older sister warned me against marrying a warrior,' Myrrima mused. 'She said that they had to learn to close off their tender feelings.'

'I've never had any tender feelings,' Borenson said.

She looked back to give him a sidelong glance. 'Really? Not even in the Dedicates' Keep?' She was trying to keep him off balance, move from one dangerous topic to another. But the expression on his face suggested that her words cut him too deeply.

'I – I'll tell you true,' he said, shaken. His voice began to rise. 'You say that I don't know what love is, and I'll admit that I don't. Love is a lie. My mother hated me from the day I was born. Even as a child, I could see it.'

'She hated your father,' Myrrima corrected. 'Averan told me. You merely had the misfortune to look like him.'

'No,' Borenson said. 'She hated me.' He tried to sound casual, but a person cannot talk casually of a wound that strikes so deeply. Pain haunted his voice. 'She spoke about love when other women would talk about their precious children. My mother would say, "Oh, yes, I love my little Ivarian." Then she would look about slyly, to see if they believed her.

'But she only spoke to reassure her friends that there wasn't something wrong with her.'

'Clearly there was something wrong with her,' Myrrima said. She couldn't change the truth. But she could take away some of the pain. 'Perhaps she didn't love you. I do.'

'How can that be?' he demanded too loudly. 'What good is a husband who cannot give you a child?'

'I can think of plenty of good uses for such a husband,' she said. 'A husband is someone who works beside you when you till the garden, and who keeps you warm in bed at night. He's someone who worries about you when no one else even knows that anything is wrong. And he's the one I'd want holding my hand when I stand at death's door.'

'People delude themselves,' Borenson said as if she hadn't seen his point. 'They want love so badly that they search for it until they pretend they've found it. Women will meet some worthless fool, and convince themselves that they've discovered a treasure, a "remarkable gem" of a human being that the rest of the world has somehow managed to overlook. What rot!

'There is nothing to such love. People breed with abandon. The world is full of fools who have no other aspiration than to procreate. I can't fathom it!' Borenson stopped. He'd been talking so fast that he was puffing.

'You don't understand desire?' Myrrima asked. 'Didn't you feel it with Saffira? Didn't you feel it when you first saw me?'

'Carnal urges have nothing to do with love – at least not any kind of love that I want. It doesn't last.'

'So you want more than carnal urges?' Myrrima demanded.

He hesitated, as if he could tell by her tone that he was falling into a trap.

'Yes,' he said. 'The best love must be founded on respect. Let desire grow from that, and when the desire wears thin, at least the respect will remain.'

'You have my respect,' Myrrima said. 'And you have my desire. But I think that there's more to love than that.'

'Ah!' he said, as if eager to hear her thoughts, but she could tell that he only wanted to argue.

'I think,' Myrrima said, 'that everyone is born into the world worthy of love. Every babe, no matter how physically marred or how colicky, is worthy of its mother's love. We all know that. We all feel it deep inside when we see a child.'

Borenson fell silent, and for first time, she felt that he was truly listening. 'You were born worthy of love,' she said forcefully, 'and if your mother never gave it to you, it was from no lack of your own.

'More than that,' Myrrima added. 'We stay worthy. You condemn people for "falling in love." You say that there really aren't any "human treasures" to be found. But people are better than you think. Even the worst people have more potential than the common eye can see.

'When a man and woman fall in love, I don't wonder that it happened. Instead I rejoice for them. I, too, sometimes wonder what qualities they saw in each other that I might have missed. But I respect people who have the common sense to love well.'

Borenson said coldly, 'Then you will never respect me.'

'I already do,' Myrrima said.

'I doubt that.'

'Because you don't respect yourself.'

Borenson was getting angry. He tried to change the subject. 'All right, I've played your game. I told you something about me that you don't know. Now tell me something that I don't know.'

'I got some endowments,' Myrrima said. 'And I learned to use the bow.'

'I can tell you got endowments,' Borenson said. 'Where'd you get the forcibles?'

Modesty forbade her from telling. Besides, she supposed that he would learn the tale soon enough. 'From the queen.'

He said nothing. She gave him just enough information to let him believe that they were merely a gift.

'So,' he said, 'tell me something that I don't know.' Once again, he was holding in his feelings. She didn't want the topic to get away from her.

'All right,' Myrrima said. 'When I was a little girl, my father and mother both loved me enough to care for me when they were tired, and to hold me when I fell, and to work long hours to feed me. Maybe I was lucky, because I got something you never had. I learned firsthand about love from people who knew how to give it.

'And I learned this: the best romantic love has a good amount of lust in it, and an equal amount of respect. But the main ingredient is *devotion*.' She wondered that he hadn't mentioned that when defining love, and suddenly she realized that he didn't even see it. 'And devotion is what you lack!'

Borenson took a deep breath, and she thought he would utter some denial. Instead, his hand drew more tightly against her belly, and he fell silent, as if he were astonished.

She was right of course, now that she saw it. Borenson could respect another, even feel compassion and envy. But he didn't understand devotion, not really. That was the part of the equation that a faithless mother could not teach him.

She wondered if she should take her words back, offer some sort of empty apology. But she knew that she shouldn't. He had to see the truth.

Maybe the truth was that it was good that he was a eunuch. He might never grow his walnuts back, she knew, despite the wizard's best efforts. Maybe it was all for the better. Making love wasn't love, she knew, and too many people confused the two. If she could help him learn to truly love, could teach him devotion, then she would have healed a wound beyond even Binnesman's reach.

She took the hand that rested on her belly, squeezed it and thus held him. But neither spoke for a long time. She had not yet broached the topic of going to Inkarra with him, and she dreaded it. Her husband had to know that she planned to go.

Seven miles north of Carris, they spotted a warhorse trailing its reins, pawing the ground as it looked for forage in the dead lands. They had to ride across a mile of blackened hills to get to it. Blood spattered across its back suggested that no owner would come seeking its services, so Borenson took the animal.

By the time they reached Carris, Gaborn had already left. People had begun to flee the city. With the reavers gone and the darkness lifted, refugees had already begun to choke every road for miles.

Common soldiers out of Mystarria and Indhopal were

heading north to repair and defend Mystarria's shattered castles. Weary footmen marched over the blackened land with heavy packs on their backs. The rest of the citizenry departed by whatever road they saw fit.

Hundreds of people had climbed to the lip of the giant wormhole.

Myrrima and Borenson stopped in Carris only long enough for Borenson to take half a dozen endowments – one each of brawn, grace, wit, hearing, sight, and metabolism. Then Borenson left orders that other endowments be added over the next day. Because of the foul air hanging over the city, he dared take no endowments of stamina, lest his Dedicate take sick and die. He would have to wait for it.

Afterward, they left the city, and Borenson stopped to hammer a pair of teeth from a reaver as war trophies, one for him and one for her. He said that he would have them carved.

Afterward they raced past Carris, and soon reached the Brace Mountains. The lower flanks of the foothills were a dim gray, but farther up the autumn colors sizzled on the mountainsides, and a fresh snow dazzled the peaks.

The reavers had cut a trail through the mountains, but Myrrima and Borenson followed the road.

Soon they would catch up with Gaborn. Myrrima dreaded the meeting; she considered what she should really say if the knights and lords asked about her husband's injury.

Chapter Twenty-one: THE SERPENT'S REACH

The bone structure of the reaver's head is extraordinary. The head is shaped roughly like a spade. Many a lord has witnessed a reaver digging with it.

Three bony plates on the head make this digging possible, forming the 'blade' of the reaver, as it is sometimes called. The plates are so heavily armored that no lance could ever pierce them. But the plates are held together with tough cartilage, and under extreme pressure, each plate can move independently.

Thus, reavers, like cockroaches, have been seen to squeeze themselves between rocks in situations where it would seem impossible. Raj Chamanuran of Indhopal once witnessed a twenty-foot-tall reaver compress itself down enough to wedge into a tunnel beneath a stone cliff that was a 'cobra' in height – about seven feet high.

These movable plates would seem a marvel of design. Yet they are also the reaver's greatest weakness.

The shovel-shaped skull leaves the reavers' brainpan close to the surface – a distance of only a foot on a moderate-sized reaver. The three plates of bone meet roughly at this spot, forming the reaver's 'sweet triangle,' its most vulnerable spot.

– *Excerpt from* A Comparison of Reports on Reavers, *by Hearthmaster Dungiles*

In the foothills south of the Brace Mountains, Gaborn's road opened to a switchback on a plateau. The sky had dusted the Brace with snow during the night, but here the morning was cool and the ground clear.

He halted beneath a trio of poplars, and his Days drew rein beside him. Their golden leaves rustled in the wind as he gazed down on the plains below. Reavers marched down there in a line, some sixty thousand strong. The reavers trekked in loose ranks eight or ten individuals across, in a line no less than ten miles long. They wove among the hills, crossing a silver stream crowded with woods. If Gaborn squinted, the reavers looked like a huge gray serpent slithering across the cold grasslands. Ahead, the old fallen castle at Mangan's Rock loomed just out of the serpent's reach, with the great statue of Mangan himself standing boldly, staring above the monsters.

Iome gasped at the sight, and whispered, 'I never imagined there would be so many.' Gaborn knew that she had seen images of them in Binnesman's Seer Stones, but somehow the stones had not conveyed the enormity of what they faced.

Even at this distance, the ground rumbled at their passage, and the hissing as they vented air was a muted whisper.

He gazed upon them in consternation. The reaver he sought had to be down there, somewhere.

Skalbairn's men had killed many reavers during the night, but Gaborn's search among the dead for the Waymaker yielded nothing. Averan had examined two reavers that nearly matched her description. Both turned out to be too small.

Which meant that the reaver he sought was still alive.

The hills were dry and nearly barren south of the mountains.

The rainstorm last night had missed this land completely. Dust rose up from the feet of the reavers like a trail of drifting smoke that mingled with the gree that flocked overhead.

To the west of the reavers Skalbairn's men rode in two separate bands. One band of a thousand knights kept pace with the reavers about six miles ahead. The noonday sun flashed off shield and helm and lance. The men looked petty, insignificant. The rest of the army, perhaps another fifteen hundred knights along with various squires and a caravan of wains, ventured near the tail of the reavers' lines, riding as a sort of rear guard to confront the reavers if they should turn back to Carris. Lances bristled up among their ranks like white spines.

Gaborn's mouth grew dry from anticipation. He could sense a rising danger. The reavers would not let this go on, would not be harried like this.

Gaborn's heralds blew their golden horns.

Down on the plain Skalbairn's men turned, looked up to the hills, and began to cheer. They waved lances and shields. Several men in Skalbairn's company peeled off, came galloping across the plains toward him. Gaborn decided to wait, get Skalbairn's latest report.

'Company, halt!' Gaborn called to his troops. Nearly half a mile back, the giants were still running hard, trying to keep up. One of them roared in anticipation of a few moments' rest.

Beside him, Binnesman's wylde spotted the reavers and cried out in delight, 'Reaver blood!'

'Yes,' Averan whispered excitedly, like a little girl talking to her best friend. 'I'll bet there's some yummy ones out there.'

Gaborn glanced over at the child resting comfortably on the saddle with the wizard at her back. She focused totally on the reavers.

'Tell me,' Gaborn said. 'This Waymaker. Do you think you could spot it from a distance if we rode alongside the reavers' ranks?'

Averan looked terrified at the very notion. 'If we got close enough.'

But he knew it would be almost impossible. The reavers were running in a horde, and no one would dare get within three hundred yards of them.

'Do you have any hint where we might start looking?' Gaborn asked in frustration.

'I . . . don't know. There are lots of reavers. He's important, so he should be up near the front. Or maybe near the back.'

'Or perhaps in the middle,' one lord offered.

'Can you add to the description?' Gaborn said. 'I might be able to put my far-seers to use.'

Averan shook her head. 'I . . . don't think I can add anything. Reavers don't have eyes. They don't see things like we do. I – I might be able to recognize him by the smell – but then, I might not. I'm not sure that people can smell as good as reavers do.'

Gaborn grinned coldly.

'If we find it,' Averan asked. 'Do I have to eat it in front of people?'

One of the lords in the retinue made a coughing noise, to cover the sound of his laugh.

'No,' Gaborn promised.

At that moment, there was the sound of galloping hooves on the trail behind, and Gaborn looked back up the road, expecting another messenger.

A young man with straw-colored hair rode into view round the bend on a plain brown mare. He slowed and warily eyed the frowth giants as he passed beneath their shadows. Gaborn tried vainly to remember where he'd seen the man. He could not place him, until he saw the pickax hanging from his saddlebags. 'Baron Waggit,' the lords began to mutter. The baron was wearing a new brown robe and leather armor, and had his yellow hair tied back. And he wore a new light of understanding in his eyes. Thus attired, his own mother would have been hard put to identify him.

The young baron rode up. He studied the king's men as if he'd never truly seen them before.

He reached the back of the king's retinue, rode past the knights and lords, and they broke into a cheer as he neared.

He reined in his mount just before Gaborn. The smell of rum followed him.

'Baron Waggit, you're looking well,' Gaborn said

Waggit wiped his nose on his sleeve in a foolish habit. 'Thanks. Um, thank you. Um, milord.' He still knew nothing of courtly graces. He might have the sense of a common man now, but he had much to learn.

'Will you ride beside me?' Gaborn offered.

'I . . . don't think so,' Waggit said. 'I mean, I couldn't. I'm not a real fighter – not like you lords. I only got one endowment, and it's just enough to make me a commoner. Don't know what I could do for you. I can't even cook my own damned dinner. I had to have a stableboy show me how to saddle this beast. I only come to say "thank you." I never dreamt . . . how it could be.'

'Not a real fighter?' Gaborn asked. 'You slew nine reavers with a pickax.'

'Dumb luck, that was,' Waggit said. He waited for Gaborn to smile at the joke. He'd caught sight of the reavers now, stared down at them.

'If you will not ride as a warrior,' Gaborn offered, 'then ride beside me as a friend. You'll learn to cook your own dinner fast enough, and maybe you'll learn some other things that will serve you well.'

'I guess,' Waggit said, 'if you'll have me.'

A lord behind him said, 'Good man!' and the other lords shouted, 'Hurrah!' as if he were some champion come to fight at their side.

More hoofbeats sounded and two riders appeared round

the bend this time: Sir Borenson and Myrrima, riding side by side. They galloped down the mountain. Gaborn's entourage could not help themselves. Knights began to cheer and wave their weapons, shouting, 'Hail Sir Borenson! See how well he rides!'

Borenson's face turned scarlet, and he nodded sheepishly. Someone shouted, 'Did you grow any spare walnuts for me?' and someone else called out, 'Riding a horse with them is only *half* the test!' Gaborn's heralds began blowing their horns in a cacophonous salute, and the men would not stop ribbing Borenson until he spoke.

He reined in his mount and raised his hands. 'Hear, hear,' he called. 'It is indeed true, thank you! I've grown three huge walnuts, and each twice as hairy as anything you've ever seen on a dog!'

The knights all laughed in an uproar, and someone shouted to Myrrima. 'Is it true?'

Myrrima blushed a deep crimson and tried to stifle a laugh. 'He's a liar. There's only two. They're perfect, but *enormous*. It's amazing that he can even walk. I fear that he'll become bowlegged!'

The knights all erupted in raucous chortles and sniggers. Some knight called out, 'Did you hear that, Sir Sedrick? Perhaps the wizard can help you with your little problem!'

Sir Sedrick's eyes grew wide, and he bellowed, 'What? I haven't got no *little* problem!'

The laughter grew louder.

Myrrima hid her face behind her hand, seeking to conceal her embarrassment.

Sir Borenson waved graciously toward Binnesman, as if inviting him to take a bow, though Gaborn felt sure that the knight merely wanted to divert attention from himself.

The wizard smiled and nodded, with a dubious grin.

The knights erupted in cheers and shouts of laughter. Gaborn could not help thinking of Wizard Hoewell. He'd fought hard to discredit Binnesman so that he could gain a teaching post in the Room of Earth Powers. Hoewell might well be a worthy wizard, but he'd never summoned a wylde, and he'd certainly never managed to grow new walnuts on a man.

Gaborn looked over at Binnesman and said gleefully, 'You're going to be famous!'

Moments later, Skalbairn finished riding up from the south with a pair of scouts. 'Milord,' Skalbairn shouted as he reined in his horse. The warlord's charger was running fast. It skidded for the last forty yards, came to a halt so close to Gaborn that his own mount danced back nervously. Skalbairn's eyes shone with excitement.

'Milord,' he said, 'the reavers froze their asses in the snow last night, and they still haven't thawed. The sun didn't warm their burrows enough to rouse them until well after dawn. Even now they're sluggish, trudging at half-pace. We only await your orders.'

Gaborn felt inside himself, wondering. He was tempted to attack, yet sensed danger. The reavers were not to be trifled with.

'Milord,' Skalbairn demanded, 'may we charge?'

Gaborn could sense layers of danger, like the peels of an onion. Many men here could die if he chose to attack.

But I am the Earth King, Gaborn thought. It's my duty to protect my people the best way that I know how.

The reavers were weak, had lost the fell mage that led them. They marched south along the very track from which they'd come, like ants following a food trail. He had the whole day to hunt. His knights were eager. The weather was excellent, and the terrain along much of the way would be perfect. In all of history, he had never heard of a lord attacking so many reavers in the open. Perhaps never again would conditions be so favorable.

But he wondered at the losses. How many brave men

might fall? He could get no clear sense of the answer. It would depend on his tactics. In the long run, could he afford the losses? What battles would he face in the coming days?

With every moment, he felt that he was marching closer to the world's doom. Men here would die today. Iome would soon face danger. Tens of thousands in Carris. And after that, the world.

Borenson spoke before anyone else. 'Damn it, Gaborn, don't you dare hold us back! Are we men here? Are we men at all?'

Gaborn looked at his old friend.

Skalbairn said in a rush, 'Milord, I cannot honestly assure you that if you order us to withhold, all men will obey. Many of the lords below are sworn to a new order, the Brotherhood of the Wolf, and acknowledge no one as their master.'

Gaborn knew what he had to do. 'Gentlemen,' he said. 'There are thousands of reavers down there, heading for the Underworld. I will not have them return in a week to scale the walls at the Courts of Tide. There must never be another Carris!'

He felt an electric thrill go through the group.

'Will you lead a charge?' Skalbairn asked.

His people needed an Earth King – a strong lord, and wise, riding out of the mists of time. Binnesman had warned that he must not fight unless he felt backed into a corner, but there was more than one way to get cornered. He was in a precarious situation. Lords on his borders were watching for any sign of weakness. Men he had Chosen only yesterday had foresworn themselves.

He needed an overwhelming victory.

Most of all, he needed to find the Waymaker.

So men would die today, good men. Gaborn would spend his friends. He pointed to the dark serpent that rumbled across the golden plains. 'We'll kill them all.'

Chapter Twenty-two: THE CHARGE

Our enemies are trained to show no fear. In Mystarria we shall teach our men to have *no fear.*

– King Therongold Orden

As soon as Gaborn announced that he would attack, he climbed down from his saddle and tightened the girth straps on his mount.

Borenson did the same. When a force horse was charging at ninety miles an hour, a knight couldn't risk even the slightest slippage.

Borenson took some deep breaths. He felt nervous on this charge. He had a good eye and a steady hand with a lance, but it had been years since he'd made a charge with so few endowments. He had only one of brawn, one of grace. Without stamina he was a 'warrior of unfortunate proportion.' His hands felt numb. The sound of men grunting and horses pawing the ground seemed unaccountably loud. Not for the first time he marveled at how fear could make sight and smell and hearing so acute, yet leave the hands and feet feeling numb and cold.

Gaborn asked Averan, 'How far can a reaver see?' Borenson leaned close to hear the answer. For ages it had been a question of much speculation.

'It depends on the reaver,' Averan answered. 'For most

of them, about from here to that tree. The howlers see a little farther, the glue mums hardly see at all. Far-seers can do better.'

'Far-seers?' Gaborn asked.

'There are none in this horde,' Averan assured him.

'About two hundred and fifty yards, then,' Gaborn said, yanking his girth strap tighter. 'Can they count our numbers by smell?'

Averan shook her head. 'I don't think so. Our world is so strange to them – so full of new scents. Every man smells so different from another. But if you put a bunch of them together – I don't think so.'

Gaborn glanced at Skalbairn. 'The wind is steady from the east?'

'It has been so all morning,' Skalbairn said.

'Call your troops back,' Gaborn said. 'We'll charge the reavers' rear flank from downwind. By the time they see us, we'll be upon them.'

Gaborn leapt on his horse as Skalbairn pulled out his warhorn and blew a short riff, ordering his troops to regroup.

Myrrima had been riding beside Borenson. She dismounted quickly and strung her bow. Her face was pale with fear.

'You can't kill a reaver with that!' Borenson said.

She looked up at him, anger in her eyes. 'Why not? All I have to do is hit it in the sweet triangle hard enough to bury the arrow a yard.'

'Can you even *hit* a reaver?' Borenson asked. He could tell that she had taken some endowments, but it wasn't just endowments that made a warrior. One needed skill in battle.

Several men in the crowd guffawed. The angry look Myrrima gave him suggested that if he didn't shut his mouth soon, she'd nock an arrow and practice on him.

With that, Gaborn spurred his mount forward and his Days rode at his side. Myrrima leapt on her own horse and charged after him, drawing an arrow from the quiver at her back. Binnesman and his wylde rode beside them.

Borenson was gathering up the reins when Iome grabbed his elbow and whispered, 'A word to the wise, Sir Borenson. Your wife has many endowments of her own now. How do you think she got them?'

'She said you gave them to her – a gift,' Borenson said.

Iome offered a wry smile. 'She *earned* them with that bow of hers. She saved me and Binnesman and the lives of everyone else at Castle Sylvarresta. She slew the Darkling Glory, and I have paid her twenty forcibles for her service.'

Borenson felt sure that Iome was waiting for his jaw to drop, but he didn't give her the satisfaction.

Instead he offered in a casual tone, 'Such things are only to be expected from a wife of mine.'

Iome smiled. 'No doubt she can roast a fine piglet too.'

Borenson laughed and climbed on his horse, raced downhill. He left only the wagon of forcibles and its guard behind, accompanied by the spidery old Kaifba Feykaald. He passed the frowth giants that loped steadily over the grass, their mail jangling like the chains to ships' anchors. They smelled strongly of sour fat and carrion.

The hooves of the horses thundered over the ground through stands of golden alders toward the bright plain. Grasshoppers, fat from eating all summer, leapt away from the horse's hooves. Yellow butterflies dipped here and there in the grass. Overhead, the sky was a blue bowl, and the wind felt brisk in Borenson's face.

Borenson wondered about his wife. She hadn't told him that she'd slain the Darkling Glory. He knew how hard it was to keep one's mouth shut about such things.

He felt sheepish. He'd killed a reaver mage in the Dunnwood, a small one that wasn't even so powerful as a scarlet sorceress, and dragged it home for his wife. It seemed a paltry prize now.

In the past few days, the world had turned upside down. He'd lost all his endowments, while she gained as many.

But he'd never imagined when he met her in the market at Bannisferre that Myrrima would someday slay a Darkling Glory, a beast of legend that he'd never even seen. He'd never imagined that she would take a bow and charge into the ranks of a reaver horde. He'd never imagined that she would want to accompany him to Inkarra.

Perhaps, Borenson thought, she's trying to earn my respect.

But, no, even that seemed wrong. Myrrima wasn't some drooling pup, eager to please. She had a toughness that did not so much beg for admiration as command it. She was that tough, right down to the core of her soul.

Borenson felt as if he were falling into a trap. He had told Myrrima himself that love was part attraction, part respect. He'd felt attracted to her from the moment he'd met her. And right now, he was feeling a whole lot of respect too.

A trio of gree whipped overhead, blacker than bats, writhing on the wind. The reavers thundered over the grasslands beneath a cloud of the winged beasts. From a distance the reavers had looked like a great gray serpent. Closer up, with the way that air vented from their abdomens, now the snake could be heard to hiss as if in anger.

Out on the plains, Skalbairn's army rode back to join with the Brotherhood of the Wolf.

Borenson worried about his mount. He'd not have bought such an uncouth animal. The piebald mare had an endowment of brawn, one of grace, and two of metabolism, but she kept fighting the bit.

As he neared the reaver horde, the mare tossed her head and shied away. She'd ridden in battle with reavers before. He needed a steady mount, one that trusted him enough to charge a reaver close so that he could bury a lance in it. The mare fought him, tried to race away from the horde.

'Get back in line,' Borenson growled. 'Don't be afraid

of them. Be afraid of me!' He slapped her ears with the reins and tried to work her toward the reavers, but she had endowments of her own. It was hard work. Reluctantly she followed the cavalry.

Myrrima had retrieved his ring mail, helm, and warhammer from Carris. With only one endowment of brawn, the weight dragged him.

He reached Skalbairn's war band. It was traveling light and fast. Most of the knights already held lances, but a hundred wains carried spares.

Gaborn rode up to get a lance. Borenson bent as a squire passed him one too. The weapon was a heavy war lance, perhaps eighty-five pounds. He inspected its iron tip, sharpened to pierce the reaver's hide. The shaft was polished and oiled, to speed its entry. Three recessed iron rings bound the ash at equal distances, to keep the wood from splitting.

Borenson hefted his lance, felt his mouth going dry. With so few endowments, it would be tough to keep the lance steady.

He glanced up and down the battle lines, saw some lords take two lances, one in each hand. They would plant one in the ground before the charge, return to make a second charge quickly. A week ago, he'd have done the same.

He saw a few knights reach for wine flasks. In the northlands, men drank wine mingled with borage to lend them courage. Borenson thought it a coward's act.

But there was little idle chatter, little boasting, the kind of thing that one hears from unseasoned lads out on their first charge. These men had fought at Carris. They'd already pounded into the reavers' lines again and again, and lived to tell about it. That was a boast that damned few men could make.

Gaborn's heralds sounded the charge, and Gaborn spurred his mount, leading the way. The cavalry was off. By now the reavers sluggishly loped nearly a mile ahead.

Gaborn circumvented their flank, taking his men to the west. As they crossed the reavers' path, it looked like a shallow trench.

The reavers had beaten this track on the way north, compacting the soil to a depth of four or five feet compared to the surrounding terrain. There were no trees in that furrow, no bushes or rocks. Everything was pulverized.

Borenson imagined that in years to come, the reavers' trail would fill with rainwater, frogs, and fish. Generations from now, people might stand in the shallows in the summer and still find the clear footprint of a reaver.

As his mount galloped along, he listened to the cadence of its hooves, imagined his heart beating in rhythm with it.

Gaborn led them west of the horde, so that the reavers moved along to Borenson's left, but Gaborn kept half a mile downwind from the monsters.

Borenson watched them intently, in case they turned to attack – huge gray beasts, corded muscles rippling beneath flesh so dense it almost seemed to be bone.

To Borenson's surprise, Gaborn did not order the charge immediately.

Myrrima rode up beside Borenson. She didn't speak. She merely held her bow, arrow nocked.

They rode along, tense, poised to attack. Borenson's palm grew sweaty on his warlance.

A pair of badgers, apparently disturbed by the trembling ground, came up out of their dens and sat staring toward the reavers.

The reavers loped ahead in a rocking motion, heads rising, and then abdomens. Their crystalline teeth flashed in the morning sun. Their huge forepaws were large enough to rip a horse in two.

Here and there, deep in the horde, Borenson spotted fiery runes branded into a scarlet sorceress. He looked up and down the length of the reavers' lines. The sorceresses kept themselves hidden.

The reavers were a wall of flesh, far more impressive than any herd of elephants. Borenson found his blood thrumming through his veins. He'd often imagined lancing reavers as a child, but always he'd envisioned them in ones and twos. Never in his wildest fantasies could he have imagined this.

Sir Hoswell rode up beside them. The small man with his dark eyes and enormous moustache reminded Borenson of an otter.

He smiled at Myrrima. 'Don't worry yourself. Killing reavers isn't so hard. Just think of them as a target – a big target. Aim for the sweet triangle. Or if they rise up on their hind legs, shoot between the abdominal plates. Other than that, don't shoot at all. You'll never get the angle to hit the soft spot under their palate.'

Myrrima did not answer.

Up and down the line, men began to make jests. Someone shouted, 'Has anyone seen a runt in the horde? Sir Sedrick wants to battle it.'

A knight rejoined, 'There's no runts, but I saw a sickly one dragging its butt on the ground!'

'I'll give a silver hawk,' another lord cried out, 'to any man who will catch a gree between his teeth and swallow it whole.'

Tradition held that a knight should face death with boldness and a good humor.

But Borenson was in no mood for it today. He could not understand why Gaborn waited to charge. They rode on thus for nearly ten minutes.

The reavers kicked up a cloud of dust a hundred yards high as they slowly loped across the plains, and all of it was drifting west, right into the knights' faces. Soon, the dirt powdered their armor and their hair, clogged their throats. It would take hours to clean it out of Borenson's ring mail.

Borenson could see every reason to speed the attack before the day and the reavers warmed up. The fields were clear, the ground dry and even, with hardly a rock or a shrub. There was no reason for Gaborn to hesitate, no reason that a trained veteran could see.

But Gaborn was the Earth King, and saw things that others could not.

After a bit, a message came down the line. Warriors ahead of Borenson said, 'The Earth King warns us not to outpace him, to charge when he does. Make no battle cry, blow no horns. Ranks three deep!'

The battle line spread out, so that each knight put ten yards between himself and his neighbor. Borenson positioned himself to be in the front rank.

Then he waited, and waited. His mare quit fighting him. Sometime during all of this, she seemed to find her courage.

Borenson never saw a signal, never heard an order to charge. Instead, he suddenly became aware that the lords began turning their mounts toward the reavers' lines. Gaborn led the way by a dozen yards.

Gaborn kept his left hand raised, so that none would outpace him. He began trotting his horse toward the reavers. For their part, the reavers did not react. The huge monsters trod across the grasslands, apparently unaware of the impending attack.

At a thousand yards, Gaborn turned his mount a bit, began racing northeast toward the reavers' lines at a forty-five-degree angle. He spurred his horse into a canter, and dropped his lance into a couched position. All the Runelords along the front followed his lead.

Borenson did likewise. The mare surprised him. She ran with an especially fluid gait, and he found it easy to keep the lance tip from bouncing.

He watched the reaver horde, prepared for the moment when they would turn to confront him.

At five hundred yards, Gaborn spurred his charger into a gallop. Borenson's mount seemed to leap beneath him, and the ground became a blur beneath her hooves. All up and down the line, a few chargers began to outpace the rest.

To Borenson's surprise, the piebald mare did the same. She did indeed seem to have found her heart, and raced now toward the reavers.

Borenson began to search for his target. The rumbling of the reavers' footsteps sounded far louder than the hooves of the charging horses. The rumbling worked into a man's bones. Gree whipped overhead, squeaking. The reavers grew closer in his field of view, yet still the eyeless heads did not swivel his way, nor did the reavers wave the philia along their necks and jaws as they did when disturbed.

He spotted a flash of opal deep in the horde, a scarlet sorceress. But there was no way he could get to her. Instead he picked a reaver in the front rank, lowered his lance.

Time seemed to freeze as his charger raced on. He concentrated on the cadence of her hooves, on the little things all around him. With only one endowment of brawn to help, the heavy lance was a clumsy weapon, but he was a skilled knight. He marveled at how butterflies and grasshoppers still flew up from his horse's path.

He tried to steady himself. For one instant the madness of what he sought to do struck him. If he missed his target on a reaver, if he fell from his horse and botched this in any of a hundred ways, he'd most likely end up dead.

He fought back a maniacal upwelling of terror, and began to chuckle.

At three hundred yards the reavers had not sensed the attack. At a hundred and fifty yards, some of them stumbled and began to swivel their heads.

But his mare was charging so fast that they had only a second or two to respond.

His reaver faltered, skidded to a halt, throwing up a cloud

of dust. It was a huge blade-bearer that bore a glory hammer in its right paw.

The black iron hammer had a handle twenty feet long, and a head that weighed as much as a horse. A bit of human hide was tied near the base of the handle. A ballista bolt had pierced the reaver's back, and stuck there still.

Up and down the lines, Borenson could hear the clash of metal against bone, the shouts of men, the screams of horses, the roaring of reavers.

His own reaver opened its mouth and raised its weapon as he approached.

Ease the tip in, he thought.

He pulled the tip of his lance up, adjusting for the change in angle, as his charger galloped. The monster loomed overhead.

Borenson began to rein his mount in, pull hard to the left. Then he was practically under the reaver, could see every crease in its warty gray hide. Its teeth flashed above him.

He guided the lance tip into the monster's sweet triangle, felt it pierce the dense cartilage there. He let the weight of the lance carry it home, made his release. The lance plunged into the beast's head.

The reaver hissed and swung its glory hammer – more in a spasm than an actual blow.

Borenson ducked violently, nearly colliding with the weapon as the hammer whooshed overhead.

Suddenly a second reaver spurred up the embankment. Borenson's mare screamed and skidded, lost her footing and rolled, throwing him from the saddle.

For a brief second, he was in the air, the smell of dirt thick in his nostrils, a reaver roaring as it filled his vision.

Then he slammed into the ground. The air came out of him in a huff, and he seemed to ache everywhere at once. He knew he had to get up, to move, and he reached out for the ground and pushed with his hands.

He thought dully that he should grab his warhammer, put up a manly fight at the very least.

But he was a warrior of unfortunate proportion. Every muscle seemed to go to jelly, and he couldn't decide which way was up.

He heard the reaver, rolled onto his back to face it.

The reaver charged, towering over him, its teeth flashing in the sun, philia writhing like snakes. It roared and raised its massive paws.

A bow twanged. An arrow blurred, disappeared into the reaver's skull.

He looked toward the source. Myrrima hunched not ten feet behind him.

The reaver lurched backward, as if seeking to escape. Her bow twanged again and the monster's legs went out from under it.

There was a hissing as a third reaver came in from the north. He saw the flash of glowing runes on its gray hide. A smell came before it in a thin gray haze, a stench that blinded Borenson and set his ears to buzzing so loudly that he could hear no other sound. His eyes burned as if they were full of acid.

Myrrima whirled as his sight dimmed. She shouted in fury and loosed an arrow.

Chapter Twenty-three: TARGETS OF FLESH

Any archer who cannot draw, aim, and loose ten arrows in the space of a minute must be demoted to the ranks of the infantry.

– Standing Decree in Heredon

Myrrima's heart pounded. Her arrow struck the bony plate of the reaver mage's head. The shaft shattered under the impact.

She fumbled for her quiver, quickly drew an arrow to the full. Her legs felt weak, as if they'd give out beneath her.

Even with her endowments, the reaver's spell made her eyes burn as if they had lye spilled in them, and there was a buzzing roar in her ears. She felt as if she were spinning.

Her hand shook as she drew aim.

She let the arrow fly. It slammed into the monster's eyeless head, buried itself in the scarlet sorceress's sweet triangle.

It did not kill her instantly.

An arrow didn't have the bulk of a lance. Shooting this monster with an arrow was the equivalent of plunging a needle into a man's brain. It would kill him, but not as fast and effectively as a heavier weapon might.

The mage roared and crouched back. She raised her crystalline staff, aimed it. A cloud of darkness, like a living shadow, hurtled from it, and Myrrima leapt aside. There was a roar, as if a huge stone had crashed to earth.

Suddenly Hoswell was at Myrrima's right. His bow sang, and a second arrow plunged into the sorceress's sweet triangle.

The monster roared in fury, and raised her arms to attack, but then wheeled as if to flee and collapsed to her belly. Air hissed from her posterior vents in rapid bursts, similar to the sound of a human panting.

Myrrima glanced back, saw the path that the reaver's shadow blast had taken. The ground was crushed and broken, the grass sheared at its roots for yards around. She did not doubt that the spell would have shattered every bone in her body.

More reavers rushed into the fray, crawling over the dead. Myrrima leapt to her feet, drew a shaky aim at a blade-bearer.

'Take your time,' Hoswell shouted as he drew on a monster to their left.

She let the arrow fly. It found its mark. The reaver lunged backward, as if looking for an easier meal. It would be dead in seconds.

'Good,' Hoswell said.

Hoswell sprinted forward, into the thick of the reavers' lines. Many of the monsters reacted to the humans' charge merely by running faster, trying to escape through their deeply furrowed trail.

Myrrima glanced up and down the battle lines. Everywhere knights had come off their horses, and many of them now were leaping into the ranks of the reavers, armed with nothing but their courage, their endowments, and their battle-axes. She saw Gaborn's standard to the north. He fought with the green woman at his side.

Myrrima followed Hoswell down into the gully, and they stopped to shoot a pair of reavers on the trail.

With her endowments, everything seemed to happen in slow motion. She knew that the reavers were charging at twenty miles per hour, but to her it seemed as if they came at only a brisk walk.

She loosed an arrow, missed again.

'With your endowments,' Hoswell said, 'you can afford to miss. If a reaver charges you, just run away.'

His assurances had a calming effect. She drew an arrow, took aim. The monster was rushing at her, and it filled her vision as it reared overhead. It gaped its mouth. Crystalline teeth flashed like molten daggers.

She dropped to a crouch, managed to fire up through its soft palate, then leapt backward as the beast kept charging on.

Her heart hammered as the reaver collapsed. But now her heart was not pounding in fear so much as in the thrill of the hunt.

Killing blade-bearers seemed easy. She felt tempted to grab Borenson's warhammer and leap into the fray, but resisted the impulse. She was gaining confidence with her bow.

But with monsters like these, any mistake would be her last.

Chapter Twenty-four: THE WEALTH OF NATIONS

The wealth of nations lies not in gold or arms, but in the vigilance of its people.
– Rajah Farah Magreb, High King of ancient Indhopal

It is amazing what an old man can learn in half a day if he keeps his eyes and ears open.

Three miles behind the battle lines, Feykaald glanced at the charging mounts, saw the Runelords of Rofehavan sweep into the reavers' flanks.

He'd stayed back with the carters and rode beside the wains that bore the king's lances and food. One wagon in particular held his attention: Gaborn's treasure wagon. It had a flat bed like others in the caravan, but this one had a tarp tied over its trunks – and guards to watch it.

He knew that the wain carried treasure of some kind. It might be as insignificant as clothing and jewels from Iome's household, but he hoped for something better.

Now, as the battle raged, the carters stood atop their wains to get a better view. Most of the guards for the precious wagon had gone to join the charge, and only a pair of them remained.

Feykaald rode along behind the wagons slowly, so as not to attract attention. He needn't have feared. Gaborn's charge this morning was the stuff of dreams, the kind of thing that children only heard about in wild tales.

The guards stood watching the battle, riveted.

As he passed the wagon, Feykaald reached down with his cobra staff and pulled up a tarp, to get a peek at the boxes.

His heart hammered.

He saw only the corner of a box. It was made of cedar from Indhopal, instead of oak from Rofehavan.

Feykaald had supervised the packing of that box himself. He knew its contents: Raj Ahten's forcibles.

Feykaald could not suppress a smile. He dropped the tarp, continued riding past the wain. One guard glanced back at him. Feykaald nodded toward the battlefield. 'It goes well, neh?'

The guard turned away.

Five boxes beneath the tarp. Five boxes – nearly twenty thousand forcibles! Gaborn still had half of his master's treasure!

Feykaald briefly considered trying to murder the two guards and flee with the boxes. But he dared not even entertain the thought.

Gaborn knew when his Chosen were in danger.

Feykaald would have to come up with a better plan.

Chapter Twenty-five: GRUDGING RESPECT

A keen blade, a fierce dog, a bold wife – these things are good.

– Adage from Internook

Borenson rolled to his knees and began to crawl over the rough stubble. He could see nothing, could hear only the vague din of battle – the screams of horses, the hissing of reavers as they pounded over the plain.

He scrambled forward, struggled to hold his breath. The reaver mage's spell made his ears more than just ring; he'd lost his balance, and could do little more than crawl.

His eyes burned like fire. Tears rolled from them. His sinuses ached as if he'd inhaled scalding smoke.

The pain was excruciating. He'd smelled curses like these at Carris, but he'd never taken one full in the face, fifty feet downwind from a mage.

Borenson clambered through the stubble as doggedly as he could. He reasoned that if he was going to be the target of a reaver's wrath, at least he would be a moving target.

After a few yards, he exhaled his burning lungs, swallowed a fresh breath. The stench had lessened, yet even now it was too much. He vomited his breakfast into the grass and struggled on.

Ten yards farther, he put his sleeve over his nose, tried

inhaling again. The stench seemed to cling to his lungs like pitch. It brought wracking coughs. He staggered up and ran.

Is this how my father died? he wondered.

He felt a terrible pity for the man.

In less than a minute he turned, blinking at the battle lines, fiercely wiping tears from his face with the back of his hand.

He strained to see. He'd reached a small rise, a hundred yards from the reavers' trail. Everywhere up and down the battle line, Runelords fought reavers tooth and nail. Few of the knights had lances. Most had dismounted and now rushed in to fight with battle-axes and warhammers.

The lords had decimated the reavers' western flank. Many reavers fled east to escape the slaughter.

At the rear of the reaver lines, frowth giants roared as they waded among the enemy, swinging huge staves, knocking the reavers' legs from under them. Runelords then dispatched the wounded beasts.

Myrrima was nowhere to be seen. Five reavers lay clumped on the battlefield where he had killed his reaver, including a huge scarlet sorceress emblazoned with runes.

His piebald mare galloped toward him, dragging its reins.

He leapt onto its back.

The reaver that he'd targeted lay dead. Usually when a man lanced a reaver, the monster would flail at the lance, trying to draw it out, thereby snapping it. But by a stroke of good fortune, Borenson's lance was still intact. He rode to it, his mare whinnying and throwing her head in fear. He drew out the shaft.

Armed now, he charged into the furrow of the reavers' trail. A dozen reavers lay dead or dying.

He reached the far side of the trail, spotted Myrrima nearly half a mile away.

Reavers were fleeing west by the thousands, trying to escape the Runelords. Borenson could see a scarlet sorceress trundling over the plains with Myrrima in pursuit, Hoswell trying to keep up. She spurred her horse faster, charged it from behind, and buried an arrow in the joint under its right leg. The leg spasmed, and the sorceress faltered, skidding on her belly. She whirled and came up roaring, bringing a staff of purest crystal to bear.

Vile energies seemed to pulse through the staff, and it blazed. A cloud of green smoke burst from it.

Myrrima reined in her mount just as Hoswell let an arrow fly into the monster's sweet triangle. The mage flipped to her side, pawing at her wound.

Myrrima and Hoswell wheeled away from the green fog, clinging to their saddles. They hastened back toward Borenson. The mage dropped her staff and rolled, as if trying to dislodge an attacker. Then she just flailed her huge arms as she died.

Borenson reined his mount.

A barbarian from Internook rode up beside him, watched Myrrima with unabashed admiration. The man had a sealskin coat, and yellow corn-braids hanging from his sideburns. He'd painted the left half of his face orange. He bore a huge, wide-bladed battle-ax in a style that his folk called a 'reaper.' It was purpled in inky reaver gore.

The barbarian offered Borenson a silver flask, nodded at Myrrima. 'If I had a hound with half her heart, I'd never hunt again. I'd say the word, and it would drag bears home for dinner.'

Borenson took a swig from the flask, found that it was mead. It tasted like warm piss, but at least it rinsed the vomit from his mouth.

'Aye,' he said. He felt an unnamable something, an unreasonable pride. He felt proud of Myrrima.

Warriors began to cheer. The charge had been an overwhelming success. The remainder of the horde fled south, redoubling speed.

Myrrima rode back, dark eyes flashing. She looked euphoric. 'I ran out of arrows!'

He'd seen her quiver when she rode into battle. She'd had at least three dozen. Suddenly he looked at the dozens of dead reavers lying around all in a knot. While he'd managed only a single kill, Myrrima and Sir Hoswell had carved a swath.

Myrrima doesn't understand me at all, he thought. Myrrima wanted his love, and like nearly all women, she thought him incapable of ever loving more than one woman at a time.

It was strange. She talked about how warriors were not really in touch with their feelings, and how she wanted that from a man. But it was a lie.

She really wanted him to have strong feelings for her, yet cut off any desires for other women.

But it seemed to Borenson that women were like food laid out in a feast. One woman might be a satisfying loaf of bread, another an intoxicating wine, a third as sustaining as a boar's ham, a fourth as sweet as a tart.

Who would want to eat only one single course at a feast? No one. And if a man would not devote himself to eating one thing for a single feast, how could a person ask him to devote a lifetime to eating that one food alone?

That was the rub. Every woman wants to think of herself as a whole feast. Would a loaf of bread say to its master, don't eat that mince pie? Or would the wine demand, don't eat the buttered parsnips?

The notion was absurd.

His feelings for Saffira weren't gone. They'd never go. She was an intoxicating wine. He'd never desired a woman as acutely as he had Saffira, and suspected that he never would again. The feelings he'd had for her weren't mere lust. Her endowments of glamour aroused a sense of devotion, a need to serve her that was so powerfully compelling that it caused physical pain.

That was the secret and the power of glamour.

While Saffira was alive, he'd been in torment, entangled by the need to serve her. He'd felt . . . that he approached a unique singleness of purpose, a form of purity.

He'd always wanted to feel that way about someone.

Yet while he was charmed by Saffira's beauty and enthralled by her glamour, he hadn't really respected her. Thus, he hadn't been able to give his heart to her fully.

His feelings for Myrrima on the other hand were growing in odd directions. His lust for her paled to insignificance when compared to his feelings for Saffira.

But his respect for her was taking on immense proportions. He sensed that while Saffira might have been wine, Myrrima was the meat of the meal. She was the one that could sustain him.

Thus as she rode back from killing the reaver mage, and the big barbarian at his side offered his highest words of praise, Borenson felt more than proud of Myrrima, he felt a respect that he'd never felt for a woman, mingled with a sense of foreboding.

To the south, a battle horn blew, calling men to regroup. He looked toward the sound. Men shouted in warning, ran toward the south. Frowth giants roared.

Gaborn's charge had been aimed at the reavers' rearmost troops. To the south, the huge line still snaked ahead for miles.

Many of those reavers had begun to turn. Thousands of the monsters charged back now toward their dead. They spread out, began forming a battle line half a mile wide with ranks twenty or thirty deep. It was a formidable front.

Gaborn's heralds furiously blew their horns. A few hundred Runelords began forming a new front of their own.

The barbarian at Borenson's side shouted gleefully, 'Looks as if they'll make a fight of it!'

Runelords spurred their mounts toward the new battle line. Borenson shouted and wheeled his charger.

He was among the first to reach Gaborn's new front. But the king seemed uncertain. The Runelords who stood with him were ill-armed. Not one in twenty had a lance.

From the west, Binnesman raced to the battle lines, with Averan astride his horse. Gaborn's Days followed on his own mare.

Averan warned Gaborn, 'It's the sorceresses, come back to feed. There was a fell mage here. They'll want to harvest her and the rest of their kin.'

Borenson had never seen reavers harvest, but he'd heard tales. They'd rip out the brains of the dead or the glands beneath their arms. Sometimes they'd devour their brothers whole.

Averan said forcefully, 'We can't let them harvest the dead. The Waymaker may be among them.'

Gaborn's brows furrowed. Blindsiding sluggish reavers was one thing. But now the child begged him to stand against a frontal assault – thousands of reavers confronting his ill-armed troops.

Gaborn's eyes flashed, and he looked at the reavers. 'Hold the lines!' he shouted to the massing troops. 'We'll allow no harvesting!'

The reavers gathered, creating a wall of flesh about five hundred yards north. Reavers that had fled Gaborn's charge now circled into the rear of the massing horde. Huge blade-bearers began to jostle through the ranks, gaining better position. Here and there, reaver scouts began to creep near, heads held high, philia waving as they scented the air.

The reavers were far enough away that they could not see Gaborn's army, yet they could smell the human host.

The air filled with energy, as if from a rising storm. Borenson's blood thrummed through his veins. This battle wasn't over. It had barely begun.

Chapter Twenty-six: HOLDING FAST

You need not fear a man who bears arms and armor – unless he also bears a deadly resolve.

– Erden Geboren

Averan studied the battle lines forming, sensed from the reavers' body language that things were quickly getting out of hand. The reaver scouts approached cautiously. They'd take three strides, then halt, rise to their back legs and wave their philia in the air, turning eyeless heads this way and that.

The reavers were worried but determined. They'd not hold back for long. As soon as the scouts spotted Gaborn's troops, learned their number and position, they would tell their masters how few men stood against them.

Gaborn seemed unsure how to withstand the horde.

'They're going to charge you,' Averan warned. 'If you want to stop them, kill the horde's new leader.'

Gaborn looked at the mass of reavers, brow furrowed. 'Which one is it?'

The question left Averan astonished. The answer seemed obvious. But she was looking at the horde now through reaver's eyes. 'The mage at the center of the front lines, hiding behind the two blade-bearers.'

Gaborn spotted the reaver slowly. She was a big brute, glittering from fiery runes tattooed on her thick outer skin.

She held a fiery red staff. Averan thought her size and the configuration of her runes should have warned anyone that she was Battle Weaver's successor. Her name was a scent, the scent of Blood on Stone.

Yet Averan saw that Gaborn had been searching to her right, where a knot of mages in the front rank acted as decoys. Blood on Stone was well concealed.

Gaborn swore. It would be hard to get her.

It was an eerie moment. Nearly all of the Runelords had ridden forward and were bracing for a charge. Eight frowth giants, spattered with reaver gore, lined up at their backs. Two had fallen in the battle.

Averan glanced over her shoulder at the wylde. Spring strolled through the midst of the dead reavers, some of which she'd killed herself, mindlessly feeding.

'Milord,' Borenson shouted, urging his mount through the ranks. 'May I suggest archers? We've a few men with steel bows.'

'Archers?' Gaborn asked. 'Erden Geboren never used archers.'

'But he didn't have bows made of Sylvarresta's spring steel!'

Gaborn licked his lips. 'I'd not thought of that. Can it work?'

'Myrrima and Hoswell killed three or four dozen of them in the charge.'

Averan found it hard to imagine Myrrima killing dozens of reavers.

'Archers,' Gaborn shouted, 'to me!'

Over a hundred Runelords rode forward. Some had their bows still wrapped in canvas. These were powerful lords. Many moved so swiftly that it baffled Averan's eyes. By the time she realized that the lords were drawing bows from their cases, many bows were strung.

'The big sorceress with the red staff,' Gaborn ordered the archers. 'Take her swiftly.'

'Kill the scouts, too,' Averan offered. 'Before they get close enough to see us.'

'Lancers!' Gaborn shouted, waving toward the scouts. Two hundred lancers rode out of the crowd.

The men prepared for their charge, and someone blew a horn. The force horses surged across the field, weaving in and out.

By the time the reaver scouts saw danger approach, and reacted by skittering backward, the lancers took them.

The archers raced within a hundred yards of the reavers' lines. Blade-bearers leapt forward, turning themselves into living shields as they sought to preserve their sorceress.

Arrows sped from steel bows, riddling the fell mage and those that sought to protect her. She lurched backward a pace, died as she bowled against the reavers behind.

For their part, the reavers in the main rank reacted slowly. The blade-bearers and common troops backed away a pace, stood up waving their forearms and weapons, but held their line, having no other command before them. Far more dangerous were the blade-bearers well behind the lines.

They began hurling stones in a deadly hail.

Gaborn's archers and lancers all wheeled their mounts and galloped away from the front. Rocks hurtled from the sky. Even though the reavers threw blindly, some stones struck their targets.

Half a dozen archers died outright.

A boulder struck a knight of Heredon nearly two hundred yards from the reavers' front. The stone slammed into his shoulder and knocked him from his horse.

For a heart-stopping second, Averan imagined that he was dead. But he crawled to his feet and staggered up, right arm hanging limp. In the fall he must have injured his hip, for he barely managed to stand. He looked about on the ground briefly, as if he'd lost something but could not recall what, then grabbed his bow.

His horse had run ahead. The archer limped for cover, using his bow as a crutch.

Around Averan, hard-faced Runelords clenched their weapons, steeled themselves for a charge.

But Averan knew that there would be no charge.

Blood on Stone's successor wasn't here. Less than a tenth of the reavers had made a stand. Her successor was fleeing with the main body of the horde.

Even as Averan watched, the blade-bearers turned to Blood on Stone's corpse and began to pry at the sweet triangle on her skull. The bony plates ripped outward, and the reavers tore out her precious brains, while others sought the glands beneath her legs.

The knight of Heredon limped back to safety, heading straight for Gaborn. When he reached his own lines, Averan saw his face. Blood streamed from his nose and mouth, and he gasped for every breath. His face was leached as white as linen.

'Sir Hoswell!' Iome said.

Some warriors helped Sir Hoswell to the ground, shouting that his lungs were burst. They laid him on a blanket. Iome got down from her own mount and held his hand. Myrrima rode back from the charge, and had retrieved his horse. Now she sat in the saddle, staring down at him.

At Averan's back, Binnesman climbed from the saddle, knelt over the dying man. He reached into his pocket, pulled out an herb.

'Chew this,' Binnesman said. 'It will make your passing easier.'

But Hoswell shook his head, refusing the herb. 'I'm sorry,' Hoswell said between gasping breaths. 'I'm sorry. I'm sorry!'

His back arched, and he stared up at Myrrima.

'It's all right,' Iome said. 'You served well. You've nothing to be sorry for.'

Sir Hoswell gasped and coughed up some red flecks. He held his bow up, offered it to Myrrima. 'Take it. It's the finest in Heredon.'

Averan had never seen a bow like it. Hoswell held it at arm's length. The wings of the bow were forged from Heredon's famed spring steel, but rather than a simple wide band of steel, this bow was made of a long, narrow piece. Many steel bows were short, the better for firing from horseback. But this was two-thirds the length of a longbow. The belly of the bow had a wooden handle bolted through it, ornately carved from oak, and the tips where the bow was strung were capped with similar pieces of oak.

Myrrima reached out hesitantly and took the bow. She did not seem glad, nor did she smile. She stared evenly at the dying knight.

Sir Hoswell began to cough, and blood foamed out of him. Averan turned away.

Beside Averan, Baron Waggit sat on his mount. He had not participated in the charge, had held back with Averan, Binnesman, and Gaborn's Days. He choked back a sob, and Averan glanced up at him.

She saw horror naked in his eyes. 'He – he's dying? Forever?'

She'd never seen that expression in the face of a man before. She remembered years ago, when her own mother had died, and Brand had come and held her tenderly and told her what had happened. He'd warned her then that it happened to everyone, that there was no escape.

She'd felt that terror then.

She suddenly realized that in some ways, she was older than Waggit. She'd learned about death long ago, as a girl of three. But Waggit had always been incapable of comprehending that death was the end, inescapable and interminable. Lucky Waggit.

'I'm afraid so,' Binnesman said softly, trying to comfort the young man.

Waggit shook his head, as if he could not accept it.

A cheer erupted from Gaborn's knights.

At first Averan thought they cheered Hoswell, but the cheer had erupted everywhere at once.

She looked across the battlefield.

The reaver horde was turning. The great monsters loped away in their strange rocking gait, running south. Even as they did, there was a subtle change. They formed into seven columns, with mages taking the center.

The warriors around Averan began to mutter. They'd never seen reavers march that way. Averan could remember nothing like it even in reaver experience.

Averan felt uneasy. The reavers had begun changing tactics, adjusting. Her experience warned her that reavers were clever creatures – perhaps even smarter than men. The moment seemed ominous.

Gaborn's own men turned their mounts, heading away from the battlefield. Binnesman got back on his horse, behind Averan, and for a moment they rode in silence.

Gaborn gave Averan a sideways glance. He smiled. 'Congratulations,' he said. 'We have our second victory, and in great part we owe it to you.'

It felt gruesome to get such a commendation now, with dead men at their backs.

'I think I shall promote you,' Gaborn said. 'Let it be known that Skyrider Averan is now a chancellor to the king.'

It was supposed a huge honor. As chancellor, she would be called upon to advise the king whenever he asked. At the age of nine, she was probably the youngest person ever bestowed the title. Averan should have been thrilled.

But she felt confused. The honor seemed hollow.

Averan looked at the fleeing reavers, at knights cheering in the battle line. Then she looked back out over the golden plains beneath the blue bowl of heaven, where reavers lay in mounds like gray stones.

She felt sad.

She realized belatedly that she did not care for a title. It was an honor that a man bestowed upon men, and she felt as if she were separating from mankind. Her calling was to serve the Earth.

Chapter Twenty-seven: IN THE CITY OF LIZARDS

The flame lizard of Djeban takes its name from the frill at its throat. When expanded, the crimson frill makes the lizard appear larger and more terrifying than it is, and the bright red patches beneath the jaw look very much as if it has been feeding on the blood of its enemies. By night, the same frill can be made to fluoresce briefly, creating the illusion of a flickering fire.

In the early spring, males will display their frills nightly for the females, rivaling for attention. Hence each evening Djeban appears to catch fire.

In Inkarra the flame lizards are used like guard dogs, and called 'draktferions,' which means 'watchfires.' In Mystarria their name was shortened to 'drakens.' In northern Rofehavan that name was changed to 'dragons.'

– *Excerpt from* Binnesman's Bestiary: Reptiles of the World.

For a long time after the baobab tree, Raj Ahten found no water. He raced his camels across the Wastes, sparing nothing in his attempt to catch up to Wuqaz.

There was sand, and more sand, and still sand, and sand piled upon the piled sand. That is how one described the Wastes.

Nothing crawled upon it but a few beetles and small web-footed geckos. All of the lizards had sand-colored backs to hide from predators and white bellies to reflect the desert sun. A few blind shrews lived beneath the sand and came out at night to hunt for scorpions, but there was little else.

Overhead, large sand-colored desert graaks flew in circles, a mile into the air, watching everything that moved. It was not uncommon for the monsters to swoop low and knock a man off his camel, leaving him to die as the camel raced for safety. But the graaks would not dare attack a party as large as this.

The camels had good runes of brawn, stamina, and metabolism burned into their flesh, but Raj Ahten soon grew to suspect that some of their Dedicate camels had died. One camel sat down halfway across the Waste, and would not get up, even when jabbed with a sharp camel prod.

Raj Ahten had no choice but to leave his man there until the camel felt ready to travel again. The Invincible drew his warhammer and stood over his mount protectively, watching the sky for graaks.

The vast bed of the White Sea was dry at this time of year, except for a few miles where the water ran little deeper than a camel's ankles. The receding sea left a salty crust that crunched under the camels' feet with every step. The wind sweeping across the dry lakebed whipped bits of salt into the eyes of men and camels alike.

Raj Ahten wrapped a rag around his face, and was happy to reach the waters of the White Sea, so named because of the white crust all along its shore. The sparkling amethyst waters were shallow and too salty to drink. But the presence of any water was welcome. No more salt crystals whipped through the air here, and the journey was safe, if slow. Giant crocodiles infested the eastern shores of this inland sea, but here in the west it was too salty even for them.

As the mounts waded through miles of water, Raj Ahten

spotted *obbatas* far in the distance – tall desert tribesmen on their ugly black camels. Whole families would ride together on one of the beasts, and the riders were as strange as their mounts, for the men and women wore little clothing. Instead, their shamans tattooed runes of water binding on the obbatas' lower lips to protect them from the blistering sun. Yet such runes had undesirable effects. They closed the pores on the tribesmen's lustrous black skin, leaving it colorless and flaky, as if covered in scales. Their fingernails and toenails became as dull as flint, while the whites of their eyes turned gray. In the south, in Umarish, the obbata tribesmen were called the 'crocodile people,' for they no longer looked human.

Whole tribes of obbatas were riding north, the sun flashing on the silver blades of their spears. Raj Ahten took their migration as a foreboding. The reticent obbatas seldom traveled by day, yet now myriads of them were driving their monstrous camels across the shallow White Sea.

They are fleeing, he realized. Could they have heard of the reaver invasion so far away?

The portent was chilling.

By early afternoon, he and his men had gained on the twelve Ah'kellah. He saw them in the distance from atop his camel, not ten miles off, and silently pleaded to the Powers, 'Let Wuqaz be among them.'

Raj Ahten's endowments let him spy the men as they prodded the camels up the high plateaus, toward the ancient ruins beneath the mountains at Djeban. The Ah'kellah rode with their backs to him, and Raj Ahten could not see if Wuqaz rode with them.

Raj Ahten, clutching his reins in his numb left hand, rode on.

Djeban, the 'City of Lizards,' lay quiet as a crypt when he reached it. All along the cliffs above the city, statues of men with the heads of hawks stood poised, gazing with dead eyes.

No sparrow peeped in the thickets; no hawk wheeled in the sky. But upon every large stone crouched huge carnivorous flame lizards that hissed and fanned the bright red frills beneath their throats in warning as Raj Ahten's men drew near.

Raj Ahten could smell his quarry strongly now. The men had stopped to water their camels at the first stream they crossed. Not far ahead was a hill, and beyond it a lush valley where the grass kept green throughout most of the year. Raj Ahten knew it well from previous journeys. The warriors would be feeding their camels there. Raj Ahten tasted for the scent of Wuqaz, but could not find it. There was a trace . . . of someone who might be Wuqaz. With so many endowments of scent, Raj Ahten felt that he ought to be more certain. He hoped that the odor of the man he sought was merely masked by the smells of other men.

He called a halt, and Raj Ahten's men strung their bows. He warned, 'Strike quickly, and take no prisoners.'

He had already thrown off his armor, which was the most recognizable part of his attire. Now he pulled his robe over a simple helm, rode with his face down.

'Bhopanastrat,' Raj Ahten called, 'take the lead'. If the Ah'kellah realized that Raj Ahten himself was attacking, they would flee.

Raj Ahten knew that Gaborn had Chosen Wuqaz and the Ah'kellah yesterday in the battle at Carris. Now he wondered at the wisdom of assailing Gaborn's Chosen warriors. He'd managed to defeat some before – but just barely. None of those men were like Wuqaz Faharaqin. That old warlord had over two hundred endowments to his credit.

The men drew out their camel prods, urged the animals on mercilessly. Raj Ahten saw blood flow on the flanks of more than one beast.

The camels snorted and raced now, their huge feet thudding on the ground with a distinctive sound. In brush and rocks the camels were of little use, and plodded along in a gangling way. But here in this terrain the creatures galloped as fast as any horse, showing that they were capable of true grace. These were force camels with endowments of brawn and metabolism.

Raj Ahten's mount topped the ridge at perhaps eighty miles per hour. He saw the dozen Ah'kellah sitting in a circle beside an oasis, cooking fry bread over a fire of dried camel dung. Their mounts were spread out along the fields, foraging on the grass.

The valley was devoid of trees and rocks, places where the Ah'kellah might try to make a stand.

At the sight of Raj Ahten's men, they leapt to their feet, peered toward the hilltop in curiosity. But when they saw a dozen men with strung bows racing toward them, they knew there would be battle. One man ran for his camel, his robes flapping wildly, but the others shouted, warning him to leave it.

The twelve warriors drew sabers and warhammers. Two men quickly strung their hornbows.

By that time, Raj Ahten's men were streaming to either side, firing arrows into the cluster of mountless men.

The Ah'kellah were trapped. They had no cover. Five men took arrows almost instantly, and stood their ground with arrows bristling from chests and legs. An enemy bowman put an arrow through the eye of a camel, so that one of Raj Ahten's men went down in a sickening thud, bones crunching. Four others of the Ah'kellah raced out of the knot on either side, attacked with battle-axes and sabers, chopping at the unprotected necks and throats of passing camels.

Five camels tumbled in a spray of blood. Raj Ahten drew his warhammer and leapt from his own mount, buried a spike through the head of the first Ah'kellah he met. Another raced up at his back, and Raj Ahten spun the hammer instantly, swiping the man across the ribs with a blow that ripped out the bottoms of his lungs.

Blood spattered his face as he charged into the crowd of Ah'kellah, seeking Wuqaz. Arrows whizzed past his head, striking two more men.

None of the Ah'kellah prostrated themselves and begged for mercy, as a man of old Indhopal might have done. It was not in their nature to ask for mercy, not in their nature to give it.

He looked into the stern eyes of one old kaif who shouted, 'Raj Ah –' as Raj Ahten's warhammer tore out his throat.

The Ah'kellah became a dark swirling mass as they rushed to attack him. These were not common troops. For one heart-stopping second he imagined that Gaborn guided them.

But Raj Ahten was not to be trifled with. Even ailing from Binnesman's curse, he had his endowments.

He kicked one man in the chest with the steel toe of his boots, crushing his heart. He dodged beneath a sword, slammed the head of his battle-ax into the man's face. He drew a dagger in his numb left hand, drove it under the chin of a third attacker, leapt up and kicked a fourth man with both feet so hard that the man's head came off.

It was too easy. He did not take even a glancing blow. This fight was nothing like the brawl he'd endured yesterday, when Gaborn guided his Chosen.

In moments it was over. Raj Ahten stood panting above the corpses of the Ah'kellah. Dust was thick in the air from racing camels. The smell of blood hung over the encampment. Camels bawled in pain, lying with their legs broken or missing.

Three of his own men were dead. Another was badly wounded – his right arm shattered and most of his face caved in.

Amid this, Raj Ahten walked back over to the small campfire, where the fry bread baked in a blackened skillet.

The bread was lightly toasted on top, and he could smell pistachios and cumin cooking inside.

He flipped out a piece into his hand, chewed it thoughtfully. A movement on the hill caught his eye. Flame lizards had begun to creep down from the bluffs and rocks. They'd caught the scent of blood. They'd feed well on the corpses tonight.

Wuqaz is not here, Raj Ahten realized. Wuqaz was not a man prone to mistakes. He would never have stopped at this oasis, barren of cover. Raj Ahten should have known that when he crested the hill.

The thought of Wuqaz running free worried him. It meant that he had either gone north into Deyazz, or more likely to the western coast – to Dharmad, Jiz, or Kuhran . . . good places to cause trouble.

Raj Ahten had sent eighty men to ride Wuqaz down. He suspected that it would not be enough.

Chapter Twenty-eight: A HARVEST

A reaver's sensory organs, its philia, circle the base of its skull and run beneath the jaws. Blade-bearers have been seen with as few as eighteen philia and as many as thirty-six. Whatever the number, they are always found in multiples of three.

Hearthmaster Magnus used to teach that the more philia a reaver had, the older it was. But I can see no evidence of this. By comparing the number of a reaver's philia to its apparent size and age (as measured by tooth wear), I see no correlation between the number of philia and the reaver's age.

Nor does a larger number of philia seem to convey any greater status to a reaver, as Hearthmaster Banes once surmised. Very powerful sorceresses have had relatively few philia, while small blade-bearers have been found with many.

Utimately, the science of counting philia on a reaver in order to make any sort of deductions is pointless. It is analogous to trying to deduce whether a man is a farmer or fisherman by counting his nose hairs.

– Excerpt from A Comparison of Reports on Reavers, *by Hearthmaster Dungiles*

Gaborn turned from the fleeing reavers. They would not

attack. His remaining Earth Powers let him feel confident of that much, at least.

He did not need to fear.

Nor did he need to count his dead. He'd felt the deaths in battle: twenty-four men. Twenty-four men had fallen, and with each death, he felt as if the man were being extracted from his own flesh.

He'd tried to warn them, tried to call to them in the battle. He sought to serve the Earth in that way, and he hoped that the Earth would restore his Powers.

But he'd been unable to reach them. He'd sensed their danger, shouted his warnings, but it was like shouting at deaf men.

Iome and Myrrima held back, stayed with Hoswell for a moment. Gaborn felt eager to begin searching among the dead, hoping to find the Waymaker. His Days rode at his side.

A frowth giant roared, off to his right. Gaborn glanced at the beast. It pointed at the fleeing reavers, roared again. There was a question in its voice. It wanted to know why Gaborn was letting the reavers get away.

'The battle was a glorious victory,' the Days said. 'It will be noted as such.'

Gaborn had seldom heard a word of praise from the historian.

In his memory, Gaborn rehearsed what he'd done. He'd ridden the reavers' flank, sensing with his Earth Powers, until he felt the moment for the charge was perfect. Now, he could see that more than two thousand reavers lay dead. The lives of so few men were a small price to pay for such a victory.

His Days was right. It was a great conquest.

Out on the battlefield, a few warriors were wounded. He saw them limping about, bandaging themselves as best they could. Binnesman went to his wylde as she broke open the skull of a scarlet sorceress and began to feed.

Binnesman had allowed the creature to enter battle. Once the charge began, she'd leapt from her horse and run to the center of the fray, attacking the monsters bare-handed with a ferocity that was hard to credit. Gaborn had not even numbered her kills.

Now lords sat down and began to clean and sharpen their weapons. A few scouts began making a count of their fallen foes.

Gaborn could not order a second charge immediately. He didn't have the lances for it.

When he dared consider the very notion of charging, he felt uneasy. There was a change among the reavers. He did not yet fathom it, but he knew that he would never be able to charge them so successfully again.

Binnesman began tending the wounded. Iome and Baron Waggit went with him.

Gaborn told Averan, 'Come with me. Let's see if we can find the Waymaker.'

With that, he climbed down from his mount, helped the child from hers. He'd promised Averan that she would not have to eat the reaver's brains in public. So when other lords and counselors sought to follow, he waved them back.

They began to walk together through the reavers, down among the furrow. Walking into it was like stepping down into a grave. The smell of beaten soil was all around. The hulking reavers lay dead and bleeding, cutting off the light. Gree wriggled in the air above them, lit on the corpses. The small black creatures scurried about like bats, with the claws at the tips of their wings hooked into the reavers' hides. But aside from the wings, that's where the similarity to bats ended. The gree, like reavers, had four small legs in addition to their wings, and their eyeless heads had tiny philia of their own. The gree scampered about over the carcasses and scaled the dirty creases of flesh to search for shelter and to feed on the parasitic skin worms that had plagued the reavers in life.

Each time Gaborn neared a dead reaver, the gree would make small squeaking noises and crawl away, or take flight.

Averan strolled along, searching the reavers slowly. Her freckled face was pinched, her pale blue eyes alert. She stopped and looked at a blade-bearer for a long time, squinting and leaning her head to the side, as if she were inspecting an apple in the marketplace.

It was a ghastly enterprise.

'This one has thirty-six philia,' Averan said. 'And he's large enough. But his paws are too small, kind of delicate.'

Gaborn felt eager for any additional information he could gather on reavers. 'Does the number of philia mean anything?'

'More philia means that a reaver *might* smell things better, and hear better,' Averan said. 'But that's not always true.'

'Do you know who the new leader of the horde will be?'

Averan thought about it. 'I'm not sure who is alive still.'

Gaborn accepted that. 'But they won't return to Carris?'

'No,' Averan said. 'I don't think so. You held your ground, and the reavers worry when humans hold their ground.'

'Why would they worry about us?'

'Because we defeated them in the past,' Averan said. 'Erden Geboren fought with the Glories beside him. To the reavers, they shone like the sun. They blinded the reavers.'

Two thousand years ago, Erden Geboren had fought the reavers, and nearly been destroyed by them. In the old songs, it had seemed to Gaborn that he fought overwhelming odds. He found it fascinating that the reavers would recall their own account of that battle, and still fear a pair of Glories.

'Why didn't the reavers harvest one another at Carris?' Gaborn asked. 'I saw the dead. None were harvested.'

'Because,' Averan said as if she were lecturing a child, 'the spoils go to the most powerful reaver lords. The dead belonged to Battle Weaver. They were hers to divide. But you killed her, and with the lightning and all of the confusion in the retreat, the lesser mages didn't dare to harvest. They were probably afraid that the Glories were returning. At the very least, they were afraid of getting punished.'

Gaborn understood. Even among men, when dividing the spoils of war, the captains and sergeants would normally get first pick of the bounty.

Averan stopped at another reaver, squinted at it for a long time. They'd gone through nearly a third of the fallen.

'This could be him,' she said at last. 'I can't be sure.' She went around to the monster's anus, sniffed at it, and staggered backward, wrinkling her nose.

'Is this the one?' Gaborn asked.

Averan shook her head. 'I can't be sure. I can't smell him well enough to know.'

'But you smelled something?'

'Just his death scream. When reavers die, they warn others away. Otherwise, I can't smell them at all.'

Gaborn went to the hole above the anus of the monster. The philia there were wet and sticky, more like sweaty glands than the philia that graced a reaver's head. He could smell something there, certainly. Though Averan described it as a 'scream,' the scent seemed mild, like moldy garlic.

'What does the scent mean?' Gaborn asked. If he was to go into the Underworld, he needed to learn to translate the reavers' language of scents.

'It means "Death is here. Run away,"' Averan said, translating as best she could.

Averan sighed, looked down at the endless string of reavers stretched out for more than a mile ahead. 'Let's mark this one. If I don't find one that I feel better about, we'll try him.' Averan acted shy, self-conscious about eating the thing in public. It was, after all, a highly unnatural act.

'All right,' Gaborn said. He glanced about, thinking to stack some rocks in front of the beast, but the dark soil here in the furrow had been trampled by tens of thousands of reavers, and seemed nearly as hard as stone. At last he took off his right gauntlet and laid it in the reaver's gaping mouth.

He and Averan trundled on. A knight came riding up through the furrow, weaving among the monsters. Gaborn could hear the jangle of his ring mail and the pounding horses' hooves before the man rounded a carcass. It was Skalbairn.

'Good news, milord,' he said. 'We've counted nearly thirty-three hundred dead reavers in this one charge alone.'

Gaborn could hardly credit such numbers. He had fewer than twenty-five hundred knights in his retinue, and had lost only one in a hundred men.

He must have been beaming. After Skalbairn left, Averan looked up at him. 'You look like the cat that ate the bird.'

'It's a good day,' Gaborn said. 'It's a great victory.'

Averan shook her little head. 'You mustn't think that, milord. Most of these reavers were innocent. Most of them were . . . like peasants.' She had a challenge in her tone.

'You talk about them as if they were people,' Gaborn said. 'But these "peasants" marched on Carris. They killed tens of thousands of people, and would have killed them all.'

'They only did it because their master told them,' Averan argued. 'It's not the little reavers you have to kill – it's the One True Master. She's your enemy.'

The child spoke with such conviction. He noted her appearance. This morning he would have thought her a normal child, a girl of nine with red hair and freckles and a determined gleam in her eye.

Now he saw that it was an illusion. Looking closely, he could detect the faintest green hue to her face, like bits of greenish mica that caught and reflected the sunlight.

She doesn't look like a common child, he decided. There's more of Binnesman to her than I'd have first thought. And like the Earth Warden who serves as her master, she seems to care as much about the health of snakes as she does about mice, reavers as much as men.

Averan neared another reaver. The garlicky scent was strong about this one, and Averan almost staggered away. 'That one is rank,' she said. 'He must have died slowly.'

Gaborn didn't doubt that she was right.

'Do you think you could learn to talk to the reavers?' Gaborn asked.

'How? In case you didn't notice,' Averan said, 'I don't have any philia.'

'But if you could mix smells,' Gaborn said. 'For example, if you took garlic, couldn't you approximate the words?'

Averan looked up at him, stunned. 'I never thought of that!' She frowned. 'No, I don't think so. Garlic isn't right. The death warning isn't really very much like garlic. It would be like yelling "breath" when you meant "death."' Yet he'd planted a seed in her mind. 'Maybe, though, I might be able to write a few words,' she mused.

Gaborn let his imagination soar. To be able to speak to the reavers! What would I say to them?

He had no idea. He didn't know their language, couldn't think how he might communicate with them.

Averan had him mark two more reavers as they went, until at length they reached the end of the line.

Then she turned back to the reaver that they had marked.

Gaborn took his sword and crawled up into the reaver's mouth. Its teeth hung overhead like green icicles. He thrust his blade into the monster's soft palate and sliced. The inky blood of the reaver drained from the wound, and rained in clotted clumps at his feet.

He stood for a long time, letting the blood flow, before he reached up and actually pulled out his prize – a huge handful of steaming reaver brains, like gray worms bathed in the reaver's dark blood.

He gave the brains to Averan, and turned his back as she fed. She chewed quietly, making appreciative sounds.

He climbed up on a reaver, looked to the south. He could see no sign of the horde at the moment. The last of them had climbed the hills toward Mangan's Rock, two miles to the south. Now they were in a depression. Only a haze in that direction let him know that the reavers still fled.

It had been a glorious battle, a stunning victory. Yet he watched as knights picked up their fallen comrades and carried them to the wains. The dead and wounded were laid in the same boxes that had been used to haul the lances from Carris. It was an economical use, Gaborn supposed, and the dead would not mind that they were carted about without ceremony. Still, it seemed an unfitting end to the battle, an indecorous end to a human life.

A contingent of lords saw him, came riding along the field. Their faces were shining, expectant. Many of them were mighty warriors: Queen Herin the Red of Fleeds, High Marshal Skalbairn of the Knights Equitable, Sir Langley of Orwynne.

Skalbairn shouted, 'We're ready to go when you are. I had lances transported from Carris and Castle Fells last night down to Ballyton, not twenty miles down the road. In half an hour, we can rearm and make another pass.'

Gaborn considered it, and the Earth's warning came almost as a wail. If he dared attempt a second charge, the reavers would devastate his troops.

'We'll rearm, and take lunch in Ballyton,' Gaborn said, stalling for time to come up with another plan. He could see by their faces that they'd hoped for instant battle. 'The reavers are forewarned. We won't take them unprepared next time.'

The look of consternation on Langley was impossible to miss. But Skalbairn said simply, 'As my lord commands.'

Gaborn climbed off his gruesome perch.

Averan had just finished her meal. She knelt down and wiped her fingers in the dirt.

He asked, 'Did we get the right one – the Waymaker?'

Averan merely shrugged. 'I don't know yet. It takes a while.'

'How long is a while?'

Averan thought. 'About three or four hours.'

At that moment, horns began to blow over the horizon. Gaborn raced out of the gully, up onto the edge of the plains, as riders came over the hill to the south.

One of them was shouting. 'The reavers are climbing Mangan's Rock! We've run them to ground.'

Chapter Twenty-nine: THE RETREAT

King Orden once asked me which I esteemed most in a knight: courage or obedience. I told him that the answer was obvious: obedience. A dutiful knight will be courageous on command.

– King Jas Laren Sylvarresta

Myrrima stood quietly in the dry grass and drew an arrow to her ear. The dyed goose pinions lightly grazed her cheek.

She faced a dead reaver at eighty yards, took aim at its sweet triangle.

'I'm going to Inkarra with you,' she told Borenson. She waited for him to respond, but he said nothing. The many times that she'd rehearsed this, she'd always imagined that he would rebuff her immediately. She held her aim, let out a sigh.

Most of the lords had ridden off, trailing the reavers that were taking refuge at Mangan's Rock. Borenson answered, 'I knew why you'd come the moment I saw you.'

'And?'

'I still think it unwise.'

A few days ago, he'd rejected her plea to accompany him out of hand. Something had changed in their relationship. She thought it a good sign.

Hoswell's bow felt sweet beneath her palms. The polished

wood at the bow's belly fit as if it had been carved for her. The long arc of spring steel drew easily and gracefully to the full.

A yew bow usually had an uneven draw. Often a warp in the wood or perhaps a wing that was shaved too thin gave yew a catch here, a loose spot there. Thus it took time to learn the range an arrow might fly based upon how far the shaft was drawn. Even metal bows suffered this defect, if the smith hammered the metal roughly.

But Hoswell's steel bow felt perfectly balanced.

She let her shaft fly. The arrow blurred, hit the corner of the reaver's sweet triangle and was gone.

Her yew bow would not have penetrated nearly so far. She'd used three dozen arrows in the charge, and had only managed to bring down fourteen reavers. Hoswell had bested her by more than a dozen kills.

'So,' she said, 'I've been thinking about it. And I agree that it wouldn't be wise.'

Borenson gave a snort of amusement. 'You agree?'

'Aye,' she said. 'I'd be a fool to follow you to Inkarra. It's much safer here with the Darkling Glories and reaver hordes and the invading armies.'

Borenson laughed a deep resounding belly laugh. She knew that she had him.

'All right,' he said. 'You've got the mettle. Come with me.'

She gave him a sidelong look.

'But –' he said, 'I don't suggest this lightly. What do you know of Inkarra?'

'The people in the Night Kingdoms live in houses as big as a village,' Myrrima answered. 'They sleep by day and work by night. Dragons guard their doors.'

'The rune mages of Inkarra protect the land,' he added. 'Those foolish enough to enter do not come out. Their borders have been closed to men of Rofehavan for three centuries, and the Storm King has not answered a missive from Mystarria in twenty years.'

She drew an arrow from her quiver, swiftly pulled it full, and planted it in the reaver's sweet triangle.

'Shall we go now?' Myrrima asked.

'You'd go without leave of the king?'

'I'm sworn to the Brotherhood of the Wolf,' Myrrima said. 'I'll serve mankind as I see fit – the same as a Knight Equitable.'

Borenson hesitated.

'What?' Myrrima asked. 'You still don't want me to come to Inkarra?'

'I'm torn. The reavers are going south, we're going south,' Borenson said. 'They make fair traveling companions, aside from their table manners.'

Myrrima grinned fiercely. She supposed that any creature that tried to eat you could justly be accused of having bad table manners.

So, he wanted to fight some more reavers. Myrrima glanced up at Mangan's Rock. 'This looks like a siege, though,' she said. 'We could be here for weeks.'

'All right, then,' Borenson conceded. 'We'll leave for Inkarra.'

Myrrima couldn't quite believe that he would take her without more argument. She'd known from the moment they met that he desired her as a woman. Now, she knew that she had earned his respect.

Only one thing remained. She would teach him devotion.

Mangan's Rock towered above the plains, a lone sentinel. Its ragged gray cliffs rose three hundred feet at their highest point, and sloped on the southern face to only ninety feet.

Nearly a thousand years before, at the peak of the Dark Lady Wars, the lords of Rofehavan had carved a fortress at the summit of Mangan's Rock, and had dug a road that wound along the cliff face.

But that was ages past. Various lords had undertaken the task of restoring the fortifications. But there was damned little water up on the rock and too little forage on the plains. In the long run, the cost of maintaining the fortress was too high.

Parts of a magnificent castle still stood. Its towers had been blasted by lightning and strong winds; some of the walls had tumbled down over the ages. Ivy climbed the walls of the castle, and where once a city had stood, oaks raised their magnificent branches. Its courtyards had become the abode of owls.

But the image of Mangan himself stood facing north, some ninety feet high. Two dogs of war flanked him. At one time, it was said that he bore a huge bronze spear in his right hand, but now the hand was gone. Still, he stared to the north, ever vigilant.

The road winding up to the castle had suffered most of all. Landslides had borne it away in places.

The reavers did not mind.

As Myrrima and Borenson rode toward Mangan's Rock, the reavers scrabbled up the cliff face as easily as a cat would climb a tree.

They clambered up to the castle walls, perched in crevasses like massive dark gargoyles. They took posts along the sheer cliff, and all of them raised their heads and stood waving their philia.

Gaborn, his Days, and the child Averan were among the last to leave the battlefield. Even the frowth had gone before them. They rode together with Iome, Binnesman, Jureem, and Feykaald.

'I'd not have thought that they would run to ground so easily,' Gaborn was saying. He studied the reavers, mystified.

'Maybe they're going to hold a tournament,' Averan

suggested. 'We killed their leader. They may have to fight to pick a new one.'

But Gaborn squinted up at the reavers, shook his head in bafflement. 'That's not it. They're planning something . . . more sinister.'

'Your Highness,' Borenson broke in. 'May I have a word?' Gaborn gave him his attention. 'I'll be taking my leave now.'

Gaborn reined his horse to a halt, sat looking at Borenson for a long moment, as if to simply hold the image in his memory.

Myrrima felt deeply aware of the fact that she might never see these people again. In only a few days she'd become a fast friend with Iome.

'May the Earth Powers guide you,' Gaborn said at last, 'and may the Bright Ones light your way.'

Iome said quickly, 'Sir Borenson, I repent of the quest I laid upon you. You are a man of honor, sir, and I was wrong to question it.'

But Gaborn raised his hand, begging Iome to be silent. She'd laid the quest upon his head in front of ten thousand men, and there could be no recalling the words. Borenson would go to Inkarra and search for Daylan Hammer, the Sum of All Men who legend said had so many endowments that he could not die. Iome hoped that he could help Gaborn defend his people against the perils to come. More than that, Borenson had killed Iome's father and had slain some two thousand Dedicates. For the sake of his own soul, he needed to redeem himself.

And Gaborn truly did need help. Whether it came from Zandaros, or whether Borenson found Daylan Hammer, or he got it from Raj Ahten himself, Gaborn needed help.

'I have the letter here,' Gaborn said, reaching back into his bags, 'for the Storm King. It explains your mission and begs his aid.

'And there is another small favor I would ask –' Gaborn broke off suddenly and whirled on his mount, as if someone had shouted an alarm.

Up ahead a couple of miles, the tail end of the reavers' forces were still marching toward the rock. They traveled as they had before, in a file seven reavers across. Nothing had changed in their configuration.

But fifty Knights Equitable with lances raced up behind, veering from the east.

'Damn the fools,' Gaborn muttered. He reached for the warhorn slung over his saddlebags, blew a retreat.

Several knights glanced toward him, then looked away and sped their charge.

'Humph,' Borenson grunted in amusement.

Instantly, Myrrima sensed that men were about to die.

Gaborn blew the retreat more vigorously. All along his lines, knights turned and raced to Gaborn, as if the summons were meant for them. But the fifty lancers held their course.

Gaborn blew more frantically.

At two miles, the men were tiny figures on the slope. Sunlight gleamed on white lances, on helm and armor. Myrrima watched as they raced up to the reavers' lines.

The charge did not go as had the previous one. The reavers were not blindsided.

Instead as lancers approached, the blade-bearers on the eastern flank did something totally unexpected. The huge monsters each spun and shoved their shovel-shaped heads into the topsoil, then stood flailing their great battle arms.

The maneuver effectively covered their sweet triangles, giving the lancers no target but the reavers' armored heads. In effect, the blade-bearers created a wall of flesh.

From behind that wall, other reavers hurled stones over the heads of their companions, as if from a flight of catapults. Scarlet sorceresses cast spells.

Thus, the reavers formed a shield wall and attacked in a way that had never been seen before.

In seconds the battle concluded. Thirty-two men and horses were cut down in an instant. Those who managed to survive the hail of stones fled, some wounded and barely clinging to their horses, others leaving fallen mounts behind.

Gaborn quit blowing retreat. He hung his head in anguish while the remaining reavers scaled Mangan's Rock.

Chapter Thirty:
THE SHEPHERD

Of all the beasts of lore, the reavers remain among the most mysterious, for the few who observe their habits seldom manage to survive the encounter.
– Hearthmaster Valen, of the Room of Beasts

Averan felt as if she carried the world on her shoulders. Yesterday as she'd run for Carris fleeing the reavers, she'd imagined that life could never get harder or more desperate than she'd felt at that moment.

Now, she knew that she was wrong.

Gaborn needed another victory from her. He wanted answers to questions, but she had none.

Almost immediately after feeding on this reaver, she began to feel ill. At first, she thought the sickness was a product of her own worries, despair at her own failings.

She knew within moments of eating the gray matter of this reaver that it was not a Waymaker.

The reaver was called a Keeper and he was intimate with all facets of animal husbandry and butchery. He knew how to gut a carcass, prepare it for his masters.

Visions of the Underworld she'd never seen unfolded to her view: she saw caverns where weird plants grew. Some were tough as gristle and did their best to look like rocks.

Others were spiny like sea urchins that thrived in open air, or hung from the cavetop like ropes.

The reavers carefully tended the plants in special chambers. But the reavers did not eat their own crops.

Instead, giant segmented worms grazed among the fields, along with strange animals that Averan would have taken hours to describe – spidery animals as large as cottages, and horned beetles the size of bulls.

So the reavers raised their herds.

Keeper was filled with a jumble of intimate details about the life cycles of each animal. He knew how to prod a cottage-sized spider with an iron pole so that she would leave her cache of freshly laid eggs. He knew how to use a knight gig by feel, so that he hooked blindfish by the belly. He knew which parasites fed on giant worms, and which scents to use to rid the worms of such parasites.

Useless information flooded Averan's young mind in a torrent, a jumble of images and thoughts and scents that left her dazed. She could glean almost nothing from it.

Yet the images were more coherent than before. Averan had eaten more of this creature than she had of the others. Maybe that was part of it. Or perhaps the difference was that she understood the context of this reaver's thoughts better than she had the others'.

She was learning the reavers' language, seeing as a reaver saw. The memories seemed not so much a tangle as they did intermittent journeys through the eyes of another.

Yet Averan felt a pang of despair as the visions began. After spending a long morning looking for the Waymaker, Averan had succeeded in eating a farmer.

So she began to think that her despair was the cause of her pains when they first began.

Gaborn had her ride his horse, his gauntleted hand wrapped protectively around her belly. Her stomach was full, cramping, as it seemed to do every time that she ate a reaver.

Gaborn's men closed in on Mangan's Rock, and he ordered various sentries and lords to form a picket all around the rock, to keep the reavers from escaping. But he kept his main force to the west, so that the prevailing wind would continue to blow their scent toward the horde.

He ordered his carters to go to Ballyton and return with supplies for a siege, and then he rode with Averan to a small brook a mile west of the rock.

The brook wound slowly through the grasslands. Cattails and willow grew thick on its banks, and a herd of deer bounded from the brush as the lords approached.

Gaborn took her to an oak tree. Averan brushed away the acorns on the ground and sat in the shade.

Iome sat beside her, wiped some sweat from Averan's face, and whispered, 'You don't look well.'

'I don't feel good,' Averan admitted.

'Just sit here, little one,' Iome offered, taking her hand. 'I'll take care of you.'

Averan looked up into Iome's face. The queen was watching her intently, full of concern.

She doesn't know me, Averan thought. She couldn't care about me. But Iome's expression informed her otherwise. Some people cared more than others did. Some people were born to love others until it hurt.

The wizard Binnesman cleared the ground nearby, dragging away tree limbs. One of Gaborn's captains, a grizzled old man with a scarred face, gave the green woman a staff. He taught her how to grip it, then began teaching her some basic combat stances and maneuvers – jabs, thrusts, and sweeps. Baron Waggit stood by, soon got a staff, and began trying to learn along with the green woman.

Averan watched them to keep her mind off her own problems. But suddenly her heart began to race in terror. Something was going terribly wrong.

'Help me,' Averan begged Iome.

Iome stared hard at Averan. Gaborn's queen was a small woman, half Indhopalese. It was impossible to look at her and not to notice the penetrating eyes so brown that they were almost black, reflecting the light. In size and build, she was much like Saffira.

'Jureem,' Iome begged. 'Get the child some water. She looks ill.'

'At once.' Jureem went to the stream to fill a skin.

'What's wrong?' Iome asked.

Averan could hardly explain. At that moment, she was being assailed by a dozen memories at once – lessons in how to transplant a rock plant, how to catch a horn beetle, the chill of racing up the mountains through an icy river, and images of lightning flashing over the battle at Carris. Terror coursed through her in gut-wrenching waves.

'I don't know . . . I feel like I'm drowning,' Averan said.

'Drowning?' Iome asked.

Averan couldn't explain. Strange fears and cravings coursed through her. She struggled. 'Maybe it's the memories. It's all these memories . . .'

Iome put her hand over Averan's forehead. Sweat rolled off like drops of dew. Jureem returned with the waterskin. Iome placed it to Averan's lips, gave her a cool drink.

Averan's mouth and throat were so dry. She hadn't felt this way before when she'd eaten reavers. Now she drank her fill until her stomach hurt, but the water didn't quench her.

She started to cry.

'It's all right,' Iome said. 'You've taken in the memories of three reavers in three days. That must be a lot for a little girl who hasn't even lived her own life yet.'

But Averan shook her head. That wasn't it. Sweat poured off her more fiercely. Her heart was racing, and she took deep breaths. The cramping in the stomach had never hit Averan so hard. She'd never had sweat wring from her before.

She wondered if this reaver had poison in its blood.

'Everyone I know is dying,' Averan said. She didn't dare say that she was afraid that she might die. 'Help me,' Averan begged.

To Averan's surprise, Iome scooted down, wrapped one arm under her neck, the other over Averan's chest. 'I'll help you,' Iome whispered. 'Whenever you need me, whatever you ask, I'll help you if I can.'

That assurance comforted Averan. She discovered that she craved a human touch.

A burst of memories welled up. Averan cried out.

'Binnesman,' Iome begged. 'Can you spare a moment?'

The wizard came to minister to Averan. He had her open her mouth, checked her eyes. 'There's nothing wrong that I can see,' Binnesman declared in a mystified tone.

'She's sweating with a fever, and she's shivering in terror,' Iome said.

Binnesman argued, 'Feel her head. She has no fever.'

Iome gave him a look that said she thought he must be daft. She checked Averan's sweaty brow, shook her head in consternation.

Binnesman peered at Averan worriedly. He took some herbs from his pocket and treated her symptoms. He warned Iome, 'Let me know if she worsens.'

So Averan lay in a torpid state, plagued by strange sensations. Pain cramped her feet and joints; dryness chafed her lungs; the consuming thirst ravaged her. She did her best to ignore the pain. She watched the green woman.

The wylde's trainer put her through her paces. He was obviously astonished at how quickly she learned. Baron Waggit couldn't keep up. The trainer quickly moved from teaching the wylde how to grip the staff and do basic maneuvers into full-body lunges, whirling attacks, spinning parries, and combination moves. 'I've taught the staff in the Room of Arms for twenty years,' the big knight said to Binnesman at one point, 'and never dreamed of a girl like this. When you're done with her, can I take her to wife?'

Binnesman laughed.

Averan felt jealous. Binnesman was desperate to get the wylde trained, and Averan thought of her as a friend. Averan didn't like what the wizard was doing to the green woman, turning her into a weapon. She didn't like it any more than she liked what Gaborn was making her do.

Chapter Thirty-one: RIDERS BEFORE THE STORM

In no contest in life does the advantage accrue to the unprepared.

– Mendellas Val Orden

Gaborn could sense danger rising around Iome. The attack against her was very close.

For a day now, he'd felt it stirring.

He checked the perimeter of his guard. He'd quietly stationed eighty men around the camp. Most of them lounged about – squatting on logs to sharpen axes, or pretending to snooze. A hundred yards away, Sir Borenson and Myrrima made a big show of packing their goods, as if in a hurry to be off for Inkarra, yet, as asked, Borenson let his keen blue eyes stray to the trees along the creek bank, as alert as any five men.

But nothing Gaborn did seemed to allay the threat.

He wandered close to Skalbairn. He'd asked the man to stay near Iome, and the big knight did. But for the moment he had a staff and was sparring with Baron Waggit. It was rough work. Sweat coursed down the baron's face, and soaked though his tunic. He'd ripped a sleeve in his sparring. His blue eyes gleamed with anticipation. He seemed to be enjoying himself immensely.

Skalbairn spoke amiably to the baron. 'Ah, you should come with me to Internook,' he was saying as the baron tried in vain to bash him with his staff. 'It's not so damned civilized. A man like you would do well there, put his past behind him.'

'Keep sharp,' Gaborn whispered to Skalbairn.

'Always,' Skalbairn said under his breath.

Gaborn made one last search of his perimeter, sauntered over toward Iome and Averan, who sat together. Iome's arm was wrapped around the child. Averan's glazed eyes stared inward. The child looked deathly ill. Perspiration poured from her.

Gaborn squatted next to Averan and Iome. 'Well?' he asked gently, expectantly. 'Any word?'

'It wasn't Waymaker that I ate,' Averan said. 'It was only some . . .' – she searched for the right word – 'worm herder.'

Gaborn squinted at her curiously. 'Worm herder?'

'Like a shepherd or a farmer, only to worms and other animals,' she said. 'I warned you that you're fighting peasants.'

She spoke sincerely, but the reavers were up to something, whether Averan knew it or not.

Could the danger actually come from this child? he wondered.

He didn't want to believe that. Averan was an apprentice Earth Warden after all, dedicated to preserving life. Yet right now he wondered if she wasn't . . . deranged. He had to test the theory.

'Iome,' Gaborn asked. 'Come here for a moment.' He purposely walked a hundred yards from Averan, stood with his back to her. He rested a foot on a lichen-covered stone, saw that there were small holes in the ground around it where mice made their burrows. A cricket sang nearby.

He briefly studied the reavers' movements on the rock. They'd climbed all over it, and now had begun to work.

A couple dozen glue mums began chewing down the great trees at the center of the rock, while blade-bearers pushed over the walls of the ancient towers, sent them cascading from the cliffs in ruins. Gaborn was so busy watching the south face of the cliff that it took him by surprise when he heard a roar on the north face. The great statue of Mangan went tumbling four hundred yards to its ruin.

Danger was rising all around him. The deaths of certain men had come this morning as predicted. Iome's moment was at hand. Tens of thousands in Carris would face their peril tomorrow. After that . . . the world. When would his enemy make the next strike? Three days? Four?

Gaborn felt desperate. Danger was everywhere. Binnesman had warned him a few days ago that Raj Ahten was not his ultimate enemy. Raj Ahten, the Inkarrans, Lowicker and Anders – all of them were like masks that concealed some greater peril. There was a mystery here.

Sometimes, he felt that they all worked in concert, perhaps without even knowing it.

Gaborn scanned the fields, searching for any sign of the impending attack.

Iome walked up to his back and whispered, 'What's so important that you must drag me away from the girl?'

He didn't know how to answer, exactly. He changed the subject, trying to buy a moment's time, in case the danger presented itself. 'It's as if they hate the works of man,' Gaborn said, jutting his chin toward the reavers. 'They can leave nothing that we've made intact.'

He reached out with his senses. The jeopardy to Iome was rising explosively. Her proximity to Averan had nothing to do with the danger.

He drew his sword from his sheath, pressed it into Iome's hand. 'Take this.'

She held it as if she'd never seen one before. 'What's this? You think I'm in danger?'

Gaborn could see no reavers nearby, no one close at all.

'Iome,' Gaborn said tentatively, 'someone wants you dead.'

She looked at him evenly, nostrils flaring. Still, he could see no antagonist. He wondered if the danger was within her – a weak heart or some hidden ailment.

Distantly there was an explosive sound – almost a scream – a crash of wind racing over the plains a mile to the south. It rose from the dead air, hurling grass and limbs from full-grown oak trees into the sky. It raised a front of dust like a rising pall nearly half a mile wide.

Gaborn had heard that sound before in the forest of the Dunnwood – the shrieking wind, the clash of lightning. He knew what creature rushed toward them.

He spun toward it. Before the storm, rode three men on pale horses. He wondered who they were.

Iome shouted her answer: 'The Darkling Glory!'

Chapter Thirty-two:
IN HIS MASTER'S SERVICE

A good servant does not concern himself with dignity. No act of service for his lord should be too mean or too small.

– Kaifba Jureem

Feykaald had seen enough of the Earth King's camp. He'd seen Gaborn's forcibles. He'd watched Gaborn order a devastating charge against the reavers. He'd seen men defy Gaborn as he sought to warn them with a warhorn.

He'd guessed at both Gaborn's strengths and his limitations. He'd learned that Gaborn would not help Indhopal, no matter how great the argument. Unlike Jureem, Feykaald could see no reason to serve the lad.

Gaborn was a fallen Earth King, nothing more.

Only one reason remained for Feykaald to stay near – the forcibles.

Not in his wildest imaginings had Feykaald believed that Gaborn would have left so many forcibles unused.

All morning he'd wondered what Gaborn planned to do with them, why he hoarded them.

Perhaps Gaborn was too cautious. Perhaps he was the kind of man who insisted on taking endowments himself, rather than vectoring. Perhaps he wanted to give his facilitators time to pick through the finest prospective Dedicates in the kingdom, those with the greatest strength, the keenest intellect, or the most perfect health.

If that were the case, Feykaald could not argue with Gaborn's purpose. Perhaps, Feykaald thought, this boy is wiser than I gave him credit for.

But Feykaald had no more time to speculate.

He waited only for the right moment. He expected that the reavers would provide it – create enough of a diversion so that he could load a box of forcibles onto a palfrey and make his escape.

The right moment came sooner than he'd anticipated, and from unexpected quarters.

The wall of wind roared toward the camp, rising in the air. Suddenly the swirling dust thrown by the front reared up and obscured the sun.

Three riders thundered before the storm. Lightning flashed along the length of their lances. On Mangan's Rock, the reavers all hissed and roared.

Gaborn sounded a warhorn. His guards rushed to his side. The wizard Binnesman had been watching his wylde. Now they both ran toward their king. Though Gaborn had thousands of knights in his retinue, most of them were scattered for miles around the perimeter of Mangan's Rock.

The treasure wagon was perhaps one hundred yards east of Gaborn, along with dozens of other supply wagons. The guards that had been standing around the wains drew their warhammers and sprinted for Gaborn, intent on protecting their king.

Instantly, Feykaald took the reins of his mount, scrambled for the treasure.

Jureem drew his curved saber, hastened toward Gaborn's back.

All morning he had been watching Feykaald, knowing that something was wrong. He'd been waiting for that moment when the old deaf spider sought to creep out of the camp.

Now as the wind and riders approached, he glanced from the corner of his eye and spotted Feykaald's dark burnoose, saw the old man take the reins of his horse. The big gray Imperial stallion whinnied and fought, frightened by the sudden roar of wind.

Soil and blades of grass hurtled through the air. Jureem raised his arm to shield his eyes. He shouted a warning to the guards, but for the moment the greater danger was to his king.

The wind screamed through the grass, came at Myrrima in a blinding storm.

She'd wondered why Gaborn had begged her to stay here in the camp with him and Iome for a little longer. She and Borenson had stayed an hour, acting as common guards.

Now she knew.

In Heredon Myrrima had slain the Darkling Glory, killed its body. But the elemental wind at its heart could not be destroyed so easily. She had been afraid that it would seek retribution.

Now she heard its vengeful screams as it raced over the grass. Now she felt its rage approach as if it were hidden in the dark thunderhead.

The three riders raced toward her.

All three warriors rode swift force horses. All three were knights of Mystarria, armored and bearing white lances.

Myrrima drew an arrow from her quiver, checked the bodkin. It was heavy steel with a narrow point, meant for piercing armor.

She spat into her palm, then slicked the shaft and quills of the arrow.

Her heart pounded. The riders thundered near, the wind at their backs. The storm raging behind lifted an ancient oak from its roots, tore the grass from the ground, made tiny spears out of pieces of straw, sent grit flying toward her. Sparrows fluttered desperately, trying to escape it.

She squinted into the howling fury and dropped to her knees as the riders advanced. They charged. She judged that they would not pass more than a yard to her left.

She would get one shot. She drew the great steel bow to its fullest, calmed herself, steadied her aim.

'I'm the one who killed you!' Myrrima shouted to the Darkling Glory. 'I'm the one you should want!'

One knight roared a battle cry, and dropped his lance so that it aimed for her heart. Ball lightning played around its iron tip.

She heard Borenson scream in fury. He raced toward her, warhammer in hand. The wind pounded her like fists.

Myrrima held her aim until the rider was thirty yards off. She loosed her shaft.

Borenson came flying as if to tackle the force horse. He hit the lance's tip with his warhammer, so that it dropped into the dirt. The lance struck the soil and cracked with a sound like a tree snapping in a storm. Lightning blasted out from it in a blinding flash, arced along the ground.

Borenson flipped in the air, smoke curling up from his boots, emitted a cry, and thudded to the dirt.

She glanced up. Her arrow plunged through the knight's neck. The force of the shaft was so great that it pierced the man's spine, nearly taking his head off.

The knight's head flapped back, neck broken, blood spurting from the gaping wound. Yet he continued to sit upright on the galloping charger for a moment, his dead hands clutching its reins.

The other two warriors charged past Myrrima, and then the dust storm hit, blinding her in its frenzy.

The elemental swept toward Gaborn like a storm from a nightmare. The front narrowed to less than a quarter of a mile wide, but rose up hundreds of feet. Dust whisked along the ground, and suddenly lightning flashed overhead.

'Take cover!' Gaborn shouted, pushing Iome behind him.

Guards, men he'd picked for this very moment, scurried to block the riders.

Langley charged up from the left, Skalbairn on his right. Both men were phenomenal warriors. Neither could have been prepared for this.

Gaborn raised his own shield: squinted over it as dirt and straw hurtled toward him.

To his left there was a wrenching of wood and metal as the storm hit his supply wagons, sent them rolling.

He clenched his warhammer.

Skalbairn dove toward one of the charging knights, screaming a war cry, his enormous battle-ax in hand.

The charging knight held his lance in his right fist, so that Skalbairn attacked from his unprotected flank.

Yet Skalbairn did not swing at the knight, as Gaborn would have. Instead he aimed at the horse, taking off its right leg at the knee.

The mount collapsed, and the rider fell with it. Lightning split from his lance, sizzled to the right and slammed into Baron Handy of Heredon. The bolt cleaved the man in two. Charred flesh flew from him.

Skalbairn rushed to the fallen warrior, stood above him with battle-ax raised high overhead.

Both men were swallowed in the onrushing wall of dust.

Feykaald watched the wind slam into wagons, send them tumbling. Bits of wooden wheel spokes popped loose while axles screamed from the abuse.

Boxes of goods went rolling away, but the forcibles were not among them.

He pulled up the bottom of his gray burnoose, ran into the wind. Wet leaves struck him in the face. He put his arm up to shelter him from oncoming debris. He had faced desert storms this fierce many times.

For long years he had feigned deafness, weakness. Yet he had some endowments of brawn and stamina to match his hearing, and he put those to use now.

Each box held four thousand forcibles, with a combined weight of five or six hundred pounds. He had packed the boxes himself, knew the contents of each. He'd put the forcibles in canvas bags, so that they could easily be loaded onto a horse.

He lashed his horse to the treasure wagon, leapt onto it, drew his dagger and slashed the bindings that held the canvas cover. It floated off in the wind as if it had taken wing. He quickly pried the lid off one box, set it in the wagonbed. He found the two canvas sacks inside. They were lashed together with a rope.

Lifting five hundred pounds was difficult, even with two endowments of brawn. Grunting and straining, he hefted the bags and managed to sling them over the pommel of his saddle. Later, when he had time, he would lash them properly.

The wind screamed around him like a living thing.

Knowing full well that his likelihood of escape increased dramatically so long as Gaborn did not know of the theft, Feykaald grabbed the lid of the box, shoved it back into place.

But now the storm was upon him, making it almost too dark to see.

He leapt on his mount, turned its back into the wind, and raced off under cover of the gale.

One lone rider thundered toward Gaborn, the rising storm cloud black at his back.

Gaborn recognized Beckhurst by the colors on his shield. He gaped at the man in confusion. Beckhurst had always seemed loyal to House Orden. Sir Langley rushed to cut Beckhurst off.

Gaborn could hear Binnesman shouting or chanting as he struggled to get to Gaborn's side, but the old wizard had no endowments of his own, and he traveled too slowly.

Gaborn lowered his shield. He felt with his Earth senses. Danger centered on Iome.

Langley ran in front of Beckhurst's charger, roaring in fury. He swung his warhammer toward the charger's legs, as Skalbairn had done.

But Beckhurst rode a mighty warhorse, replete with endowments and well trained for battle.

It leapt over Langley and cleared him as effortlessly as if he were a rail fence. Indeed, to Gaborn's eye for that moment, it almost seemed that the charger flew.

Gaborn raised his shield and set for the charge. Blinding dust rose everywhere, a billowing black front that roared over him.

He reached out with his Earth senses, felt no danger to himself. Only to Iome. He knew where his Chosen were, knew when they were in danger. She had turned and run from him.

'No!' he screamed.

He whirled to see Iome racing toward Binnesman. She had almost reached the wizard.

Jureem ran in front of her, trying to block the onrushing foe with little more than his bulk and a curved dagger.

Beckhurst's mount leapt again as it brushed past Gaborn.

'Strike!' the Earth commanded.

For a brief second, Gaborn hesitated. He hurled his warhammer. It hurtled end over end through the air, but fell behind its mark.

His heart seemed to freeze in his chest, fearing that his hesitation would cost Iome her life.

The wylde raced forward, staff at the ready. She whirled

it forward. The staff nicked the lance, and lightning erupted from it. For a moment, the wylde was bathed in light as ball lightning danced over her skin. But her staff continued its arc, slammed the warhorse in the knees, and the lightning blasted the poor mount.

The horse screamed in pain, stumbled. As the charger fell, the wylde reversed her swing, aiming a blow at the back of Beckhurst's head.

Beckhurst reared back and hurled his lance.

With his endowments of metabolism, Gaborn saw it all in slow motion. The white lance racing for Iome's back.

'Down!' he shouted.

Jureem had nearly reached Iome, his jeweled dagger drawn. Jureem saw the lance and leapt in front of it. He screamed as the lance struck home, and light exploded all around, burst from Jureem's feet.

For a moment Gaborn stood in a daze, saw the lance plunge clear through Jureem. The lance took him in the chest, wedged his ribs wide open, and continued on.

Blood rained down as the wylde clubbed Beckhurst with a furious blow, decapitating the man.

The lance slammed into Iome's right shoulder, and Gaborn saw a flash of red as blood spattered from her robes.

She fell.

The elemental wind roared overhead, lashing. Lightning played at its crown. Horses neighed in terror. Binnesman stood with his staff in hand, singing words of warning against the storm. He touched Iome's still form with his staff.

And then the elemental was past them, howling in its glory, as if to mock the efforts of puny mortals.

Chapter Thirty-three: REVELATIONS

Study brings wisdom. Wisdom brings power. Power brings responsibility.

– Inscription in the Room of Numbers in the House of Understanding

Iome woke with a pain like fire in her shoulder. The camp was in disarray.

Binnesman had her lying on her belly on the ground, or perhaps that was the way she had fallen. She remembered it now, running from the knight, hoping to draw him away from Gaborn, dropping to the ground at Gaborn's warning, feeling the lance tip slam into her shoulder.

She could not have been unconscious for long. Distantly she could still hear the roaring wind. It raced northeast, toward the mountains.

As quickly as the Darkling Glory's elemental had struck, it was gone. It left the camp all but destroyed. Horses galloped about, having slipped their tethers in the storm.

Everyone gathered round her, looked on with relief.

Binnesman applied some balm to her wound. It felt as sweet to the skin as warm honey would to the tongue.

She groaned in pain, tried to climb up to her hands and knees, and caught a glimpse of bloody corpses nearby. Jureem was not twelve feet off, shielded from her view by a knot of onlookers. She suspected by the fact that no one was kneeling over him that the good servant must have died. She knew that he had died to save her.

'Jureem?' she called, in case he was still alive.

'Don't move yet,' Binnesman said. 'Even the worst shoulder wound often doesn't hurt as badly as you would think.'

'And Jureem?' Iome asked.

Binnesman shook his head. 'Jureem and Sir Handy are both gone.'

The news left her numbed and saddened. She'd known Handy since she was a child. He'd been a shy boy of eight when his father first brought him to court. And Jureem had been an impeccable servant. Iome glanced at her own small wound. The men hadn't just died to save her. Gaborn had set them as guards. He'd spent his men. 'I'm all right. It just grazed me.'

'You're lucky it didn't skewer you through the heart,' Binnesman said. 'If not for the wylde, I think it would have.'

Iome tried to get up again. Binnesman held her down for a moment, until he tired of resisting. 'Ah, well,' Binnesman said. 'The bleeding has stopped. With your endowments, no doubt you'll be healed by tomorrow.'

Binnesman went to tend to Borenson, who lay gasping in pain, while Myrrima knelt at his side.

Iome climbed to her knees, found herself circled by friends. Averan, Gaborn, Langley, Skalbairn – all looked on in concern. Just two dozen yards away lay the body of the man who had tried to kill her, a gory mess. The knights of Rofehavan had made triple sure of him.

Iome crawled over to Jureem. The lance had opened him wide, and there was no chance that he could be alive. Still she took his hand, found it limp and warm.

Who knows the moment of death, or what the dead can hear? she wondered.

'Jureem,' she whispered into his ear, the hot air of her breath fogging his golden earring. 'You did well, my faithful servant. I thank you. If there is any way I can reward you in this world or the next, I will do so.'

She stayed with him, held his hand for a long moment. She looked up and saw Baron Waggit standing over her. The man had tears in his eyes, and looked on in confusion.

'Is there anything we can do for him?' the baron asked.

She wondered how it would be, to learn of death so brutally. He could not have had his endowment of wit for more than a few hours, yet he'd seen dozens of men die savagely before his eyes.

'There is,' Iome said. 'We can live so that our deeds become a monument to his memory.'

Waggit's mouth moved, and for a moment she thought that he would beg to enter the king's service, take his endowments and go to war. But he said nothing, merely turned and stalked away.

As a fool at Carris he had killed reavers without knowing what death was. Now, he seemed to have no nerve. She thought of the old adage 'Make a fool to cure a fool.' Gaborn had wasted a forcible on him.

She let go of Jureem's hand, placed it over the gaping wound in his chest. A pair of knights came to take him away.

Iome glanced at Averan. The big oak that Averan had rested under lay on its side, twisted roots rising twenty feet in the air. The wind had swept all of the straw and grass nearby bare. Averan crouched by the tree, her arms wrapped around her legs, and Iome marveled. The gale had been so fierce, she somehow expected that the girl would have blown away.

A couple dozen yards farther off, Binnesman was asking Sir Borenson, 'Can you breathe all right?'

Borenson grunted in pain. 'It just knocked the wind from me.'

Iome looked up, found Gaborn staring at her as if he would bore through her with his eyes.

Others drew close and whispered things like, 'Honor be to the Powers,' but Gaborn just stared accusingly. With a curt motion he ordered all the others away.

'Why?' he asked, when the well-wishers had left. 'Why would the Darkling Glory come after you?'

Iome did not want to burden him with another worry. 'I don't –'

'Please,' Gaborn said.

'It wants your son,' Iome said. 'It knows that I'm carrying your son.'

Gaborn asked, 'My son?'

'Yes,' Iome admitted. 'When it was stalking me at Castle Sylvarresta, it said that it could smell a son in my womb.'

Iome did not know how Gaborn would react. She had not wanted him to find out this way. She feared that he would be angry with her for withholding such news.

'That's why I took more endowments,' Iome whispered. 'I wanted to give birth to him quickly. If the Darkling Glory wanted him dead so badly . . .'

Gaborn's eyes grew bright as he blinked back tears of joy. Or perhaps they were mingled with tears of sadness. Both he and Iome had taken endowments of metabolism – too many to ever live normal lives again. They would age and die before their child reached adulthood. With half a dozen endowments of metabolism each, by the time the child was a dozen years old, Gaborn and Iome would have aged to nearly a hundred. Though endowments of stamina might keep them healthy to that point, in time the human body was meant to wear out. This child might be born safely, but Iome and Gaborn would never live to see it reach adulthood. Gaborn had to realize that, had to know the price that she'd already paid for her child.

Gaborn knelt beside her, put his hand on her back. 'Here, lie down.'

'I'm all right,' Iome said.

'You're more than all right. You're magnificent,' Gaborn said. 'But lie down anyway.'

Gaborn took off his cloak and laid it on the grass. Iome lay on it. Her head was ringing, but she felt well enough to stand. Binnesman was still tending Borenson.

'When were you going to tell me?' Gaborn asked.

'I don't know,' Iome admitted. 'I thought I'd wait until there was a lull in the battles – or until the child was two or three. Whichever came first.'

Gaborn forced a smile. She could see worry pent up behind it. 'Then I'm glad there was a lull in the battle.'

As the roaring of the Darkling Glory faded, the sound of thunder followed. In the distance, two more lightning bolts struck in rapid succession.

Averan sat in the grass, staring inward, lost to internal nightmares. The stomach cramps and sweats were abating, yet she felt as if the bolts pierced her.

In the distance, on Mangan's Rock, the reavers hissed in alarm.

The memories that the thunder aroused were terrifying: racing up through the narrow canyons in the Brace Mountains, running with thousands of reavers, the sky erupting in its display of pyrotechnics, the horrible lightning storm that had left her blind and dazed.

Those were some of the last memories that Keeper had formed.

Even now, she could feel his pain. The cold last night had been so bitter that it nearly froze his joints, until at last he huddled in a burrow with the others, sharing their warmth.

Even now, sitting in the sun, Averan shivered at the thought, and her feet ached from endlessly running. The weariness that Keeper had endured after days of marches, of fighting, of working without stop, also assailed her, along with an endless burning thirst.

But most of all she felt the horror of last night, Keeper's fear of the lightning.

The fear it aroused was almost primal. It moved her beyond all bounds of reason. While others cleared the battlefield, Averan sat wondering why this was so.

But though the reavers' memories flowed into her, they came at their own pace. She could not choose to discover what she wanted to know.

So she sat for long minutes, peering deeper into Keeper's dark soul. Memories assailed her: reavers digging trenches to channel steaming water to newly opened caverns, reavers herding immature worms from one tunnel to another, reavers cleaning their kills.

In so many ways, Keeper had just been a peasant.

Yet gradually she realized that Keeper was like no human farmer she'd ever known. She'd watched milkmaids with their cows, and shepherds with their sheep. She'd tended graaks in an aerie.

There was a bond of affection that grew between a man and his animals. Averan used to love to pet her graaks, to feed them and stroke them between their eyes, or to scratch them roughly beneath the jiggling folds of skin at their throats.

But Keeper had felt none of that. He tended the creatures he ate, watched them grow. But all of the time that he did so, he could barely restrain himself from tearing his charges to pieces.

Keeper had been a creature of monstrous appetite.

And suddenly she knew that he had come here with a charge – to learn to capture and harvest men and women.

She saw it clearly now, through Keeper's memory. There had been a cave deep in the Underworld. Keeper had gone there to help tend the human charges, to learn how it was done so that he could perfect the techniques.

In the reaver's memory, Averan recalled people huddled in that black place, too terrified to move as Keeper crept among them. The humans were thin, emaciated. Averan saw them through the monster's eyes as potential meals. They had all been counted, and Keeper knew that he could not eat one, could not even take a nibble.

But he happened upon a mother with her newborn child. The other keepers had not counted the babe.

So he quickly snatched the infant from its mother and swallowed it. The flavor was bland.

Averan felt horrified – not merely at the thought that Keeper had eaten a child, but that she had then eaten Keeper in turn.

She was filled with revulsion.

Gaborn depended on her. He wanted another victory. Timidly, in the aftermath of the attack, she got up and walked to him as he hunched over Iome.

Her body felt strange, as if her hands and feet were all disconnected. In her memory, she always ran on four legs.

She stepped over a dead sparrow to reach Gaborn.

'You were right,' she told him. 'The reavers are monsters. They're nothing like people.'

Gaborn shot her an inquisitive stare.

'What makes you say that?'

'Because of what they plan to do to us. Because of how they feel inside. I know how they feel when they look at us: it's a burning hunger.

'You wondered why the reavers stopped here?' she said. 'I can't say for sure. Maybe they did it because they are cold, tired, and starving. They aren't built to walk in the snow, to charge up through rivers of ice like they did in the mountains last night, or to go for days on end with nothing to drink. They're dying of thirst.'

Gaborn stared off at the reavers in wonder. 'So, have we run them aground?'

'Maybe. But I know what they're thinking, and mostly they're just afraid.'

'Of what?'

'Of you!'

Gaborn chuckled as if she had paid him an undeserved compliment. 'How could they fear me?'

'They smell you,' Averan said. 'Yesterday, in the battle, the fell mage tasted your scent. She knew that you caused the earthquakes, and that men fought more fiercely when you came. She sent your smell to all of her warriors, warning them that you were a danger.

'She did it just before the world worm destroyed the Rune of Desolation, and lightning flashed in the sky.'

'Yes?' Gaborn said. He didn't understand her point.

'Don't you see?' Averan asked. 'They think that you're Erden Geboren, their ancient enemy. They think that you summoned Glories into battle. The reavers aren't fleeing back to their caves just because they're afraid, they're going back to warn the One True Master!'

A sudden silence formed around Averan. Iome, Gaborn, and dozens of other lords all leaned close to listen.

'And what happens if they warn the One True Master?' Gaborn asked.

Averan found herself breathing hard. 'She'll summon her armies to destroy you.'

Chapter Thirty-four: THE NETHERWORLD

In the beginning, there was one world, and one sun, and all men were Bright Ones who thrived beneath the One True Tree.

– *Opening of the* Creation Saga

Erin Connal could not leave the door to the netherworld in the ruined village of Twynhaven behind – not really. Oh, she turned her back, rode away, but the knowledge that it existed preyed upon her, and her heart stayed, even when urgent matters demanded her attention.

Two hours after leaving Twynhaven, she and Celinor stopped on a lonely hill that afforded a view of Castle Higham, some five miles off in southeastern Beldinook. 'There's a hornet's nest for us,' Celinor said.

The riders from Fleeds had warned that Lowicker's daughter was waging a tantrum, but from the hilltop it looked like war. Carpenters and masons were fitting hoardings on the castle walls. Perhaps three thousand mounted knights wheeled about on its greens, practicing with the lance. To the north, a column of footmen snaked over the hills. Wains filled with supplies rolled in from the east. Beyond them a dirty brown haze hung in the air as if an army moved, but Erin could not see what caused it.

Erin and Celinor headed west, through the forests, circling Beldinook, not daring to take a road. They cautiously followed a dry streambed through the pines.

For much of the day they kept silent, alert. Or at least Celinor remained alert. Erin could not.

As she rode through a quiet glen in the early afternoon, shafts of sunlight spilling upon the moist leaves, the drone of mosquitoes buzzing in her ears, time and again her thoughts returned to the door to the netherworld at Twynhaven. She imagined the green flames swirling there among the black ashes of the ruins.

She was transfixed. She'd found a gate between worlds. Who could guess what wonders might be on the other side? All she had to do was step through. That would be an adventure!

But could she make it? Wizards might visit that realm, but Erin doubted that a common person could do so.

Yet her dagger had disappeared. It had plunged into the flames. Perhaps it was destroyed, or even now, it might lie upon that far world.

The call of a rook on the hill startled Erin. Its raucous cry indicated that something lurked there.

It might have been nothing more than a boar or a bear. But both she and Celinor were edgy. They drew reins, made no noise, listened for other riders. Pines shadowed the ridge above them. Long after the rook fell silent, Erin urged her mount forward.

They entered a canyon where deep pines closed in on both sides of the streambed. The trees stood so thick that Erin did not fear other riders. No horse could make it through the dense undergrowth.

So as the shadows played upon her back, cooling her, Erin closed her eyes. She'd slept little in the past few days. She now took a moment to rest as Runelords do, letting her mind wander through realms of dream.

She dreamt of Twynhaven – gray ash that blanketed the ground, smelling bitter and dry. She dreamt of families lying dead in the ashes, while a vivid green circle of fire shone upon the blasted earth like a flickering eye.

In her dream she stood by the circle, and leapt.

Her feet struck the ground of a new world with a jolt. For a moment she crouched in deep grass as thick as a carpet. Full night lay upon the land, and she smelled moisture rising from the fields. Overhead, scintillating stars filled the heavens – not the tens of thousands that she'd tried counting as a child upon the plains of Fleeds. Instead hundreds of thousands simmered in the sky. Each was a fiery crystal on a blanket of blue, and their combined brilliance gave more light than a harvest moon. Erin gasped in wonder.

Just ahead atop a small hill stood a monolithic oak. Each limb was wider than the trunk of any oak she'd ever seen. The limbs snaked around, and a cottage could have fit in a crook of one of those limbs.

The One Tree! she thought – the great tree that legend said sheltered men in the netherworld. But a glance told her otherwise. To her left, more majestic oaks raised their proud heads along the rolling hills. Each was perfect in its own way, as if some higher mind had first conceived it and then given it form.

Not the One Tree, she realized – just a tree.

She looked about. The fields were empty. No cricket disturbed the night. A strange creature, perhaps a bird, gave a throaty call in the distance, miles away.

Having no destination in mind, Erin set out for the nearest tree, but stopped after a few paces. The green grass reached almost to her knees. But all around, the stalks were bent and crushed in a circle a hundred yards wide. She smelled burned grass. In a scorched patch ahead, something gleamed like water in the starlight.

She drew forward. It looked like a scorpion, perhaps three

feet in length. At least it had a tail like a scorpion's, and it had claws, but it gleamed like silver. One claw was broken. Black soot suggested that lightning had struck it.

Was it a statue? Had it been alive? Or might it still be alive? A trail had been trammeled in the grass. The thing had certainly crawled to its resting place.

She drew her warhammer from her sheath, and tasted the air. Yes, the grass smelled sweet, almost honeyed, but lightning had struck. She could make out burned patches – arcane symbols burned into the grass.

She walked around the circle and found thirteen runes – each different, each unknown, at equal distances. Deep hoofprints suggested that riders had combed this area. She could taste the scent of horses.

She tried to understand what might have happened. Someone had burned runes into the grass. Perhaps in doing so, they had attracted attention – a patrol. She could not tell who had killed the scorpion.

Warily, Erin stalked uphill toward the great tree. It was a mountain of a tree. A grove of normal trees could have sheltered beneath its boughs. Each leaf was as large as a knight's breastplate, and a single acorn would have fit in a helm.

She had not gotten beneath the boughs when she became aware of distant sound, the grumble of thunder.

Erin wondered. She tasted cool moisture rising off the fields, but the air was not thick with the scent of water. The still heavens heralded no wind. Yet distant lightning split the night. She glanced toward the source.

The sky was black along the horizon for a dozen miles, blotting out the stars, as if a storm were rolling in. Tongues of flame darted in the blackness.

But it was no natural storm: funnels of fire appeared high up. By the flicker of lightning she could make out vast shapes, like enormous men with the wings of bats.

Erin had seen such a thing only once – when the Darkling

Glory struck at Castle Sylvarresta. Now thousands of them streamed across the horizon in a flock. They were half a dozen miles away, closing fast.

Erin raced for shelter, hoping the vast tree would hide her as a bush might hide a mouse from the hawk.

It was no easy feat. The hill was steep, and as she sprinted, boughs overhead blotted out the starlight. It was nearly half a mile from the shade of the nearest limb to the deepest recesses at the bole of the tree.

The limbs rose high overhead as she entered the shadows. The pungent leaves smelled so strongly that Erin realized that she'd never truly tasted the scent of an oak before. Her feet thudded over the ground, muted by a thick carpet of decaying leaves. Darkness and cold reigned under the tree. Sunlight had not warmed the soil here for a thousand years. Under the vast tree, nothing grew.

Erin stumbled. Dry bones clacked beneath her feet. Fallen leaves had hid them. She saw a greatsword thrust into the ground, a monument to a battle. The bones of creatures that might have been men lay all about. She saw the glint of bright armor, and a skull that was too wide of face to have been human.

Lightning struck closer, only a mile or two off by the sound of it. It threw stark shadows. Erin feared that it would show her up to anything that flew above. The cries of Darkling Glories sounded, an unearthly howling.

Erin ran deep under the great oak. The trunk was old, twisted, and no less than ninety feet across. Lightning flashed close to the ground, and a scream involuntarily tore from Erin's throat – for in the stark light, she saw that the tree had a face: eyes and a wide mouth.

She drew to a halt and peered into the shadows, until a flickering bolt revealed the scene again.

The enormous trunk was old and wrinkled, bent in on itself. Moss and lichens covered the hoary thing. But someone had hacked away a face on its surface – a woman's face. Her features were beautiful and unearthly. Her mouth was wide, as if she were calling out. Her open mouth led to a hollow beneath the roots of the tree.

Shelter. The mouth was a vast cavern twenty feet wide. She raced through the opening, tripped and rolled down a long hill. She landed, clattering among bones.

She smelled the musky scent of some animal's den. The tree's shadow had eclipsed the bright starlight. Everything was black, except when lightning split the sky. The heavens snarled. A tempest rose.

Erin climbed back to the opening, kept herself low to the ground. Lightning flickered. Perhaps half a mile off, a hart bounded across the open fields. It floated over the ground as if in a dream.

But the Darkling Glories came. A howl of warning rose from their throats, a hunting cry that froze the bones, like the call of a wolf mingled with a screaming wind and the rumble of a distant storm.

A lightning bolt was hurled before the hart. It leapt right, making for the shelter of a tree. A second bolt struck the earth. The hart veered again.

Shadows descended. Winged beasts swirled out of the sky like bats dropping into a cave, and the hart was gone.

A shadow blotted out all light overhead, and Erin heard the rush of wings. Something enormous swept through the air above her, then rose again, into the den. Erin felt the wind of its passage.

A Darkling Glory, she realized, her heart thudding. She threw her face into the dirt, and dared not move.

But there was no hunting cry. No claws raked her. Instead, she heard the sound of wings shifting, an enormous bird primping its feathers. It made a soft throaty noise, the sound of an owl, 'Whooo.'

But the bird was much larger than any owl. Its wingspan

could not have been less than twenty feet.

The lightning continued to strike out on the plains.

The tree shook with the rumble of thunder and the roars of Darkling Glories. Lightning flashed overhead. Wind screamed through the tree boughs, and leaves rained down.

Erin clutched the haft of her warhammer, turned to try to glimpse her companion, to see if it posed a threat.

By the flickering thrill of lightning, she saw the beast perched above her, about fifty feet away. A passage looked as if it led down, into a deeper chasm, but the owl crouched upon a knob of moldy root. The raptor was a downy gray, with bits of white at its breast and a collar of black at its throat. Its golden eyes were as large as saucers, and lightning reflected from them.

The owl watched her, unblinking. Its beak was large enough to rip off a man's arm. It held something dainty in its beak.

Then her light was gone. An afterimage formed in her mind. She'd seen the gleam of bones on the floor. She recognized the owl's musty smell. This had to be its den.

Lightning flashed, weaving a webwork from horizon to horizon. The owl had closed its eyes, and she saw now what it held in its beak – her dirk!

The owl let the blade fall, and it flashed as it tumbled end over end in the unsteady light, to plunge into a skull on the floor with a whack.

The owl spoke, a whisper that pierced Erin to the core, 'Warrior of the Shadow World, I summon you!' The words did not merely ring in Erin's ears, they spoke to her flesh and trembled through her bones.

You're dreaming, she told herself. Wake up.

She found herself back in the forest, with a brilliant blue sky overhead. Celinor rode beside her as their horses picked their way through a streambed. A squirrel in a nearby pine raced round its trunk, chattering.

Erin's heart pounded. In memory she still smelled the musty den beneath the great oak, and heard the grumble of thunder. A surety grew that on some far world, some*thing* had found her dagger.

Chapter Thirty-five: THINKING LIKE THE ENEMY

How oft the jailer becomes the jailed! Therein lies the danger of learning to think like the enemy.
– Adage from Mystarria

'For one little girl,' Gaborn replied to Averan, 'you're sure full of bad news.'

He gave her a worried smile, stroked her face, and wondered at the portent of her words.

As Earth King, Gaborn had ridden to Carris in hopes of saving his people. He'd managed to do it in glorious fashion. But in doing so, he'd called attention to himself. The enemy knew his name, and would come to hunt him. Binnesman had warned him that the more people he tried to save, the more his enemies would try to destroy them. Perhaps in freeing Carris he had triggered the battle that would destroy the world.

He hadn't considered this.

He wondered at his own wisdom. Even now he planned to hunt down this One True Master. Was it possible that in doing so, he might provoke the very catastrophe he sought to avoid? No, he didn't believe that. The Earth had whispered to his soul that this was the right course.

Yet doubt nibbled at him. He'd lost most of his powers,

and now felt bereft. Could it be that he was mistaken in his designs?

He peered up at Mangan's Rock. The reavers had nearly cleared the trees from its crown. They'd bulled them over the cliff to the ground.

A vast contingent of reavers manned the cliff face as if it were a castle wall. They stood with blades and knight gigs and staves, gazing out like sentries. The philia on their heads waved about, tasting the air.

They'd taken a nearly unassailable position.

'You said that they were racing to the Underworld,' Gaborn asked. 'But if they plan to warn their master, why stop now?'

'Maybe it's because you killed their fell mage.'

'So we killed a mage. Does that alter the plan?'

'Yes!' Averan said. 'A new sorceress has to take the lead, and she'll . . . make changes.'

'What do you mean, "make changes"?'

Averan huffed. 'You killed a mage. That proves that her ideas weren't good enough. The new mage will try new things against you, and pick new leaders for the blade-bearers. Killing one mage can change everything.'

Of course, it made sense when Gaborn thought about it.

'There's no telling what they're plotting,' Skalbairn said.

Gaborn could see a weakness in relying on Averan for information. She could see into the reavers' minds better than any human had ever done. But all of her news was hours old. She couldn't tell Gaborn what he needed to know now.

'If they are ill and thirsty,' Jerimas offered, 'I can see no outward sign of it. But every moment that they sit there on Mangan's Rock is another moment that they'll stay hungry and thirsty.'

'So what is their new mage thinking?' Iome asked.

'Perhaps she's merely waiting for the sun to warm them,' Binnesman offered. 'That's what lizards do before they hunt.'

'Or maybe they just want rest or time to think,' Iome suggested.

'Not likely,' Skalbairn said. 'That rock is like a fortress. I think the reavers hope to draw us into battle.'

That seemed most probable. Gaborn looked from face to face. Jerimas's eyes twinkled. To the scholar this was merely an elegant puzzle. Skalbairn was already eyeing the rock, trying to figure out how to pull the reavers down from it. Iome looked scared.

Skalbairn said, 'Maybe it's a diversion. By taking a defensive position here, the reavers could hope to draw reinforcements away from nearby castles. They may even have reinforcement of their own on the way.'

That was a frightening thought. Gaborn gave Skalbairn a look. 'Right,' he said. 'We'll check into it.' He nodded toward a captain nearby, who rushed off to gather scouting parties.

'You know,' Jerimas said, 'maybe the reavers have more than one objective.'

Gaborn suspected a plot. Tens of thousands of people in Carris were still in danger. He reached out with his Earth senses, touching them – and immediately noticed something odd. Those people weren't in Carris anymore!

Instead, most had already fled the city, bearing southeast so that now they were just forty miles east and a little north of him. Others of his Chosen were heading west or northward, but Gaborn sensed no trouble around them or those that stayed in Carris – it was only the people traveling southeast. And not even all of those were in danger.

None of the roads in that direction were any good. Most travelers moving southeast took boats on the River Donnestgree to the large cities downstream.

With a sinking heart, he recalled the wounded he had evacuated from Carris. There had been legions of sick and dying – more than ten Binnesmans could have handled. Now they spread for miles along the river. Were they heading into an ambush? The danger was rising. By this time tomorrow it would be upon them. It could be anything – reavers, a flash flood, or an attack by Lowicker's troops.

Gaborn turned to Skalbairn. 'While you're sending out scouts, have a dozen men head downstream along the Donnestgree.'

'Yes, milord,' Skalbairn said. He nodded toward his captain.

'You know,' Skalbairn offered in a dangerous tone, 'if these reavers do want to warn their master about you, you'll have to stop them.'

'Perhaps my best chance would be to ambush the One True Master,' Gaborn said, 'before she hears the news.'

But he had no idea how to reach her in the Underworld. The only person who might decipher the reavers' trails was Averan, and she'd need the Waymaker's knowledge to do it.

She hadn't agreed to lead him. He hadn't even dared to ask her. He didn't want to sacrifice her.

A dozen lords had gathered round. Gaborn asked, 'Gentlemen, may we have some privacy?'

He took Averan by the shoulder and led her away from the knot of warriors. Only Iome and Gaborn's Days dared follow.

'Averan,' Gaborn said. His stomach knotted. 'I have an enormous favor to beg.'

'What?' Averan asked in a small voice. She was trembling. She looked very timid, though she tried to be brave.

'I'm going to the Underworld, to look for the Place of Bones and the One True Master. Can you lead me to her?' He'd known that he would have to ask this of her, yet asking was hard.

Averan swallowed and began to tremble harder.

'You can't ask that of a child,' Iome said.

'I have to,' Gaborn replied. 'We're running out of time.'

'Perhaps the wylde can do it?' Iome said.

'I thought of that,' Gaborn said. 'But it doesn't speak well enough yet. I doubt it could understand our questions, much less give us answers.'

'But she's just a little girl. Even if she said yes, she doesn't understand the question.'

'Yes I do,' Averan told Iome fiercely. 'I know what it means better than he does.' She jabbed a finger in Gaborn's direction. 'He's the one who doesn't know what he's asking. The path is long and dangerous. The reavers crawled through the Underworld for days to get here.'

'How many days?' Gaborn asked.

Averan shook her head. 'I don't know. Reavers don't measure time like we do.'

'Averan,' Gaborn said, 'this is important. I feel danger approaching. I feel a great danger to every man, woman, and child I've Chosen. We have to leave soon. We don't have days to waste looking for the path. Is there any other way that you know of?'

Averan shook her head emphatically.

Gaborn wasn't sure that he believed her. 'The reavers left a groove in the ground on the way here. Can't we just follow it?'

'Probably much of the way,' Averan admitted. 'But we'll have to go to the deepest nesting grounds, where the sorceresses lay their eggs. All of the tunnels have well-beaten paths, and the sentinels keep watch.'

Gaborn sighed, rubbed his temple, trying to relieve the tight muscles.

'If you want me to lead you,' Averan offered, 'then you must get the Waymaker off that rock!' She pointed toward the monolith on the horizon.

'I will,' Gaborn said. 'And before we go, you'll need to take endowments. We have to make the journey swiftly, and I cannot afford to have you lag. You'll need brawn, grace, stamina, and metabolism. Most of all, you'll need endowments of scent so that you can smell the reavers' markings.'

'Averan –' Iome began to say. But Averan cut her off.

'It's all right,' Averan said. 'Everyone dies. All my friends are gone. He wants to know if I'll die down there with him.'

'That's right,' Gaborn said. 'It could come to that.'

Iome bit her lip, shot Averan a mournful look. Yet she had to know that Gaborn could not ask this lightly.

Averan took Iome's hand, squeezed it. 'I know what I'm doing. It's better for one person to die, than a whole world. Don't you think?'

Gaborn was not surprised at the tears that filled Iome's eyes. She had always loved her people, but he felt overwhelmed by the way she grabbed Averan, and hugged her fiercely. 'I could never be good at that kind of math.'

Gaborn knelt, wrapped his arms around them both.

'Iome,' he whispered into his wife's ear. 'I want you to go someplace safe. I can't think of any place safer than the Courts of Tide. I need you to carry a letter for me to an old friend. He'll know where we can get the endowments we need.'

'It will take days for the dogs to bond with her,' Iome objected.

'We'll have the dog handlers take the endowments,' Gaborn said. 'That way it can be done in hours. Then we'll give them to the girl as vectors.'

Iome nodded her consent. Gaborn quickly penned his missive. As he did, his mind turned to other matters.

He knew the value of stepping outside himself, of learning to think like his enemy. He'd discovered it when he was Averan's age, and for a moment he was lost in a memory.

When Gaborn was nine, he'd gone on an autumn hunt

with his father and some Runelords near the headwaters of the river Dweedum.

On the hunt, the lords found a few salmon running weeks before expected. Gaborn's father set up camp, and mentioned that he wanted fish for dinner.

The lords couldn't let such a challenge lie. Catching the salmon suddenly loomed large.

It was one of those cool dawns in autumn when the sun barely filters into the canyons, and the morning mists spend half the day trying to climb up the ridges to make their escape into the sky. The larks and finches had been hopping in the pines, and the spores on the ferns along the hillside were so thick that the whole of the forest carried their scent, so that a tang like iron mingled with the pine needles and a carpet of moss.

With the river running low, the riverbed held more round gray boulders than water.

The lords rode their horses up through the shallows of the river, driving the salmon up to Wildman Falls. The falls soared a hundred and seventy feet. The water tumbled like silver hair, leaving a cold spray in the air that misted Gaborn's shoulders. No salmon could leap those falls, so the basin beneath was a good place to hem the salmon in. The tumbling water had carved a nice little pond, cool and deep. A few strategically placed boulders all but blocked the shallow exit downstream, and that could be easily guarded.

There weren't many salmon. Gaborn had only spotted three or four on the ride up, and saw only one swim into the deep waters, making it all that much more desirable.

The older lords thrust a spear into Gaborn's hands and told him to stand in the shallows and 'try' to bag any fish that headed downstream.

Meanwhile, the lords all rode their horses out into the deeper pool, till the water reached their mounts' bellies.

Then they launched themselves at fish with spears that were meant for boars.

It was a mad episode. The horses lunging around in the pool soon muddied the water so that no one could see. If one man did spot a fish, he'd give a shout and spur his horse forward, and all of the others would give chase, for they'd made a game of seeing who would spear the biggest fish.

For the most part, they spent their time chasing around trout that weren't much longer than Gaborn's forearm. After an hour of this, only one knight had speared a salmon, a little jack that was small by way of having swum upstream to spawn a year or two early.

But Gaborn was his father's son, and he decided that if he were going to get a fish, he'd have to think like a fish.

The knights all held to the deep, splashing and muddying the water so that a fish wouldn't be able to breathe.

So Gaborn went to the shallows at the edge of the stream, where a few overhanging weeds provided cover and the water was fairly clear. Soon he spotted the tail of a salmon poking out. A quick thrust with his spear won Gaborn the salmon that his father had ordered.

The lords had talked about it for days afterward – this little lad, going out and spearing the only salmon in the pool while a bunch of force soldiers and Runelords made fools of themselves.

If I were a reaver, Gaborn wondered, what would I do? The reavers were all fleeing along the exact same trail that had brought them here two days ago. At least, that's what it looked like.

But a smart reaver would take another trail.

'Sir Langley, Marshal Skalbairn,' Gaborn said, calling the men to his side. 'Is it possible that this main force of reavers is acting as a decoy? Could some others have left the trail?'

'I had men watching,' Skalbairn said. 'But it's hard to say for sure what they did in the night.'

'Send a hundred men to check for tracks,' Gaborn ordered. 'In particular, have them search back where the reavers dug in last night. Unless I miss my guess, some of them waited to leave. Your men must kill any that they find.'

'Yes, milord,' Skalbairn said.

'And after you've done that, call the lords together for a council. We have to get the reavers down from the rock.'

Gaborn turned to Averan. 'Could the reavers be digging a well up there?'

'On Mangan's Rock?' Iome asked.

It didn't sound feasible even to Gaborn. The rock had to be hundreds of feet thick. But reavers were inordinately strong, and there were thousands up there to work. They had a virtually unassailable position.

Gaborn frowned in concentration.

He felt . . . rising danger around some of his men.

He looked up. The reavers were sculpting a shallow dome atop Mangan's Rock. Glue mums had begun to spit out pulpy strands into a configuration he recognized. A brown haze rolled from it, and actinic blue lights flashed beneath. An enormous flameweaver crawled atop the thing, raised a crystalline staff to the sky.

Gaborn's heart seemed to freeze.

Binnesman breathed out in wonder. 'They're making another Rune of Desolation.'

Chapter Thirty-six: MAYGASSA

Maygassa is the oldest city in the world. For twice ten thousand years it has stood, and if a man digs anywhere beneath its streets, he will find the ruins of older buildings and the bones of the ancients. The meaning of its name is lost in time, but the oldest texts argue that it means 'First Home'.

– Excerpt from Cities and Villages of Indhopal, *by Hearthmaster Arashpumanja, of the Room of Feet*

On the western slopes of the Anja Breal, in the Valley of the Lotus, lay sprawling Maygassa, the capital of old Indhopal. It was a city that produced nothing but people – a myriad of people.

The rajahs of Indhopal had long ago built the Palace of Elephants here, a stronghold along the river. On the west, above the city, the palace stood atop an enormous gray stone nearly eight hundred feet high. All along the base of this huge stone were pictographs in ancient Indhopalese that gave the Enlightened Texts of the ancient Rajah Peshwavanju. The texts covered the gray rock, forming an exquisite pattern that was much admired throughout Indhopal. The pattern was called 'Lace of Stone.'

Some legends said that the texts were not carved by human hand but had appeared overnight, written by the Earth for those who sought enlightenment.

Raj Ahten glanced up at the palace, read the uppermost verse, 'Bow before the Elephant Throne, O haughty traveler. You upon your proud camel: know that you are nothing.'

The words struck Raj Ahten with the force of a portent. The warnings from Binnesman, the way that the Earth Powers had withdrawn from him – even his failure to catch the insolent Wuqaz Faharaqin – all seemed evidence that the Earth was against him. Now the inscription in stone seemed to blaze.

It was only a coincidence that he read that verse, of course. Peshwavanju's masons had known that merchants traveling the Old Spice Route would ride by on camels, and would of course glance up to read the verses.

Still, it felt a portent, and Raj Ahten halted along the road to rest his camel, as he looked down on Maygassa.

He admired this city. Conquering it had been the high point of his life. He remembered well his ascent to the Elephant Throne here at the palace. Raj Ahten's father, Arunhah, had once told him that the name Ahten meant 'the Sun.' His given name, Avil, was so common that Raj Ahten had held it in contempt. So when he seized the Elephant Throne, he renamed himself Raj, 'Ruler,' as did all of the kings of Indhopal. Thus, on the day that he took the capital of Indhopal, he became known throughout the world as the 'Sun Lord.'

Below, the walled city sprawled beside the broad banks of the Djuriparari River. The walls of the city, and of every palace within it, were carved of stone that was grayish white, almost a pale lavender, so that the city shone bright in the sun. The Djuriparari River was a broad band of copper beside it.

Fleets of sailing boats, carved from teakwood, each sporting a single mast of brown canvas, plied the sluggish waters. They brought rich spices, rice, sugar cane, silk, gold, melons, and fruits from the jungles. Even from miles away, Raj Ahten's keen nose could smell the thick scent of cloistered humanity, of commerce and rotting fruit, of poverty and hope.

But as he watched the river below, he knew that he would find trouble in Maygassa. The boats were all heading downstream today, and their four-pointed sails had been unfurled to hurry the pace. People were fleeing.

More than that, from the upper passage he could see along the highway that led to Majpuhr. It was thick with oxcarts, horses, and people. From a distance, the seething mass of humanity marching up the broad winding road between the trees looked like a python twisting through the grass.

None here dared to head northeast, along the trade routes into the desert – not at this time of year. The Wastes were too dry for any but the best force camels. Instead, the refugees were following the curve of the jungle through the hills northward, toward Deyazz.

'What is happening?' Bhopanastrat asked. 'Are the reavers coming?'

'Yes,' was all that Raj Ahten said. He gripped the reins of his camel in his numb left hand, prodded the beast with his right, and rode down into the valley.

Maygassa was bustling. A nervous buzz filled the air, the sound of thousands of worried voices talking quickly, punctuated by shouts and cries. Beyond the markets, the city still crawled with men and women, each packing their families' goods and abandoning their homes. Raj Ahten saw women in their apartments throwing bundles of clothes and food down to children below, while men with daggers and swords guarded their horses and wagons.

All of this Raj Ahten gathered as he rode in from the north, through the Gate of the Blind and along the broad avenues. The city was in a state of panic. The first few people he passed were so preoccupied with flight that none paid him or his men any mind. The one man who looked his way was eyeing his camel, as if wondering if it might be worth stealing. When at last he bothered to look at its rider, he fell back, speechless.

Raj Ahten suspected that men had already begun killing one another in their haste to flee.

Dull consternation began to settle over him, a creeping numbness. He was still nearly two hundred and sixty miles from Kartish.

But he dared not show concern. He prodded his camel and held his head high as he rode into the market, past the Fountains of Paradise with their tubes of polished silver twisted like vines that spurted water in flowery shapes, above basins carved of rhodolite and filled with live crocodiles.

Refugees had evacuated from the south with their whole families – children, animals, and all that they owned. Those who had mounts at all were lucky. The peasant men and women of Maygassa had a hungry, frenzied look in their eyes as they shouted, 'Horses? Camels? I pay gold for camels!' 'Food? I want food!'

Babes cried in panic. The bazaar was normally a hive of eager merchants hawking their wares. Maygassa was home to the busiest markets in the world. Here by the north gates on the outskirts of the market, medicine men sold healing herbs – goku and ginseng – or potions made from ground white cobras to ward off old age, or lizard testicles to make a man virile. And down near the docks were merchants of fish, vegetables, hemp, wood, copper and iron. Farther into the finer merchant district were vast stalls for the traffickers in silk and linen, cloth of gold, muslin, cotton, and wool, all dyed in ten thousand colors.

On a busy day, the bazaar was so crowded that one could not ride a camel through.

But now the northern bazaar was nearly empty, the stalls vacant, the wheedling cries of the merchants unheard. Most of the traffickers had already fled Maygassa. Those who remained were the most mercenary sort, rapacious men who would charge a peasant twenty times the normal price for a horse, only to deliver a sickly mule. He saw women with eyes that shone from greed selling saffron rice at forty times its customary value.

Desperate peasants crowded round them.

'Raj Ahten!' a woman cried. 'Our deliverer!' All eyes in the market began to turn to him. For years Raj Ahten had warned his people that the reavers would attack. He'd promised to be their savior. Now people muttered hopefully. 'O Great Light!' 'He will save us!'

Into the midst of the bustle and confusion he rode. The cries of the hawkers died on their lips. Everywhere, the people fell silent.

Raj Ahten raised his hand. 'What is this commotion?' he called. He pinned his eyes upon a man who was offering a handful of rubies for a camel so old that its muzzle hairs had gone gray.

'Great One,' the man said, 'the reavers – they surfaced in Kartish! The very Lord of the Underworld marches at their head . . .'

Raj Ahten nodded. 'Are they marching here now?'

'No, O Light of the Universe, it is much worse. There is a blight upon the land – a creeping stench that kills every plant it touches. It is moving this way, just a bit faster than a man can walk – unless the wind bears it faster. Last night, the winds blew very hard indeed.'

In rising trepidation Raj Ahten made some quick calculations. The reavers had surfaced yesterday at dawn, and had swiftly created a Seal of Desolation in Kartish, as they'd done at Carris. If the resulting blight crept forward at a steady pace, it could be over two hundred miles in diameter.

'It covers all of Kartish?' He tried to imagine the consequences. There would be little food for his troops, so he would not be able to lay siege to the reavers' stronghold.

He'd have to strike quickly, and with all of his might. If the reavers managed to hold the blood-metal mines, it would bring his ruin.

But there were other dangers. The bulk of Raj Ahten's Dedicates were currently housed in the Palace of Canaries, not far from the mines themselves. They would be at risk.

I am dead now, he thought. If my Dedicates die, I will die with them.

'Indeed, Enlightened One. The blight covers Kartish and Muyyatin as well. But last night the winds drove it into Dharmad and Aven. Soon it will swallow all of the Jewel Kingdoms. Every plant in them will be blasted by nightfall.'

Raj Ahten could not imagine the pepper trees at Aven lying blackened and twisted in their groves, or the passion fruit orchards of Dharmad with nothing but rot beneath their trees. The apiaries of Osmol would be devastated, along with the vineyards and jungles and the rice paddies at Bina.

The farms and orchards of southern Indhopal, of the Jewel Kingdoms, were the richest in the world. With them gone, all of Indhopal would suffer famine this winter.

'All gone,' the kaif said. 'All destroyed. The people are fleeing as fast as they can, but the blight spreads even at night. A common man, even on horse, cannot outrun it! To wait until it catches up with you is folly, for it means certain death.'

'And what of my warriors?'

'Armies are converging on the mines at Kartish,' someone yelled from the crowd. One of his soldiers was there, a man in a saffron surcoat with the three-headed wolf emblazoned in red. But he wore his surcoat hidden under a black cloak, so that Raj Ahten had not seen him from behind. 'Aysalla Pusnabish leads the charge, with three million footmen and eighty thousand lancers – every able-bodied man in the Jewel Kingdoms.'

Pusnabish was Raj Ahten's most trusted warlord – the

captain who protected his Dedicates. He was marshaling every troop available, but nearly all of those three million men would be commoners, and it might take days for them to gather.

If the Lord of the Underworld led the reavers, if she uttered curses as the one had at Carris, the commoners would become as dross burning in a forge.

Raj Ahten asked, 'Yesterday the reavers took Kartish?'

'Yes, O Wise One,' the soldier said.

'And Pusnabish is throwing every man against them?'

'As I have said,' the soldier agreed.

'And the blight still spreads?'

'Even as we speak,' the soldier said. 'I raced north from the borders at dawn, and saw the decimation spread with my own eyes.'

It could mean only one thing. Pusnabish had failed to dislodge the reavers, failed to destroy the Seal of Desolation. Perhaps he had simply been unable to break the reavers' defenses. Perhaps he did not know what needed to be done, or was still gathering his troops. But Raj Ahten suspected the worst: Pusnabish and all his millions might already be dead.

Raj Ahten could not reach Kartish before nightfall, not if his camel was to live through it. Once he hit the blasted lands, there would be no fodder for the beast.

And as the blasting spell spread, it would make it more and more difficult for anyone to reach Kartish, to mount an attack on the reavers lodged there.

There was a slim hope that Pusnabish and his men still lived, that Raj Ahten could marshal a charge against the reavers and break the Seal of Desolation there. A slim chance.

He prodded his camel through the streets of Maygassa, and as he did, he calculated quickly. If the Desolation spread, then by tomorrow at dawn it would swallow the Jewel Kingdoms and lead to a terrible famine in Indhopal. A day later, it would swallow Maygassa and begin taking the rich jungles to the north. Five days later, it would eat through the vast deserts of Indhopal, destroying all but Deyazz.

Within a week, it could devastate all of Indhopal. After that, the world.

Chapter Thirty-seven: MANY FAREWELLS

True friends must be cherished beyond all worldly measure, for in our memory they shine brighter than gold and last longer than diamonds.
– Jorlis, Hearthmaster from the Room of the Heart

Myrrima's heart felt heavy as she prepared to leave Gaborn. Men had only begun to cart off the bodies of Jureem, Handy, and their attackers.

The assault on Iome had happened so quickly that Myrrima's nerves still jangled. The reavers were brewing some new trouble on Mangan's Rock, while Gaborn spoke of going to the Underworld to fight their master.

Langley rode out onto the plain to gather up several lords for a council. As the council prepared to convene, Gaborn gave Myrrima and Borenson a message case to carry to King Zandaros. 'Be sure that this gets through,' Gaborn told them. 'Algyer col Zandaros would be a powerful ally, and we cannot afford to have him as our foe.'

'It will get through,' Myrrima promised. 'And I'll take good care of Iome, so long as our roads lie together.'

'I know,' Gaborn said. 'May the Earth protect you.' He drew close, hugged her to say goodbye. The act surprised her. Though she saw Iome as a friend, Gaborn was still the King, and therefore too high above her station for such a show of affection.

Myrrima went to Averan. The little girl's eyes were glazed. She looked forlorn. Myrrima took her hand, 'Little sister. I'm going to Inkarra, and I've come to say goodbye.'

'Oh,' Averan said. 'That means I'll never see you again.'

'No,' Myrrima promised. 'I'll be back.'

But Averan shook her head. She said matter-of-factly, 'No one comes back from Inkarra, and I'm going to the Underworld.'

Myrrima wanted badly to comfort the girl. 'Have faith in yourself and your king. And have faith in me. I'm your big sister now.'

But Averan just shook her head. 'Not really.'

She was right. Roland had never petitioned the duke to adopt Averan as far as anyone knew. Averan had never been made Borenson's sister, and Roland's promise was left unfulfilled. This girl had no one.

Myrrima's own father had been taken at an early age. She'd had a mother and sisters to help care for her, and knew how vital their support had been in her life. Averan's own loss seemed a small matter, easily corrected.

Myrrima turned to Gaborn. 'Your Highness, Roland Borenson planned to petition Paldane to become Averan's guardian. But he died before he could make his plea. I wonder now if you can grant Roland's petition, my petition, now.'

Gaborn looked to Averan. 'Would you want this? Would you take Myrrima as your sister?'

Averan appeared more thoughtful than excited. She nodded.

Gaborn glanced at Sir Borenson. 'If I grant this, you become her brother indeed, and her guardian.'

Binnesman cut in. 'She's an Earth Warden. The Earth will clothe and feed her as it sees fit. And you may leave her training to me.'

Myrrima was taken aback by the wizard's statement. 'I'm sure you intend well,' she told Binnesman. 'And you might train Averan in the ways of magic. But you're not used to caring for children. Can you give her the love that she needs? And when she's hungry, will you feed her, or merely let her grub around for roots and nuts?'

'I'm sure you mean well too,' Binnesman said. 'But remember, dear lady, you are the one going to Inkarra. How well will you care for her?'

Myrrima argued, 'Our estate in the Drewverry March is large enough to accommodate a child. She could stay with my mother and sisters, when she's not training.'

Binnesman warned, 'Wild birds like cages as much as she'd like a house, I think.'

Gaborn eyed them both. 'The child can live in a house and eat at a table and still be an Earth Warden. I see no reason why Roland's desires should not be granted. But I still haven't heard from Sir Borenson.'

'My father made that choice already,' Borenson said.

Gaborn said softly, 'So be it. Then Averan, I grant you into the care of family Borenson. Even if it be in name only, you have the right to call yourself Roland's daughter.'

Myrrima nodded, looked at Averan gravely, and said, 'Now we are sisters.'

It was a small act of decency, but the words brought tears to Averan's eyes.

Myrrima hugged Averan and said, 'My mother and sisters will be going to Drewverry March.' She took a necklace from around her throat, placed it on Averan. It was a small pendant of a silver fish. 'When they see this, I'm sure that they'll welcome you. It was a gift from my father. Drewverry will be your home, whenever you want.'

Averan hugged Myrrima fiercely, choked out, 'Good-bye.'

Then Myrrima shook hands with Binnesman, and even his

wylde. In moments she, Borenson, Iome, and Iome's escorts began packing for the quick ride. Iome would take Gaborn's forcibles to the Courts of Tide.

Gaborn called a man out of his ranks especially to lead the group, a swarthy fellow with a single black eyebrow who looked as disreputable as his namesake would imply. He was called Grimeson.

But as Grimeson began tying down a tarpaulin over the treasure wagon, he shouted, 'We've been robbed!'

There was a great commotion as he tore the lid off one crate, threw the empty box to the ground, and began opening each crate in turn.

Several men rushed to the wagon. The guards protested, 'But it hasn't been out of our sight!'

'How well were you watching when the Darkling Glory attacked?' Grimeson asked.

The guards let out a cry of consternation, began shouting, 'Search the camp.' There were hundreds of horses tied up and down the creek in small enclaves. Myrrima didn't know where to begin searching, who to look for.

Gaborn closed his eyes, seeking inward. 'Don't bother. The thief is gone. Feykaald is riding to Indhopal.'

Borenson said, 'He has less than an hour on us. We can catch him!'

The old Wit Jerimas urged Gaborn, 'Milord, you must retrieve those forcibles. Make no mistake. If Raj Ahten learns that you still have so many, he *will* come after them.'

But to Myrrima's surprise, Gaborn shook his head. 'No. I feel a pall settling over Raj Ahten. There is trouble in Kartish. Surely the children of Indhopal need those forcibles as much as we do.'

Myrrima thought that someone would speak out against the notion. Knights Equitable and lords from half a dozen lands stood within hearing. But no one spoke against Gaborn.

For days he had been saying it: all of the world's people

were Gaborn's charge. Perhaps now they had begun to believe.

So Myrrima, Borenson, and Iome's retinue mounted up. They waited for Iome.

She and her king walked together and stood under an oak by the brook, talking for a long while. Myrrima saw tears stream down the queen's face. They were far enough away that no one could hear what they said, but Myrrima could imagine.

Iome was leaving Gaborn, and he would go to the Underworld to hunt for the One True Master. Iome feared for him even as she held him. When at last she was able to tear herself away, Iome got on her mount and spoke not at all.

Force horses pulled the treasure wagon so fast that it sang over the highways. They raced southeast through grasslands, following the river Donnestgree as it surged toward the ocean and the Courts of Tide.

Few villages dotted the plains. Myrrima asked Borenson why. He pointed out that the driving winds would not allow many trees, and the soil here blanketed a thick crust of volcanic stone. Without wood for fuel, few people wanted to settle here, though the land was bountiful enough for wild cattle.

But people had lived here once. She saw the remains of castles on many a lonely hill. Borenson pointed out the site for the Battle of the Five Wizards, and halted once to show her bones of a giant encased in a rock by the wayside. She saw the very tower where Leandra had pushed her mother to her death upon hearing that Andreas was no more.

Near the old altar at Rimmondy they scared a flock of young wild graaks up from the carcasses of some cattle that had been chased over a cliff.

In the late afternoon they reached a crossroads two hundred miles southeast of Carris where silver birches bent over a still river, their leaves perfectly mirrored in the waters.

To the south lay the road that Myrrima and Borenson would take, while Iome headed northeast. They stopped to let the force horses graze and drink.

'We can't stay here long,' Borenson warned Myrrima. 'The sun will be going down soon. We'll want to be clear of the Westlands.'

'The Westlands?' Myrrima asked. She couldn't keep the edge of fear from her voice. She had heard children's tales of the wights that haunted them. 'Are they close by?'

'Oh, you'll get a close look,' Borenson assured her with a grin. 'If you spit that way, you'll hit them.' He nodded toward the south.

'But I thought they'd be farther . . . west,' Myrrima said.

'They're west of Old Ferecia, and that's all that matters.'

'But there's supposed to be bogs and swamps.'

'They start just beyond that rise,' Borenson assured her. He nodded toward a rise where the remains of a castle wall still thrust up like a dog's tooth. 'That's Woglen's Tower.'

Myrrima shuddered. She knew the tales. The land here had been black with Toth, and blood had once filled this river. For three months Fallion's armies had fought to break their siege and win that tower, only to discover that Fallion's bride was dead inside.

Somehow she'd expected Woglen's Tower to still be standing. In the old tales it had seemed indomitable. And she'd imagined bones here upon the ground.

She didn't feel prepared for Borenson's news. She'd thought only about getting to Inkarra, not about any dangers between. But there would be bogs full of wights and mountains with hazards of their own.

'Can't we go around the Westlands?' she asked.

'It will be faster if we go through them,' he said, obviously amused to see her dismay.

Myrrima and Borenson sat for a few moments counseling about what they should take with them south. Borenson had found gold in his father's purse. He assured Myrrima that the city of Batenne near the Alcairs would carry all the supplies that they needed. Iome walked downstream as they spoke.

When it was near time to leave, Myrrima went looking for Iome. She walked down along a grassy trail beside the river and scared up a family of mallards.

She smelled an apple tree somewhere in the band of woods nearby, and found Iome there, leaning with her back against it, looking to the northwest. The head of a kingly statue lay in the grass, gazing upward with blank eyes. Wind-fallen apples carpeted the ground at Iome's feet. Deer had nibbled many of them. Iome thoughtfully chewed a yellow apple. The sunlight striking the golden fields was piercing, brilliant.

'Are you worrying about Gaborn?' Myrrima asked.

'No,' Iome said. 'My thoughts are far more selfish.'

'Really?' Myrrima said. 'Good.'

'Good?' Iome asked. She turned and stared into Myrrima's eyes. Over the past three hours she had been so preoccupied that she had not said a word to anyone.

'You don't indulge yourself that way enough,' Myrrima suggested.

'Well, I'm making up for it today. I was just wondering if Gaborn would even spare a thought for me this afternoon.'

'I'm sure he will.'

'That's the trouble,' Iome said. 'He'll think about me, and with a thought he'll know whether I'm safe, and where I am.'

'I imagine so,' Myrrima said.

'I wish that I could go with you,' Iome confided. 'Jerimas said that Gaborn's nearest kin should deliver the message.'

'Gaborn couldn't risk that,' Myrrima assured her.

'I know,' Iome said. 'Now that he knows that I carry his son, he'll send me to "safety." No doubt he'll want me to lie comfortably in bed until it's time to spread my legs and deliver his child.'

'Your Highness!' Myrrima said, affecting a shocked tone that she really did not feel.

Iome grinned wickedly, dark eyes flashing. 'I'd go with you if I could. But Gaborn would know. He might even use his Earth Powers to hunt for me, and in wasting his precious time, I might place others in jeopardy. I can't risk that. So it seems that I must do as I'm told.'

'At least you'll be safe,' Myrrima said.

'There is no place in the world safer than at the Earth King's side,' Iome countered. 'That's where I want to be.'

Iome tossed her apple to the ground, and took Myrrima's hands. 'I'll miss you. Though you've saved my life twice now, I think of you as far more than a protector. I want you for my friend. Each day, I'll beg the Earth to guide you, until you hurry back.'

'I'll think of you too,' Myrrima said. She found it hard to speak, could add little more. Words didn't suffice. 'I wish you well, in the birthing of your son.'

Iome grinned, placed her left hand low on Myrrima's stomach, just above her womb. 'May you have a child of your own,' Iome intoned.

It was an old tradition in Heredon for a pregnant woman to offer a blessing upon her barren friends this way. It was merely a gesture of goodwill. Yet Myrrima felt a muscle spasm beneath Iome's hand, and stepped back quickly. For half a second she imagined that Iome's touch really could fill her empty womb.

Iome laughed. 'It will happen soon enough, now that your husband . . . I'm sorry if I've offended, or upset you,' Iome quickly added. 'I know that you and your husband have your troubles. I – only want the best for you.'

'No, it's all right,' Myrrima said. 'Thank you.' She couldn't hide her uneasiness. Myrrima dared not tell Iome that Borenson had never slept with her, and that she had lied about his miraculous restoration.

'Let me give you another gift,' Iome said, as if hoping to

atone for an unintended offense. 'You need a necklace – to make up for the one you gave away.' She reached around her own throat, where a necklace lay hidden beneath her tunic. 'I've been wearing this, for luck. You'll need it more than I.' She brought out the opal necklace that Binnesman had used to fight the Darkling Glory.

'Your Highness,' Myrrima said, 'I could never – I have no present to give you in return.'

'You gave me my life, and the life of my son.'

Iome put the necklace around Myrrima's neck, hugged her, and they walked hand in hand back upstream to find Borenson brushing the mounts.

Borenson said goodbye to the queen and leapt up into his saddle in a single fluid move, as Runelords do. Myrrima swung onto his warhorse, her back straight, her movements quick and efficient.

Myrrima wondered why Borenson didn't ask for his warhorse back, for it had more endowments than the little piebald mare he rode. Perhaps he no longer wanted it. His horse was a kingly mount, and Borenson was no longer the king's guard. The piebald mare he rode was more appropriate for a minor lord. The two rode south along the river, turned at a bend and waved back through the trees.

Iome stood among the silver-barked birches at the edge of the wood, waving in return.

Myrrima had a strange view of her then. It seemed right for Iome to be there in the woods, as natural as berries on a holly tree. There with the golden limbs hanging above her head, wearing her traveling robes of green, with a son growing in her womb and horses at her back, Iome looked a proper wife for an Earth King.

Iome waved farewell to Myrrima and Borenson. She felt miserable. Gaborn wanted her to be safe, protected. He wanted what was best for her.

But right now, she felt very much alone.

Her friends were riding to Inkarra. Gaborn planned to go to the Underworld. And she . . . would go where she was told while the world collapsed around her. She yearned to do more.

Iome had Sergeant Grimeson call the guard together and they headed east with the guards and wagons.

The golden plains soon dissipated, replaced by lands so rich that they remained green even at the last of summer, and great oaks pocked the fields. Cottages began to dot the landscape, and stone fences lined the highway.

People were soon everywhere, and as Iome's horse raced by, more often than not the farmers with their pigs or sheep or wagons would hardly have time to recognize her, much less doff a hat or bend the knee.

So their party was continually followed by cries of 'Was that the queen?' and 'Look, quick, there goes the queen!'

By late afternoon, Carris was but an evil memory. The aroma of living wheat fields supplanted the smell of dead grass; lordly pear orchards where starlings soared in riotous clouds were exchanged for the gray soot; the lowing of cattle as they grazed in the fields replaced the cries of children.

Iome felt invigorated.

Grimeson named the villages and cities for her as they passed, and sometimes would point out an ancient battlefield or spot of ground where history had unfolded. She soon realized that this unsightly little man had a fine head on his shoulders, and was cordial enough. But she wondered why Gaborn had chosen him to be her escort.

As evening gave way to night, Iome kept wishing to stop for a real meal at one of the inns that they passed. Time after time, she would smell the delicious aromas of ham cooking in a bed of leeks, or chicken savories, or warm bread fresh from the oven.

But the need was on her, and so she rode like a gale through the night, until, as Runelords do, she slept in the saddle, passing through a dream with a cool wind in her face, her hair flying.

Under starlight they rode, until one of the guards said, 'Milady?'

Iome blinked her eyes as she woke.

They came to a stop on a rise, and the dark ocean spread before them in every direction. Iome had never seen an ocean, had never smelled the bitter tang of salt so strongly mingled with life and decay. She had not conceived how endless its horizons would be.

Ahead lay several small islands, all spanned by elegant bridges made of white stone that were almost indiscernible from wisps of cloud in the moonlight.

She saw stretched out above them the soaring towers at the Courts of Tide, like silver spears taking aim at the horned moon.

Chapter Thirty-eight: A WIZARD'S PERSPECTIVE

Wizards never infringe upon the affairs of common men. It's just that common men sometimes get entangled in the affairs of wizards.

– The Earth Warden Binnesman

As afternoon dimmed into night, Averan watched Gaborn and various lords gathered in the council. They all sat on rocks and stumps that they had pulled into a circle near the creek. The reavers had been up on Mangan's Rock for nearly three hours, roosting there like crows. The sun slanted toward the horizon, and a cool breeze wafted out of the mountains, carrying with it the scent of pine.

The Rune of Desolation that the reavers formed was only just beginning to take shape. Many scarlet sorceresses had been slain in the march, along with the glue mums, so that this construct was growing slowly. But the sickly design was evident, and foul-smelling smokes rolled off the hill as if bubbling from a cauldron.

Still, Averan had to wonder. From Battle Weaver's memories, she knew that Battle Weaver had been sent here precisely because she had mastered the Rune of Desolation. Other reavers might duplicate portions of the rune, but each sorceress knew only a small piece of the whole.

Gaborn's men still held the plains in a vast circle. The

reavers' smoke burned a man's sinuses and made his eyes water. It was bad enough so that the frowth giants moved their camp well upwind of the rock. Yet there was still no sign of the blasting that had destroyed crops for miles around Carris.

To Averan, that seemed proof that the reavers were destined to fail at duplicating the rune.

But Gaborn was worried. He wanted the rune destroyed, and he wanted the Waymaker.

He huddled with dozens of lords: Skalbairn, Sir Langley, Queen Herin the Red, Duke Groverman, Jerimas, and dozens of others. They raised loud voices and planned to assault the rock.

Averan sat quietly at the edge of the circle.

There was a thrill of expectation in the air, the sense of a rising battle. 'I say we take artillery to them,' Skalbairn was saying. 'We put ballistas south of the rock, and shoot the reavers down until they retreat. Then we send Runelords up the cliffs on scaling ladders.'

Gaborn looked evenly at Skalbairn. 'I told you before: artillery won't work.'

'Of course it will work!' Skalbairn argued.

'The king's right,' Jerimas said. 'The reavers would just throw rocks back at us. There's no getting at them.'

'There has to be a way,' Queen Herin offered. 'What if we built large siege towers, attacked from downwind? We could draw the towers in fast, using force horses. We might gain some element of surprise.'

Gaborn shook his head sadly. 'The Earth warns against it.'

So he had said of every plan that the men propounded. The Earth did not grant him leave to act.

If only he could summon an earthquake, Averan thought, as he did at Carris. I'd see the reavers shaken from their perches, the whole hillside sliding into ruin.

But Gaborn could not summon earthquakes or world worms anymore. He could not even come up with a plan of attack. Always the Earth's counsel was the same: no.

Averan glanced up, found Gaborn gazing toward her, as if hoping she would come to his rescue. Averan leaned forward, wrapped her hands over her head. She felt as if it were crammed to bursting. Memories still rushed into her, even though her mind was full. It was as if she'd devoured a huge feast, and now sat torpid, bloated, and kept shoving snacks down her mouth.

She had a sudden vivid vision of the nesting site of the Soft Stone Clan where Keeper had hatched, down where the rocks were warm from magma. She recalled cutting her way out of a leathery sack at birth by using her egg tooth, only to be attacked by one of her older siblings while still weary from the ordeal.

Keeper had wrestled with his sister, ripping off a hind leg as she fled. It was a hollow victory, for Keeper would have been better nourished by his sister's corpse. Still, the leg provided him with his first real taste of flesh, and he fashioned the broken bone into a weapon, which he used to stab the next few hatchlings. He tore off the sweet musk glands beneath their forearms for nourishment and ate their brains, so that he quickly grew strong and wise.

Keeper's memories were macabre, fascinating, although sketchy. She remembered haunting fragments of incidents: reavers desperately placing huge stones to form a conduit so that magma rising around them would shoot up to heat an underground lake.

The discussion had hit a lull. In the background there was a yelp and the sound of a staff smacking flesh. Beneath the fallen oak behind them, Gaborn's captain was still training the wylde. He'd shown her how a runelord could use a staff to vault over the head of an enemy. Now he taught her how to whirl her staff to engage multiple attackers. Even without endowments of brawn, the green woman matched his expert maneuvers.

A voice of reason suddenly spoke up. It was Jerimas. 'We've been talking for hours now, and each time we come up with a plan, Gaborn says that the Earth forbids it. Are we sure that we even want the reavers off that rock?'

'What do you mean?' Skalbairn said in his deep voice. The huge warrior was sitting on a stone, sharpening his battle-ax. He tilted his head to hear the answer.

'I mean,' Jerimas said, leaning forward eagerly, so that his long silver beard nearly swept his knees, 'that Averan tells us that the reavers are suffering from thirst. Once they come off that rock, they're likely to head for the nearest drinking water – the water they left in Carris. Perhaps that's why the Earth warns us against attacking.'

'Aye,' Queen Herin said. 'I'm all for letting them sit up there till they dry up like jerk.'

'We can't wait,' Gaborn said. 'I have greater worries than Carris. I need the Waymaker.'

'For what it's worth, I don't think they'll go back to Carris,' Averan said. 'The mountains were too cold last night. They'll be afraid to try them again.'

'The weather has turned,' Skalbairn reasoned. 'It won't be that cold tonight.'

'The reavers don't know that,' Averan said. 'The weather is a mystery to them. To them, weather is just something that happens.'

Old Jerimas said, 'If the reavers feel too desperate, it may be that once they come off the rock, they'll simply attack in full force. We must leave them an escape route, a way that looks safe.'

'Agreed,' Gaborn said. 'We'll give them an open road to the south – for a while.' The wilds of Mystarria to the south were scarcely inhabited. Keep Haberd had been one of the largest fortresses, and now it was gone. 'But I'd still like to know what can get them off the rock.'

Averan glanced up. Everyone was looking at her expectantly. She shook her head. 'I don't know. I can't understand what they're doing up there. Only Battle Weaver knew how to build the Rune of Desolation.'

'They learn fast,' Gaborn said. 'Perhaps this new leader is feeling confident.'

'I'll tell you what can get them off that rock,' Skalbairn said to Averan. 'Fear. They have to be more frightened of staying up there than of leaving. What is it that reavers fear in the Underworld?'

Averan dredged up what images she could. There were lots of things. She recalled one reaver that had stepped on a creature that burrowed in the ground. It was long, with a thin tail that poked up. The tail had pierced the reaver's foot, and the small creature had injected its eggs.

Battle Weaver had used a spell to burn the eggs, but the wound was too deep, and the eggs were already in the reaver's blood. Thousands of parasites soon began hatching in the unfortunate reaver, so that it had to be cast into a pit.

There were other denizens of the Underworld that reavers feared or respected.

But one thing came to mind more than others, 'Smoke.'

'Of course,' Skalbairn said. 'Smoke in a closed tunnel. It would kill reavers as fast as it does men.'

Gaborn shook his head. 'Carris was burning, yet the reavers didn't flee. They're afraid of smoke, but not mindlessly so.'

A sudden disjointed image came to Averan's mind of Keeper handling a clutch of spider eggs, turning them over one by one so that the fluids inside wouldn't settle, and the eggs would eventually hatch. When no other reavers were near, he stuck one in his mouth.

To her surprise, Binnesman came to her rescue. 'Lords,

ladies,' the wizard said, 'I'm afraid my charge is done for a while.'

Binnesman took Averan's hand, drew her from the crowd.

'Binnesman?' Gaborn asked, surprised at his move.

But the wizard planted his staff in the ground. 'You ask too much of the girl. She's not a warrior, and she's not your counselor. She's an Earth Warden. It's time that she began her schooling.'

'Can't it wait?' Skalbairn demanded. His tone suggested that he would gladly fight the wizard.

'I think not,' Binnesman said. 'It's an important lesson. It has to do with obedience, and remembering one's place in the world.'

Gaborn stood up as if to challenge the wizard, but Binnesman stuck a gnarled finger in Gaborn's chest. 'It has to do with *obedience*, milord. You are not the Earth's warrior any more than this child is. When it is time to strike the reavers, the Earth will warn you as it has in the past, or maybe a lightning storm is already on its way, and will drive the reavers from the rock. Trust me – or trust the Power that we serve. The Earth knows the danger better than we do, and will prepare an escape. We must only do our part when the time comes.

'So, for now, I suggest that all of you lords get some rest. Have some dinner. Feed your horses. Maybe play a game of chess.'

Gaborn grinned coldly at the wizard. He had a twinkle in his eye. He nodded. '*That*,' Gaborn said, 'is the best advice I have heard all afternoon.'

Averan couldn't quite fathom it. She knew how desperately Gaborn needed to go to the Underworld. Time was so short.

Yet he agreed to bide his time, in hopes that the Earth would guide him. It seemed to Averan to be a terrible gamble.

Binnesman led Averan to his horse, helped her into the saddle. 'Where are we going?' Averan asked.

He nodded. 'Up into the mountains, to start your training.'

'Can Spring come with us?' She was still sparring with Gaborn's captain. He'd set down the staff, now began to teach her the use of the longspear.

'She has more important things to do,' Binnesman said, nodding in approval.

He climbed onto the saddle behind Averan, spurred the big gray Imperial stallion out over the prairie. The golden fields seemed to roll back beneath the horse's hooves, and the Runelords' camp fell behind.

'Why did you take me away from them?' Averan asked.

'Gaborn is trying too hard,' Binnesman said. 'He wants to attack, though the Earth warned him against it. He needs to learn his lesson. And you need a rest.'

His answer made sense, but Averan couldn't stop feeling guilty. She wanted to help Gaborn.

Binnesman reached behind his saddle, pulled his old oak staff from a sheath at his back, handed it to Averan.

As soon as her palm touched it, she felt . . . the wood thriving beneath her fingers. It was as if she touched a living tree, sun-warmed on a hill. She turned the staff over, studied it. The staff was perhaps five feet long, made of an oak limb that seemed to be polished a rich orange-brown from long handling. Near the top, a bit of leather had been tied around it as a grip, and the laces to the bindings held the only decorations: four large beads – one forged from silver, one from iron, one carved of reaver bone, and one of obsidian. The knob at the top had no fancy decorations, only a few runes delicately carved above the grip. There were no holes from woodworms, no cracks or blazes from a fire. All in all, it looked unremarkable.

But Averan could feel power surging within it.

'Do you sense it?' Binnesman asked. 'Earth Power is bound into that staff.'

'Yes,' Averan said.

'You must find your own staff. Any limb will do. All you have to do is ask a tree for it.'

'Any limb?' Averan asked, eyeing some willows along the creek up ahead.

'Not quite any,' Binnesman said. 'You must find the one that is right for you.'

'Is one kind better than another?' Averan asked. 'Could I take a willow limb?'

'A willow limb is good,' Binnesman said. 'A wizard who bears a willow staff will be strong in the healing arts, and will be closely allied to Water. Do you feel drawn to the willows?'

Averan studied the willows, their leaves flashing green and yellow in the sunlight. She didn't feel drawn to them, not the way that she'd felt drawn to sleep in the ground.

'No.' She pointed out, 'You have oak.'

'Oak is strong, and resists Fire,' Binnesman said.

Averan peered over her shoulder at him. There had been an odd tone to his voice, almost reverence for the oaks.

'What of other trees?' Averan asked. 'Do they have certain powers?'

'I wouldn't call them "powers,"' Binnesman said. 'Different trees have different personalities. The tree that you pick, the tree that picks you, is something of a gauge of an Earth Warden. Your choice will give me clues about the kinds of abilities that you will develop.'

'Are there kinds of staves you shouldn't want?'

Binnesman frowned. 'Some are weaker than others. There are some that I would not want. . . . But I'll say no more on the subject, child. I don't want to influence your decision.'

Averan glanced back at the willows that she was passing. They looked pretty with their leaves all going gold. She bit her lip. No, not willow.

Nor did she feel drawn to the oaks that stood like lonely sentinels on the plains, their limbs all twisted and bound with ivy. She barely glanced at a stand of prickly hawthorn by an outcropping of rock.

'Must I find one today?' Averan asked.

'No.' Binnesman chuckled. 'Your staff is important, and here at the base of the mountains are many kinds of trees. That's the only reason I mentioned it, so that you would be aware in that moment when you feel the trees calling you.'

He neared a second small stream.

'See the yellow clover,' Binnesman said as they passed. Averan nodded. 'It's called melilot. If you roll the golden leaves between your fingers and apply them to varicose veins, you can heal them in moments. It can also relieve swelling from bruises, and can be added to a compress of lamb's ear to stop bleeding wounds.'

The horse leapt the stream, and Binnesman said, 'As for the willows, you may not want a staff made of one, but you can steep the leaves to make a tea that will cure most pains, including those of a weakened heart. I find that if you pick them at midsummer it is best. Some old women prefer to strip the bark from the willow and use it, but the plant dies.'

Averan knew about willow bark, of course. The wizard drew rein and climbed down from his mount.

He picked the leaves from a flower with purple petals on the tip, light yellow in the center. 'This is heartsease,' he said. 'Silly girls not much older than you use it for love potions. Personally, I think that clean hair and an inviting smile do as much good. But if you chew the fresh leaves for a few minutes, you'll find that your mood brightens, and cares weigh less heavily on your mind.'

Averan put the leaves in her mouth. They had a pungent odor that seemed to open her chest, allow the air in easier. She chewed them thoughtfully as Binnesman remounted and rode along.

'If someone is following you, tie morning glory in a loop and cast it on the trail behind,' Binnesman said. 'Your enemies will get tangled in the brush.'

For long minutes he extolled the virtues of goosegrass and feverfew, elder flowers and smallage. As he did, his horse climbed the foothills until they reached the forest. There he stopped in the shade of some alders. In the higher hills Averan could see the red leaves of maples, tan leaves of beech, the greens and blues of pine and spruce.

Averan looked out over the fields to the south. Mangan's Rock was miles away. She cried out, 'From here you can't see the reavers at all!'

'It helps put the problem in perspective, doesn't it?' Binnesman said. 'Up close they're monsters, towering over you with dripping fangs. But from here . . . the Earth swallows them.'

Averan stared off. She didn't know what to say. The falling sun cast its slanting shadows. She could see the folds and undulations of the ground that she hadn't noticed in the full sunlight. The air had begun to cool.

'Gaborn wants me to come to the Underworld with him. Was I wrong to say yes?'

'What does your heart tell you?' Binnesman asked.

Averan felt inside. She hadn't noticed it, but all of her concerns, all the fears that had paralyzed her today, were suddenly gone, lifted by the heartsease. For the first time she felt as if she could really look at her problems.

'I'm not afraid. Not now.'

'Good,' Binnesman said. 'You're not a child going into the Underworld: you're an Earth Warden. The Earth can hide you. The Earth will heal you. The Earth will make you its own. You must understand that. You're not a child any longer. You're a powerful wizard. And I'm coming with you, of course, as is Spring.'

'Good.' Averan felt genuinely relieved.

'But you must promise me something,' Binnesman said. 'You must promise to remember what you are.'

'A wizard?' she asked.

'An Earth Warden. You are here to protect the small things of the world.'

'Yes?' She could tell by his tone that she had done something wrong.

'Don't let Gaborn mislead you. You are not here to fight reavers – that much I can assure you.'

'I'm protecting people,' Averan objected.

'It's only natural to want to protect your own kind,' Binnesman said. 'But mankind is not your domain. You aren't called to serve it.'

'How can you know?' Averan asked.

'Because it is my domain,' Binnesman said forcefully. 'There is only one Earth Warden to a species. It is my duty to watch over and heal mankind. You – I don't know what you're here for.'

'You're getting old,' Averan said. 'What happens when you die? Won't you need a replacement?' She liked the idea of carrying on in his stead.

'When the Earth no longer needs my services,' Binnesman said, 'then I'll be released. Not before.'

'I won't take over your charge?'

'No,' Binnesman said. 'When I am gone, mankind will either be saved or destroyed. But in either case, the danger will have run its course.'

Averan looked up and, despite the heartsease, his words filled her with sadness. She could not comprehend how he must feel, knowing that he bore such a weight on his shoulders.

'How can you even talk about it?' she wondered.

'If mankind is swept away,' Binnesman said with a wise nod, 'I will grieve. But in time a new kind of men will arise to take their place. They may be as different from us as we are from the Toth. But life will go on.'

Binnesman stared off toward Gaborn's army at Mangan's Rock for a long moment. His blue eyes seemed unnaturally clear in the fading sun, and shadows filled every crease in his face.

'Now, girl, to work.'

For a long hour he schooled her. He pulled seven small white agates from his pocket, and laid them out on the ground. 'I apologize that these are all I have. Such small stones are of limited use, but they may come in handy.'

He drew runes about them in the dirt, and then called forth images in the stones. At first it was simply mountain ridges as seen from the ground – blue in the distance with a dusting of snow. Averan could look uphill and see the same ridges, overhead.

But then Binnesman began to move the stones about. Each time he set a stone down, the viewpoint changed. She saw the roads that they had traveled this morning as they followed the reavers' trail – all as if she were standing on some high escarpment, looking down. The sound of wind rushing over the hills issued from the pebbles, and she could smell the twisted pines there among the rocks.

The stones are showing me what stones see, she realized.

She saw more than just roads. She saw lakes and hills, a bear running over a ridge, huffing and grunting. She saw carters driving wains south from Carris, their wheels squeaking and horses whinnying, and a long line of people fleeing that city.

Binnesman dabbled with his stones, as if searching for something in particular. At last she witnessed movement in one valley. Binnesman adjusted his stones, twisting one. The scene changed to a much closer view. She saw Skalbairn's knights in the mountains, flushing a scarlet sorceress from the pines on a ridge. It was growing dark now. Thirty men had her surrounded, and the monster was digging in the sod, desperately trying to escape by burying herself.

Just downhill, eight blade-bearers lay dead.

'That's what I was looking for,' Binnesman whispered. 'Gaborn sent his riders to hunt for any reavers that might have escaped. It looks as if they've found some.'

'A throng of nines,' Averan corrected. Reavers often traveled in threes or multiples of threes. For an important mission, nine was a minimum number.

Several men charged into the trees, rode the sorceress down, lancing her from behind. Averan could not merely see the men, she could hear their shouts, the jangle of armor, the pounding of horses' hooves, the wing beats of a startled grouse, and the rasping breath of the reaver.

When he finished, Binnesman waved his hands over the agates, and the image dissipated. He seemed thoughtful. 'So, Gaborn was right. The reavers down on Mangan's Rock were trying to divert his forces while they sent a warning.'

Averan knew that the danger was far from over. Perhaps he'd won a small round, but there were still nearly sixty thousand reavers down on Mangan's Rock, and they would not wait for long.

Binnesman moved three of the pebbles and said, 'Now, look into the stones yourself and draw forth an image. Do not try to picture what you will see. I've moved the stones so that nothing I've shown you will appear again. Instead, I want you to merely open yourself to what they will show you. Once you unlock the power of the stones, you can change your viewpoint by moving them.'

He instructed her for long minutes, but no matter how hard she tried, she could not manage to draw forth any image at all. She struggled to imagine things, tried not to imagine anything – it didn't matter.

The stones remained mere stones under her hands.

Binnesman pocketed them at last and said, 'Don't worry. It may be that in time you will develop the skill.'

'What if I never learn to do it?' Averan said.

'Not all wizards need all powers,' Binnesman consoled her. 'You already have a gift that I don't: you can learn from reavers. That's a very strange gift – a powerful one, I'd think.'

He sighed, looked contemplative.

'I know,' he said. 'I have another idea. Try this: close your eyes and imagine a deer in the forest, any deer at all.'

Averan did. At first she tried to imagine a spotted fawn, lying in a bed of ferns.

But Keeper's memories still flowed to her, and she recalled a scene of herself learning to gut one of the great horn beetles. Her master was instructing her in the art, saying, 'Pull off its head-plate first, to get at the brains.'

Averan recoiled from the image that assailed her. For a moment she stood blinking, trying to dredge up any image of a deer.

She imagined a stag, a huge stag with antlers as wide as tree limbs.

'Do you have it?' Binnesman asked.

'Yes,' Averan said.

'Good. Hold the image in your mind. Think of nothing else. Try to look closely at the animal, imagine its details. Every deer is different. There are males and females, different ages, different shades of red or tan. How does it look? What sounds does it make? How does it smell? What details separate it from any other deer in the woods? Hold the image in your mind and think of nothing else.'

For ten long minutes she did just that. She imagined a stag, an old buck with silver hairs in his coat, a ragged right ear from a battle. He had six tines on his left antler, and eight on his right.

The image came so vividly that she could see his nostrils

flaring as he breathed, the way he ducked his head and flashed his tail at a strange scent. She could smell the musk of him, strong now that mating season was on.

She pictured him in her mind until she *heard* the buck. Sounds came, and at first she was not sure if she just imagined them: the buck snorting as it tested the air for her scent. She heard it swish through brush, step on a dry twig, and bound twice downhill as if startled by its own noise.

The sound wasn't fantasized. She felt sure of that. The snap of the twig echoed twice in her memory. The first time it came loud and clear, as if she heard it with the stag's ears. The second time it was a distant snap, up the hill. The same was true with its bounding.

She felt . . . as if she didn't merely hear it. She felt as if she were dredging the creature up from a dream, giving it form.

She waited, heart hammering, expectant, until she discerned the thud of hooves draw close. Still she kept her eyes closed.

'Hold out your hand,' Binnesman ordered.

She did. She reached out with her palm upward, and the stag drew near. The moist hairs of its muzzle brushed against her wrist, and his warm breath spread over her palm.

'Now open your eyes,' Binnesman instructed.

When she did, Averan gasped. She'd expected a stag, any stag, to have appeared at her summons.

But the stag nuzzling her hand was exactly the one she'd envisioned, complete with the fly that it flicked from its rump.

She stroked its muzzle, and the stag stood for her touch as if he were a faithful pet.

'Did I *make* him?' Averan asked.

'What do you think?' Binnesman said.

'No, I couldn't have made him. But he looks . . .'

'You envisioned him because he was near. Your mind

sought for him, and found him, and he answered your call. It is a common enough power among Earth Wardens. And because you have it, I suspect even more strongly that you are here to protect an animal of some kind.'

'Not a rock?' Averan teased.

But Binnesman's lesson was not done. He said sternly, 'This is not a small matter. Each Earth Warden has his own charge, and each is of equal import. To answer his calling, each Earth Warden develops different powers. I could never summon animals. All that I know of the art is hearsay. But you are quite powerful. I tested you with a deer, and you summoned it the very first time.'

'Are deer hard?'

'The more complex the intellect, the keener the mind, the more difficult it is to summon an animal. Had you failed with a deer, I'd have had you try a mouse or a bug.'

'So a deer is harder than a mouse, and a man is harder than a deer?'

'Only the very greatest of summoners can call forth a man.'

'Can they be summoned even if they are dead?' She was thinking of Brand, Roland, and her mother.

'They can,' Binnesman said. 'It is nothing at all like summoning a living being. It is far easier to summon the dead. Even I can do that.'

'Really?'

'Who do you think called the spirit of Erden Geboren to Longmot?' He pointed a finger at his own chest.

Averan wondered at that. Her summoning seemed a marvelous power. 'Can a creature refuse the summons?'

'Yes,' Binnesman said. 'In a sense, the stag here thinks it came of its own volition. And it did. You performed the summoning, and the stag answered in return. But it could have refused.'

Averan placed her hand on the stag's muzzle and stroked it. She smiled.

Binnesman stepped closer, gazed at the stag. 'Now,' he said softly, 'look into its eyes. Peer into them, and tell me what you see.'

Averan continued petting the stag, scratched under its jaw. She'd never imagined that she could get so close to a wild animal and have it become so tame. But she remembered how Brand always used to say that even with the graaks, she had a gentle touch.

She peered into its deep brown eyes, looked far behind. She smelled the scent of men – woolen cloaks and horse sweat and armor and the sour odor of human flesh. It came strong to the stag's nostrils, and involuntarily the muscles in its calves quivered. It remembered a hunt long past – the yammer of hounds as it fled mounted archers. It started backward, as if to leap away.

'Fear,' Averan said. 'The stag's fear is a terrible thing. There are too many men in the woods today, Runelords charging about on horses. It's made him wary.'

Binnesman crouched at her side as Averan let the stag bound away. It took six great leaps, then stood at the edge of the trees, head held high, as it froze in profile for a moment. At last it stalked back into the shadows, and began to feed.

'Very good,' Binnesman said. 'You have a power that I never gained. I could never summon animals, and I could never see into the minds of people. I've always had to settle for talking to them.'

'But – the way you looked at me when we met! I was sure that you knew what I was thinking.'

'Ah, well. When you're as old as I am, you don't need Earth Powers to read the minds of children.' Binnesman said, 'My mentor, on the other hand, used his powers often. He looked into the minds of birds and rabbits to find out who had passed along a trail before him, or who might be following. . . .'

By now the shadows had grown long. Night was enfolding the land. The sweet smell of autumn straw from the plains below mingled with the scent of alder bark and dying leaves in the woods above. Wild pigeons cooed in the hills.

Binnesman and Averan sat in the grass. Campfires burned like diamonds upon the black plain, and strange blue lights flickered and throbbed over Mangan's Rock.

Book 10:

Day 3 in the Month of Leaves

A Day of Mages

Chapter Thirty-nine: ASGAROTH

Our world is but a shadow of the One True World.
You are but an intimation of the Bright Ones.
– *Excerpt from the* Creation Saga

Erin and Celinor rode through the day without event. Their journey around Beldinook had slowed them to a crawl, for even their fast force horses could not negotiate the rocky streambeds and steep trails easily. By nightfall they'd skirted the southern tip of Beldinook and reached the plains of Fleeds. Clouds were rolling in, and now darkness and an approaching storm slowed them once again.

They stopped at a good roadside inn and had their first decent meal of the day – rye bread and a trencher of gravy made of stewed starlings in rosemary. On the side were scallions and parsnips cooked in butter and honey.

After dinner they went to bed and lay in one another's arms. Celinor held Erin for a long while, and she wondered at it. She'd never slept in a man's arms before. She loved his touch, but knew that it would not make for a restful sleep. She wondered how long men and women needed to sleep together before they got used to it.

Celinor seemed distracted, Erin more so.

'Tomorrow is the day,' he whispered. She knew what he meant. Tomorrow they would reach South Crowthen, probably late in the afternoon. They would meet his father, and try to discover how deep his madness went.

'Promise me that you won't do anything rash,' Celinor asked. 'My father has always been a good man. He treated me well as a child. If he has gone mad, let me deal with it in my own way.'

She knew what he wanted. Celinor had said that his grandfather had gone mad, and had to be locked away beneath the castle, until he finally died of old age. It was a family curse, apparently. Celinor had promised his father that if the curse ever struck, he would lock him away. Erin did not envy Celinor his duty.

'All right,' she conceded. 'But be careful. Some men, you can see the madness in their eyes. Others can hide it. Your father is dangerous.'

Celinor nodded. His father was plotting against the Earth King, and had already gained some support. Anders claimed that Gaborn had masterminded the death of his own father in order to gain the throne.

'My father isn't a danger to us,' Celinor said. 'He's just . . . so confused. I'll talk to him.'

'Be careful what you say,' Erin said. 'Your father is a smart man, a cunning man.'

Celinor seemed to think a moment, then said, 'He would think it a compliment if you told him so. Why do you call him cunning?'

'I've been thinking about what you said. Your father told you that I was Gaborn's sister . . .'

'It's an interesting deduction,' Celinor said. 'Given the habits of the horsesisters, it makes sense that your mother would choose a sire from a noble line. You look as if you could be Gaborn's sister. And you were born nine months after old King Orden's hunting party passed through Fleeds. . . .'

'I know who my father is,' Erin said. She did not know if

she dared tell him. The truth was as bad as the lie. 'I've seen the genealogy. My mother chose a sire from House Orden, but it was not Mendellas. She thought there was a better man in the party – Paldane.'

'Of course – you're not his sister, but his cousin!' Celinor said. 'Better breeding, but without the title.'

He saw her dilemma. Paldane was Gaborn's uncle. As Paldane's only offspring, Erin was still his heir by Mystarrian law. So even though she wasn't Gaborn's sister, her predicament remained.

Celinor held silent for a long moment. She knew what he was thinking. By the laws of her people, they were wed. Celinor was a prince of South Crowthen, and now he had married into the family of House Orden. If Gaborn died, Celinor could assume the throne of Mystarria.

She wondered if he was tempted by the prospect.

At last he whispered, 'You must never reveal that to anyone, especially to my father.' Erin didn't plan to, but she wondered just how much Anders knew, or guessed at.

Erin tried to sleep, but her mind could not rest. She kept recalling her dream during the afternoon, the great owl of the netherworld summoning her.

She knew that dreams were often just bits and pieces of memories. Could it have been that alone? It had seemed so real. Yet some things did not quite make sense, if the dream came only from memories. The owl had called a 'warrior of the Shadow World.' Erin had heard that the netherworld was sometimes called 'the One True World,' but she'd never heard of her world referred to as a shadow world. And the details of the place were like nothing she'd ever conceived.

For a long time, she lay, afraid to sleep, but finally slipped off to slumber. . . .

She woke in the owl's lair. It was daylight now, and an early-morning sun streamed under the branches of the tree. It barely lit the burrow. The owl sat high up on its perch, as it had before. Beneath it lay a pile of bones: squirrel, rabbit and fawn. Her dagger still sat there, piercing the skull of some froglike creature.

The owl's eyes were closed, and it breathed softly. She could smell it more strongly now, its oily feathers, the scent of blood and old bones.

The burrow descended farther into the ground, a tunnel. Sconces in the wall suggested that it had been dug with human hands, but had long lain unused. Arcane symbols were carved into the living wood of the tree, runes unlike any that Erin had ever seen before.

'You have returned. Thank you for coming in our hour of need,' the owl whispered. Erin glanced up. The owl still breathed softly. The beast did not speak in her tongue, yet its words pierced her, filled her with understanding and communicated emotion all at once. She felt its deepest gratitude.

'I didn't come,' Erin said uneasily. 'You brought me. I don't deserve your gratitude.'

'Don't you wish to be here?' the owl asked. 'You answered the summons. Is this not your dagger?'

Erin blinked, looked around in the shadows for some avenue of escape. 'I only thought of coming because I was looking for help.'

'Ah, you have troubles in your world?' Erin sensed amusement in the question.

'To put it mildly,' she said.

The owl shifted on its limb, peered at her. 'The hope of our world may rest on you.'

'The hope of *your* world?'

'Perhaps the hope of both our worlds. Asgaroth has come to your realm.'

The name Asgaroth struck Erin like a mace. The owl's words were heard by the heart more than the ears. They conveyed knowledge, seemed to inscribe it upon Erin's bones. Asgaroth was the Darkling Glory that had attacked Castle Sylvarresta. He was a lord of tremendous power. His name struck terror into the hearts of Bright Ones and Glories alike.

'Asgaroth!' she said. 'He's dead.'

'Dead?' the owl asked. 'A mighty warrior you may be, but even a Fury Blade could not kill a *locus*.'

Erin bolted awake, sat up in her bed. Celinor stirred beside her, tried to hold her close. But her heart still hammered. She could not rest, could not sleep. She felt certain that if she slumbered, she would only awaken in the netherworld.

And right now, her head felt near to bursting. The owl's words had pierced her so. This was not the stuff of dreams. The words that the owl used were unfamiliar. In all of Rofehavan, there was no word for a being called the 'locus.'

Yet in a flash she understood. A locus was a creature that housed itself within the mind of a vile man or beast. It entered like a parasite, but soon assumed control of its host.

Asgaroth was a great ruler among them, an evil that had existed from time immemorial. He was not a Darkling Glory. He was something much more, a powerful servant of a darker master. A thousand, thousand Shadow Worlds he had helped to destroy in a war that would rage through eternities.

Chapter Forty:
A MIGHTY WIND

The beings that men call 'ferrin' have their own names for themselves, which are known to the wise. There are three distinct subspecies. The woodland ferrin are the largest, and perhaps the least fierce. Their range covers hills and woods throughout most of Rofehavan. The water ferrin have a darker fur, prefer moist habitats, and are excellent swimmers. The desert ferrin has short, sandy hair, and seems well adapted to its own harsh environment.

None of the breeds survive well in the snow. I have seldom seen one even fifty miles north of Castle Sylvarresta.

It is well documented that ferrin were brought from beyond the Caroll Sea by one Yakor the Bold, apparently for the express purpose of ridding his realm of rats and the plagues that they carry. They serve the purpose well in southern climes, but are considered a nuisance even by those who benefit from them, for though ferrin spread no disease, they eat far more than their smaller counterparts.

– *Excerpt from* Binnesman's Beastiary: Mammals of the World

As King Anders took dinner, the dying screams of men suddenly filled his castle.

They came in through the uppermost tower and whirled down the stairwell. The wind carried the sound down to the Great Hall, then swirled up again through the chimney.

To an ear that was not attuned, it sounded like a simple moaning wind. But Anders had been listening for that sound all afternoon.

For a moment, the fire flared.

Anders's wife felt the draft and said, 'Oh my.'

Anders had hoped to hear a woman's dying cry. But only five voices mingled in that scream, and all were male.

Anders raised his head and held a goblet of wine up to his latest guests: a Duke Stote from Lonnock, and Prince Grunensen from Eyremoth.

The prince was talking. He was a big strapping lad with soft dark hair and the mannerisms of a girl. 'I can't abide travel by ship,' he was saying. 'The last time I rode one, the galley was full of rats. They spread diseases, you know. That's why I travel by land. At least in the inns, the ferrin keep their number down.'

'I thought it was too cold in Eyremoth for either rats or ferrin,' Duke Stote jested.

'Milord,' Anders's wife hissed into his ear, dismayed at the turn in conversation at the dinner table.

He smiled. The conversation would surely turn to grimmer matters than rats. 'A toast,' King Anders said, 'to friends from far lands.'

The guests smiled coldly, drank. It was a quiet dinner, filled with clumsy conversation and long silences. Anders excused himself between courses and climbed his tower.

There he stood looking far to the south. Iome was so far away. He could do little from here.

His attack had been clumsy, inelegant. His master was not pleased. Perhaps . . .

For a long while he thought about rats. Huge rats, black as

coal, burrowing beneath houses. Fat rats on the wharf, feeding on fish heads. Sleek rats in the woods climbing the trees. Rats that carried pestilence and disease.

A notion took him. There were few men so susceptible to his spells that they would fight in his behalf. He had used up three already. But wars did not always need to be fought with men and arms.

Still, to send rats? To call down a plague upon a whole nation – the old, the infirm, women, and children?

In some bright corner of his mind, the man that Anders had once been cried out, The notion is monstrous!

Anders thought himself to be a hard man. He was a king after all. He'd ordered the execution of a highwayman when he was twelve. He'd fought men in battle.

He'd thought little of sending men to kill Iome.

But he'd never brought death upon innocents in such a wholesale fashion.

A cold wind tugged at the hair around his ear and whispered, It would please me.

'No!' he said aloud, shaking his head vehemently

A cold gust slapped his back. The iciness took his breath. His head seemed to reel, and for a moment he felt dazed, as if he were drunk and spinning.

He suddenly trembled in fear, realizing that the rough paving stones stretched wide below, so close, so very close. He clung to the merlons as the wind rushed at his back. It would take so little to push him over.

Please me, a voice whispered in his ear.

For a second, Anders felt desperate. He'd sought to serve the wind, hoping that it would serve him in return. To some degree it did. Now, he saw that it could turn on him at any moment. He was in its thrall, would either do its bidding, or be discarded.

The cold wind pummeled him, slashing at his thin robes and tunic like a blade. It pierced his heart.

He suddenly stood tall and let the coldness seep into him. 'Come, my warriors,' he whispered. 'Come.'

The wind had been blowing from the south all day. Now the wizard on the weather vane of the highest tower turned and pointed to the west.

The wind beat down with a new ferocity.

Presently, Anders could hear sounds in the streets, the patter of tiny feet, the squeaking of small voices. He looked down in the deepening shadows, saw dark shapes darting across the cobblestones.

A terrier leapt out, barking, grabbed one of the small beasts. It shrieked in pain as the terrier broke its back.

But the rats continued to rise up from beneath the city. They scuttled out of drains and sewers, came leaping out of barns. They scurried down from trees and crawled up from beneath rotting floors. They went racing over the rooftops in furry little packs, flowing out the castle walls in a dark tide, casting off dank turds in their wake.

Here and there in the city below, a woman would cry out as she discovered a pack of rats scampering beneath her feet.

People would talk about it for days, Anders knew, the mysterious exodus of rats. But he needed them, the dirty little beasts, with their penchant for spreading disease.

They fled the city under the cover of darkness, traveling east with the wind.

Anders whispered softly to the south, 'Iome, come home. Your land needs you.'

He had hardly finished when his wife came up to the tower. 'Are you going to stay here all night? You have guests, you know.'

King Anders smiled.

Chapter Forty-one: FARION'S FATHER

Farion is the Queen of Slumber. She rewards good children by leading them into fair realms of dream, and punishes the wicked by directing them along dark paths into the lands of the twisted phantasms.

To win her favor, a child who has been bad may leave a piece of fruit or a sweet by his bed.

– A myth from Ashoven

Stars smoldered in the cold heavens above Mangan's Rock. Sunset was gone an hour ago, and still the reavers sat on their pile of stones, casting their spells.

Wains filled with supplies had arrived from Castle Fells, and Gaborn's army was well fed for the night. Many lords lay in their bedrolls, taking the first real slumber they'd had in days.

Everything seemed quiet, yet Gaborn sat beside his campfire, poised, pensive. He could sense danger approaching his perimeter guards.

Baron Waggit, who was acting as a sentry, called out to Gaborn from the edge of his campfire, 'Milord, Skalbairn says that there's something you should see.'

Immediately Gaborn came alert, sensing danger. Yes, he could feel trouble brewing along the perimeter. He got up, with his Days in attendance, and followed Baron Waggit.

The big man's yellow hair shone like silk in the starlight, and his back looked broad enough to ride. Watch fires burned steadily in a ring around Mangan's Rock, every two hundred yards.

Sounds carried preternaturally in the cool night air. Gaborn could hear the rasping of the reavers' breath, as if the monsters had crawled closer in the darkness. Smoke still roiled from the top of Mangan's Rock, and blue lights crackled around the Rune of Desolation.

As Gaborn followed, he spotted other sentries out on the plains in their pale livery, starlight reflecting from arms and helms.

He came upon Skalbairn. The big High Marshal had saddled his mount, and stood in the darkness bearing a lance in one hand, the reins of his horse in the other. He gazed longingly over the plains. Marshal Chondler stood watch at his side. They were nearly a mile from the base of Mangan's Rock.

Chondler was whispering, 'You are either the bravest man I ever knew, or more of a fool than I'd have given you credit for.'

'He's no fool,' Waggit boomed. 'You have the word of an expert on that.'

Skalbairn slapped the baron on the back in a friendly greeting.

Gaborn strode up behind the men. 'What's going on?'

'A reaver, Milord,' Skalbairn said. 'A monstrous big one, behind those rocks. I want to kill her.'

Gaborn followed his gaze. Behind three humped rocks, a scarlet sorceress ambled on the valley floor. The huge creature glimmered softly, her entire body covered in fiery runes. She circled as if in a daze, dragging her rear legs like one wounded. She was less than half a mile off, about midway between the men and Mangan's Rock.

'How did she get there?' Gaborn asked.

'We saw her climbing down the cliff,' Chondler said. 'She was about a hundred yards up when she slipped and fell. Since then, she's been wandering all over the field, much as you see her now.'

Gaborn considered attacking, felt inside himself. The notion aroused a sense of near panic.

'Leave her,' Gaborn said. 'She's not as helpless as she seems.'

'Ah, if only I had a ballista out here,' Chondler said, 'I'd plant a bolt through her gizzard.'

'We have ballistas,' Gaborn told him. 'They came on the wains about an hour ago.'

Chondler and Waggit looked at each other gleefully. Gaborn felt inside himself. . . . Yes, it would be safe to get in range of the monster. He urged, 'Go get the ballistas.'

Chondler and Waggit hurried off into the darkness, leaving Gaborn alone with Skalbairn.

'You've taken a liking to Waggit,' Gaborn observed.

Skalbairn grunted. 'He's a good man, I think. Perhaps good enough for the likes of my daughter, Farion. I've long thought that she'd need a kind man, someone who will not condemn her for her weakness. She's a bit simple, you see.'

Gaborn said nothing.

'You know,' Skalbairn said, nodding toward Chondler, 'that man may serve you yet.'

'You mean he doesn't now?'

Skalbairn shook his head. 'He's sworn to the Brotherhood of the Wolf. He doesn't completely trust your judgment. He thinks you . . . too much a gentleman.'

Gaborn chuckled at the notion.

'He's serious, milord,' Skalbairn said. He related Chondler's tale of the charitable mother and her grasping son, then said, 'Chondler claims that there is only one virtue, milord: moderation. And even that is not a virtue when practiced to excess.'

'By his argument,' Gaborn countered, 'I should account myself worthy so long as I give as much as I steal, or tell the truth as often as I lie.'

'He'd say that a good man gives *more* than he steals,' Skalbairn said, 'and rescues *more* than he butchers.'

'That seems a damned convenient argument.'

'Very convenient,' Skalbairn said. 'It saves the mind a good deal of contemplation and assuages much guilt.'

Gaborn felt angry. He saw Chondler's points: men do train themselves to see their vice as virtue; and a virtue carried to excess can become a vice.

But Gaborn believed that wrongs were more solid, like rocks jutting in a harbor. Any man of conscience could steer the course between them. To do anything else led to guilt and suffering. Chondler's arguments were not merely circular, they seemed contrived to deceive. 'What do you think about this?'

'I can't very well fault you for your kindness,' Skalbairn said. 'After all, I am the recipient of your generosity.'

'I was wrong to Choose Raj Ahten,' Gaborn said. 'I see that now. Was I also wrong to Choose you?'

Skalbairn shook his head. 'I don't know. Obviously, I wouldn't think so. You saved my life six times yesterday in the battle for Carris. I'm in your debt. I intend to repay you.'

Gaborn looked at the man. He stood holding his lance, gazing out toward the scarlet sorceress on the plain. A falling star flashed through the heavens above Mangan's Rock, blazing a trail of light.

During the height of the battle yesterday, Gaborn had sent warning to many people, so many thousands of times, that he could not guess how many lives he'd saved.

Out in the fields behind Skalbairn, there was a sudden *whunk* – the sound of falling dirt and stones. Gaborn turned, saw a plume of dust rising. Not a hundred yards west of a watch fire, the ground had caved in, leaving a gaping hole some thirty feet wide.

'What's that?' Skalbairn shouted.

Instantly, Gaborn realized what had happened, why the feeling of portent around his guards kept rising. The reavers were digging underground, trying to flank his men!

But they'd tunneled under a rock that could not hold.

He saw their plan. Averan had said that none of the reavers here could build a Rune of Desolation. The reavers had stopped because they were thirsty, terrified, and desperate.

Now he suspected that she was right.

A plan blossomed in Gaborn's mind. 'Strike,' the Earth said. 'Strike now!'

'Blow retreat!' Gaborn shouted. 'Get our men away from the watch fires. Have our troops form up by the creek.'

Gaborn turned and raced into the darkness. 'What?' Skalbairn called, 'are we going to flee?'

'No!' Gaborn shouted. 'We're going to attack. I know how. I should have thought of it before.

'We have seen wonders today. Wait a moment, and I will show you one more.'

Chapter Forty-two: CROW'S BAY

Nine worldships built Fallion of old,
and set them sail from the Courts of Tide.
And filled them all with warriors bold,
to hunt the Toth, across oceans wide.
– From the 'Ballad of Fallion'

Iome had sometimes tried to imagine the Courts of Tide, but imagination had failed her.

She knew that the city was set upon a number of islands, and she'd heard of the famous bridges that spanned them. The bridges were carved of crystal shipped from the Alcair Mountains on huge barges.

The stones did indeed vault from island to island, and though she'd fairly imagined the bridges to look as pale and translucent as ice in the moonlight, she had never envisioned their fine pillars. Each was cut in the form of a heroic figure that represented some virtue that the Runelords of Mystarria aspired to. Nurture was a woman who nursed a daughter in her arms. Courage was a stout warrior with a wavy-bladed dagger in hand, straddling a serpent that sought to entangle him. Charity was a lord hunched beneath a sack full of fruits and wheat, bearing it to the poor.

The sheer scale of the works was impressive. Ships could sail beneath the soaring bridges.

Though Iome had heard of the king's Great Tower in Mystarria, the tallest edifice in all Rofehavan, she'd never visualized a tower that was three hundred feet tall. Even now she could make out the tiny figures of Mystarria's vigilant far-seers, making their rounds on its highest ramparts.

Yet upon entering the city, she also saw the price that Mystarria's kings paid for this haven. Land was at a premium, and though the streets were free of clutter and well tended, they were also remarkably narrow. She rode as if through a chasm. In many places overhead, marble walkways and plazas spanned from building to building, so that as Iome's retinue neared Gaborn's palace, they traveled through tunnels where crystalline lanterns hung from black iron rungs. The sea wind cut through with its chill breeze.

Iome gaped up at the soaring citadels and remarkable stonework and tried to keep from gasping at each new fountain or frieze or hanging garden.

Sergeant Grimeson and the knights of Mystarria tried to keep from looking too pleased by her reaction.

But over and over again, she found herself letting her mouth fall open no matter how hard she tried to keep it shut. She didn't want to look like some bumpkin who'd never strolled beyond the border of his village, but that is precisely how she felt.

'You should have seen it first in the morning,' Sergeant Grimeson said, 'when the rising sun colors the towers gold.' They had to ride slowly now, and he seemed thoughtful, as if the words did not come easily to him. 'The sunlight slants down through those towers, and fills the streets. You'll see hummingbirds and sunbirds in shades of emerald and scarlet and streaks of blue streak through the hanging gardens to search for nectar. It's like – by the Powers, it can be pretty.'

Hummingbirds were the pride of Mystarria. Before the Toth wars, they'd never been seen here. But after Fallion destroyed the invading armies, he sent ships to far lands beyond the Carroll Sea to hunt down the last of the Toth. In those far lands his men found many wonders, and King Fallion himself brought back the hummingbirds as a gift for his people. They first began nesting here at the Courts of Tide.

I am the queen of this realm, Iome had to remind herself, the richest and finest in all of Rofehavan. Yet I feel like some barbarian from the frozen north.

She fell in love with the Courts of Tide, and just as quickly knew that she could never belong.

So she rode to the palace at midnight, and entered. Sergeant Grimeson ordered servants to 'throw together a feast' in the grand reception hall while his men delivered the forcibles to the treasury.

Iome pulled out Gaborn's instructions. He'd given her a note commanding Grimeson alone to contact a certain Abel Scarby so that he could secure the dogs that he needed. Gaborn wrote directions for finding the man's house down an alley near the docks. But a cryptic message near the bottom warned Grimeson never to reveal where Scarby lived.

'Who is this Scarby fellow?' Iome asked Grimeson. 'Why would Gaborn want to keep his whereabouts secret?'

'He's the best damned dogfighter in the realm. He spends most of his time evading the King's Guard. I can handle him.'

A dogfighter. He *sounded* thoroughly disreputable, as disreputable as Grimeson looked.

'And my husband knows this man well?'

'Well?' Grimeson said. 'Of course! Why, they're old friends.'

Iome was astonished that Gaborn knew either man on a first-name basis.

Gaborn needed good dogs. Though she suspected that Grimeson could handle this Scarby fellow, curiosity drove her to say, 'If he's Gaborn's friend, I'd like to meet him. I'm coming with you.'

'But Your Highness, dinner is cooking!'

'It can wait until we get back. This is far more important.'

Grimeson nodded reluctantly, for there was nothing more that he could do.

In moments they were on fresh horses, and Grimeson let them canter through the city. The streets were empty so late at night, except for the occasional alley cat or ferrin.

In minutes they reached the seamy side of the city, in Crow's Bay, where cramped shanties and inns perched along the sea wall, and the smell of dead fish, whale oil, urine, and boiled crab hung heavy in the air. Soot blackened the stonework on ancient buildings.

Though it was late of the night, music and raucous laughter escaped the open doors of the hostels. Everywhere, bandy-legged men lounged about on ale kegs, and painted whores laughed and advertised their wares. Old women cleaned and mended fishnets by lantern light, while seagulls wheeled and cried in the night as they scavenged for scraps. Children scampered to and fro like wharf rats.

This part of the city never slept. Near dawn, the boats would go out with the tide, and so long as no leviathans were sighted, they'd not return until sundown.

From time to time Iome could glimpse between various shops, inns, and fisheries out to the thousands of fishing boats – coracles and trimarines – moored in the horseshoe-shaped bay. They bobbed like bits of cork bark on the star-dusted water. Many boats had serpent heads carved at the prows, with white runes of steadiness and wayfinding painted on as eyes.

Sergeant Grimeson slowed his mount and entered one dark alley where sooty buildings leaned together. Iome had the good sense to know that she should never go in there alone – at least not if she were a commoner.

But she was Runelord, and rode with a guardsman. That lent her courage.

The hooves of their horses clattered over salt-crusted cobblestones. Swarthy men slouched on narrow porches, and the only light in the alley spilled from an open door far up the street. A pair of mastiffs with spiked collars lunged from behind a crate, barking and snarling at the horses.

Grimeson's mount reared and pawed the air while Iome's danced backward. In the confusion, as she struggled to regain control of her horse, half a dozen men swarmed from dark doorways.

One man began shouting at the mastiffs, aiming rough kicks into the flanks of the dogs while he cursed in language so amazingly coarse that Iome had never heard the like. Another young man jumped out, and with grimy hands took the reins to Iome's mount and stood staring at her, his gap-toothed face hardly visible in the wan light.

Other men closed behind. One big fellow with white streaking his beard separated from the shadows. He held a spiked cudgel in hand. While the mastiffs barked, he challenged Grimeson, 'Here now, lad, that's a fine horse you've got, and a fine woman! And I'm sure you've gold in your purse besides. So tell me one reason why I shouldna slit your weasand and take them all?'

Iome fought her horse as the mastiff growled and snarled, barking at its feet. The gap-toothed man holding her reins didn't let go, even when Iome reached down and drew the dagger from her boot. With her endowments, she could have gutted him like a fish, but she held back.

'You couldn't handle either the woman or my horse,' Grimeson replied, 'but you can have some gold, for "Much wealth is surely a curse."' He pulled out his purse and tossed it to the scoundrel. Iome stifled a cry of outrage.

The scoundrel aimed his cudgel at one of his dogs and sent it yapping into the shadows, then began to laugh deeply.

'Grimeson,' he said, 'what are ya doing down here among the galley rats? Surely ya can find men of lesser character to hobnob with? Or has Gaborn finally decided to arrest me?'

'It's not men of character I'm looking for tonight,' Grimeson said easily. 'For if I did, I wouldna be down here with you.'

As he spoke, a door opened in a nearby shanty. A trio of curious children dressed in rags peeked out to see the cause of the commotion.

The rogue hefted Grimeson's purse curiously, then tossed it back to him. 'How can I do for you?'

Grimeson threw the purse back, and the villain's eyes went wide. 'The king is in need of some dog flesh. And he says that Abel Scarby always knows where to find the best pit dogs in the city.'

Abel grinned broadly. 'Fighting dogs, is it? Mastiffs? Bulls?'

'No, a peculiar breed,' Iome said. 'Yellow dogs, and small, but known to take a liking to man quickly, and have certain other valuable assets. Some lords would take exception to such animals, but perhaps you know of them?'

Abel Scarby peered up at her. Iome had her hood pulled up to hide her face, but he could not fail to notice the quality of her mount, or of her clothes. She could tell that he was used to dealing with rogues, for he did not ask her name.

Abel spat on the cobblestones. 'Na a popular sporting dog, but they can be had. And pound for pound, there's na a more vicious dog in the pits. I remember one unlikely bitch – as treacherous as a sack of weasels –'

'Can you get some dogs?' Iome asked. 'Tonight? Now? They're not for me. They're for the king. We'll want thirty at least, more if you can find them.'

Abel said, 'I'll have 'em for ya by sunrise.'

Iome bit her lip. 'One more thing. The men who sell the dogs must take endowments of scent, and vector them to the king's agent. I will pay well for this service.'

Abel Scarby swallowed hard and suddenly realized whom he was talking to. He bowed to one knee. He growled at the fellow who held Iome's reins, 'Kador, take your paws off the queen's horse.'

Kador backed away and raised his hands, as if to ward off a blow.

'Excuse us, Your Highness,' Abel said. 'We're hard men, used to guarding our own backs. We keep the law in this alley. We meant no offense.'

'None was taken,' Iome said. 'Any friend of Gaborn's is a friend of mine.'

Abel stared up at her with solemn eyes and a troubled expression. 'Is't true, Your Highness? Gaborn is really the Earth King?'

'It is.'

'An' . . . dark times are 'pon us?'

Iome nodded.

Abel tossed the purse up to her and said loudly, 'Yer Highness, I'll want na coin.' He rested the knob of his cudgel on the ground in parody of a lord offering his sword, and his bright eyes shone with a mixture of hope and fear of rejection as he explained, 'Milady, I'm na a fancy-pantser. Ya won't find me wearing silk hose on feast days, and if ya ventured into my hovel, ya'd find it smelly as a bear's den, and na a chair at the table clean enough for the likes of you to sit at. But my heart is as right and proud as any lord's who ever bent a knee to ya. I'm na a knight, but I've got as much gristle in me as any animal what ever lived. An' I've seventeen sons and daughters to my credit. So, I'm beggin' you to ask the king – him what's called me a friend, to Choose me an' me kids.'

The young thugs around Iome all looked up at her expectantly, like dogs begging for scraps at their master's table. The children in the doorway, wearing grime instead of cloaks and rags instead of clothes, timidly stepped out and crept to their father's side. He threw his arms around the young ones. Iome hesitated.

Gaborn had no power to Choose the man, yet she dared not tell him. The man looked hopeless, forlorn.

Seventeen children. She thought of the one in her womb. Could she bear to have it torn from her?

'Gaborn is far away,' she said, 'fighting reavers. I'm sure that he would Choose you, if he could.'

'When he comes, then?' Abel said. 'Ya'll ask him for us?'

There is a chance he will get his powers back, Iome assured herself. Yet she suspected that he never would.

'I'll ask him,' she promised.

Abel's lips were quivering, and his eyes shone dully from tears of gratitude. He stifled a sob, and his children all stood with wide eyes, till one young girl ran back into the house shouting, 'Ma! Ma!'

Abel said through a tight throat, 'Thank ya, milady. I'll try ta be worthy of ya.'

Iome tossed back the purse. 'Please, keep the money too. If not for your own sake, then for your wife and the little ones.'

Abel dropped his head, bowed lower. 'My condolences for your father. He was a great king, from all I hear.'

'Thank you,' she said. Iome no sooner began turning her mount than Abel shouted, 'Ya heard 'em, boys, look lively!'

Iome spurred her horse from the alley, and for a moment Grimeson was hard-pressed to keep up with her as she fled. Half a mile up the road she left the squalid waterfront at Crow's Bay.

Iome reined in her mount and dropped to the street, then stood for a moment, looking out to the water.

Her hands would not stop shaking.

'Will you be all right?' Grimeson asked.

'By the Powers, I have never felt so dirty and ashamed,' Iome said, shaking. 'I couldn't tell him no. I couldn't tell him that his children might die, not with the little ones standing there. What can I do? I never imagined I could feel –'

Suddenly she realized how Gaborn must feel. Only for him it had to be a thousand times stronger.

She leaned against the wall of a fishery and emptied her stomach. Grimeson said nothing. There could be no consolation.

Iome wept for her people.

Chapter Forty-three: THE ROUT

The horseman's warhammer is the favored weapon of Mystarria. The handle of such a hammer can be from four to six feet long, and is made of the finest steel. The crosspiece is narrow, spiked at each end, and of sufficient depth so that it is suitable for piercing a reaver's skull – or a man's armor.

– *Hearthmaster Bander's* Guide to Weapons

Averan and Binnesman sat on the hillside under the starlight. The sun had fallen hours ago, and a horned moon lingered on the horizon. In the distance Averan could see fires winking around Mangan's Rock.

Deer had come down from the hills to feed in the meadow. They walked around Averan on dainty hooves, as unmindful of her as if she were a dandelion.

Binnesman had planted his staff in the ground, left it sitting upright, and explained to Averan that an Earth Warden always did so, that the staff might draw power from the soil.

Afterward, he fell silent. He did not take Averan aside and show her plants in the dark, fretting about how little time he had. For once he merely sat, resting, gazing across the fields, as if he could see to the ends of the world. He'd done nothing more for hours.

Perhaps he only remains silent to keep from frightening the deer away, Averan thought.

'Are you casting a spell?' she asked at long last, afraid to disturb him. The doe that grazed beside her did not so much as twitch an ear at the sound of her voice.

Binnesman turned his head, glanced at her from the corner of his eye.

Binnesman pondered a moment. 'Yes, I am casting a spell of sorts,' he said. 'I'm taking time to renew. The touch of grass, the smell of pines in the wind, the taste of soil – they invigorate me. Sometimes, rest can feel magical, can't it?'

'I suppose.'

She said nothing more for a long minute, then asked, 'Binnesman, what happens when people die?'

'Their bodies go back to the Earth, and their spirits . . . do whatever spirits do.'

'You saw Erden Geboren,' Averan said. 'Was he happy?'

'About as happy as wights get,' Binnesman grumbled. She could tell that he turned aside hard questions. In her experience, adults seldom liked answering hard questions. In time, they even learned never to wonder about things at all.

'But . . . not all spirits rise, do they? What happens to the others?'

Binnesman glanced at her. 'No one knows, really. It is said that some are reborn in the netherworld, or perhaps are born into worlds that are shadows of ours, just as our world is but a shadow of the one world. But not all spirits go away, it seems – for some remain behind as wights.'

'I think I'd rather be a wight,' Averan said. 'I like it here.'

'Why?' Binnesman asked. 'Do you want to cheat death?'

'Of course,' Averan said.

Binnesman smiled. 'You can't cheat it, but some people learn to face it calmly. Some even embrace it as a friend.'

'That's just conquering fear,' Averan objected. 'Anyone can do that. I want to cheat death too.'

'Well,' Binnesman said. 'So you want to know how to come back as a wight. I'm not sure I know the answer. I think that the dead may hear our thoughts. It's almost as if we can summon them by thinking about them, or wishing them near. Or maybe by thinking about them, we merely lend them greater form. I don't know. . . .'

He fell silent a moment, then added, 'I've noticed that wights are almost always creatures of great will in life. By far, most of them are people who desired to do good, who sought to create rather than to tear down.'

'But not all?'

'Not all,' Binnesman said. 'Some were people or creatures of great will alone, beings with black hearts.'

'What else makes a wight?' Averan asked.

'Who knows?' Binnesman said. 'You see the stars in the sky. There are millions of them, and all of them have worlds like ours whirling around them. Or at least they have bits of world like ours.'

'I've heard that before,' Averan said. 'Beastmaster Brand sang that – part of the *Creation Saga*.'

'Really?' Binnesman asked. 'He must have been a wise man. Few know it nowadays.'

'He only knew part of it,' Averan said.

'Then I will tell you what I know. You see, once there was only one world, and one star, and beneath it grew the One True Tree.

'And One Rune bound them all together. But an enemy sought to change it, to take control. The enemy smashed the rune, and the pieces flew apart. They dashed out like shards of glass, and scattered through the cosmos.

'Now there are a billion, billion worlds or more, each one spinning around its own sun. Each a broken piece of the One True World, each one more or less true in its own way.'

'So there are people like us on those worlds?' Averan asked.

'Not exactly, I think. We are all distorted reflections of something greater, of what we once were. We might not pass for human on their worlds; they might not pass for human on ours. But we are similar in our hearts, if not in appearance. We all yearn to return to the One True World. Some say that our spirits, our wights, our pieces of our true self, longing to return home.'

Wizards had traveled to the netherworld, Averan knew. Raj Ahten's flameweavers had summoned a Darkling Glory from the One True World, as it was sometimes called. And she'd heard of other creatures from that mystic realm.

Binnesman furrowed a brow. 'Averan,' he said. His voice suddenly sounded choked. 'Averan, the Earth . . . needs us to be strong now. The future is rushing toward us. I can feel it like a rising storm.

'I created the wylde to fight the Earth's battles, but I have not had time to finish her, to train her. There will be no time. I can see that now. Though I cannot unbind her, we'll take her with us. I'm sure she'll be of use.'

'What are you talking about?' Averan asked. She was afraid that he would take her into the Underworld at that very moment, just lead her down into some cavern.

Suddenly the ground began to tremble and rock beneath Averan. There was a hissing from the forest, and Averan imagined that some world worm was about to rise, like the one she'd seen at Carris.

But no, it was only an earthquake.

She looked at Binnesman for comfort, but the wizard stood up and pointed to the sky. Eight stars fell in rapid succession.

'What's wrong?' Averan asked. 'What's happening?'

He jutted his chin down toward the grasslands, toward Mangan's Rock. Averan gaped in surprise.

The watch fires around the rock all suddenly blazed. They were coming together in a huge crescent.

Gaborn's men were setting fire to the plains!

'Come now,' Binnesman said. 'We'll get no more rest. Let us join the battle.'

As Binnesman's mount galloped down from the hills and over the grasslands, Averan watched the flames shoot higher, filling her vision.

Gaborn had sent horsemen charging over the fields, spreading logs from watch fires upwind from Mangan's Rock.

Now the flames leapt skyward, the fire spreading. They roared palpably, and rose a hundred yards in the air. Firelight smote against clouds of smoke, making them glow a ruddy orange, and through those glowing clouds Averan could glimpse the reavers on Mangan's Rock, beginning to pace, their philia waving frantically.

What is he doing? Averan wondered. The fire could never climb the rock. The sides were too steep, too high. The few vines and grasses along the slopes would not catch.

But the reavers might well have sealed their own doom. They'd pushed the vast old oaks from the top of the rock, hurled them over its sides. The dry bark of the trees would burn, sending up clouds of smoke.

Did Gaborn hope to suffocate the reavers?

The very idea somehow terrified her.

She had smelled the world as a reaver, knew something of the beasts' darkest fears. The smell of smoke loomed huge among those fears.

More than that, Fire itself scared her. It was the enemy of Earth, the antagonist to her Power.

'Can you feel that?' she shouted at Binnesman.

'What do you feel?' he demanded.

'The Fire. It's aware of us. It's angry that Gaborn seeks to use it against itself.'

'Don't be afraid,' Binnesman said. 'Fire consumes. Its appetite overwhelms its intellect. It destroys, and will spread devastation when it can. It cares nothing for life, either human or reaver. But that is also its weakness. Remember that. Fire will consume everything around it, until it burns itself out.'

She'd never sensed Fire as a power, at least not as strongly as she did now. Her growing Earth senses made her aware of the rising danger.

'What's he doing?' Averan cried, even when they were two miles away.

She could see men outside the line of flames, knights mounted on chargers, bearing down with lances. The firelight gleamed on burnished mail.

A scarlet sorceress suddenly came thundering out of the wall of fire, her runes glowing fiercely, her staff held in a great foreclaw. Smoke roiled around her, came rushing with her.

She strode out of the fumes and blaze, and brought her staff to bear as knights charged her from three directions.

One fellow lanced her side, and she spun to meet him, hissing furiously. Suddenly other sorceresses came loping out of the inferno in her wake. Clouds of noxious fumes hovered around them.

'They're coming from underground!' Binnesman shouted.

Averan saw it now. The reavers had been digging under the men, hoping to ambush them from beneath. Gaborn must have discovered it, broken into their tunnel. So he had lit the fires, thus filling their caverns with smoke.

The reavers burst up from a single chasm, just beyond the wall of flames, and made straight for Gaborn's warriors.

Binnesman wrapped his arms tight around Averan's waist, spurred his charger on.

As they drew near, she saw that not all of Gaborn's troops rode. Hundreds of men now manned smaller blazes at the edge of the creek. They stood there over the logs, cooking huge slabs of meat.

In rising horror she realized what they were doing: they

had cut the philia from the bungholes of dead reavers, and were throwing them onto the burning logs.

Even now she could smell the garlicky scent of them cooking, a stench that sent words shrieking in her mind. 'Death, beware! Death! Death!'

She glanced back toward Mangan's Rock. The wall of flames blew quickly to the east, had just begun to engulf the base of the cliff. It struck the wood and dry leaves, sent a tower of flame soaring up three hundred feet along the sheer walls.

She had no sooner realized what Gaborn was up to than it started: the reavers panicked.

All along the top of Mangan's Rock, they scurried to escape.

A moving mass of monsters stampeded to the south, heading for the lowest cliffs, and began to rush down.

Reavers slipped from the top, pushed by their fellows behind. Black crablike monsters flailed their arms and legs as they fell.

Some of the plunging reavers slammed into their fellows below, knocking them from the cliffs. Rocks crumbled beneath their mighty claws. Some of the reavers' carapaces shattered as they met stones below. Others flailed about on broken legs.

Another tremor struck, and Averan wondered if Gaborn had suddenly regained his powers. Was he making the earth shake?

An entire escarpment collapsed, and the resulting avalanche hurled two thousand reavers into a pile. Those on the bottom died, while those on the top scurried off. Walls of flame shot up along the eastern slope of Mangan's Rock, sending clouds of smoke billowing.

And all through it, Averan could hear the death screams of the reavers in her mind. The scent of the burning philia nearly overwhelmed her.

Binnesman rode to Gaborn, who sat on his mount. Gaborn stared at the destruction with eyes that gleamed from reflecting fires. His charger stamped its feet nervously.

'Isn't it beautiful!' he shouted. 'The reavers were bluffing, like Averan said. They couldn't build another Rune of Desolation. They only hoped that we would spend ourselves trying to dislodge them.

'Once I figured that out, and thought of setting fire to the plains, the rest was easy. Not a man will die!

'Knowledge!' he shouted. 'Knowledge is better than a fine warhammer!'

Reavers threw themselves from the rock. Instead of merely climbing down, some dared to try leaping a hundred yards to safety, only to shatter legs under the impact.

From out of the smoking tunnel, the last few scarlet sorceresses and blade-bearers fled.

Averan had given Gaborn the weapons he needed to dislodge the reavers. A sense of horror welled up in her. She had not meant to cause such mindless slaughter.

A sound like rising thunder rose on the plains south. The surviving reavers formed into columns and began to retreat. The earth trembled at the sound of the stampede.

Gaborn glanced at her and jutted his chin toward the cliffs. 'Let's go see if we can find the Waymaker.'

Chapter Forty-four:
PRAYERS IN THE DARK

When seeking the aid of higher powers, any place of power is suitable. Wizards of the Air will climb a mountaintop, sorcerers of Fire need only stare into the flames, wizards of Water bathe in a pool, while those who serve the Earth seek the touch of soil.

The higher powers often answer our petitions.

Men seldom listen.

– *Excerpt from* The Child's Book of Wizardry,
by Hearthmaster Col

Raj Ahten and his men hurried along the Old Fortress Trail south of Maygassa. He'd hoped to get fresh horses, but rode his camel still.

The trickle of fleeing humanity had become a flood – a surging tide of bodies that could not fit within the confines of the trail, but which spilled out on both sides, so that hundreds upon hundreds marched abreast through the jungle. For long hours Raj Ahten had to ride slowly along the side of the road to make it through the throng.

Overhead, in the dark of night, monkeys leapt through the trees shouting in panic and hurling bits of fruit and leaves, until the very jungle seemed to shake.

On the banks of the Kelong River he stopped near a bridge an hour past midnight and watched his people all in one sweep. The Kelong was wide, with rice paddies planted along both banks, and afforded him a good view of the exodus. What he saw made him tremble:

The people hurried along the river by torchlight. At any moment, he saw tens of thousands of them – men with walking sticks and immense bundles on their backs, struggling forward like oxen, wearing only loincloths and a thick coating of sweat. Women carried baskets on their heads or babes strapped to their chests.

Too many men and elephants had tried to cross the bridge at once. Now the bodies of elephants lay among the shattered timbers in the shallows.

So the people slowed to wade across the river.

All of humanity was there – a proud lord rode beneath a silk canopy upon a white elephant, arrayed in a coat made of cloth of gold. His guards sported fine red silk trimmed with otter fur. They surged through a throng of peasant women adorned only in shifts of crudely dyed cotton. Wealthy merchants traveled as merchants will – in rickshaws pulled by poor laborers so blunt-faced and brutish that they seemed more animal than human.

Whole families rode in rugged flatbed wagons drawn by water buffalo. One man pulled a handcart, with his infirm wife loaded in the back as if she were a sack of gingerroot on its way to market. An old philosopher had students, their heads all shaved except for their scholars' knots, carrying cases of scrolls. Elsewhere, caretakers used bamboo rods to herd madmen and fools who were naked and chained together at the ankle.

The waters of the Kelong flowed slowly. Burning torches reflected from its surface, while smoke hovered above it in a blue haze.

Fathers and mothers groped for a foothold as they bore their young. Raj Ahten spotted a small girl who looked much like Saffira's eldest daughter, riding in a pack on her mother's back.

The mother stumbled and slipped beneath the muddy waters of the Kelong. When she surfaced, her child was gone. Peasants nearby shouted and peered into the depths of the river. Some dove under the dark water, seeking the girl by feel alone.

But their panicked search yielded nothing. Soon the child would surface, Raj Ahten knew. She would float facedown for a while, perhaps, until she washed up on the shore with the others that failed to make the passage.

The people kept coming. The exodus stretched beyond the horizon.

A peasant who had nearly crossed the river spotted Raj Ahten's camel. He pointed and began to shout, 'O Great Light, protect us! O Sun Lord, we beg of you!'

Other men and women heard the call, spotted Raj Ahten in the darkness. They began struggling to reach him, staggering in the muddy water. Soon a vast throng began shouting, clasped hands raised before their faces.

Distantly, he could smell death – the familiar stench of reavers' blight.

He ordered his men to bypass the throng, and quickly forded the river, while pleas for his aid rose up as if on dark wings into the night.

An hour later he reached a hillside that looked over the plains. Three miles off, the jungles and grasslands steamed, turning gray before his eyes.

Masses of humanity snaked over the road in a vast throng. Their lanterns shone like a river of light. They would never outrace the reaver mage's curse.

On each side of the road, an ancient city carved of white stone lay like broken bones upon the jungle floor.

The air filled with hissing, as if wet flesh sizzled in a fire. Not half a mile downhill the reavers' curses struck: leaves instantly curled inward, then fell from the trees, leaving branches naked. Vines and smaller limbs drooped or writhed under the onslaught. Entire trees cracked as if lightning had taken them.

Clouds of parrots, weavers, and finches rose up and wheeled above the destruction.

The horizon showed an empty landscape of blight for as far as the eye could see. He was still a hundred and eighty miles north of Kartish.

'There will be famines this year,' Bhopanastrat said, 'no matter what we do.'

The enormity of the destruction overwhelmed Raj Ahten. It would take days to truly settle into his bones.

Raj Ahten swatted his camel's nose with his riding prod, forced it to kneel. He climbed down. 'Let the animals forage,' he told his men. 'It might be the last food they get for days.'

The eyes of Bhopanastrat and his men bored into his back. He could tell that they all wanted to know what he would do. But no man dared ask.

All day long, his muscles had felt weak somehow. Now his left hand was trembling.

Despite all that he could do, despite his endowments, Binnesman's curse threatened to destroy him.

He rode through the night, past vacant cities over a landscape that was a surreal horror.

Creatures still lived. Tarantulas crept through the ruins, feeding on mice and linnets. But the trees were down. From horizon to horizon, not a blade of grass survived. The stench of rot filled his nostrils.

His people fled, but not all could make it. Raj Ahten found the dead along the roadsides – men who had worn their hearts out in a single day of running, the old, the infirm. Some of the dead had had their throats cut for a morsel of bread or the use of an ox.

The utter desolation drove out all worries of Wuqaz

Faharaqin crying for his blood in the streets, or of Gaborn plotting his downfall. Nothing that men could do would ever compare to the malice of the reavers.

Hours later, just before dawn, he came upon one of his armies – three hundred thousand common soldiers twelve miles north of the Palace of Canaries.

They'd camped in a deserted city for the night to chew their rations and make peace with themselves. Their sullen faces stared up as he rode through the city, men in straw hats or turbans, eyes clouded with despair.

Even if they managed to drive back the reavers, there would be no food for man or horse for more than a hundred miles in any direction. Judging by the grim expressions on their faces, the warriors knew that they went to die. Here and there he heard men muttering solemn prayers in the dark.

When they saw Raj Ahten, some raised a shout of triumph, but most just gazed at him with sullen curiosity.

Hovering over the midst of the camp was a silken balloon shaped like a graak.

Beneath it, his flameweavers sat cross-legged before a campfire, along with his Days. The hairless flameweavers gazed up expectantly as he neared.

'What news from the front?' Raj Ahten asked.

'Aysalla Pusnabish leads your men,' Rahjim answered. 'All day yesterday he probed the reavers' defenses. Many men died.'

'How many?' Raj Ahten asked.

'Most of the knights in your cavalry, O Great One,' Rahjim said.

Raj Ahten breathed out a curse. The mines at Kartish were an open pit with steep sides and tailings piled haphazardly. Such terrain favored reavers, not cavalry.

'How can this be?' Raj Ahten asked.

Rahjim shrugged. 'The reavers have built a fortress. The

fell mage who guards it is mightier than the beast you faced in Carris. But all is not lost. Pusnabish has prepared well for the battle tomorrow.'

Raj Ahten stood rubbing his numb left hand, trying to increase the circulation.

The flameweaver Az nodded toward it. 'You are feeling worse?'

'I'm well enough,' Raj Ahten said.

'I can heal you,' Az offered. But Raj Ahten wanted none of his healing – not at the price of his humanity.

Raj Ahten cast a cold eye on his army. These were troops of old Indhopal, dressed in simple breastplates with spiked helms on their heads, and round targets clamped to their left forearms. They bore weapons fit to kill reavers – oversized longspears, warhammers, and axes. But men without endowments would not fare well with such weapons. Even if a man could swing these warhammers, he'd tire quickly.

Three hundred thousand common troops would be ineffectual against the reavers. But Raj Ahten could think of some use for them. At the battle for Carris, when confronted by masses of men, the reavers balked. They could not detect which men might be Runelords and which were commoners.

The reavers' ignorance might be his best weapon.

Raj Ahten called upon the powers of his Voice and his glamour, and shouted. 'Honorable warriors of Indhopal, I salute you! Now is the hour we have feared. Desolation is upon us. Only your strong arms and brave hearts can save the day. Tonight the kingdoms of Indhopal live or die by our valor. Tonight I will lead you in a war like none that mankind has ever known! Ride with me now, ride for Indhopal!'

The power of his Voice surprised even Raj Ahten. The weary men raised their weapons and cheered like berserkers.

He leapt on his camel and raced before them so that even the wind could not catch him.

* * *

In the winter, snow fell heavily in the Alcairs, leaving the mountains white. It melted throughout the summer, feeding the rivers that tumbled over the green slopes. In the Valley of Om on the southern verge of Kartish, twelve waterfalls spilled down from the hills.

It was Raj Ahten's favorite place in the world. Every year on the first day of the month of Poppies, he would journey to Om. Always the pecan blossoms were in bloom, and the new grass grew lush and fragrant, and the red poppies covered the valley while the waterfalls spilled from the freshets into languid pools, misting the air above the Palace of Canaries.

The grounds around the palace were pristine. No man or animal was allowed to trample them, and the palace itself was a gem.

Its walls were made of thin slabs of yellow marble, and at night when the lanterns were lit within, the whole complex shone like burnished gold beneath the starlight. On such nights the palace earned its name: for the palace took its name not from canaries, as some supposed, or even for its yellow walls – but rather from the songsters who vied for the honor of performing within its great arching acoustic hall.

Many were the pleasant nights that Raj Ahten had spent listening to songsters in the jasmine-scented hall, wandering the pristine poppy fields, gazing at the waterfalls and the palace in the moonlight, seducing young women.

He'd lain with Saffira here.

Raj Ahten shook the memories away. There was nothing for it. The joy of his life was gone.

Among the Jewel Kingdoms, blood-metal mines had always made Kartish the richest. The kaifs of the land had grown fat over the centuries. They had controlled the blood metal, and could set the prices they saw fit. Beyond that, they knew precisely how many forcibles each lord purchased over the years, and thus by regulating shipments ensured that no one ever built a force powerful enough to strike against them.

Over centuries they acted as puppetmasters, orchestrating the rise and fall of nations that they knew only by rumor. The fat old men had kept their knives to the jugular vein of the world, and congratulated themselves on their cunning.

Of course, they made mistakes. From time to time, shipments would fall into the wrong hands, and the kaifs of Kartish would be slaughtered wholesale. The world hardly noticed, for the sun set on one despot only to rise on another.

Raj Ahten had killed them all easily enough.

When Raj Ahten reached the Palace of Canaries, the palace itself shone as usual, and the falls tumbled like a silver mist in the starlight.

But on his pristine grounds, an army had settled, blackening the land with tents and bodies. The valley would never heal from the double curse of the reavers' blight and the damage done by the troops.

Dingy fires guttered in the vale. No fewer than two million men bivouacked for miles around the palace. The stench of men, horses, and elephants was unbearable. All through the camps, horses whinnied and elephants trumpeted in hunger while men short of rations sounded loud and raucous in turn. So the valley filled with a noise of pandemonium.

Raj Ahten rode down through the hills while an army of three hundred thousand men raced to keep up.

As he did, heralds bore torches on either side of him, both ahead and behind. Men beheld his countenance, and were cowed by his glamour.

He shouted to the common troops huddled below, his voice a roar. 'Men of Indhopal, how can you sit here idle while the reavers call us to war? Rise now! Grab your weapons and armor. We go to battle at dawn. I promise you victory!'

He met Warlord Aysalla Pusnabish at the palace gates. Pusnabish dropped to his hands and knees and did obeisance.

'O Great Dawn of Our Lives,' he said, 'we thank you for delivering us.'

'My Dedicates are safe?' Raj Ahten asked.

'We hastened them away at the first sign of trouble, O Great One. By now they have reached the coast, and are sailing north for the Palace of Ghusa in Deyazz.'

Raj Ahten felt weak, disjointed. His left hand trembled. 'What of my forcibles?'

'They are in the treasury, O Sun of Our Morning,' Pusnabish said.

Raj Ahten did not want to hear more. His troops were preparing for battle, and he had enough men that he suspected he could swarm the hills, take the reavers in their lair.

He pushed past Pusnabish and strode through the gilded halls of the Palace of Canaries, up toward his treasury.

'I'll need my facilitators,' Raj Ahten said, 'and men to grant me stamina.'

Pusnabish snapped his fingers at a servant, and the man ran to get the facilitators.

'There is some good news,' Pusnabish insisted, running in his wake. 'Our miners struck a new vein of blood ore. It is quite promising, as you will see.'

Raj Ahten smiled grimly.

Chapter Forty-five: THE NIGHTRIDERS

Many adventures await you upon the road of life. Enter these doors, and take your first step. . . .
– From a placard above the Horn and Hound Pub, the first stop in the Room of Feet

Myrrima didn't fancy being followed. It was doubly worrying that she wasn't sure whether the creature tracking them was human or not.

Borenson did not speak as they rode. He peered about, his bright blue eyes alert. Each time she started to open her mouth, he would raise a hand, begging her to be silent.

So she held her tongue.

She was a wolf lord now, with endowments of scent from a dog, and sight from a man. Borenson's nervousness kept her wary, and she strained her senses, sniffing the air and keeping her eyes open for signs of danger.

In the Westlands, the barren plains gave way to woods where hoary trees grew among craggy rocks, limbs heavy with moss. The trees were tall and dark, with only a few ragged gray leaves clinging to them. The earth smelled of mold and fungus. Toadstools thrust up from the detritus in the fens.

It was not hard to envision the wars fought here against

the Toth so long ago, or to imagine that the dark pools still held traces of blood.

She wanted to ride through quickly. But the muddy roads forced them to slow their horses to a walk.

It was a stagnant land. In spite of the yawning emptiness, time and again she found herself reaching for her steel bow, slung in its case on her saddle pack.

The forest was dead. No squirrels danced round the sides of the trees to hide when they passed. No deer were startled from the grass if they happened on a glade. Only once in a great while would she catch sight of some dark-winged bird as it darted for cover in a shadowed glen.

She strained for any sound – the buzz of a locust, the pattering of a woodpecker, or the caw of a crow.

But the woods held little in the way of life, and none of it was pleasant. Myrrima imagined that nothing much could live here. Biting flies and mosquitoes swarmed in clouds over brackish pools, and in places they seemed so thick that she imagined that they'd simply strip the hide off any animal that held still long enough.

She did not hold still.

Wights haunted this place, Myrrima knew.

That's why Borenson shushed her every time she wanted to speak. Wights were drawn to sound, to movement. They hid in shadows. Their icy touch would kill a man.

The shrouded bogs where oily water gave rise to night mists, the creepy woods with their folds and hollows, both were the perfect abode for such creatures.

And while the wights of the Dunnwood back home protected the realm, the same was not true of the Westlands. Sixteen hundred years ago, nomen and Toth had died here by the uncounted score. Their revenants craved vengeance. At times it was said that the shades of men could be seen fighting them still, as if reenacting their deaths on old battlegrounds.

Once, they came upon a hill and heard the rush of wind

through the trees in the valley to their left, a distant sigh like the beating of waves upon an endless shore.

Myrrima imagined that the wind heralded a coming storm, and that soon all of the trees would begin bobbing and creaking in the gale.

Instead, the wind merely passed – as if it were an invisible rider heading south through the forest.

When it was gone, Borenson whispered, breaking an hours-long silence, 'What was that, do you think?'

'Wights?'

'There are wights here,' he admitted, 'and they're aware of us. But that wasn't one. Something else passed by.'

Myrrima's mind returned to the Darkling Glory, to the howling tornado that had issued from it. Binnesman had warned that it was capable of great evil still.

'If we ride slowly,' Borenson whispered, 'we won't reach Fenraven by sunset, but if we ride fast, we might catch up to whatever passed us by.'

Myrrima bit her lip. 'Ride fast,' she whispered.

Myrrima glimpsed another rider just before sunset, and knew for sure that they were being followed.

They'd been cantering through the hills, and had come down for the hundredth time into another marsh. They let their horses forage for a few short minutes, and had then ridden on for half a mile, until they reached a bog so wide that the road itself was submerged.

The forest ended here. A few gray skeletal trees struggled up from fetid pools, but otherwise there was no cover for nearly a quarter of a mile. In midwinter the bog would have been a lake.

So Myrrima slowed her horse and let it pick its way through the water, wading through muddy pools where it sank up to its withers. With every step, the smell of rot rose from the depths, and the splashing of the horse obscured any other sound. Myrrima had to lug her saddlebags on her own shoulder, lest her provisions get wet. Mosquitoes buzzed around her in a starving cloud.

As her horse waded through the pools she saw someone – or something. She happened to glance over her shoulder, checking the road behind, when she glimpsed a horseman on the hill three quarters of a mile back.

A dark, hooded figure sat ahorse under the trees, peering toward her intently. In the gloaming woods, she couldn't see the color of his horse. So well concealed was he that at first she wasn't sure if he was real or simply an unhappy confluence of sticks and shadows, an invention of her fears.

But a moment of squinting through the cloud of mosquitoes convinced her otherwise.

It was a man, hiding in the trees just off the road.

Myrrima swallowed hard, thinking, Assassin? Or the wight of some long-dead wolf hunter?

It could be anyone. Perhaps it was only a fellow traveler who had been frightened to hear a force horse riding through these lone woods, and had decided to exit into the trees.

She haltingly waved at the fellow in greeting. But he didn't move. He held as still as a deer as it tastes the air for the scent of the hounds.

'Who are you waving at?' Borenson hissed.

'There's a man in the trees,' Myrrima said.

'Are you sure it's a man?'

She suddenly realized that she hadn't seen fresh-cut tracks in the road. Nor had she smelled warm horseflesh along the trail either. Which meant that the fellow had not been ahead of them on the road.

That left only two possibilities. He might have been riding cross-country through the bogs – something only a madman would try – or he might be following them.

Only a man on a fast force horse could have kept up.

Muyyatin assassins rode force horses.

She reined in her mount, and sat for a moment, braving the mosquitoes, pointedly staring at the fellow. At last he turned his head and urged his horse forward, onto the road, spurred it north into the shadowed woods, and was gone.

His horse made no sound as it trotted through the trees.

'I saw him,' Borenson whispered. 'Can't tell if he's alive or dead.'

A wight, she decided, one that has no interest in us. Or perhaps it was still too light yet, and he would come after them in the full darkness.

Her heart was pounding. She suddenly recalled a tale of Muyyatin assassins who booted the hooves of their horses with layers of lamb's wool, so that they could ride quietly.

'Water and cold iron can sometimes turn a wight,' Borenson whispered. 'But if that fellow is alive, just give him cold iron.'

Myrrima reached into a pouch, pulled out an iron spear tip that Hoswell had once showed her. It had a flaring blade, and fit nicely onto the end of her steel bow. She twisted it in place.

She spurred her horse through the fetid swamp, and rode on for five miles. The woods grew darker as night thickened, and in many places the roots of huge trees snaked out into the road, creating a hazard for any who dared ride at night.

A dim haze covered the sky, muting the stars, and Borenson convinced her to abandon their journey for a while as they waited for moonrise.

They reached a dark copse on a hillside, where the roots were especially thick, and turned off the road. They led their mounts into blackness under the trees. Myrrima's horse lowered its head, then sniffed at molding leaves as it sought forage. She'd ridden far, and the mount had got nothing to eat for the past two hours. It whickered in consternation.

'Quiet,' Myrrima whispered. The beast had endowments of wit from other horses, and was well trained. It suddenly went still as a statue, ignoring even the mosquitoes that eagerly settled on its rump.

For long minutes, Myrrima and Borenson waited.

She hated the silence, wished that they could speak. She occupied herself by watching the heavens. Almost immediately a trio of shooting stars arced across the sky. One was a fireball that left a guttering trail of ash. She'd seldom seen such a display. No crickets chirped. No frogs croaked.

The night seemed perfectly still.

Until a wailing cry arose that was like nothing human. Goosepimples formed on her arms immediately, and the sound sent a shiver down her spine. Her horse pawed the ground nervously, and Borenson's danced forward.

On a windswept hillside not a mile away, she saw the gray ghost light of a wight – incredibly thin and tall. At first glance, it seemed vaguely human in shape, until one made out its impossible form. Its gangling arms were as thin as branches, a crepuscular white in color, like a warty fungal growth, that ended in scythelike talons. Its four legs were also inhumanly long and slender. The rearmost legs were attached to flaring hips that tilted up like a grasshopper's, with an inverted knee. But the rear hips were set no more than two feet from the forelegs, so that it squatted oddly. Its narrow skull tapered so that the protracted muzzle looked almost like a bill. The flaring at the back of the skull was not from bone, but from philia.

Though from a great distance one could almost mistake it for a human in shape, the beast was far more closely related to a reaver than a human.

A Toth.

Myrrima's heart hammered in her throat. Sweat spilled down her forehead. She dared not move, lest she attract its attention.

The Toth enchanters from beyond the Carroll Sea were all

but legend now, and most of their specters had faded. This could only be the shade of a powerful sorcerer.

Water and cold iron wouldn't be enough to ward it. Only a great wizard might drive the monster away.

The wight stood upon the hillside, its head tilted upward, as if it were a hound tasting the air. As it did, the philia hanging like a thick beard beneath its long jaws quivered. It swayed on its legs, an incredibly graceful gesture, then went striding northwest with a determined gait.

He's caught the scent of something, Myrrima realized. And given that I'm riding from the north, it could be me.

She was about to leap on her horse when Borenson stopped her.

Almost immediately she heard hoofbeats. A rider came galloping along the road behind them, whipping his mount with his reins.

A heavy warhorse charged past, its cloaked rider hunched low in the saddle, wheezing in terror. She heard the muted *ching* of studded mail. Even the heavy sheepskin slippers that quieted the horse's pounding hooves couldn't silence it completely.

Muyyatin. And the wight was after the assassin.

The only problem was, she was hiding in these woods, too. The wight wouldn't care who it caught first.

Which do you want to risk, she asked herself, death from an assassin, or death from the wight of a Toth?

Borenson decided for her. He gouged his horse's flanks with his heels and was gone.

Myrrima reined her mount around. She kicked his flanks harder than she'd wanted, and the stallion lurched beneath her in a dead run.

It was nearly all that she could do to hang on. She grabbed her steel bow anyway, hoping against hope that its iron spear tip might keep the wight at bay.

The force horse galloped under the trees. Behind her, a

quarter mile back, Myrrima heard that inhuman cry. It was not a wail of sorrow, but more of an ululating shriek, like the sound an eagle makes as it stoops for the kill.

Her force horse redoubled its speed in blind panic, and Myrrima bent low in the saddle, clinging tightly. Borenson's mount set the pace ahead. His robes flapped behind him.

She came up on a strait where the trees thinned. She spared a glance backward.

Her blood froze in her veins. The wight was leaping toward her on incredibly long legs. It glowed with its own inner light so that she could see it clearly now, only a couple hundred yards behind. Its skin shone pale as polished ivory, and its huge eyes glowed a deep, deep crimson. Upon its arms, faint blue runes burned, ancient wards against death. Philia swayed from its narrow chin like a beard, and scythelike teeth glimmered in its lipless mouth. It made grasping motions with its right paw, as if grabbing for her. Its paws were incredibly long, each with three talons that had many joints.

'Fly!' she shouted at her mount, and the force horse redoubled its effort again, shooting through the shadowed copses, leaving the wight to flounder in its wake. Her beast had four endowments of metabolism, and two of brawn. With those endowments it could attain incredible speeds. Given the choice, she'd not have dared a run like this even in daylight.

Myrrima suspected that she was racing at eighty miles an hour when she heard Borenson's horse stumble.

He was galloping through a copse ahead when its fore-hoof clipped a root with a report like a lance shattering.

As the beast floundered, Myrrima's first thought was for her husband.

He's as good as dead, she thought. Yet she saw Borenson jump or fall free of the saddle, roll to the grass.

Myrrima reined her own mount, leapt from her saddle while the horse continued to run. She tried to land on her feet, but they slipped from beneath her on the slick road and she fell on her right hip. She skidded over some roots or rocks, then flipped onto her chest.

Pain wracked her, surging from hip and arm.

She climbed to her feet, ignoring the agony. Her horse was gone. But during the fall she'd managed to cling to her bow.

She spat on the iron spear tip. Water and cold iron, she thought hopefully, the same as she'd used against the Darkling Glory.

A shriek sounded as she looked up.

The wight was nearly upon her, mouth gaping as if to swallow. It was too late to stand still like a terrified rabbit, too late to hope that it might pass her by.

She lunged with her bow, sent its spear tip into the sweet triangle between the monster's eyes.

The Toth shrieked, and there was a blinding flash. Invisible shards of ice seemed to fly through the air, sending pinpricks of cold that rushed through her.

Myrrima stared at the Toth. Its runic death wards suddenly blazed into blue fire, and for a brief second she had a vision: she thought she stared into a blinding haze, and in that light she saw warriors dressed in the ancient mode, with rounded helms and round shields. They surrounded the Toth on all sides, and plunged their spears into its flanks. She could hear them shouting, 'Arten! Arten da gaspeilten!'

The vision faded, and Myrrima was thrown backward by the icy blast. The world went bitter cold. She'd never faced such cold.

Myrrima felt as if a glory hammer had slammed into her chest. Every single muscle in her body ached. In a daze she struggled to sit up, but her head reeled too much, and she fell backward.

Borenson grabbed her, picking her head up. 'Are you alive? Can you hear me?'

'Wha –?' Myrrima managed to blurt.

His breath steamed in the icy air. Her right hand felt as if it had frozen at the knuckles.

'By the Seven Stones!' he swore. 'That – that's not possible!'

She pulled herself up, ignoring the ache in her bones.

For fifty yards in every direction, the ground was blasted with hoarfrost. White crystals glistened under the starlight.

The wight was gone.

Yet her right hand ached, as if it blazed in a cold fire. She held it up, realized belatedly what had happened. She'd plunged her spear tip into the wight so hard that she had struck the beast with her hand. Her fist was as white as ice, and crystals shone brightly on the pale skin.

Chapter Forty-six: THE DAYS

For as long as there have been Runelords, there have been Days. But the number of Days in the world is never precisely known, and seems to swell and wane from time to time. Mad King Harrill, it is said, had three Days in his attendance at all times, and went to great lengths to evade them. One can well imagine that he needed more watching than others.

Yet we know from the chronicles of Erendor that not even one in twelve kings had a Days in attendance during his lifetime. This state of affairs lasted for nearly four hundred years. Hence, because so much of our history is lost, we sometimes speak of the Dark Age of Erendor.

– *Excerpt from* Chronicles, *by Deverde, Hearthmaster in the Room of Time*

While the world slept, Iome retreated to the palace at the Courts of Tide, there to wait while Abel Scarby gathered the dogs that Gaborn needed.

The guards ushered her in and called a chambermaid who would have waked the whole staff in a panic if Iome had not forbidden her to do so.

The immensity of the palace overwhelmed Iome. Her

father's entire keep back at Castle Sylvarresta would have fit in the Great Hall. Sixteen huge hearths lined its walls.

Around the room hung dozens of lanterns backed by silver mirrors, their bright flames subdued beneath rose-colored crystal. The oil that they burned gave off a pleasant scent of gardenias. Enormous windows facing south would have lit the room throughout the day.

The tapestries on the walls, depicting scenes of ancient kings in love and in battle, each looked as if they might have kept a village full of women weaving for a year.

The postern and lintel above each doorway had been intricately carved to show scenes of foxes and rabbits racing over trails in an oak forest.

The king's table was set with golden plates, brightly polished. Iome took one gasping look, and just stared in amazement. She'd never grasped how wealthy Gaborn might be. She'd never imagined how insignificant Heredon's splendor must seem to him.

Before one great hearth, a girl in a plain scholar's robe sat hunched on an elegant couch. Her brown hair was long and braided in cornrows, then tied together in back.

Upon hearing footsteps, she turned to look at Iome.

'Oh, there you are!' she said in a pleasant voice. The girl's face was freckled, her eyes an ordinary brown. Iome took one look, and felt as if she'd known her all her life. She was perhaps sixteen, a little younger than Iome.

'Are you my new Days?' Iome asked.

The girl nodded. She had a pimple on her chin. 'I heard that you had arrived. Did you have a good ride?'

'It went without incident,' Iome said, sure that the girl wanted only the historical details.

The girl's face fell a little, as if she'd expected more. 'But – it was pleasant, I hope?'

Iome's mind did a little twist. She'd never had a Days inquire as to whether something pleased her.

'Very pleasant,' Iome said. 'I have to admit, I'd never imagined how vast Mystarria was. The land here is so rich and fertile, and this castle overwhelms me.'

'I was born not far from here,' the Days said, 'in a village called Berriston. I know everything about Mystarria. I can show you around.'

Iome had never had a Days offer to show her anything. Most of them were cold and aloof. But she recognized immediately that this girl felt just as lonely as Iome did, just as overwhelmed by her responsibilities.

'I would like that,' Iome said. She took the girl by her hand, squeezed her fingers.

It felt distinctly odd. At home, friends had always surrounded Iome. Whether they were dried-up old matrons or other young women in waiting, she'd always had a female companion nearby. She'd come to the Courts of Tide knowing that she would feel out of place.

Now she wondered what it would feel like to have a Days as a friend. 'Do you know the castle?' Iome asked. 'Can you show me to the tower?'

'Indeed,' the Days said. 'I've been here all afternoon.'

The girl took Iome to the base of the tower. Together they climbed the long stairs until they reached the room where Gaborn's father had slept.

A guardsman in Mystarria's colors stood at the door, opened it with a key.

Upon opening the door, Iome smelled King Orden's scent – his sweat, his hair – all so strong that it seemed impossible that her husband's father had been slain only a week ago. The scent belied his death, made Iome expect that at any moment old King Orden might appear on the parapet outside the window, or stir from an antechamber.

At the very least, his shade ought to be here, she thought.

The room was overlarge, with rich furnishings and a huge canopied four-poster bed, draped with woolen curtains. Iome went to it, patted the firm mattress. This is where I am destined to sleep, she thought. This is where – the Powers preserve us – I'll bear my son. This is where Gaborn will get more sons upon me.

Iome's Days went to a window, opened it wide. 'I've heard that the view of the city here is beautiful,' she exulted. 'We should see it from the promenade.'

Iome wouldn't be able to sleep, she knew. With so many endowments of stamina and metabolism and brawn, she needed very little of it. From now on when she did take rest, she would take it as powerful Runelords were wont to do – by standing quietly and staring off at private dreams. She still felt rested, and the Days' tone was infectious.

Iome went out to the promenade. It was three stories beneath the very topmost ramparts of the tower, where the far-seers kept their vigil. The promenade was well lit. A huge red lantern hung just beneath the far-seers' outlook.

'That wasn't lit a while ago,' Iome remarked.

'The queen wasn't in residence a while ago,' the Days replied. 'It is lit in your honor.'

In her castle back home, there had been no such practice. Castle Sylvarresta served as the bastion of defense, and Iome had seldom left it. But Mystarria was another matter. Gaborn's family maintained half a dozen castles that could serve as resorts during time of war, along with palaces that had sometimes served as homes during times of peace.

Below Iome the various buildings of the Courts of Tide hunched in the darkness – lordly castles with their proud towers raised high, manors and estates squatting in their splendor. Markets cascaded to the west, the light of the horned moon glinting on their slate roofs; while beyond them, in the poorer quarters, the pitched roofs of thousands upon thousands of shanties jutted up like sharp stones.

Beyond it all was the vast ocean, placid. Salt tang tickled her nostrils. It was not a cold night.

'It's beautiful up here,' the Days said. 'Just as I always imagined.'

She went on, 'When I was young, my mother told me a child's tale. She said that there was a castle filled with giants on each edge of the world, and that those of the east are making war with those of the west. Each day, the giants to the east load their catapult, and send a flaming ball high overhead, to smash against the roofs of the castle to the west. And each night, those same giants send a great stone hurtling overhead. The ball of flame is the sun. The ball of stone is the moon. And when the day comes that the sun no longer rises, you'll know that the war has ended.

'The commoners in their shanties in town say that the King's Tower is so high,' the girl continued, 'that a far-seer standing here can look across the ocean, and spot the giants working to load their catapults.

'It was from this very tower that Fallion's far-seers spotted the gray ships.'

Iome smiled. Overhead, several stars lanced through the sky at once. One, in particular, was a huge fireball that hurtled slowly, leaving a flaming trail. She teased. 'It looks as if your giants must have run out of rocks. They're hurling shot tonight.'

The Days laughed. She turned, her eyes sparkling. She knew her history and she loved it. The girl's dream was to stand at the side of a queen and watch history unfold. But assuming that Gaborn even could stop the fell mage that led the Underworld, Iome would be stuck in this tower for weeks, doing nothing. The notion wrung her heart.

How long, Iome wondered, before this girl grows bored with me and regrets her choice of occupations?

Iome scanned the far horizon where water sparkled in the night. She couldn't discern any ships, or even a pod of whales. 'No giants,' Iome said. 'No ships either.'

At that, the girl stiffened involuntarily just a bit, and her fingers tightened on the stone rail around the parapet. She laughed again, but her laugh sounded forced.

Ships are coming, Iome realized. The Days knows it. Ships are coming to attack the Courts of Tide.

But whose ships?

Iome began to think furiously. To the south were the Inkarrans, who had never made war upon the north, though they were doing so now. Still, sending fleets was not how they practiced war. To the north were half a dozen countries that could muster a fleet – Lonnock, Toom, Eyremoth, Alnick, Ashoven, and Internook.

I'm jumping to conclusions, Iome thought. Yet she had to wonder. This Days was young, perhaps the youngest she'd ever seen. The rest had always been far more mature. Perhaps she wasn't fully trained.

For long centuries there had been rumors that Days sometimes acted as spies. Could this be the source of such rumors – a Days who involuntarily twitched an eye or looked away nervously when the conversation strayed to dangerous topics?

'So,' Iome said. 'You said you grew up here, in Berriston?'

'Yes, it's nearby,' the girl answered.

'Can we see it from here?'

The Days took her to the north side of the tower, pointed up along the coast four miles. 'You see the village there, the one with just a few lights.'

'Ah, so close,' Iome said. 'You could see the towers here from your home every day.'

'Not in the winter,' the Days said. 'Not when the fog rolls in.'

Iome had never known a Days who spoke so much. 'Does your family still live there, your mother, father, brothers, sisters?'

'My mother died years back,' the Days said. 'But my father is here, and my older brothers. They're twins. I never liked my stepmother.'

'Have you visited them recently?' Iome asked.

Now the girl clutched at the railing again, nervous. 'No.' Was she worried for her family, or did the idea of visiting them make her nervous?

'Would you like to?' Iome said. 'Perhaps I could take you.'

'No!' the Days answered. 'Time does not roll backward. We should not try to make it do so.' She did not speak this last with full conviction.

'I suppose not,' Iome said. 'I shall certainly never see my parents again, and nothing I can do will ever bring them back. It seems a shame, though, that your family would be so close, and you not able to see them.'

The Days clutched at the railing again, then looked away to the northwest, avoiding the subject.

Iome strolled around the promenade, until she faced west. Overhead, a star streaked across the sky, followed almost instantly by another.

'My husband is out there,' Iome said, 'fighting the reavers. He fears that the end may be coming, three or four days from now. But I suppose you know all that.'

The girl fell silent and leaned forward, gazing west.

Iome continued, 'He's facing so many enemies. It's not just the reavers. It's the Inkarrans to the south, now, and Raj Ahten. And mad King Anders. I worry for him.'

The Days did not clench the rail. She merely stood gazing out. Iome read her reaction: Gaborn is safe. Don't worry.

Iome's head felt near to bursting. She suspected that she was on to something. This girl was not fully trained. So long as she did not suspect that Iome could read her, she would continue to reveal what she knew in her reactions.

Iome circled the promenade. 'It's getting late. You'll probably want some sleep. I hope that your quarters are adequate?'

'They're wonderful.' To a girl of peasant stock, any quarters here would seem luxurious.

'And you've had dinner?'

'Yes.'

'Good,' Iome said. 'I've never given it much thought before, but I suspect it must be hard for a Days at first, to be stuck here without any friends.'

'Oh, I have friends,' the Days answered.

Iome knew of them. She knew that the girl had given an endowment of wit to another, a friend who granted the endowment back, so that now they were of one mind. Gaborn had spoken of how he himself envied those who had such deep relationships.

Beneath Iome, the tower began to sway slightly, and stones bucked under her feet.

At first she thought that she imagined it, and she reached for the railing more worried that she would look silly than from any concern about the safety of the tower.

Then the tower really did sway, and the ground trembled and shook. Iome's heart pounded.

'Earthquake!' the Days cried.

Her mouth opened in surprise, just as a rumbling sound rolled through the city.

The great tower began to thump up and down as the soil rolled beneath it in waves. Of all the places in the world that Iome would want to be during an earthquake, this tower was the last.

She heard glass shatter down in the palace as the huge windows in the Great Hall burst.

Throughout the Courts of Tide, people began to scream in alarm. Dogs barked and horses whinnied. In a castle on an island nearby, a whole tower collapsed, went sliding into the sea.

The Days grabbed the railing around the parapet, as if afraid that she might fall.

'Let's get out of here!' Iome shouted. She grabbed the girl's hands and pulled her through the door, into the tower proper.

The king's books tumbled from a shelf, along with a helm that clattered loudly. The canopy above the bed swayed.

Iome pulled the Days into the room just as a sound of cracking rock split the night air. The parapet outside splintered and fell.

The Days shouted and grabbed Iome, clutching her for support.

Still the tower swayed as if it might topple any second.

'Come on,' Iome said. She began dragging the girl from the room. Overhead, Iome could hear shouting as the far-seers raced for safety.

She leapt into the stairwell. Lamps were hung along the wall, and they swayed, spilling flaming oil. As the tower leaned, plaster on the walls buckled and fell in heavy chunks. The air inside the castle filled with dust and smoke.

Iome ran downstairs with her hand shielding her head from the debris. With her endowments of metabolism, the plaster seemed to slough off slowly. With her endowments of brawn, she was able to knock chunks of it aside, protecting herself and the girl.

She leapt past a wall of fire.

Enormous slabs of plaster skittered down the steps, and Iome had to fight for decent footing. The farther down she ran, the more it felt as if she were negotiating a landslide.

She felt inside her. Gaborn did not warn her of any danger as he had at Castle Sylvarresta. She felt only panic. At any moment the whole tower might collapse.

She had not reached the bottom of the stairs when the first tremor stopped.

The Days halted for a second. 'Wait. Wait. It's over.' She wiped tears of terror from her eyes and began to sob.

But Iome had seen more than one quake in Heredon, and she knew better. 'You can't know that!'

She grabbed the Days and urged her down the stairwell, out of the castle. It was good that she did.

Iome had just fled the building when a stronger tremor began to humble the Courts of Tide.

Chapter Forty-seven: SEARCHING FOR THE WAYMAKER

Honor often goes to the warrior who gives his life in battle. But few properly venerate the bravest of all: those who willingly endure endless agony for a higher cause.

– Lord Mangan

At the base of Mangan's Rock the ground lay scorched for a mile around. Here and there, small shrubs still burned, so that the land grew blacker than a night sky, even though a thousand small fires lit it.

To the east, Gaborn's fire raged, blowing into the foothills of the mountains. In all likelihood, it would continue to sputter and blaze into the forests for days.

With each step that Averan took, ashes stirred in the air, clogging her lungs. Averan, Binnesman, Gaborn, his Days stalked toward the dead reavers that lay in sordid humps, each monster taller than an elephant.

Thousands had leapt or fallen from Mangan's Rock in a grisly hail. Some had actually died. The land was covered with them at the south end of the cliff. In a few places, bodies lay three or four deep.

Thousands of the wounded retreated over the plains, legs broken or carapaces cracked. The rest of the horde outran them. Most of Gaborn's knights went to hunt down the injured, but he'd sent some scouts with torches in hand to search among the grim carcasses for the Waymaker.

Averan did not want to eat another reaver. The last one had wrung sweat from her, sickened her, caused her profound pain. Her nerves still jangled, and her muscles ached. It was too soon to eat again.

But dead reavers lay everywhere, and Gaborn didn't dare waste an opportunity.

Averan stalked through the ashes. A falling star streaked above her. She looked up, saw another almost immediately, and noted that only a few gree remained with the dead reavers. Either the smoke had killed them, or they'd flown off after the rest of the horde.

The ground shook again, and a few stones tumbled down from Mangan's Rock, bouncing among the reavers.

'Did you make the earthquake?' Averan asked Gaborn.

'No,' he said. 'It's none of my doing.'

She recognized a dying glue mum ahead. It lay on its back, gasping, drawing air in massive gulps. The sacs beneath its jaws excreted oozing mucilage.

'Don't go near,' Gaborn warned her.

'It's all right,' she said. 'Its philia aren't even moving.' She stared at it. 'This one was called Maker of High Things. It built the nesting hall for the One True Master.'

She went to it. This glue mum had been a fine beast. Many glue mums were trained to use their mucilage to reinforce ceilings in caverns and tunnels, but this one had excelled. Her vaulted arches and buttresses were a marvel of strength and grace.

'You feel sympathy for the monster?' Gaborn asked.

Averan closed her eyes, peered into a snatch of memory. 'They're alive,' she answered. 'This one – was an artist. It should have stayed where it belongs.'

Binnesman said, 'Good, child. You are learning. All life

is precious. All must be revered.'

For a long while Averan and Gaborn hunted, along with a hundred scouts. Word came to them after an hour that more than a thousand reavers had died in the stampede, and Skalbairn's men were still lancing the wounded, having made another two thousand kills. The main body of the horde was heading south, running along their trail to their bolt-hole in the Underworld.

So Gaborn and Averan hunted among the dead.

At Mangan's Rock the bodies lay thick against the cliffside, stacked to a depth of five or six deep, so that the corpses rose in morbid piles. The scouts searched as best they could, climbing down through little gaps where a reaver's leg or head wedged open a crawlspace.

But in some cases, it was simply impossible to see what might lie beneath the pile. Even Runelords with force horses couldn't easily move the massive carcasses of the reavers, and Gaborn was left to worry that the Waymaker would lie forever hidden.

'Milord!' a scout shouted. 'I think I've found him!' The scout appeared three hundred yards down the cliff, and stood atop a pile of dead reavers, waving his torch eagerly.

Averan jogged to the pile of corpses against the cliff. 'He's a big brute,' the scout said as she neared, 'just like you told us. And he's got thirty-six philia, and big paws. It's hard to see much down there, but there's a rune on his right shoulder, just like you said. The rest of him is buried down where I can't see it.'

Averan scampered up a jagged rock, the lichens on it rubbing her hands raw.

She climbed up on the corpse of a reaver with Gaborn's help. The pile of dead reavers here was deep, and to get to the one that she wanted, she had to go up and over. She was on a sorceress when the reaver twitched, and for one heart-stopping moment she dared not move, thinking it was alive.

She watched the scout crawl into a little cave formed by dead bodies. He squeezed under one reaver's leg, into a grotto. The torch lit the way.

Averan followed him down. The path was precarious – step on this reaver's leg here, watch out for the spike on that one's elbow, climb onto that one's head, don't let the torch burn you. And try not to worry that one of the reavers might twitch or shift, and the whole pile of them collapse on top of you.

Gaborn and Binnesman followed her down.

The scout reached the bottom, stepped back into a smaller space, and stopped. Averan followed. Smoke swirled in the still air, and the torch burned hot. She looked up in the torchlight and saw a reaver's head. She stifled a cry.

That's him! she thought immediately. Four dead reavers covered much of the corpse. But one huge paw protruded near his muzzle, and part of his shoulder could be made out between the legs of another reaver.

In size and shape, it looked like the Waymaker. Averan closed her eyes. Her only memories were seen from a reaver's point of view. They didn't see the world exactly like people do. To a reaver, the whole body glowed in different shades of blue light. So it was hard to tell.

'Yeah,' Averan said, her voice coming out rough with anticipation and dread. 'It could be him.' After hunting through thousands of reavers today, she felt skeptical.

The body of another reaver squashed the Waymaker's face so that the bony plate on its skull angled back, distorting the reaver's visage. 'Maybe if it wasn't squashed, I could be more sure.'

'What of the rune?' Gaborn asked. The reaver had a rune on his shoulder, still glowing in smoldering colors.

'I don't know,' Averan admitted. 'Reavers can't see those colors. To them, the runes are just smells, magical incantations written in smells.' Averan's memory didn't let her see the shape of the rune, and she couldn't tell if it was placed properly on the body.

She stared for long minutes. She couldn't smell anything but smoke. If she'd had a reaver's strong nose, and if she'd been able to get at its bunghole, she would know. 'I just can't be sure.'

'Will you eat from this one?'

Averan looked up. Fear made her breath come out ragged, and she found herself clenching her fist, so that her nails bit into her palm. 'I'm not sure. It might not be him.'

'But it's the closest match you've seen?'

Averan's stomach cramped in fear. 'Yes,' she said. 'But I can't do it.'

Gaborn took her chin in his hand and looked into her eyes. 'Listen, the world needs you to be strong. We may have driven the reavers from the rock, but already I sense a rising threat. Men are going to die in battle tomorrow, hundreds of men, maybe thousands. And tens of thousands more are at risk.'

'Is that supposed to make it easier?' Averan asked. 'I'm afraid. I got so sick last time –'

'Men are taught to give their lives,' Gaborn said. 'They give them in war. They wear themselves out working to support their wives and children.'

'Women wear themselves out too,' Averan said, thinking of her mother.

'Agreed,' Gaborn said. 'I'm not asking you to do anything more than what every man and woman does. When you grow up, you have to give yourself away. Sometimes you give your life all in a moment, but mostly you give yourself away laboring one minute at a time. I need you to grow a lot now.'

Binnesman hugged her close, offering comfort. Gaborn could give her none. He couldn't let her back down from her duty.

'My men have searched most of this pile in the past two hours,' Gaborn urged. 'We've found no other match.'

Averan swallowed hard. Gaborn was only asking her to grow up. That would happen whether she wanted to or not. 'I'll eat.'

As soon as she agreed, relief overwhelmed her. She'd only have to do it this one more time.

Gaborn let out a heavy sigh, knelt down, and put his arms around her. 'Thank you,' he said.

Gaborn felt exhausted – not just physically exhausted, but mentally and emotionally drained in a way he'd never felt in his life.

'Get her what she needs,' he told the scout. The reaver's sweet triangle was exposed enough so that a man ought to be able to get some of its brains out.

He patted Binnesman on the shoulder, and whispered, 'Stay with her. Give her what comfort you can. I need some rest.'

He went to his horse, rode his mount north for a mile along the cliff face. His Days followed, until they reached the fallen statue of Mangan.

The warrior had broken into a dozen chunks when he fell. Gaborn dismounted, scaled the side of Mangan's pitted head, and just sat with his hand against the rock, feeling a sort of reverence.

Little was known about Mangan – a few sayings, this statue. Over a thousand years ago he had built a fortress here. He had stopped the warriors of Muttaya from overwhelming western Mystarria. He'd built his castle and withstood enemy forces in a dozen fierce battles. He died young in some ignoble skirmish, and fifty years later his son had artisans carve the cliff face in his honor. Now the weathered stone felt rough under Gaborn's hand. The lichens grew thick.

Gaborn gazed up as a star streaked across the horizon. He'd seen a hundred in the past three hours.

Gaborn sat wondering. Things were changing, he realized. He sensed the rising danger to the wounded of Carris, who were floating down the river Donnestgree, along with some of his warriors.

He was becoming more adept at discerning such things. Sometimes, he could sense the danger well in advance. Other times, it seemed to flare up suddenly. It was like trying to stare into a pot of boiling water and decide which of the bubbles forming inside the cauldron would rise next. It seemed an inexact science, and Gaborn suspected that it had to do with agency, with the choices that he and his enemies made.

Out of nowhere, he could sense great jeopardy to Borenson and Myrrima. He desperately tried to warn them to hide, but could not reach them. He wondered how long this might go on. Would the Earth punish him forever? Would it really let his Chosen die? Or dared he hope that his powers might be restored in his hour of need?

He could not bear the thought that his Chosen might be torn from him. It wasn't just others' lives that were lost. In some small way, when one of his Chosen died, a part of him was lost also.

But it isn't just me, he realized. If a man dies, then perhaps a wife loses a husband and child loses a father. A whole village might feel the blow. Perhaps he was a breadmaker, or someone who could ease another's pain with a joke – make them feel lighthearted. The loss of one man's skills weakens his whole community, and in a small way his nation suffers, and his world.

We are all one fabric, humankind. To tear out a single thread unbinds us.

And, oh, how many threads have been torn.

Gaborn felt pangs of loss for his own father, for Iome's parents, for the hundreds of thousands who had already died, and for the millions that stood now on the threshold of death.

He sighed. 'Raj Ahten is near Kartish,' Gaborn quietly informed his Days. 'He is fading. He killed more of my Chosen today – a dozen men.'

'You spend a great deal of time worrying about the welfare of your adversary,' the Days pointed out.

Gaborn turned and looked at the skeletal scholar. The man sat on the cold rock, his feet drawn up to his chin, his robe pulled low over his face. Gaborn said, 'I would not have any man for my enemy, if I could choose it. Do you know what Raj Ahten faces in Kartish?'

'Time will reveal all things,' the Days answered.

Gaborn said, 'I sense a great danger rising. I suspect that Kartish is already destroyed.'

'I can neither confirm nor deny such suspicions,' the Days said.

After a lifetime of living with a Days, Gaborn expected nothing more. Gaborn had tried his best to evince aid from this man, to no avail.

Gaborn had memorized the drawing made by the Emir of Tuulistan. It revealed the Days' secret teachings from the Room of Dreams in the House of Understanding. As Gaborn studied the scholar before him, the image flashed through his mind.

The drawing detailed how each man saw himself as the lord of his own realm. It showed how men gauge good and evil based on whether another person enlarges one's territories or tries to diminish them.

Gaborn struggled inwardly, and suddenly had an insight. It seemed to him that a man could not truly be good in isolation. To develop such virtue, he had to recognize that he was inextricably tied to his community, to the brotherhood of mankind.

A truly good man, he reasoned, could not live for him

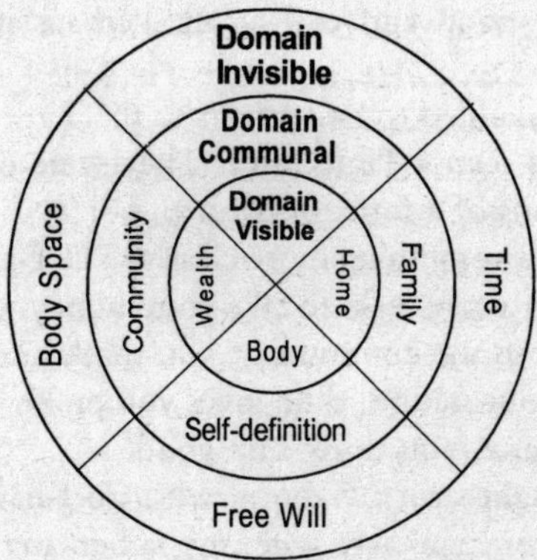

alone. Like some of the mystics in Indhopal who refused to wear clothes or to eat food that others might need, he gave himself in service.

Gaborn keenly felt the need to become that kind of man. Though he was born to be a lord, he wanted to dedicate every waking moment to protecting his people. He wanted to consecrate every thought in their behalf, every deed. Yet . . . nothing that he did seemed enough.

There was something in the nature of good and evil that he did not yet comprehend, some mystery that still eluded him.

He blinked his eyes. They felt gritty, overused. The Days merely sat on the rock.

Why? If the Days understood the nature of good and evil, why did they not act?

Was the Days even human anymore? Had he no compassion?

Suddenly connections seemed to weave together through Gaborn's mind, like lightning weaving across the clouds. He considered the diagram. Everything about it seemed to converge. He felt as if he were on the verge of revelation.

'Time!' he whispered in triumph. Perhaps the diagram wasn't about good and evil at all. Perhaps it was about *Time.*

The Days claimed to be servants to the Time Lords. Yet, who had ever seen a Time Lord? They were only legends, personifications of a force of nature.

Now he saw something more clearly. The Days' teachings said that when a man seeks to take your money, or your wife, or your place in the community, you think him evil. But if he enlarges your stature, if he gives you praise or wealth or gives of his time, you think him good.

But a thought struck Gaborn: what do I have that *Time* won't take from me? My wife, my father, my family? My wealth, my life? All that I am, Time will steal from me. I *have* nothing!

Obviously, the Days recognized this. But something about the recognition ate at Gaborn. One could deduce by this argument that Time was the ultimate evil, for it would surely strip a man of all pride and pretentiousness.

Gaborn wondered about his Days. He could not expect one of them to elaborate on his observation, or even to verify his suspicions. The order that they belonged to required them to remain aloof from the lords, to watch only, and never to influence the course of events that Time decreed.

So they merely watched events unfold. But to what end? Why would they give themselves in service to Time if it was the ultimate villain?

He had to be missing something.

If it was true that Time strips a man of everything that he thinks he owns, Gaborn wondered, then perhaps the Days see ownership as an illusion? Perhaps they believe that good and evil are mere phantasms?

Or maybe, Gaborn wondered, his thoughts coming in

a rush, they recognize that Time also gives us all that we have. It brings us our homes, our wealth, our loved ones. Time gives us every precious second to enjoy.

So Time may ultimately be a paradox: creator and destroyer, bringer of joy and sorrow.

Perhaps the Days saw themselves as enlightened, standing aloof from that paradox. It certainly fit with their actions – and inaction.

But what could they hope to gain from their service?

Time. The Days served the Time Lords. Could they hope to gain more *Time* for their service? Binnesman had lived for hundreds of years. The Earth had extended his life. Water wizards also were known to live for long ages.

Could his Days hope to similarly extend his life? It was a curious thought.

A nagging suspicion took hold of Gaborn. In all of the chronicles of the lives of various kings, nothing was ever said of the Days. The authors did not name themselves, remained completely anonymous. From time to time, they were reassigned. Gaborn's own Days had come to him when he was still only a child. He had looked then much as he did now – skeletal, fiftyish. His hairline had not receded farther, no age spots had appeared in, what, fifteen years?

Yet Gaborn could not credit the notion. If the Days did live to a long age, someone would have noted it before – unless, like other wizards, the Days each had varying degrees of power.

Perhaps there really were Time Lords. If one of them stood before Gaborn, would he even know?

'How old are you?' Gaborn asked the Days.

The Days' head swiveled. 'How old do I look?'

'Fifty years.'

The Days nodded. 'That would be about right.'

The answer was imprecise, an obvious evasion. 'Whose

life did you chronicle before you began writing my history?'

'Picobo Zwanesh, a prince of Inkarra,' the Days replied.

Gaborn had never heard the name, or even one similar to it. Nor had he known that his Days could speak Inkarran. 'He was the first person you chronicled?'

'Yes.' It was spoken slowly. Another evasion?

'How long do you hope to live?'

'From all that you say, anything beyond a week would be a great boon.'

There was a puzzle here. Something was still missing. For a moment he'd thought he was on the verge of a revelation. Now he wasn't sure he'd come any closer to the truth at all.

His Days certainly would not provide him with any clues. Gaborn couldn't afford to ponder it anymore. He was too appreciative of how every precious second passed. The future rushed toward him. He needed to rest. The time was coming when he'd not be able to afford the luxury.

Every couple of minutes, a falling star would arch through the sky like an arrow shot from the bow of the heavens. Shortly after midwinter for three days after Bride's Feast, it was normal for the heavens to put on a display like this, but not now.

'When you write the book of my life,' Gaborn asked, 'will you tell the world that it pained me to use my friends? Will you write that I wished evil upon no man, even my enemies?'

The Days answered, 'It is said that "Deeds reveal the inner man, even when he would cloak himself in fine words."'

'Yet sometimes deeds tell only half a tale,' Gaborn said. 'I don't like using this child, Averan. She should be allowed to grow into a beautiful woman, with sons and daughters of her own, and a husband that loves her true. Your book will only tell that I used her badly. It shames me that I must use her at all.'

'Your sentiments will be added as a footnote,' the Days said.

'Thank you,' Gaborn said sincerely.

A shout rose in the distance, hailing Gaborn. Gaborn looked south. A knight rode hard toward him, a flaming brand in his hand. He recognized the scout who had been with Averan and Binnesman.

'Yes?' Gaborn called.

'Milord,' the knight said, riding closer, 'I've been looking for you. I thought you should know: the girl Averan ate of the reaver. She's very ill.'

Gaborn went cold. 'How ill?'

'She cried out a few times, and sweat began to pour from her. Then she fell to the ground and began to convulse. She bit her tongue badly, and swallowed some blood. She was choking on it –'

'By the Powers!' Gaborn swore. What have I done?

'I got a knife between her teeth and pried her mouth open, but we had to put her on her belly lest she smother in her own blood. We can't get drink down her at all.'

Gaborn leapt down from the rock, ran to his horse.

'Binnesman and his wylde are doing their best to keep her alive,' the scout said.

He swung up onto his mount, urged it galloping back to the south. He came up on a small knot of men all in a circle.

Two lords held Averan pinned to the ground, so that she wouldn't hurt herself as she convulsed. Her eyes were rolled back in her head, showing white, and her eyelids quivered. Her breath came out in great wheezes.

Binnesman stood over her, swinging his staff slowly, as he finished a higher incantation.

The stench told Gaborn that she'd retched, and wet puddles in the ash showed the remains of her meal.

He turned away in disgust. After long minutes, Binnesman came to his side, put a hand on his shoulder.

'The reaver she ate must have been near death. It was suffering greatly. She had hardly finished eating, when she cried out, "I'm dying. I'm dying."'

Gaborn dared not say anything.

'She regurgitated most of the meal,' Binnesman said. 'In doing so, I suspect she saved her life.'

Gaborn shook his head, confounded, unable to think what to do next. 'And perhaps because of it, we have lost ours.'

Chapter Forty-eight: MATTERS OF THE HEART

I know not which to fear most – the asp's poison, the wight's touch, or my wife's wrath.

– King Da'verry Morgaine

Borenson stared by starlight at Myrrima's right hand. The knuckles and middle three fingers were icy and almost as white as the hoarfrost that blasted the ground for fifty yards in every direction.

He touched her flesh, found it so bitter cold that it felt hot. Her teeth were chattering, and she trembled from the chill.

The Toth wight had cast some sort of spell on her.

'Damn,' he swore. Her fingers were as good as gone. She'd lose them for sure – maybe the whole hand.

Borenson's heart was still pumping frantically. The wight's dying scream echoed endlessly in his mind. His thoughts were racing. His wife had banished a wight. *That* couldn't happen. Only a powerful mage might have done it. And it looked as if she would lose her hand.

She did it for me, he realized. She stood over me and fought the monster, just as she fought the reavers near Mangan's Rock.

He couldn't think clearly. He breathed on her hand, trying to heat it.

'Let's wrap it and try to keep it warm,' he offered, pulling off his own cloak. He gingerly bundled the cloak around the injured hand.

'There's no warmth left in it,' Myrrima said. 'The cold is spreading.'

The touch of the air around him was surprisingly bitter, as if this place might not thaw in a week. Ice clung to his beard. The very air felt as brittle as the crust of ice at his feet.

A fire? he considered. But his fire kit was in his saddlebags. He looked down the road. The horses had both run off. With a wight on their tails, they'd probably keep running until dawn.

'Can you walk?' Borenson asked. 'Fenraven can't be far.'

'I can walk,' Myrrima said through chattering teeth. 'But can you keep up with me?' She was a Runelord now, with more endowments of brawn and metabolism than he, and endowments of stamina to boot. She could run farther and faster than he.

'No,' he said. 'There's bound to be a healer in Fenraven, a midwife at least. Maybe you should go ahead.'

Myrrima climbed shakily to her feet. Even with all of her endowments, the effort seemed to drain her. She grabbed her bow, used it as a staff, and began to hobble forward. In his mind, Borenson recalled how Hoswell had fled the battlefield only hours ago using the same bow in just such a manner. He'd not survived.

Borenson jogged along beside her.

She looked down the road determinedly. 'We've got to find the horses,' Myrrima said between chattering teeth. 'I put some of Binnesman's healing salve in my saddlebags.'

Passing out of the blasted area was a relief. The warm night air seemed to surge around Borenson. He felt refreshed by it, more hopeful. He realized that moments before he'd felt . . . depleted of some vital essence. He hoped that Myrrima would feel it too.

Starlight shone overhead, a powder in the heavens that

barely pierced the gauzy clouds. Soon they topped a small rise, and he looked eagerly along the road ahead. Night vapors spread over the muddy trail in patches. Black trees raked the sky with leafless limbs.

He could see no cheering lights for miles ahead, and no sign of his horses.

It looked like a good patch of road in which to find another wight.

There is a rider ahead of us, he recalled. Most likely he is an assassin out of Muyyatin.

Borenson had few endowments. His warhammer remained sheathed on his horse's back. His only weapon was the long knife strapped to his leg.

Myrrima took a look at the horizon, groaned in despair. 'How big is Fenraven?' she asked as she stood panting.

'Not big,' he said. He'd never been there, but knew it by reputation.

'So, maybe – maybe we just can't see its lights. It could be close ahead.'

Borenson knew that Fenraven was situated just beyond the bogs on a small island. The flowing water around it was a bane to wraiths, but the people of Fenraven also kept lanterns outside every doorway, to make doubly sure.

If we were even close, he knew, we'd see those lights, or smoke rising from the town. But there was nothing. 'You could be right,' he lied, trying to offer some comfort. 'It could be anywhere.'

Myrrima nodded, hobbled on.

For nearly half an hour he jogged to keep pace with her. He pulled off his armor, threw it to the ground, along with his helm.

Myrrima's breath came in quick, shallow gasps. She held her wounded arm cupped against her chest like a claw, Borenson's cloak wrapped around it. He could tell that she was in great pain.

They ran through the fog-shrouded woods, and Borenson listened for the sounds of danger or for his horses. Water dripped from tree limbs, landing in the mud with sucking sounds. The wind blew softly, making leaves skitter nervously. Borenson recalled the elemental of the Darkling Glory that had attacked Gaborn's camp earlier in the day, and the gale that had raced ahead of them inexplicably this afternoon.

Was this some kind of vengeance? he wondered. Myrrima had done the creature great harm, after all. He only wished that she could have killed it.

Myrrima slowed and began to move erratically after the first half hour, scampering forward in little starts and stops. He could walk as fast as she could by then.

He was winded. He figured that they had covered nearly three miles. He felt numb all over. He kept watching her. She seemed more drained with each passing moment. He feared that she would collapse with nearly every step.

They reached another hillock, looked down the road below. Stars fell, as if to empty the heavens.

The hills were rising, becoming a bit taller. The fog lay thicker in the folds beneath. Finally, a horned moon began to climb above the horizon, limning it with light. In the distance to the south, he could make out the jagged white peaks of the Alcairs. No sign of horses, no sign of town.

He glanced at Myrrima, and what he saw made chills lance through him. Her face had a deathly pallor and she breathed roughly, shallowly. With every breath, fog rolled out of her mouth and hung round her face in a little cloud.

Yet it was not so cold that his breath did so.

The Bright Ones protect her! he swore inwardly.

'Are you all right?' he asked.

Weakly, she shook her head, no.

'Let's have a look at that hand,' he said.

Myrrima shook her head no, pulled back, but he took her gingerly. Her right arm would not move. It felt as if it were frozen at the elbow. He began gently unwinding his cloak from around her arm. The folds of cloth had frozen to her flesh.

He got it off, and found that more than her knuckles and fingers were white now. The ice reached all the way up her arm, and was spreading to her shoulder.

It was as if death crept through her flesh.

He stared at her, stricken with horror.

Myrrima nodded, as if the sight only gave her visual confirmation of how she felt.

'It will kill me,' she said.

Borenson looked about, bewildered. There was no fighting otherworldly powers. He was no sorcerer, had no weapons.

'Maybe . . . if we cut it off . . .' The very notion horrified him. He had never performed an amputation. He had no bandages, nothing that would relieve her pain. And from the look of it, the arm would have to come off at the shoulder. He wouldn't be able to control the bleeding.

Myrrima shook her head. 'I don't . . . I don't think it will work.'

'Here,' he said, 'lean against me for a moment.' He still wore the padding that he'd had beneath his armor, and his sweat was slick beneath it. He unlaced the front of it, along with his tunic, then put her arm against his side. Her touch was like bitter ice, and he wondered for a moment if the wight's curse would take him too.

He no longer cared if it did.

Early in the morning, he'd asked Gaborn what more he might be required to give. Borenson had already lost his manhood, and his virtue. Now he realized that he was about to lose something more, something so precious he had never even guessed at its worth: his wife.

Myrrima leaned against him heavily, as if to steady herself, as her breath came quick and frightened.

This isn't how it was supposed to be, he thought. When

he'd left Castle Sylvarresta four nights ago, he'd imagined that he was leaving Myrrima forever.

I was the one taking the road to Inkarra. I was the one who was never supposed to return.

He'd been protecting himself from that knowledge. He'd refused to give himself to her in hopes that he would protect her, too. He saw that now, all in flash. Myrrima was right.

He'd tried to divorce himself from any feeling for her. But he'd loved her from the moment he saw her.

He began to suspect that he *knew* what that meant. He'd stood at Gaborn's back as he studied in the House of Understanding. Borenson had never been a student, had kept his eyes and ears open for danger. But he had learned some things.

Now, he tried to recall something he'd heard once while Gaborn listened to a lecture in the Room of the Heart. The memories came slowly, and Borenson wondered at that. Perhaps they came slowly because he'd lost endowments of wit when Raj Ahten destroyed the Blue Tower. Perhaps they came slowly because he'd never paid much attention to Hearthmaster Jorlis. Who could take a man seriously who spent his whole life thinking about emotions?

In the Room of the Heart, Hearthmaster Jorlis had taught that every man has two minds, the 'scant mind' and the 'deep mind.'

Jorlis had said that the scant mind was cold, logical and rational. It knew little of love. It was the part of the mind that fretted about numbers and accounts.

But Jorlis said that every man has another mind, a deep mind. It was the part of the brain that dreamed and struggled to comprehend the world. It was the creative mind that made unexpected insights. It was the part of the mind that assured you when you'd made a right choice, or that warned against danger by sending feelings of uncertainty or fear.

Borenson had always felt skeptical of such teachings. After

all, Jorlis was a bit of a pansy – a big-boned man with red cheeks and soft flesh.

But Jorlis claimed that the deep mind would ponder problems for weeks or months, independent of the scant mind, until it discovered solutions that the scant mind could never fathom. Thus, he believed that the deep mind was far wiser than the scant mind.

Jorlis had said that when a man fell in love with a woman at first sight, it was a warning from the deep mind that the woman before him matched his vision of an ideal mate.

The deep mind created that image. It told a man that his perfect love would have the kindness of his aunt, and the eyes of his mother. She might treat children as tenderly as a neighbor did, and have his father's sense of humor. All of these traits were then bound into an image, woven from borrowed threads into a crude tapestry.

'The recognition you feel when you meet the woman of your dreams, that rush of dizziness and thrill of discovery,' Jorlis had taught, 'is merely the deep mind speaking to you. It is warning you that it recognizes in someone some virtues that you've long sought. The deep mind is not always right, but it is always worth listening to.'

Nonsense, Borenson had thought. Jorlis had always seemed to be a touch off.

But with Myrrima, everything that she had done was beginning to convince Borenson that in his case, the deep mind was right.

She was everything that he'd ever hoped for in a woman. She was full of warmth and compassion and endless devotion. All his life, he'd felt as if he were but half a man.

Myrrima completed him.

So he held her.

The cold of her wound seeped into his side, and if his attempt to warm her did any good, he could not tell. He bore it for long minutes, as her face went pale and her trembling increased. The fog around her mouth came out thicker with every breath.

'Hold my hand,' she begged weakly, through chattering teeth. He took her frozen right hand in his, but she shook her head. 'Not that one. I can't feel anything.'

He gripped it anyway, took her left hand too. The cold from her right hand was like a fire, burning up his arm. It could not easily be borne.

He wondered if he could divert the cold, let himself become a conduit for her death.

Take me, he begged of the Powers. Take me instead.

She leaned against him heavily, her head resting against his shoulder.

'I love you,' he whispered into her ear.

She nodded slightly. 'I know.'

In the distance, a lone wolf howled at the rising moon out in the woods, while stars streaked through the night sky.

He kissed her brow, and Myrrima fell into him, a dead weight. He held her up for a moment. She was breathing still, but he could not guess how much longer she might hold on.

It was late, past midnight, he figured. He felt hungry and exhausted. He had few endowments to help him, none of stamina, and he had no idea how far Fenraven might be. Miles, he suspected.

He considered abandoning Myrrima while he went for help. She was a large woman, and he didn't know how far he could carry her. But the wolf was howling, and he dared not leave her. Besides, he knew that she would not want to die alone.

He carried her.

Chapter Forty-nine: STARFALL

Catastrophe teaches us humility, compassion, courage, and perseverance. Beyond that, it's an absolute bother and I have no use for it.

– Duke Paldane

At the Courts of Tide, yet another tremor struck. Messengers from all over the countryside carried reports of the damage to Iome. In the hours since the quakes first hit, towers in a dozen castles had collapsed, along with a bridge that joined two of the larger islands in the city.

More frightening were reports of damage in the poorer quarters. There, cheap shanties collapsed and caught flame, so that even now the people of the Courts of Tide battled fires on a dozen fronts. Worse, huge waves beat the northern shores after the first temblor. The waves capsized boats and swept more than a thousand cottages into the sea.

The death toll would not be known for days.

So fires lit the city, while pillars of smoke rose.

Servants and guards from Gaborn's palace all took refuge outside, bringing blankets and furs to lie on.

No one slept.

Lanterns brightened the courtyard. The cooks carried out stores of bread, huge hams, and slabs of beef. In an attempt to lighten the mood, the king's minstrels decided to play.

It made for a macabre carnival.

Iome felt almost as if she were accursed by the Earth.

But as reports came in, she realized that the tremors had nothing to do with her. Apparently the devastation was worse a dozen miles north, where whole villages had been flattened.

Messengers inundated the castle, requesting men to help in rescue efforts. Chamberlain Westhaven, who handled the normal duties while the king was gone, deferred judgment on such matters to Iome.

For hours Iome sat in the open courtyard while the minstrels played and couriers bore tales of woe. With the help of various scribes and minor lords, she levied lords for men to help with the rescue efforts and to feed and shelter the homeless. She appropriated funds to begin rebuilding.

In one night she spent twelve times as much gold as her father would have in a year, until she began to worry whether she squandered Gaborn's wealth.

She had no experience running such a large kingdom. The problems threatened to overwhelm her. Time and again, Chamberlain Westhaven offered advice at crucial moments. He was a competent man and knew the realm far better than she did.

As she worked, her Days curled up on the ground and merely watched, trying not to sleep. A dozen times after Iome had brought the girl out of the tower, the Days thanked her profusely. For long minutes, the girl could not help crying, and Iome longed to give her comfort.

Obviously, the Days worried for her family, a few miles to the north.

Yet Iome could not feel any comfort herself. There had been strange tremors in Heredon before she left. She'd felt them again south of Carris, and now here at the Courts of Tide. Were they related?

Gaborn claimed it was a message: The Earth was in pain.

But if the minor tremors had been a sign of its pain, Iome wondered, what could this devastating quake mean?

Intuition told her that these matters were related. She tried not to worry about it.

Thus the ground shook and fires raged throughout the city when a tall, gaunt scholar came through the crowd that had gathered in the courtyard around the King's Keep.

He wore a blue robe with silver stars sewn upon it, marking him as a stargazer. He had a long silver beard and piercing eyes.

Chamberlain Westhaven leaned close and whispered, 'Hearthmaster Jennaise, from the Room of Stars. I suspect that his watchtower has fallen. But may I remind Your Highness that we do not spend funds repairing their buildings. The House of Understanding has always been supported solely by its patrons.'

Iome nodded.

The stargazer strode to Iome and said in a Ferecian accent, 'Your Highness, I beg the queen's ear. We have a great problem, an unprecedented problem.'

'How may I help you, Hearthmaster Jennaise?'

'I'm not sure where to begin,' the stargazer said in a befuddled tone. Of course not, she thought. Ferecians never know where to begin, or how to finish, or when to get to the point.

'Your watchtower has sustained damage?'

'The observatory? It's a mess – charts and scrolls everywhere. And there was a fire! My assistant nearly died trying to save the maps. It will take weeks to clean it. I'm sure the water we threw on the fire did as much damage as the flames themselves – but, er, uh, that is not your concern, is it? Indeed, I'm not sure if any of this is your concern.'

'Nor am I,' Iome said quite frankly, for she had no more idea what his problem was than when he had first opened his mouth.

He looked at the crowd of servants and whispered, 'Your Highness, may we speak privately?'

Iome nodded, and together they strolled through the courtyard over to the shadows beneath a pair of pecan trees, in a dark corner by the castle wall.

'Milady,' he said, 'what do you know of the stars?'

'They're pretty,' Iome said dryly.

'Yes,' Jennaise said. 'And you may also know that as the seasons progress, the constellations rotate about the sky. At the first of the year, Elwind rides over the mountains of the north. But at high summer he is almost straight overhead.'

'I know,' Iome said.

'Then it is with great . . . bewilderment that I must report that the stars are wrong.'

'What?' Iome asked.

'The stars are wrong tonight. It is all very baffling. Tonight is the third of the month of Leaves. But by our charts, the stars read as if it were the twentieth of the month of Harvest – off by two weeks.'

'How can that be?' Iome asked. 'Could the charts be wrong? Perhaps –'

'The charts are not wrong. I've been over them a hundred times. I can think of only one explanation,' Jennaise answered. 'The world is taking some new path through the heavens. Even the moon – by my preliminary measurements –'

A moment before Iome had felt overwhelmed. Now she was staggered. She stared at him with her mouth open, and finally managed to ask, 'What can we do?'

Jennaise shook his head. 'I – perhaps no one can help. But your husband *is* the Earth King.'

Suddenly she recalled Averan's words. The One True Master was binding the Rune of Desolation to the Runes of Heaven and the Inferno. She planned to make a new world, where mankind would not survive.

Could she wrest the Earth from its appointed course?

'Of course,' Iome said. 'I'll – send word immediately.'

Even if the One True Master had done this, how could Gaborn stop her? He'd lost most of his own powers.

The stargazer turned to leave, and Iome desperately cast her eyes over the courtyard. She called for a courier, thinking to pen a message to Gaborn.

But even as she began thinking how to frame the words, she realized that she wasn't telling Gaborn anything that he didn't already know.

He'd warned Iome that if he did not destroy the reavers' lord, his people would all die. He knew the danger as well as she did.

Or did he? she wondered. Gaborn could sense danger, but he could never tell from what quarter it might come. And nearly all of his Chosen in Mystarria were still near the city of Carris. He couldn't sense danger to those outside the city. She wondered what Gaborn would say if she warned him of her suspicions of an impending attack here at the Courts of Tide. Would he ask her to go, or to stay? She wondered what he would say if he knew that the world was out of its course.

Just then, Grimeson came into the courtyard with a facilitator in tow. 'Milady,' he shouted. 'We got them endowments that Gaborn wanted.'

Iome's thoughts had been a jumble. She'd forgotten about the endowments. Gaborn had ordered the facilitators to prepare vectors for Averan. Now, the facilitator would need to escort the vectors to Gaborn.

'Get horses and set off immediately,' Iome told Grimeson. 'Every second counts.'

'Milady,' Grimeson said, 'these vectors have been up all night. I wouldn't want one of them to fall off his horse. There's royal carriages that would be almost as fast as a horse.'

'By all means then, we'll take carriages.'

'We?'

Iome felt as if the world were falling apart around her. Gaborn had sent her here to be 'safe.' But the quakes had struck and towers collapsed and the stars were falling. The world was out of its course.

No place was safe.

Her place was beside Gaborn, but she couldn't follow him into the Underworld. There, she would only be a liability to him. He was the Earth King still, and though his powers were diminished, he alone might stand against the reaver lord.

Yet there had to be something more that she could do than wait here at the Courts of Tide. She glanced back over her shoulder, saw Chamberlain Westhaven taking a few moments to advise half a dozen lords in her absence. He knew this realm better than she did.

'Grimeson,' she said with finality. 'Get my escort. I'm coming with you. I need to speak to Gaborn.'

She penned a note to Chamberlain Westhaven, warning him to prepare for an attack from the sea, and handed it to a page.

In moments she was gone.

Chapter Fifty: REMEMBERING SUMMER

A thousand blows struck in battle bring a man less honor than a single act of compassion.

– Ivarian Borenson

Borenson staggered through the dark moors, carrying Myrrima in his arms. She was a big woman, and even with an endowment of brawn, he could not carry her easily – he tired too quickly.

As he carried her, he clung to her right hand, gripping it for life, hoping that by some miracle he could help her hold on for awhile longer.

It made little difference, he suspected.

In fact, after an hour, he knew that it made no difference. The bleak cold from her hand froze his bones, making them hard as iron. His own right hand became locked to hers.

He did not regret his decision to hold her, to warm her. He regretted only that he could not feel her hand anymore, for his own flesh seemed to have frozen as solid as midwinter ice.

So he bore her over uneven ground. He listened to her teeth chatter, and each time a puff of icy air came from her mouth, he thought it a small miracle.

It became a chore to walk. Sweat poured from him and his legs burned. Without an endowment of stamina, he tired as quickly and deeply as any other man. He dared not rest, for fear that if he stopped, then he would not regain the will to move again.

So he staggered on beneath the dripping trees and starlit skies over a land so dank it was fit only for newts and worms. The wolf continued to howl. He no longer feared assassins or wights. He knew his own death would not be far away. The cold of the Toth's wight stole the heat from his own hand, had worked its way down to his elbow. His prayer had been answered in part.

Myrrima would die. He could not stop it. But he also knew that he could not live much longer. He had taken her death into himself as well.

So it was that as he walked, he felt an odd sensation between his legs as his testicles suddenly dropped.

He had had no premonition, no tingling or warning. Indeed, he had forgotten that little boys are not born with hanging walnuts. Instead, they ripen in small sacs between their legs, and drop after a couple of years.

The wizard's balm had worked its miracle. There could have been no more natural way for it to happen.

'I'll pay that damned wizard no more than a pint for the both of them,' Borenson choked, and laughed at fate's cruel jest.

He kept walking. Lift a foot, plod forward. Lift a foot, stagger on.

He could no longer hold his head up. With every step, the world seemed to swim, and his eyes would not focus.

He lost consciousness, and walked for a while in a dreamscape where Myrrima's shade floated beside him.

'I'm coming with you to Inkarra no matter what,' she said. 'Leave my body here, and I'll follow. It's all gone cold anyway.'

An overwhelming sadness took him, and he looked down to discover if it was true. He couldn't see whether she was breathing anymore. Icy cold ran up the length of his own arm, pierced his shoulder now.

He wanted nothing more than to lie down with Myrrima to die.

He thought about the message for King Zandaros. He wasn't sure that he could deliver it any longer. He'd always tried to be faithful to Gaborn. It hurt to find that he had failed him at last.

It was bound to happen, Borenson told himself.

And Daylan Hammer, that mythical figure, was still supposed to be in Inkarra. What of the Sum of All Men? Did he even exist?

He kept walking, and must have slept as he did. He stumbled into a streambed, slipped on round wet stones. One of them drove into his knee, waking him. It was hazy. Mist rose up from the brook, filling its channel with a thick fog. He got up, waded in water up to his hips across the stream, under the dark trees.

I must be getting close to Fenraven, he thought.

He heard a horse whicker. He jumped, realized that he had passed it in the dark, or fog, or perhaps in his sleep.

His own warhorse, the one he'd let Myrrima ride, stood beside the brook, its reins tangled in a limb. He went to it, held Myrrima still as he dug into the saddlebags.

He found the wizard's balm, as she'd said.

He pulled it out, managed to open the tin with one hand. He looked at Myrrima for a long moment. It was dark and foggy. He could hardly see for the burning sweat that stung his eyes. He could not tell if she breathed anymore. If her chest rose and fell, he could not detect it.

He gazed up at the sky, saw a pair of stars plunging through the night. The horizon seemed to be lighter. Soon dawn would come. He wondered if he would live to see it.

He sat down with Myrrima, and smeared the wizard's balm

up her arm, over her wrist, and between each finger on her right hand.

He spared only the tiniest bit for himself. There was precious little of it left.

Then he lay down with her beside the stream. He tried to listen to the plink of water as it tumbled over stones. He gazed at the odd way that fog coursed along the channel. He sniffed the scent of moist ground. A cricket chirped in a thicket of brambles, adding a lonely serenade to the music of the water. He could feel nothing in his right hand. He lay against Myrrima, hoping to warm her.

His thoughts came muzzily. He felt weary nigh to death, but could not sleep.

For a long hour he remained as the stars began to fade, and if his wife breathed, he could not see it, could not feel it. He caressed her chin. It was cold to the touch.

She's dead, he finally admitted, his mind reeling in a daze.

The balm had warmed his hand, brought some life back to it. He pried it loose from Myrrima's frozen grasp.

There was no use pretending any longer, or hoping that she might live. On the Isle of Thwynn, where Borenson was born, the dead were not consigned to the earth, but to the sea.

So he kissed Myrrima goodbye, and begged her forgiveness for loving her poorly. Then he carried her back to the brook, and waded in to his hips. The water seemed warmer than the night air. It still remembered summer.

Somewhere in the distance, a cock crowed. His mind was a muddle from fatigue. He gave his wife to the stream and to the mist, let her float along the brook. Part of him could not believe that she was gone. It is that way with death. He stared into the mist, listened to the stream's music. 'Let her find peace in your embrace,' he whispered to the brook, 'as you carry her to the sea.'

He felt as if he had somehow betrayed his wife. But in his spent and confused state, he couldn't figure out why. He turned and staggered to his mount. There would be an inn at Fenraven, but he doubted that he would find comfort there.

Chapter Fifty-one:
THE POINT OF NO RETURN

Life is a journey, and with every step we reach a point of no return.

– Gaborn Val Orden

Dawn found Averan lying in a fetal position beside Spring in the back of a wagon as it thundered along a road, heading south from Carris. Averan's tongue had quit bleeding where she'd bitten it, but sweat soaked her thin robe. A large praying mantis rode on the buckboard above her, having turned as gray-brown as the wagon. It stood perfectly still.

Averan lay trembling in pain, wrung out. But the convulsions had mostly stopped an hour ago. She knew that she would live.

Worst of all, she knew that she had failed. She'd fed upon the wrong reaver again. The Waymaker was still out there in the reaver horde, waiting for Gaborn to hunt him down. Waiting for Averan.

She shook her head in despair. The reavers were suffering more than men could suffer. She knew that now. Their capacity to endure pain far exceeded that of a man. Averan feared that if she tried to eat again, she'd die. Yet if she found the Waymaker, she couldn't refuse to try.

She knew little of the blade-bearer she had eaten.

Cunning Eater was its name. His few memories tormented her.

Cunning Eater had often tunneled beneath enemy hives and masterminded his queen's wars of genocide. The visions Averan faced were atrocious – charging through enemy tunnels, tearing off the sweet meat of enemy corpses and gulping them down with a ravenous appetite. In her memory, none were spared. Even the eggs of enemy queens became food for Cunning Eater's horde. No human lord had ever been as rapacious as the monster Averan had eaten.

He had been a master of war, one who had studied ancient battles against mankind and sought to devise new strategems.

Averan closed her eyes against the rising sun, tried to forget.

Still the wagon raced on, chasing the reavers' trail. In the still dawn the high clouds blanketed the skies like a sheet of white silk, while behind it the sun was a rose-colored lamp, all incandescent. A morning mist roamed the fields.

The reavers thundered over the plains, black in the wan morning light, like a vast stampede of elephants as they rocked across the golden grasslands, stirring up dust and sending starlings to wheel through the sky in fretful clouds.

But the reavers plodded slowly now. In five hours during the night they had traveled fewer than forty miles.

The reavers had spent themselves. Averan could feel it from Cunning Eater's every memory. Sweat still squeezed from her every pore. A ravenous thirst still assailed her. She drank, but water did not satisfy. She craved more, but when men offered it to her fresh, she sniffed at it and panicked. She wanted sulfur in it.

The reavers themselves had begun to show signs that they were failing. In the night, first one reaver and then another dropped from the marching line. They did not stop, just simply began loping in circles. Their left legs kept marching while their right could not, so that they spun around on the ground like water beetles on the surface of a pool.

Gaborn himself had ridden up to her wagon in the predawn darkness an hour ago, pointed out the afflicted reavers by moonlight and asked, 'Do you know what it means?'

'They're dying of thirst,' she confirmed.

'Let's hope for a warm day then,' he'd said. 'Maybe a bit of sun will hurry their end.'

Now, Averan's left arm spasmed in a cramp. She cried out. Spring crept up beside her in the bed of the wagon and began stroking Averan's hair.

A memory carried Averan back to when she was small. She remembered a picnic with her mother at Kellysbrook, just outside the Boar and Stag back home.

She must have been very small. It was the first time she remembered ever really seeing a stream.

The water of Kellysbrook tumbled down from the hills, burbling over round stones pounded as smooth as porcelain by the waves. Water so cold that it should have been ice spilled upon the gravelly banks. The taste of the freshet was like freezing rain in the air, and the jingle and chink of water on rock became a soothing music. The water misted her face.

In places the stream slowed and dropped into languid pools. There, minnows darted in the shadows of moss-laden logs, and water striders danced upon the deep.

For hours she had searched among the pools for shy crayfish that walked about with their bouncing gait.

Afterward, Averan lay beneath a willow in a patch of sunlight as her mother told her stories, stroking her hair.

But Averan was a long way from Kellysbrook now. It seemed like forever ago.

As Averan shivered in the green woman's arms, she looked up into the creature's eyes. Spring's touch was soothing, and Averan could feel Earth Power in her, but it wasn't soothing like a mother's touch.

Something enigmatic, wild and feral, gleamed in Spring's eyes. The green woman was not a woman at all, not her mother or a friend. Spring was not even an animal.

'Can you help me?' Averan asked. 'Can you help me find the Waymaker?'

The green woman made no answer. She didn't even understand the question.

Suddenly, from the wagons and men all around, a cheer arose.

Averan climbed up, looked around. The soldiers were riding slowly across the plains, the frowth giants following in their trail. The reavers kept to their formation. She could see no cause for celebration.

'What's going on?' Averan asked the wagon driver.

He glanced back over the buckboard. 'We've passed the point of no return. It's closer for the reavers to head to the Underworld now than to turn back for Carris.'

The men cheered as if it were a great victory.

Gaborn spurred his mount past the line of wains, and a wounded knight in a wagon ahead called, 'Are we going to make another charge?'

'Not yet!' he warned. Gaborn studied the reavers pensively, looked to Averan as if for advice, but asked nothing. Instead, he continued to ride alongside her wagon.

The reavers dragged themselves homeward at a plodding pace as Gaborn's armies rode their flanks.

The sun had just topped the horizon when Gaborn suddenly blew his warhorn, calling retreat. He shouted to the wagon drivers. 'Turn the wains around, quickly! Go back!'

'What is it? What's going on?' Averan's driver asked.

He studied the reavers uncertainly. Nothing had changed. They still moved south. He slowed the horses, wheeled the wagon. He snapped his whip over the horses' heads, and the wagon began to bounce over the highway as the force horses gathered speed.

Still, he couldn't give the animals their heads. These were big draft horses used for carrying goods swiftly, but few had more than a single endowment of metabolism. The train could move along the road only as fast as the slowest team.

'Get off the road!' Gaborn shouted to the drivers. 'Give your horses their heads. The reavers are going to charge!'

Averan climbed up from her blanket, and watched the reavers for any sign of danger.

She could see no hint of it. Her driver pulled off the road and snapped his whip. The wheels sang and the wagon bounced over rocks and roots. The wagons and their drivers threw long shadows in the early morning light.

After two or three minutes, suddenly the whole horde halted in their march, and a hissing erupted from the reavers' lines.

Thousands of the behemoths rose up on their back legs and stood for several long seconds. They faced east into the morning light, philia waving excitedly.

The hissing grew louder and louder. The reavers seemed agitated, or maybe frightened.

Averan's driver cursed his horses and asked, 'What's going on?'

'They smell something,' Averan warned. Gaborn's men had been riding their flanks. Averan's wagon was perhaps two miles up the side of their lines.

It looked almost as if the reavers were trying to catch a glimpse of something, or to taste an elusive scent.

Averan turned east, but could spot nothing on the horizon – only golden plains with oaks rising here and there, some distant hills.

Do they smell another war party? she wondered. Were they hoping for reinforcements, or was an army riding to Gaborn's aid? She doubted it.

She searched the skies for sign of thunderclouds on the horizon.

As she did, the reavers charged straight toward Gaborn's troops. The lords on their force horses easily outpaced the monsters, but the frowth giants were hardpressed. They loped along the field, swinging their arms hugely in a bouncing gait. The frowths' nostrils flared, and they called out to one another in their own tongue.

Now the wagon drivers whistled and cracked their whips, shouting, 'Haw, there! Haw!'

Horses whinnied in terror.

She saw one team of horses swerve into another. Their lines tangled and a horse tripped. A wagon spilled lances to the ground, throwing the drivers down like dolls.

One driver limped up to grab the back of the closest passing wain. The other driver did not move.

Reavers thundered toward Gaborn's flank. They ran with renewed vigor, faster than she'd have thought possible, their teeth flashing in the morning sunlight.

Averan couldn't understand why the reavers suddenly took the offensive.

Gaborn's knights wheeled northeast. The men on chargers could easily outpace the monsters. But her wagon was another matter. It bounced over the plains, and threw Averan into the air each time a wheel hit a rock. She heard a crack as an axle split.

She clutched the sideboards. The frowth giants raced along now, almost to the wagons. The reavers closed the gap. Her heart hammered.

Spring stood up in the wagonbed. The wylde watched the monsters intensely, as if she would pounce on the first one that drew near.

A reaver close to the front ranks grabbed a fair-sized boulder and hurled it. The stone streaked ahead two hundred yards and slammed a nearby wain.

The wain shattered. Its driver and horses disintegrated without a scream, becoming a bloody spray. Splinters of the wood hurtled dozens of yards in the air, and spokes and bits of metal rained down over the plain, among gobbets of flesh.

Other reavers quickly repeated the feat, demolishing another dozen supply wains.

Averan's driver cracked his whip, sent his wagon bouncing over the prairie even faster. It hit a dip, and Averan heard the axle crack again.

A reaver roared, went striding past her wagon.

One reaver galumphed forward, an enormous blade-bearer with a knight gig in its front paws. She recalled from Cunning Eater's memories how brutally effective such a weapon could be in experienced hands.

'Help!' Averan screamed.

She needn't have bothered. Her driver was snapping the whip at the horses' ears, shouting for them to hurry. He urged the team east, nearly tipping the wagon, but effectively racing from the monster's path.

The enormous blade-bearer cut off the retreat of the wagon behind them.

Averan saw the driver's face. He was an old man with silver hair and a worn leather coat over his ruddy tunic. He screamed in panic, tried to veer east too.

The blade-bearer's huge paw snaked out, and she feared that the monster would impale the man before her eyes. Instead its knight gig snagged the lead horse by the neck. The reaver jerked hard, tearing the horse away. But it was tied to its traces.

The whole wagon jerked violently, and the second horse went down as the singletree snapped. The wagon's front wheel hit a falling horse, and the wain bounced high in the air. Then the whole wain came down hard, flipping end over end.

Averan closed her eyes, didn't want to see what happened to the wagonmaster.

Suddenly she realized that her driver was pulling away from the reavers' lines.

The reavers could have turned to press the attack, wiping out another thirty or forty wagons, but they didn't. Instead the horde flowed together, taking a new formation, as they rushed to the east.

Huge blade-bearers joined ranks in a pentagon nearly a mile to each side, while smaller reavers made up a star at its center. Within each arm of the star, a few scarlet sorceresses gathered in an elongated triangle. A fell mage and her escorts took up the center of the star. Averan recognized the formation, dredged it from Cunning Eater's few memories.

The reavers called it the Form of War.

It was not a formation designed for speedy flight. It was designed for a military charge.

She clung to the side panels of the wagon, heart pounding in terror, thinking furiously. Her stomach knotted. She fought to calm herself.

The driver let his wagon slow. The reavers had passed them now, were charging away.

Averan had flown over these plains before, knew every city, every hamlet. To the east lay only hills for a bit, and beyond that the Donnestgree River twisted lazily over the plain. Villages and farms were everywhere along its banks. But the only city of import was Feldonshire, forty-five miles east.

Feldonshire was a sprawling tangle of cottages, shops, wheat mills, farms, and breweries set in wooded hills. From the sky it didn't look like a city quite so much as a cluster of villages strung together.

Averan could think of nothing there that the reavers might want – no fortresses, nothing.

Gaborn shouted as his charger raced up, paced beside the wain. 'They're attacking Feldonshire.'

* * *

Gaborn, riding hard, watched the reavers' lines in confusion. He could feel danger rising rapidly in Feldonshire, some forty-five miles to his east. Many of the wounded from Carris had floated downriver in the night. Now they were bivouacked in the city. His Earth senses screamed a warning to his Chosen, 'Flee! Flee!'

The horde stampeded in a strange new formation over the golden plains. Dust and chaff thrown in the air during their passage rose for thousands of feet. The morning sun arcing through the clouds cast a strange, yellowish pall.

But why Feldonshire?

'Water!' Averan said. 'They're going to water!'

'In Feldonshire?' Gaborn asked.

'No, to the ponds at Stinkwater, just three miles past the city!' Averan said. 'I've seen them from the air – like green gems. The water has sulfur in it!'

Gaborn knew of the ponds. The hot mineral water that flowed up from the ground was a curse to those who lived nearby. No one farmed for miles around, and on cold winter mornings, vapors from the ponds sometimes blew all the way to Feldonshire.

Could it be? he wondered. 'But Feldonshire is forty-five miles from here!'

Averan nodded vigorously. 'We know it's forty-five miles, but maybe the reavers don't. To them the water is just a smell in the air.'

Could a reaver scent water that far away? he wondered. Wolves could smell blood at four miles, and the Stinkwater probably had an odor stronger than blood.

So the reavers charged east, straight into the wind. A line of oak-covered hills rose up. The reavers would bull through the woods, blazing a trail of devastation a mile wide.

Gaborn licked his lips. Some reavers had already fallen out

of the ranks, too weak to keep up the grueling pace. Several hundred lancers chased after them.

Forty-five miles. How long could they run before they exhausted themselves?

One way or another, he was determined to kill the Waymaker. He'd have to move quickly to head them off.

'Skalbairn,' Gaborn shouted. 'Send a dozen of your fastest riders to Feldonshire. If it's water that the reavers want, make sure that they don't get it.'

'Milord?' Skalbairn asked.

'Poison the ponds,' Gaborn ordered.

'Poison them?' Binnesman demanded.

Gaborn frowned. He was the Earth King, and the Earth was allied with Water. For generations, his forefathers had allied with Water.

'It's not a choice I make lightly,' Gaborn said.

'What should we use?' Skalbairn asked.

'Anything at hand,' Gaborn said. 'Go to the woodcarvers' guild. Ask Guildmaster Wallachs for help.'

'Aye,' Skalbairn said. He called out to some men, sent them racing off for Feldonshire. Baron Waggit rode with them.

But poisoning the water wouldn't be enough. The reavers would head through Feldonshire.

Gaborn sensed danger to thousands of refugees. He could imagine what the banks of the river must look like, with the camps of the wounded there.

He would need to turn the horde if he could, block their path – or at least delay them long enough to save his people.

At the rate the horde was running, they'd reach Feldonshire in two hours. Even his fastest couriers would have to ride up the road nine miles to Ballyton, then cut southeast. Their trail would be sixty miles. Even on force horses, that would take the better part of an hour.

That would leave the people of Feldonshire only an hour to evacuate.

'You men,' Gaborn called to another dozen Runelords. 'Go get the philia from some reavers' bungholes. We'll set another fire against them! Perhaps we can scare them off again. Does anyone here know Feldonshire?'

A young lord answered from the ranks. 'Your Highness, my family is from there. I grew up in Darkwald.'

Darkwald was a forest of black walnut north of Feldonshire. The local craftsmen used the wood for carving tables, placards, wooden bowls, fine chests and wardrobes, decorative mantels, and ornate doors. Many of Mystarria's finest treasures had been carved in Feldonshire.

'Then you'll know where to start the fire?'

The lord glanced at the reavers' trail. 'Shrewsvale.'

'You'd burn a village?' Gaborn asked.

'I don't want to – I have a sister who lives there. But that's where the reavers are heading, if I have my guess.'

Another lord spoke. 'He's right. The hills rise up on either side, and Shrewsvale is in the midst of the pass. There'd be no better place to stop the reavers.'

Gaborn had heard that there was a good inn at the top of the pass.

He jutted his chin at Langley. 'Take a thousand lancers on slow mounts, along with the frowth, and follow the reavers. Cut down any that fall behind, but don't engage the main force. Be sure to note the position of any that might be the Waymaker.

'I'll take the thousand fastest men to Shrewsvale.'

Chapter Fifty-two: THE FORTRESS

'If we must die, at least let us die in splendor.'
– A Prayer of Indhopal

The slow dawn rose above Kartish, painting a pink haze above the gray and blasted lands. Raj Ahten prepared for his attack on the reaver fortress. No birds sang. No cattle walked the fields. Not even a lonely wind sighed.

Shadows puddled in the hollows, while sunlight gilded the hilltops. Overhead, a single flameweaver rode the spy balloon, along with two common troops. The graak-shaped balloon hovered in the still air like a seagull.

Raj Ahten stood on a ridge, glaring down. Below him, the reaver fortress was a monstrosity. A vile brown haze circled the place, swirling in a vast circle as if it were a slow tornado. Through wisps of fog he could see hundreds of thousands of dead men lying on the battlefield. Pusnabish had led his men to war, but the fell mage's curses were so strong that no commoner could survive that swirling mist. Men and mounts with as many as three endowments of stamina stepped into the nebula and could only stagger a dozen yards before collapsing.

Worse than that, Raj Ahten's sorcerers warned him that the mist was bound to its course. Even a driving wind at sunset had not diminished it. Instead, the haze circled maddeningly, as if it occupied its own space and time.

Raj Ahten would not be able to send commoners into this fray. They would only avail if the reavers sought to escape.

At Carris, Raj Ahten had seen glue mums erect a single black tower that leaned at an odd angle. The tower had twisted around like a narwhale's horn.

Here, the reavers had constructed nine such spires in a circle, each leaning out. It reminded Raj Ahten of a glistening black crown of thorns.

Within that circle was a nest, or fortress, concocted of strands of blue-white mucilage laid out in a bizarre and complex pattern. Smaller black spikes and spires shot out of the fortress like the spines of a sea urchin, and everywhere were diminutive holes – similar to kill holes and archery slots in a human castle.

Raj Ahten could see no exterior guards. Yet through the kill holes he spotted an eerie sheen the color of life, a color that only his eyes could see.

Reavers hid inside their fortress in vast numbers.

Around the fortress, steep trenches would prevent a charger from drawing near. The trenches looked to be twenty feet deep or more. Even a Runelord in armor would be hard-pressed to climb their sides.

Beyond the fortress itself, amid the piles of tailings from the mine, was a reaver city. The entrances to burrows reared up by the thousands.

This is folly, Raj Ahten told himself. At Carris his knights had fought to hold the walls of a sturdy castle with only one entrance. It had proven to be nearly impossible. Here he would have to attack the reavers in their own fortress, a stronghold of unknown design.

Strange-looking reavers clung to the top of each black spire. He had not seen such reavers at Carris. They were a new subspecies, never described in the old bestiaries.

The bony plates of their heads jutted back at a peculiar

angle, making their muzzles exceptionally long. Each of these reavers had thirty-six philia. Their forearms also seemed to be longer than those on a blade-bearer. Their hides were a tannish-gray. They stood atop their spires, and their heads swiveled.

Though Raj Ahten crouched on a ridge nearly two miles away, the reavers swung toward him and waved their philia questioningly.

A common reaver would not have spotted him.

Even reavers have their far-seers, he realized. This breed must be rare, indeed, if only these few keep guard here.

He took it as a sign. Truly, the legendary Lord of the Underworld had surfaced. Now Raj Ahten would battle the monster.

He studied the reavers' fortress in mingled wonder and confusion. No castle had ever survived Raj Ahten's attack.

A fortress is merely a shell for the cornered enemy to hide in, he reminded himself.

Raj Ahten squinted, checking the strange building for signs of weakness. He could see none, but he was not dissuaded. He had shattered fortresses with his Voice alone, and though it had proven ineffective when he tried it with the reavers' construct at Carris, he felt certain that he would find some weakness in the reavers' defenses.

Pusnabish had served him well in preparing for this battle. For the past two days, he'd kept his troops busy. Force horses had brought ballistas from every fortress within two hundred miles, raiding the defenses of the richest castles in all of Indhopal.

Pusnabish had sent to Aven and retrieved the volatile powders that Raj Ahten's flameweavers had been experimenting with.

He'd gathered ten thousand elephants, including fourteen war elephants that had endowments of brawn, metabolism, and stamina.

More than that, Pusnabish had recognized that fire might be the key to driving out the reavers.

Kartish was not known for its many trees, but figs and citrus grew along the creek beds. The blight had devastated the orchards. So his men had scavenged every dead tree for thirty miles and piled them north of the reavers' fortress. The hot sun had dried them over the past two days.

So it was that from the moment Raj Ahten arrived at the Palace of Canaries, his men were ready for war.

Now Raj Ahten blew the winding horn of a ram, and his men prepared the attack.

A mile behind him, two hundred thousand men began dragging twenty-five thousand pieces of artillery in place. With them marched a million well-armed common troops as escorts.

Beyond that, two million more men and ten thousand elephants began to drag dead trees toward the fortress.

Raj Ahten held to the ridge, and four thousand Invincibles – every lord in Southern Indhopal – rode up to join him.

They were a glorious band, wearing the riches of Indhopal. For this battle, they abandoned the heavy splint mail and scale mail that men wore into battle in northern climes. Instead, they donned armor in the styles of the ancients – tight-woven silk a dozen layers thick. It was both lighter and stronger than lacquered leather, and it would still breathe in the heat.

So the lords of Indhopal rode to war in bright silk long-coats dyed crimson and gold. Their turbans were pinned with rubies, emeralds, and diamonds as large as hens' eggs. Their horses and war elephants were caparisoned as if for a parade. They bore bright lances, richly carved and decorated with gold foil, and their scabbards glittered with gems and silver.

Never in all the history of Indhopal had such an army gathered. Raj Ahten rode proudly at their head, dressed in armor of shining white silk, as befitted his station.

The ground rumbled from the feet of Raj Ahten's troops,

while clouds of dust rose over the plains, thrown up from dragging logs and artillery.

The reavers did not stir.

For an hour the commoners approached the swirling mists, and began laying down their logs. Raj Ahten watched the fortress, saw reavers frantically scurrying about near the kill holes. But they did not flee, did not seek to attack. He'd expected some form of resistance, but the reavers did not so much as hurl a stone against his men.

As he considered, the reason seemed obvious. The swirling nebula of vapors extended for nearly a quarter of a mile outside the fortress. The reavers couldn't see his army.

So their horde elected to wait.

Hills of logs began to rise. The flameweavers supervised the commoners and their elephants. They set the logs in two piles, one to the east of the reaver fortress, one to the west.

Raj Ahten had expected the sorcerers to pile the dead trees in simple mounds, but there were copious logs, and the flameweavers ordered each pile to be arranged in a vast rune nearly a quarter of a mile across. To the east was the Rune of Fire. To the west was the Rune of Night.

Tens of thousands of workmen still toiled among the logs when the flameweavers reached up into the heavens. Night fell from horizon to horizon as they drew fire swirling from the sky and sent it sizzling through the logs.

The screams of burning men filled the air, and they began the lurid dance of the dying.

Raj Ahten took it stoically. He did not like to watch his people die, but Rahjim had assured him that a sacrifice was necessary. 'A few thousand men will die. But it is better that a few thousand men are lost, than all of us.'

The smell of singed hair and cooking fat filled the plains. Now Rahjim and Az stood in the runes, glowing in flame.

Raj Ahten had seldom sacrificed to the greater Powers. But he felt desperate. Despite the fact that he'd taken endowments of stamina last night, the numbness in his left arm was spreading.

Raj Ahten's sorcerers, clothed in fire, began to dance among the flames, twisting and writhing until they almost seemed to become flames themselves. Heat from the burning runes smote Raj Ahten on the hillside even half a mile away. Logs screamed in protest and sent up a cloud of smoke.

Atop the spires of the fortress, one of the reavers' far-seers collapsed, while the others began to back from the heat.

Pusnabish held his hand before his face, and called, 'O Great One, the fire is too hot. Even men with many endowments will not be able to charge the fortress.'

'Perhaps the reavers will do us a favor and bake in an oven of their own design,' a second lord chimed in.

Raj Ahten's heart hammered. He felt the heat, but did not fear it. The coldness in his left hand eased a little. It felt more alive.

Az had promised him again and again that fire would heal him, but only if he let it burn away his humanity.

Raj Ahten's pulse quickened.

For several moments the inferno grew more murderous. Flames danced hundreds of feet in the air, and billowed up in clouds.

'There is a great rune carved in the ground at the center of that fortress,' Raj Ahten shouted to his nobles. 'I will grant a chest full of rubies to the first man who buries his warhammer in it.' He blew his horn again, preparing his men for attack.

His lords shouted their war cries.

Above the reaver fortress, the commoners in the graak began dumping bags of volatile powders into the air. The powders fell in dirty streaks – curtains of red, gray, yellow. The heat was so intense that the men themselves succumbed. One man tumbled over, unable to throw the bag. For a moment, one of the silk wings of the graak began to smolder, but the flameweaver Chespot quickly drew the heat to himself, kept hurling out the powders.

Suddenly a ball of fierce white light came screaming from the west, ignited the fell powders.

The resulting fireball erupted high in the air, sent out a deep boom that went echoing for miles. The ground trembled, and three black spires on the reavers' fortress shattered. The reavers could endure it no more.

From the warrens to the south, thousands of reavers came streaming from their burrows, weapons in hand.

Meanwhile, from the fortress, the fell sorceress hurled a counterspell. A thundering *gasht* sound erupted, and noxious fumes billowed from every kill hole in the fortress. The flames near the fortress sputtered and died.

'Attack,' Raj Ahten screamed, filling the hills with the power of his Voice.

The artillerymen south of the flames loosed volleys of rocks and ballista bolts into the onrushing horde. His army of commoners did not balk. They split into two wings and raced to meet the reavers.

Raj Ahten did not concern himself with the battle on the plains. He spurred a great Imperial warhorse toward the fortress, drew his hammer. Men charged around him and ahead.

Flanked by burning runes, he felt a sudden sense of serenity. There was a presence here in battle that he had never sensed before. It had no body or form, only a vast appetite. He felt as if it were a cloud, hovering above the battlefield, like an eagle waiting to feast.

It did not speak, yet he felt certain that it was mindful of him.

He hit the swirling mists, held his breath as his charger plunged through. His eyes and nose burned at the very touch of the air.

His mount reached the pits, and Raj Ahten leapt down.

The sky went black as he scrambled up the other side. The flameweavers drew fire from the heavens. In moments they would begin hurling massive fireballs toward the kill holes of the fortress.

Screams filled the battlefield as his armies clashed with the reaver horde.

The sky brightened again, filled with fiery light and a whooshing sound. A fireball streaked from Az.

Half a dozen warriors gained the entrance to the fortress, ran inside. The reavers' lair was painfully dark.

Kill holes were set above and below the entrance. The first warrior who raced inside halted for half a second as a knight gig dropped down, hooked him beneath the chin, and jerked him upward.

A second man took a reaver's blade through the crotch. The force of the blow drove him upward a dozen feet into the ceiling. He rained a spray of blood as he fell. A third man saw the danger and leapt through quickly, dodging past a blow from above, another from a side slot. The entrance became a deadly gauntlet.

The tunnel sloped up along a sinuous curve into perfect blackness. Raj Ahten smelled the rising danger of a reaver's curse back at the end of the tunnel, and it issued forth before he could warn his men.

He leapt from the entrance. A cloud of green-gray shot from the gullet of the lair. Twenty men disappeared.

Raj Ahten leapt through before the sorceress could hurl another spell.

He realized that he might well be the only man in the world fit to breach the reavers' fortress. He had endowments of sight that let him see the reavers' shimmering forms even in perfect darkness. His metabolism and grace let him leap past deadly blades faster than the reavers could move.

In less than a second after the sorceress had cast her spell, he was up the tunnel.

He leapt into her open mouth, thrust his warhammer into her soft upper palate before she knew he had even charged. Brains and blood rained down as she opened her mouth in alarm, staggered back.

He rolled from her mouth, ducked beneath her legs. He felt a rush of peace and comfort. There was something deeply satisfying about killing reavers.

The walls around him shuddered as a fireball slammed against the fortress, spilling light through a thousand kill holes. Up ahead he saw his next target, another sorceress.

He had gained ingress to the reavers' fortress.

Chapter Fifty-three:
THE HEAD OF THE BLACK QUEEN

What avails a blow that does not take a man's life? It only alerts the prey to danger.
– From the Teachings of the Silent Ones

'Hear me! Hear me, O People!' a man shouted in the dawn, filling the streets with the sound of his voice.

The Emir Owatt woke from his slumber in the Dedicate's tower at his palace in Bel Nai, a city near the sea in the small country of Tuulistan, just north of Kuhran.

The emir was blind. He had given the use of his eyes to Raj Ahten. And because the emir was beloved by his people, he had been made Raj Ahten's vector.

As such, he was pampered here in Bel Nai, like some woman's old cat.

The emir did not stir, did not stumble out to the balcony to better hear. The fellow who shouted had great endowments of voice, so that his words flew above the dusty streets and trumpeted above the noise of the city – the bawling of camels, the crowing of roosters, the first morning cries of vendors in the bazaar. 'Hear the words of Wuqaz Faharaqin, Warlord of the Ah'Kellah, as I raise the Atwaba against a murderer most despicable: he who calls himself "Lord of the Sun," Raj Ahten.'

It had been but six short years ago that Emir Owatt was captured in the Palace of Weeping Vines at Ma'al. At the time, Raj Ahten's Invincibles had surrounded the entire city. By surrendering, the emir had hoped to save his people from outright slaughter.

Now he climbed from his bed and hobbled to the small open window, grasping the bars with both hands. The cool night air off the ocean slapped him like a woman's open palm.

Nine-year-old Messan came rushing up the tower stairs. 'Father! Father! Do you hear?'

'Yes, I hear very well,' the emir said. 'Come, be my eyes. Tell me what you see?'

The boy grabbed the elbow of his father's burnoose, and stood on tiptoe. The smell of dust, camels, and smoke hung over the city, along with the scent of wet hemp, which women in the markets wove into rope and baskets.

Emir Owatt could hear the scuffle of feet as people went running. Guards shouted at the gate.

'There is a great crowd gathering outside the keep,' Messan whispered. 'Three Invincibles sit on their horses in the square.'

'You are sure they are Invincibles?'

'They are sitting on Imperial warhorses, and all wear the surcoats of Invincibles among the Ah'kellah. One man has wings on his breast and helm. He is holding something – the head of a man. He has it by the hair!'

Owatt could hear the ring of mail, the scuff of boots over stone down below him.

'What are our guards doing?'

'Some are running to the gates, others are taking posts on the towers. Some have strung their horn bows, and look as if they will shoot.'

'Our guards will not shoot,' the emir predicted. 'Wuqaz Faharaqin has great respect. They must listen to what he has to say.'

'Hear me!' Wuqaz shouted. 'In Rofehavan, an Earth King has arisen, Gaborn Val Orden. He has wed Iome Vanisalaam Sylvarresta, and is now our lord's own cousin by marriage. The Earth King has warned that we are in great danger, and begs Raj Ahten to put aside his conflict until the enemies of mankind are laid low. But Raj Ahten dishonors our nation. He champions the reavers' cause by battling his own kin!'

At that there were shouts of horror and cries of disbelief from the square. Some people shouted, 'Liar. This man is lying.'

'Wuqaz is holding up the head, to show the people,' Messan said.

The boy fell silent as Wuqaz relayed what had befallen Carris. Wuqaz told of a battle, with reavers surrounding a castle. He told how his men fought to defend Carris, for in doing so they defended all mankind.

But Raj Ahten tried to flee the city by boat, leaving women, children, and his own common troops to suffer the ministrations of reavers.

And when the Earth King charged from the hills, Choosing for his army Raj Ahten and all of his Invincibles, Raj Ahten sought to restrain his troops from giving aid, leaving the Earth King to die.

'Even when his favored wife, Saffira, appeared and bade our king lay aside his war,' Wuqaz shouted, 'Raj Ahten withheld aid. She had endowments of glamour and voice from thousands, and only the strongest being could have resisted her. Raj Ahten resisted.

'He let the reavers slaughter his own wife, as the Earth King faced the reaver horde alone!'

At this news, Emir Owatt gasped, then dropped to his knees, leaning against the wall for support. Messan grabbed him.

The emir had long feared this. He'd feared it ever since that dreadful night when Raj Ahten laid his siege at Ma'al.

He had known then that he in his tiny kingdom would never be able to fight Raj Ahten.

His mind flashed back to that night. He could not fight, but he'd devised another plan, one that offered hope that he might yet vanquish the Wolf Lord.

He took all of the forcibles in his treasury, and had the facilitators forge them anew, so that each held a rune of glamour or voice. Then he'd used them on his tender daughter, Saffira.

Raj Ahten was a man of fierce appetites. The emir had suspected that the Wolf Lord would not be able to resist the child. 'Beg him not to kill us,' Owatt had warned Saffira. 'He will spare us for your sake. Ask him to prepare a place of honor among his Dedicates.'

After the surrender, Raj Ahten demanded the use of the emir's tongue, believing that the emir must have great endowments of voice with which to beguile his people. After all, how else could a lord be so beloved by the commoners?

But a search of the emir's scars showed that he bore no endowments of voice. Owatt offered instead his eyes, saying to Raj Ahten, 'Take them, for I do not wish to see how you will make my people suffer.'

It had been a poor choice. Too often Owatt had heard the cries of his people in the markets.

He'd long suspected that Saffira would die by violence. He'd been afraid that in some petty fit, Raj Ahten might strike her. With his endowments of brawn, any blow he delivered would destroy the girl.

But Raj Ahten became fond of Saffira – as fond as his nature allowed. He'd pampered her, conceded to her wishes, sired her children, and showered her with gifts. She was as much a wife as he would ever know.

Now, the emir learned that, indeed, Raj Ahten had murdered Saffira – pretty little Saffira.

* * *

In the square, an old woman began to cry out angrily, 'Liar! Tongue of the snake!'

Always, the emir felt surprised to hear any common person rise in defense of Raj Ahten. To speak against him was outlawed, and so one could go for months without hearing a single whisper of discontent, yet he often imagined that others kept their discontent hidden inside, as he did.

I am a blind man, the emir thought, and even I can see his evil.

Wuqaz shouted, 'I do not lie. Let me tell you all: Here is the head of an Invincible – Pashtuk by name – whom Raj Ahten slew in an effort to kill the Earth King.

'By the Atwaba, I call upon all good men: Throw off the yoke of Raj Ahten! There must be only one king – the Earth King!'

The emir's heart pounded fiercely in his chest. He knew that Wuqaz spoke to him. True, he was in the market more than a hundred yards below, but he had come here to shout outside these walls, knowing that the emir was here, knowing that Owatt might be cowed, but would never surrender.

As Wuqaz cried these last words, bowstrings twanged and arrows hissed through the air. From the streets below a roar of panic rose.

Emir Owatt did not need eyes to know what was happening. Archers in the tower fired at the Ah'kellah. Arrows struck among the crowd, skewering men, women, and children. From the sounds of it, fighting broke out even among the crowd – some going to battle against Raj Ahten, others fighting to protect him.

'Father!' Messan cried. 'One of Wuqaz's men is hit. He took an arrow in his eye. He has fallen from his horse. Wuqaz and one other are trying to ride away.'

Now a battle raged. A woman shrieked in pain, a horse

whinnied, accompanied by the sound of hooves smacking flesh. Men roared. Children cried in terror.

People shouted as horses broke into the streets, and fled.

His son said, 'Wuqaz is gone!' But the sound of fighting continued.

'Who is winning?' the emir asked.

'The guards who fight for Raj Ahten,' his son confirmed.

In that moment, a realization struck the emir. He had always thought of the throng below as 'his' people. But by surrendering to Raj Ahten, he had given those people away – given them to a man without conscience, a man without honor, who would use them as cattle.

He had not saved himself, his daughter, or his people. He had *surrendered* them.

Now was the time to take them back.

'Hurry,' the emir said. He went to a box and pulled out a bag of coins that held a particularly large ruby. 'While the guards are busy at the front gate, I want you to slip out into the streets by the back. If the guards there try to stop you, tell them that today is my purifam, and you are going to buy me some figs for breakfast.' He handed the coins to the child and urged, 'Once you leave the palace, go to my sister's villa. Do you remember the place?'

'On the hill?'

'Yes. Beg her to hide you. Do you understand? You must never come back! I will not be here.'

'Why?' his son asked. 'Where are you going?'

'I am going to war,' the emir said.

Down below, in the Dedicates' Keep, Raj Ahten kept his most valued vectors. The air here at Bel Nai was especially healthy, and so over the years Saffira had convinced Raj Ahten to house here in abundance those who vectored stamina.

The emir was well prepared for this day. He'd long known that he could not strike a meaningful blow against the Wolf

Lord of Indhopal from the front lines. But here, from behind the lines, he could be devastating.

He'd have struck a year ago, if not for his children. He'd once held great hopes that his daughter might persuade Raj Ahten to turn away from his evil. Later, the emir knew that Raj Ahten kept Messan here as a veiled threat. If Owatt moved against him, the life of his son would be forfeit.

'What do you mean?' his son asked. 'I want to stay with you.'

The emir did not dare tell his son what he was about to do. Instead, he went to the chess set where he and his son had played now for years. Over and over he had warned his son that he must sometimes make sacrifices if he hoped to win a game. He hoped that his son would understand. He twisted the head off the black queen, pulling out a poisoned needle. The body of the queen was like an inkpot, filled with the deadly stuff.

The guards would kill Emir Owatt for what he would do. He only hoped that he could save his son.

'Go quickly now,' he whispered. 'Keep your head up and your manner easy.'

Chapter Fifty-four: SMALL SACRIFICES

Every day, we each make small sacrifices to ensure the continuity of civilization. In our own way, each of us is a Dedicate.

– King Mendellas Val Orden

Gaborn's troops began racing north in hopes of cutting off the reavers. Langley led the other half, along with the frowth giants, on the reavers' trail, to slaughter any that fell behind.

Binnesman rode to Averan's wagon, took her by the arm, and scooped her up into his saddle. In the skirmish, a lord had fallen from his horse. Binnesman pointed at a white mare, a mile off, standing over her dead master.

'Would you dare ride a warhorse without help?' Binnesman asked.

'It's easier than riding a graak,' Averan assured him. 'And if you fall, the ground isn't a mile below.'

'I daresay,' Binnesman agreed.

They galloped over to the animal, Spring following on her own gray stallion. Binnesman hopped down, and Averan held the mount's reins. She tried not to look at the dead knight while Binnesman used his knife to cut the leather straps of the horse's heavy chaffron.

But she had to look, if only to be sure he was dead.

He'd surely never ride again. He'd fallen badly, snapped his neck and scraped his head against the rocks. The flies were already at him.

In moments Binnesman stripped the animal of its precious barding, leaving only its saddle beneath a quilted blanket. Now the horse was ready for a quick ride.

By that time, Gaborn's troops had all fled north, and the wagons followed. Averan imagined that she'd be eating trail dust for lunch.

Instead, Binnesman swung onto his mount, got her on the white mare, and spurred east, in the wake of Langley's men.

'What are we doing?' Averan asked.

'We'll carry a warning to Feldonshire,' Binnesman said.

'You mean we won't take the road?' Averan asked.

'We can make it through the forest faster than Gaborn's men can travel the roads.'

Averan found that hard to credit. The huge Imperial stallion that the wizard rode was built for speed on the plains, not in the hills. Her own mount, with its small hooves and sturdy legs, might do better in the mountains, she thought. Yet she knew that earth mages had an uncanny gift for finding trails in the forest.

'All right,' Averan said. 'But won't Gaborn disapprove? He'll want me at his side, to give him counsel.' The thought of riding with him terrified her. He'd ask her to eat another reaver if they found one that looked anything like the Waymaker.

'Hmmm . . .' Binnesman said, frowning in concentration. 'I've never seen the Stinkwater. How large did you say the pools are?'

'Not large,' Averan said. 'They get bigger in winter when the rain fills them, shrink in the summer.'

'I have an idea,' Binnesman said. 'It may be that I can heal the Stinkwater, cleanse it rather than poison it. But we must hurry. It's a slow magic.'

'Do you think?' Averan asked. 'You're no water wizard.'

Binnesman sighed uncertainly. 'I can only try.'

So they rode hard for the hills, the horses racing over plains beneath a yellow cloud. They bypassed Langley's troops.

The wizard spurred his mount up a steep ridge. He stopped a moment, while Averan and the wylde caught up. The forest ahead was a tangle, with only a few wild game trails. Boars had been rooting for acorns here recently. The ground looked as if it had been plowed.

Just to the south, the reavers had gained the woods. Trees began to snap under the onslaught of their charge. A hart came bounding down the trail in a frenzy, its huge antlers clacking against the brush. It saw the wizard, leapt away.

Binnesman raised his staff and chanted, 'The road is long, and short the day. Make for us now, a swifter way.'

Ahead a rustling sound broke from the trees, as if a great beast trudged through the woods, scraping against boughs and papery leaves. Suddenly Averan spotted a trail that she'd not seen before. The branches on each side were bobbing.

'There!' she shouted.

'Indeed,' Binnesman said wryly.

He spurred his mount up the trail, galloping like the wind. Averan let him take the lead, followed by Spring. She didn't want to meet any low branches.

But she noticed after the first mile that there were no low branches. The trail remained clear ahead, and almost straight. Though leaves covered the forest floor, the game trails they rode over seemed as free of rocks and limbs as if it were a well-traveled road.

Yet when she looked behind, she could see no trail at all. Branches flung backward like arms, blocking her retreat.

Averan's heart hammered, and she rode in awe. She'd seen the fell mage in battle, casting her destructive spells, and she'd seen Spring kill a reaver with a single blow. But she suspected now that Binnesman was far more powerful than the wylde or any reaver mage.

Thus they raced. The mounts galloped tirelessly, until they gained the main road. Long before Gaborn's men arrived, Binnesman reached the village of Shrewsvale.

She saw it when they came up out of the woods. White cottages with thatch roofs dotted the green meadows along the northern slope of the vale. Stone fences that had stood for a thousand years sectioned off acreage: here was a meadow speckled with sheep, beyond spread a field of barley. There lay a garden where sunflowers grew tall. Along the southern ridge of the valley, the road wound up to town. A huge inn with a tile roof loomed over the main street, while shops with stone walls squatted to either side.

Binnesman raced to the first shepherd's cottage. Red chickens scrambled from their path as they neared the door. He shouted, 'Flee from here, the reavers are coming!'

A shepherd's wife rushed out, wiping her hands on her apron. She was a blunt woman with graying hair and a wide mouth. 'What?' she asked gruffly. 'What are you yelling about out here? I'm baking.' Obviously she thought that some madman called.

'I'm sorry to disturb you, madam,' Binnesman said in a tone of mock formality. 'But reavers are coming, and King Orden is about to fight a war on your doorstep. I suggest that you warn your neighbors, and prepare to flee.'

Averan watched the woman in pity.

The same reavers had destroyed her home at Keep Haberd, and had laid Carris to waste. Now they would tear through this valley, destroying cottages that had stood for generations.

The old woman finished wiping her hands, gave Binnesman a stern look. 'You'd best not be telling tales,' she warned. Even as she did, she gaped up at the wylde in confusion. It obviously wasn't every day that she'd had a green woman and wizard show up on her doorstep, warning of imminent peril.

'You'd best run,' Binnesman said.

Then they spurred their horses onward, onto the cobblestone streets of Shrewsvale itself.

It was a pleasant town. Averan could tell by the architecture that they were nearing Feldonshire. The doorposts and lintel of the inn were intricately carved of fine oak. The post on the left depicted a minstrel with a lute under his arm. The one on the right was a lord talking to him amiably. The perspective was skewed, so that it looked as if both were walking through the door. A carved frieze overhead showed a table filled with fine foods: grapes and apples, bread and a rabbit.

The sign above the inn was gorgeously carved to show travelers on their journey. The sign itself named the place as the Loaf and Brew.

Binnesman's shouting soon drew every shopkeeper in town. The mayor of Shrewsvale owned the inn. He rang the city bell.

Averan said little, only nodded vigorously to second Binnesman's warnings. She caught the eyes of a dark-haired girl who held a doll woven of reeds in one hand, and the chubby fist of her little brother in the other.

The girl could not have been seven years old, and Averan suddenly realized that in the next hour she'd face terrors that many a graybeard had never met.

They left Shrewsvale and raced along the dirt road through village after village. Binnesman stopped in each hamlet, relating his tale. At every stop, the village bells began to ring, so that one could listen to the path that they followed. With each stop, the people were already gathering, waiting for the news.

They were only halfway between Shrewsvale and Feldonshire proper when Gaborn's messengers passed them on the road.

By the time they reached the city, the bells were already ringing out in warning. Word of the attack had raced ahead.

People scattered to and fro in the streets. Horses whinnied

and snorted and pranced with ears back and nostrils flaring. They could smell their masters' terror. Eight miles to the west, smoke could be seen rising from the hills.

Averan imagined that Gaborn had already set fire to the woods at Shrewsvale.

The citizens of Feldonshire fled from their shops and cottages, and became a steady stream, heading north out of town, across the bridge that spanned the Donnestgree.

Peasants in plain hooded frocks ran along with all their belongings stuffed into tote sacks made by tying four corners of a sheet together. Farmers thundered away in wagons filled with grimy children. A wealthy merchant rode through town with his family in a carriage, shouting in his hurry and snapping his whip over the heads of anyone who dared to hinder his escape.

Commoners all. Without force horses or endowments, they would travel slowly. Worse, they were taking time to pack their things. Husbands at work in their shops had to run about fetching children. There was food to gather, belongings to save.

Loaded under the weight of their goods, the peasants would not be able to run fast or far.

Already the bridge was turning into a bottleneck.

Worst of all, on the banks of the Donnestgree camped thousands of wounded refugees from Carris. The tents lining the river were a city to themselves, and the wounded lay attended by their healers. Fires hugged the riverbank, and most of the cooking pots there were not for food, but for boiling the dressings for wounds. Rags and cloths were draped over every bush to dry.

Averan had never seen a sickyard, as the soldiers called them, where the battle-torn lay in the open air like this. Between the drying bandages and the gray canvas tents, and smoke smudging everything, the sickyard looked like a city formed from rags.

Most of the wounded were heavily bandaged. Few could yet rise or walk on their own, and there was no way to move them easily. The boats that had brought them downstream had all departed – returned north for another load. Evacuating these people on foot was not something that could be done in hours. It was a labor that would take days.

They knew what would happen.

Wounded men and women cried out in terror and pain. Pleas of 'Help me! Help!' and 'Have mercy!' rose from dozens of throats, adding to the general din of people scurrying for shelter.

Some invalids climbed to their feet in heroic efforts, and staggered across the bridge. They shuffled slowly, blocking the exit for those who followed. Staves or canes might have helped speed many of them, but every stick along the riverbank had already been salvaged. Two men dressed in the bright red of the City Guard stood on the bridge, pleading with everyone. 'Help the wounded. Grab someone and help him across! There's plenty of time!'

But everyone knew that time was far too short.

Among the rows of tents, healers and townsfolk sought to save many of the injured. Wains from farmhouses lined the river roads. But the healers were taking only the children and the women, the vast minority of the wounded, leaving the men to die.

She saw one fellow nearby lying on a cot before his tent, curled into a fetal position, merely waiting.

She recalled Gaborn's words last night. He'd tried to tell her that men did most of the dying in this world, that they wore themselves out. She hadn't wanted to believe it. Now she saw the proof of it, and wondered how it would be.

As Binnesman rode up to the woodcarver's guildhall, Averan sat on her white mare and stared down at the men, and felt the most profound pity and sense of desolation.

I'm not like them anymore, she realized. Her horse

could carry her away fast. She didn't feel their terror, felt only pity.

Once, when Averan was small, Brand had picked up an old door that lay in a field below the graaks' aerie back at Keep Haberd. Averan had seen a family of mice scurry about in a panic, blinded by the sunshine.

Three generations of mice lived there – a mother and five children, along with six little pink babes. Neither Averan nor Brand meant the mice any harm. Yet they watched them scurry in panic for a moment, before setting down the door.

That's how Averan felt now, distanced from the turmoil, high and above it all. Yet the loud noises and confusion made Binnesman's wylde jumpy. The green woman's eyes darted this way and that, and she flinched at every nearby noise, as if she were a caged fox just captured from a field.

Binnesman had come to the guildhall to speak to the officials. He dismounted, saying, 'Watch the horses while I speak to Guildmaster Wallachs.' Wallachs was more than just the guildmaster of the woodcarvers here in Feldonshire. He served as mayor of the city, and though he had no endowments, his people held him in as high estimation as if he were a lord.

Binnesman led his spooked wylde into the guildhall. Averan held the reins to the mounts, sat alone outside.

The guildhall of the woodcarvers dominated the center of Feldonshire. The massive building was an advertisement for the guild's wares. It stood five stories high and was made of finely cut multicolored stone set in mortar. The high ceilings of the upper stories were supported by abutments, with flying buttresses made of black walnut, all elegantly chiseled to show woodland scenes from the Darkwald: wild bears and stags in the forest, geese winging majestically over the Donnestgree.

Every gable, every panel on every door, every lintel and every shutter was a minor miracle of precision and detail. The carvers had carried their motif of the woods throughout the building. Perfectly sculpted squirrels raced over pine boughs carved into the gables and support beams. The front doors were carved to look like a path leading into the woods, with a pair of grouse preening beside a rock not far ahead. A gallery near the top of the building boasted wooden statues of renowned carvers at work with chisels, hammers, and saws.

The guildsmen had taken great pains to care for the exterior. The dark wooden surfaces all gleamed, as if the craftsmen had applied a layer of shellac only days ago. With winter coming, Averan realized that this was likely true.

The building served as a monument to the beauty of wood in all its forms. Walnut trees bordered its front, and wrapped around the east lawn along the river. The leaves had gone a dark brown with the coming of winter.

Too bad the building is all coming down, she thought. I'd best admire it while I can.

She was staring up at the guildhall when someone said, 'Here, girl, let me help you down from there.'

A man put his hands around her waist, and yanked. She turned to see a fellow with a grizzled face and a mouth full of rotting teeth. His hood was pulled up over his head.

'What?' she asked. She gripped her reins, but he had her off her horse so fast, she hardly had time to wonder what happened.

He set her on the ground near her mount, taking the reins in his hand as he did, and said urgently, 'Here, now. These aren't your horses. They're worth a lot of money. What do you think you're doing with them?'

She thought that maybe he knew the owner of the white mare, and had some fair argument. She was about to object when he slugged her. One moment she was standing there, and the next his fist came up in a quick jab, and Averan went reeling.

The world spun and went dark for a moment. Pain

lanced through her head and jaw. Everything seemed to go cold.

She found herself lying on the cobblestones, while people shouted, 'Thief! That man stole her horses.'

She could hear the fellow shouting, 'Haw!' as he raced away. Hooves clattered over the stone.

Averan looked up to see where he'd gone, but a crowd was closing in on her. ''Ere now, poor dear,' some old woman said, bending close to pull Averan to her feet. Averan could smell cooked vegetables on her woolen shawl.

Averan's jaw stung, and she worked it experimentally, trying to see if it was broken. Her stomach churned, as if she would lose her breakfast. She'd slammed the back of her head on the cobblestones when she fell. Averan reached up and touched it, winced, and stared blankly at the blood on her fingers.

A moment ago she'd felt so smug and self-contained. Now she was no different from everyone around her.

Averan felt furious at the stranger who had stolen her horse. She felt furious at herself for letting him do it.

Almost without realizing it, she cast a spell.

She pictured Binnesman's big Imperial stallion and focused on it. She saw it running down the road, its new master dragging it in tow.

The horse's mind was frenzied. It could sense the fear of the people around it, could hear the distant thunder of the horde. It longed to escape, to reach the open plains of Indhopal.

It dreamed of sweet grass, and running through fields at night, nostrils flaring while its mane and tail floated out behind it. It remembered the mares of its herd, and the sweet taste of streams that flowed from the mountains.

The thrill of it all was marvelous, and utterly alien. Averan touched the horse's consciousness, and immediately realized that she felt almost no kinship to this magnificent beast.

Averan called to it, and immediately the image slipped from her mind. She could not hold it. Binnesman's charger would not respond to her summons. It wanted to get away from here.

She tried another tactic. She considered instead her attacker. She focused on his face. She could envision his grizzled beard, his rotting teeth, the warty mole just beneath his left eye.

He was racing from town, leading the spare horses, glancing behind to make sure that no one followed. He chuckled in glee, thinking he had escaped.

Averan reached out with her mind, tried to touch him more fully. She inhaled with his inhalations, exhaled as he did. She could feel that his bladder was full. He felt so excited, he really had to take a pee.

She delved deeper into his mind, could hear the whisper of his thoughts. 'Fine horses. Sell 'em in Gandry – and this time, won't settle fo' no pint of ale, neither!' She glimpsed flashes from his imagination – the thief cavorting with naked wenches.

His mind was a seething place, full of filth. She almost dared not touch it.

She summoned him, commanded him to turn the horses. 'Go back,' she sent the warning. 'You may be leaving a child to die.'

For an instant the thief caught his breath.

Where'd a thought like that come from? he wondered. He muttered in a prissy voice, 'You may be leaving a child to die!'

Then he cackled in delight and spurred Averan's white mare on.

Averan withdrew, snapped back into her own consciousness, and her legs nearly buckled beneath her. Her attempt had drained her, and drawn beads of perspiration on her brow.

Maggots would be easier to summon than that piece of filth, she realized. And they would be a whole lot cleaner, besides. Binnesman had warned her that it was harder to reach a complex mind.

Maybe I should have stuck with the horses, she thought regretfully.

Averan went to the guildhall. Just inside, Binnesman was coming down a grand staircase, talking urgently to Guildmaster Wallachs, an imposing man who wore wooden chains of office and bore himself with great authority. Spring walked behind them.

The guildmaster was saying, 'I understand your concerns, but my men left fifteen minutes ago. I suspect that the first wagons full of poison are already in the water.'

'What did you send?'

'Nothing much – lye soap and lacquer. I thought to use ale. Not all of it that comes out of Feldonshire is fit for consumption. I'd rather see it used to poison a pond than to affront my gut.'

The men were so deep in conversation, neither of them even noticed Averan. 'Binnesman,' she called, grabbing a nearby wall for support. 'We've been robbed: a man took our horses!'

'What?' Wallachs demanded. 'What man?'

'A stranger,' Averan said, searching for a way to describe him. 'His . . . his breath smelled like rye bread and . . . fish.'

'Where is he?' the guildmaster demanded.

'Long gone!' Averan said. Outside, the noises of the city could be heard, the shouts of people, the tumult of horses.

The guildmaster sighed deeply. He apologized. 'Don't worry. You can ride out of town on my wain. I'm sorry about your horses. We're good people in Feldonshire. But –'

Binnesman looked to Averan. 'Did you try to summon the beasts?'

'I . . . tried that, and the thief too. He won't come back.' Averan crossed the room and collapsed into a chair in defeat.

Chapter Fifty-five:
A FIRE IN THE HILLS

In ancient texts it is said that Fallion's men scouted the Underworld, searching for Toth. It was only in the deepest recesses, many miles below the surface, that they began to find 'much foretoken' of reavers. Most of Fallion's men died not in battle with reavers or Toth, but from the 'arduous heat which grieved us unto death.'

– Hearthmaster Valen, of the Room of Beasts

An unending thunder rumbled through the hills beneath Shrewsvale. With it came a sound as if a million dry leaves hissed to the forest floor at once.

The horde forged onward.

Crows flapped up from the old forest, black pinions groping the sky as they sought to escape the onslaught. They winged about in a dirty haze amid the gree. A cold sun glared down through a thickening yellow brume. Huge oak trees, browned by autumn, shivered and cracked, leaving holes to gape in the canopy.

The reavers advanced in a formation that men had never seen, the strange new Form of War. Gaborn stopped his mount on a hilltop and peered at the forest. He saw the reavers scurrying forward, glimpsed gray carapaces beneath the trees. They loped with a newfound fury. A hundred times he considered sending men to ambush the reavers, but his Earth Powers warned against it. No lancers dared attack. To even send men within archery range was futile. Something had happened to the horde.

The hope of water lent the reavers new heart. They were learning, surely. Averan said that they knew his name, and feared him.

Gaborn had beaten them easily enough at Carris, when the lightning threw them into a panic. But he'd lost so many of his powers. Now, he dared not attack.

Perhaps they sensed his weakness.

The very fact that they were learning how to defend themselves alarmed him. What if they taught other reavers their secrets?

With each minute, Gaborn more strongly suspected that he could neither stop the horde nor turn them from their destination.

He worried about whether his men could reach the ponds at Stinkwater in time to poison the pools. A cold terror seized him.

He'd passed through his ranks on the way up, and had expected to find Binnesman near the lead, riding his fine gray warhorse. But the wizard was nowhere in sight.

He reached the green fields and meadows of Shrewsvale barely half an hour in advance of the reavers. When he arrived, he found Baron Waggit ringing the town bell.

'Have you seen Binnesman?' Gaborn asked Waggit.

'He's gone to warn Feldonshire,' Waggit offered.

Gaborn breathed a sigh of relief.

In the village, peasants and merchants had already harnessed horses to wagons. They were pulling goods from their homes and barns – pillows, food, blankets, piglets and lambs. One woman outside the inn stood beating a pan, shouting frantically for her son. Another man was not fleeing at all. Instead he had opened the door to a root cellar, and Gaborn watched him usher his wife and eight children down into it; then he came back up and started carrying a lamb down in one hand, and a rooster in another.

Gaborn shouted to Waggit, 'Go and get that man and his children out of there!'

He could not hide his despair. He was not just a king, he was the Earth King. Yet his subjects would not always follow his counsel, even to save their own lives.

Gaborn sized up the terrain, decided where to set his battle lines. No one had ever built a siege wall here at Shrewsvale. A sheep stockage bordered the woods, and would have to serve as the only barricade. The low wall would not hold back reavers, wouldn't even slow them down. The carefully piled slabs of gray stone were no more significant than a line drawn in the sand.

He went down into a field where an old haycock sat, the straw in it having grayed with mold over the past year. He fumbled with flint and steel to get a fire going. In five minutes the haycock was ablaze.

The wind worked against him. Down on the plains the wind had gusted to the east. But here in the vale at mid-morning, the air grew still. He'd not have a driving fire.

He'd hardly got the haycock to blaze when the main force of his army began to ride in, just over a thousand men, with lances held high. Lords hurried down to the vale and formed up in ranks behind the sheep stockage, as if they would hold fast if the reavers charged.

Skalbairn reported, 'Milord, the reavers are less than six miles off, and they're running faster now. They know that they're close to water. We got word not half an hour ago that Langley's men are making a good accounting. Many reavers can't keep up the pace.'

Gaborn nodded, numb. He looked uphill. 'Where are those men with the philia?'

Skalbairn just shook his head in consternation. 'They'll be here soon.'

Gaborn couldn't wait. 'Put a torch to the trees,' he ordered. Fifty Lords came forward in a rush. They tied cords of twisted straw to their lances, then set them afire. The mounts leapt the low stone wall and charged into the trees.

The autumn leaves had begun piling in the woods, and the ground here had been dry for a couple of days. Yet the fire did not rage as Gaborn had hoped. It fumed and sputtered, filling the sky with a dim gray.

Still the reaver horde marched. The mass of bodies running and heaving themselves over the rocks and trails became a dull roar.

Baron Waggit rode down the hill, pick in hand. Gaborn looked at the young man, felt deeply troubled. Waggit was in danger, might not survive the battle.

'So,' Gaborn said. 'You've decided to join the fight?'

'If I may. I'll give it a go. But . . . I'm really not sure what to do.'

'You rang the bell in town, and already saved a man and his family,' Gaborn said. 'You don't have to give yourself in battle. Certainly not in this battle.'

'I . . . I want to stay.'

'I'll see that you begin training for knighthood soon.'

'Thank you,' Waggit said softly.

'Stick close to me,' Gaborn said. 'Move when you see me move.'

Waggit nodded.

Skalbairn caught sight of the baron, rode up and shouted, 'Good man! Good man!' He looked out over the Knights Equitable gathered in the ranks, and shouted, 'Did I tell you that he's going to marry my daughter?'

Waggit shook his head at Skalbairn's jest. 'I said no such thing!'

But the knights all cheered as if it were a made match.

Gaborn's senses screamed in warning. A few miles west, the wounded refugees were still puttering around in Feldonshire. He struggled to send the message, 'Flee!'

But if his people heard, none obeyed.

The thousand knights had all joined ranks across the field. Gaborn shouted, 'Gentlemen, we'll hold here as long as we can. We've got to make the reavers believe that we'll fight, in hopes that they'll retreat. But be ready to fall back on my command.'

Even as he spoke, gree flapped overhead, squeaking with a sound like aging joints. The ground began to tremble, and he looked down the valley to the south. Two miles off, trees creaked and toppled.

On the slopes of the vale, a couple of fires had begun to rage. Pillars of red and yellow twisted up, enveloping oaks whole. The heat smote Gaborn's face, and the smell of it came drier than before. Limbs crackled and branches hissed. Yet the center of the valley floor merely smoldered.

We should have been here an hour ago, with barrels of oil and pitch, Gaborn realized.

For a moment he dared wish that he had a flameweaver in his retinue.

The reavers were two miles away, and then one. The front of their formation filled the valley from north to south. Distantly to the northwest, beyond the thunder of the reavers' pounding feet, a single warhorn blared, signaling that troops had been cut off behind enemy lines.

Gaborn realized what had happened.

The men who bore the philia were cut off, surprised at the reavers' pace, no doubt. Gaborn sniffed at his own hands. He could still smell the garlicky mildew scent that Averan told him was a reaver's death cry. He hoped that there was enough residue on his men's hands so that the reavers would feel some trepidation.

'Hold your positions, men,' Gaborn shouted. 'Hold your

positions.' The warriors were ranged on horseback about fifty feet behind the stone wall. If Gaborn ordered a charge, the force horses would merely leap the wall.

Among his troops, lords began to lower their lances. Others had already strung bows. Now they nocked arrows.

The faintest breath of a breeze swept down from the hills, teasing the flames, raising Gaborn's hopes. A flickering wall of incandescence licked the forest floor in some places, making a low curtain of fire beneath the trees.

Just as quickly, the wind dropped off.

In the distance he glimpsed reavers between the boles of oaks now. They had been traveling in a loose pack, but they smelled trouble ahead. The reavers closed ranks, making a wall half a mile wide. Blade-bearer walked shoulder to shoulder with blade-bearer.

Charging into those lines would be suicide. Reavers with stones behind that wall would provide artillery cover, while mages cast their noxious spells.

The reavers came slowly, philia waving. When they reached a tree, the blade-bearers merely lowered their massive heads and rammed. Thus they cut a huge swath through the forest.

The reavers were a quarter of a mile away now. Gaborn sought to put on a bold face, yet his Earth senses warned, 'Flee! Flee!'

Every man under his charge was at risk.

'Not yet,' Gaborn whispered to his master. In Feldonshire, his Chosen still lay abed, while others puttered over the bridge of the river Donnestgree. He hoped to buy them time. Every minute that he slowed the reaver horde might win him another hundred souls. 'Not yet.'

Then the reavers were two hundred yards ahead, almost to the smoldering woods.

The reavers did not slow. In fact, they seemed to lope faster as they neared the flames, as if in welcome.

When they reached the fire, they lowered their heads into the dirt, bowling over and burying the burning leaves. Even trees that crackled with flame fell back under the onslaught.

The horde marched forward, irrepressible, trampling the flames. Reavers hissed in warning to their neighbors.

'Retreat!' Gaborn shouted.

The reavers began to hurl a hail of stones. Boulders that weighed as much as a man came soaring overhead, falling into his front ranks.

'Dodge,' the Earth warned, and Gaborn spurred his charger to the left. A great boulder slammed into the stone sheep wall, toppled it. Flaming debris and flakes of stone hurtled past Gaborn and into the ranks of his men behind. Horses and riders burst into a spray of bloody gobbets. Gaborn felt sickened to the core as half a dozen men were ripped from him.

He glanced over his shoulder, Baron Waggit rode on his tail. The young man had followed his instructions precisely, and it saved his life. The pasty color of Waggit's face showed that he knew how close it had been.

To the left of the battlefield, another boulder hurtled from the reavers' ranks and slashed through Gaborn's lines.

His men wheeled their mounts and raced for safety.

Chapter Fifty-six: LORD OF DARKNESS, LORD OF THE SUN

Many men dream of doing well, but few give form to their dreams.

Therefore, we cannot insist that greatness is a condition of the heart or mind in abeyance of deeds. To do so would diminish the achievement of those who prove their greatness by their deeds.

– *Arunhah Ahten, Father of Raj Ahten*

In the reavers' fortress, darkness reigned. Fireballs hammered the outer walls, and briefly illuminated the reavers' kill holes. The hive shuddered under their impact. But deep in the heart of the lair, no outside light could pierce.

With his keen ears, Raj Ahten heard the cries of war out on the plains.

He raced through a tunnel, a string of dead sorceresses and blade-bearers strewn behind him.

There were no kill holes so deep in the lair. Only a little light issued from the flickering blue runes tattooed on the dead sorceresses.

Darkness was the reavers' element. They did not need light to hunt by. Even the watery lights of the runes were most likely an accident. The reavers would not know that their tattoos glowed.

But ahead of Raj Ahten, a room seemed to be filled with fire. He raced to an entrance and looked down from a parapet to a floor twenty-five feet below.

The Seal of Desolation spread before him, pulsating with color, throbbing. It was nearly two hundred yards across. A dozen scarlet sorceresses filled the room. At the center of the seal, like a great spider in its web, hunched a great mage.

Indeed, she was larger than the one at Carris.

Raj Ahten dared not give the reavers time to react. His left arm was still numb, and he could not hold his breath much longer. Soon he would be forced to take the foul air, and learn just how vile it tasted.

He ran several paces, leapt from the parapet, vaulted onto the head of the great mage. His right leg snapped from the impact, just below the knee.

He bore the pain, slammed his warhammer into the mage's sweet triangle. He feared that for such a huge monster, the blade itself was too short. He reversed the weapon and plunged the handle into the hole as if it were a lance.

She seemed unaffected by the wound. The mage shook her head and tossed him. Even with all his metabolism, all his stamina, Raj Athen's leg had not yet healed when he slammed painfully to the ground.

The Seal of Desolation itself looked to be made of molten glass, but felt as solid as stone. The mucilage of the glue mums had hardened into knobby shapes. Ghost fires in shades of deepest purple flickered through the thing, bursting out in actinic flashes. A sorcerous smoke filled the room.

The Rune of Desolation was powerful.

Raj Ahten swung his hammer, broke off a knob. A blinding flash of white light burst from the broken rune.

The great mage wheeled to confront him. Gree flew up from her bloated body in a swarm, and her staff blazed a sickly yellow.

Raj Ahten leapt aside as a bolt of pure night shot from the

staff. It slammed into the rune where he'd stood, demolishing a wide swath.

The rune simply shattered. A scarlet sorceress caught in the blast hissed in agony, was bowled over on her side. The left half of her body had disintegrated or been blown away, as if it had been eaten by acid.

Raj Ahten dared not give the mage time for a second attack. He raced across the Rune of Desolation, darting left and right.

The huge mage reared back in alarm.

She stood a full six feet taller than the monster at Carris. Never in legend had a reaver grown to such a size.

Surely, he told himself, this is the great Lord of the Underworld.

He would never be able to leap high enough to slam his hammer into her massive brain, and she had the wisdom to close her mouth so that he could not strike up through the palate.

His best target was the soft spot of her thorax, but he would have preferred a lance to pierce so deeply.

He reversed his warhammer. The handle was nearly six feet long. With his endowments of brawn, it was no great feat to leap high in the air. He hurled the hammer with all his might, wrenching his shoulder from its socket as he did.

The warhammer buried itself into the monster's thorax, and the fell mage reared higher, trying to escape. Raj Ahten hit the ground, scurried out of danger.

The fell mage threw down her staff, reached up with her huge clumsy paws and began trying to yank the warhammer out. She got it between two claws, thrust it away from her. It rang against the roof, then clattered a dozen yards off.

She reached for her staff. Raj Ahten lunged for his warhammer.

He had not struck deeply enough. A sound hit to the

thorax should have caused her to die almost instantly, similar to a blow to a man's kidneys.

All around, scarlet sorceresses rushed to join the fray. The great mage lowered her head and charged him, gaping her jaws wide at Raj Ahten.

That was what he needed. He gripped his warhammer, and vaulted into her mouth. The dry, raspy surface of her tongue felt as if it were made of gravel.

Her jaws snapped closed around him, and she tilted her head back in an attempt to swallow. He jumped, plunging the warhammer deep into her soft palate, raking a long gash.

He pulled out the hammer in a rain of gore. Blood and brains cascaded down, spattering.

The fell mage staggered a few feet, wobbled.

Raj Ahten slammed his hammer against the back of her throat to make her gag.

As she coughed him out, a dozen other Runelords in fine silks came leaping into the room. Bhopanastrat shouted, 'Kill them all, secure the fortress!'

The scarlet sorceresses backed away, tried to retreat. But there would be no escape. The fortress was surrounded. Raj Ahten had already cleared a path into it, and ripped out the heart of the reavers' defenses.

Pusnabish entered seconds later. Runelords swarmed into the fortress by the hundreds.

Raj Ahten ran for the open air, leaving lesser men to complete the job.

He imagined how the world would now sing his praise. There would be parades at Maygassa as he ascended the Elephant Throne. The people would carpet the road beneath his feet with petals of rose, gardenia, and lotus. The enormous golden gongs outside the city's western gate would pound night and day for a month. The most beautiful women in the realm would seek him out, hoping to bear his sons, while wealthy lords and merchants showered him with gifts.

His victory would far outshine any deeds that Gaborn Val Orden had accomplished. He, Raj Ahten, had killed the greatest of reaver mages, had saved the earth.

Songs would be sung about him for a thousand years. Children as yet undreamed of would sit around the campfires at night and hear how Raj Ahten stood against the Lord of the Underworld. Their mouths would gape in wonder, and they would try to hide from their fathers how they shivered in fear.

All of this, and more, Raj Ahten envisioned as he cleared the mouth of the fortress, came back into the daylight. The poisoned air swirled round the reavers' hive in a dingy cloud.

He plunged down the ridge into the reavers' dry moat and suddenly felt a nauseating wrench.

He knew the sensation far too well.

His Dedicates were dying.

At the palace in Bel Nai, the markets were awash with morning light. White doves fluttered about the spires of the citadels, or strutted along rooftops, cooing contentedly.

In the bazaar, a merchant cried as always, 'Fresh roasted pistachios, still hot!'

Camels lay in the street, chewing lazily.

Here, a thousand miles north of Kartish, word had not yet reached the city of a reaver attack in far lands. Raj Ahten's ministers had not wished to alarm the populace.

Yet in the deepest heart of the Dedicates' Keep, four men lay dying. Three were men who vectored stamina to Raj Ahten. The Emir Owatt knew them by voice. One was Korab Manthusar, a Dedicate who had acted as a vector for nearly twelve years. Another was Jinjafal Dissai, who had vectored stamina for less than five.

Between them, they accounted for hundreds of endowments. They had been sipping tea as they played chess when the emir came upon them and jabbed each with his poisoned needle.

The resin of the malefactor bush paralyzed the lungs, and would leave the men gasping on the floor. Without stamina, they would not resist death for long.

But though the poison promised to make quick work of them, it did not do so soon enough. Both men managed to cry out a brief warning.

The emir spun and stabbed a third Dedicate.

A nearby guard heard the noise, rushed into the common room, and sliced the emir in half.

As the old king died, the guard held his hand.

For a moment, the emir imagined the man sought to offer him comfort. But only in his final seconds did he realize that the guard held him to keep the poison needle from piercing another victim.

Raj Ahten gasped outside the reavers' stronghold, choking on the fetid air. Even now he could taste the great mage's curse: 'Breathe no more.'

The power of it was undeniable.

The curse reached into his lungs, its decimating grip clutching them like a vise. He fought it desperately, but all his remaining endowments of stamina would not keep him alive.

Dedicates were dying, his vectors. His defenses were crumbling. Binnesman's curse had undone him. He was not the Sum of All Men.

He struggled for air, and his heart beat wildly. Moments before he had imagined the praise that would be his as savior of the world. Now, he lay beneath clouds of darkness, gasping in the pit.

Over Raj Ahten's head, a fireball hurtled toward the fortress, slammed into its side. Delicious heat spilled out in a hundred directions. Flames roared nearby.

He felt the warmth like a soothing balm, recalled how delicious it had felt against his skin at the campfire high in the Hest Mountains.

'I can heal you,' Az whispered in his memory.

The skies went dark as Az enticed fire from the heavens again. It swirled down into his hands, a brilliant maelstrom, a webwork of light piercing the darkness.

Unable to walk, Raj Ahten crawled toward it. His frame shook. Despite all his endowments of brawn, he trembled like an old woman, and gasped in the fetid air. He gained the lip of the pit, and looked up at the burning rune only three hundred yards away.

A wave of nausea rushed over him. He gasped as if he felt his own heart had been ripped away. Another vector gone.

There is an assassin at Bel Nai, he realized.

I will never live to reap my reward. I will not hear the songs I have earned.

He tottered up the lip of the pit, began stalking toward the great fire.

Az stood at the heart of the Rune of Night, drawing flames to himself, stealing the very light from heaven.

'Az!' Raj Ahten shouted with the last of his strength. His voice rang over the battlefield. He collapsed to his knees, struggled even to hold up a hand, pleading.

Az glanced down at him, saw his failing condition, and hurled the fireball.

It expanded as it roared near, until it filled Raj Ahten's vision.

In one instant, the white silks on his back seared to ashes. The fire pierced him with a thousand burning fangs. The flesh of his face bubbled. Ears and eyelids roasted to nothingness.

Old parts of him, unneeded parts, the dross of his humanity, melted away.

An intense light burned into his mind, expanded his vision. In an instant he saw that he had been traveling toward this destination all his life. He had imagined that he fought to serve mankind by becoming the Sum of All Men, while others said that he only served himself.

But at every juncture in the path of his life, he had chosen to serve Fire.

Even as a young man, he had appropriated for himself the title Sun Lord.

Now his master seized him and, like precious ore, purified him in the flames. The dross melted away, and that which remained was hardly flesh at all – only a vessel that veiled an immaculate light.

Raj Ahten was no longer human. He was the power that he had served so faithfully, and now, all of the lesser flameweavers of this world would bow before him and call him by his secret name.

Burned, naked, transformed, and trailing glorious clouds of smoke, he climbed to his feet. The flames hissed his new name: Scathain.

Chapter Fifty-seven: FELDONSHIRE

I crave peace. I would that all the villages in my realm would continually overflow with peace, like foam overflowing a mug of warm ale.

– Erden Geboren

Guildmaster Wallachs led Averan, Binnesman, and the wylde out the back of the guildhall to a cobbled square bordered on one side by shops.

Here, draftsmen designed the works to be created while young wrights cut the timbers and master carvers did the detail work. Averan was surprised to see two blacksmith forges for the smiths that fashioned the carvers' myriad tools.

In a finishing shop where pieces were stained and varnished, four burly men were loading wooden barrels into the back of a wagon. The team was already in its traces. The odors that arose from the wagon were noxious – the barrels were filled with spoiled linseed oil, denatured alcohol, poisonous lac, bags of salt crystals, and colored powders that she didn't even recognize. All of them seemed to be ingredients for various types of varnishes and wood preservatives. The woodcutters were carting off virtually anything that they hoped might poison a reaver.

'Are the other wagons gone?' Wallachs asked.

'Aye,' one of his men muttered. He wiped an arm across his sweaty face.

'Leave the rest,' Wallachs told the laborers, indicating the poison. 'Go save your families.'

The workers leapt from the wagon. Binnesman and Wallachs sat on the driver's seat. Averan and the wylde climbed in.

As they left the stable, Averan could hear a distant roar, like the pounding of the sea. The reavers were coming.

She tried to judge her distance from the reavers by sound alone. Over the past two days, she'd become good at it. 'They're maybe three miles out, I think. They'll be here in five minutes, maybe less.'

Her words seemed to have caught Wallachs by surprise. 'So soon?'

'Maybe less,' Averan emphasized.

Wallachs glanced at Binnesman for verification. The wizard arched a brow. 'Less than that, I'd say. The reavers are racing full tilt.'

Wallachs snapped his whip over the heads of his mounts, whistled and shouted. The horses erupted from the stable, went charging up the hill.

They're slow, Averan realized. So slow.

These weren't force horses. They were common animals, and big. Pulling logs and heavy loads over the years had strengthened them. But even with a light wagon racing at full speed, they'd be hard-pressed to outrun a reaver even.

So Wallachs went stampeding south along the road, shouting, 'Clear the way,' when anyone dared stand in front of him. 'Five minutes. In five minutes the reavers will be here!'

Only then did Averan begin to see the danger. Heading east of town, where workmen's cottages lined the dirt road, she still saw people everywhere. Many were emptying their houses, packing goods onto horses. One old woman quickly tried to pick an apple tree clean. Another young mother was grabbing laundry off a drying bush while her children tugged at her apron strings.

Dogs yapped at the wagon as it passed.

The road climbed a small hill, and for a couple of minutes Averan could see all of Feldonshire spread out below her. To the northwest the Darkwald was a brown blot along the silver waters of the Donnestgree. To the south lay a dozen hamlets in the folds of the hills. Boats plied the river, floating downstream on a glimmering road. Everywhere on the east of town, the highway was black and cluttered with travelers. Many of them were folks from Shrewsvale and villages to the west. They raced across the country on horse, on wagon, on foot.

Beyond them, three miles away, a cloud of dust rose in the hills where the reavers raged. From up here, the sound of their advance was louder, a continuous thunder.

People screamed across the miles.

'They're all going to die,' Averan whispered. She climbed to the back of the wagon and stared out, feeling helpless.

She'd thought that she and Binnesman had done some good. They'd given the people all the warning that they could. But it wasn't going to be enough.

'Not all of them,' Binnesman said. 'We've saved some. Perhaps many.'

But as the buckboard topped the hill, she saw the reavers' front ranks charging over a distant rise. Wagons and people fled before them.

A man's legs would not carry him fast enough. Hiding would do no good. Men were less than mice before the reaver horde.

Gaborn's troops fled in a long column, their armor flashing in the sun. They headed south into the hills, helpless before the onslaught.

Binnesman pulled Averan back. 'Come away,' he warned. 'Watching doesn't do any good.'

But it does, Averan thought. Watching made her angry, and anger made her strong.

On a bald hill above Feldonshire, Gaborn tried to decide whether to make another stand. Hundreds of commoners had ridden up here on horseback. Most were young men who bore bows or spears. They were eager to prove themselves, hoped to earn the Choosing. Thus, Gaborn's small army had begun to swell.

Still, he could do nothing for Feldonshire.

Below him lay his last hope: a stream cut through a narrow defile, and would provide some small distance between men and reavers. Farmers had built stone walls to keep their sheep from wandering into the ravine. Perhaps a hundred local men had taken position behind the eastern wall, and now stood with bows ready.

The reavers advanced on Feldonshire.

Too few people had left the city. Gaborn's men could see the peasants down in the valley, still loading food and wagons. Their hearts went out to the commoners preparing to die down there.

'Milord?' Skalbairn asked.

Gaborn warned, 'Stay back. We can't do any more good. The cover is inadequate, as anyone can see.'

Gaborn dared not tempt fate. He knew that he could not turn the horde.

Skalbairn's men chafed at his command.

Beside him, Baron Waggit was breathing heavily, almost unable to restrain himself from riding down into the valley, to join the doomed men. The minutes stretched interminably, though the wait was short.

Nearly a mile below, the reavers marched in the Form of War. The ground trembled from their passage.

He could not stop them.

When the reavers neared the far side of the ravine,

the hundred archers rose up and let loose a volley of arrows.

Few men had bows powerful enough to penetrate a reaver's hide at a hundred yards. Fewer still had the skill to use them effectively at such a distance. Yet three or four men managed to make kills before the reavers retaliated.

Blade-bearers hurled stones, then leapt through the ravine. Mages blasted with their staves.

Some of Feldonshire's archers raced for their horses. A few lucky ones ran fast and lived. But most of the commoners died by the droves.

Then the horde was beyond the ravine, into the borders of Feldonshire itself.

Reavers knocked down orchards in their path, smashed cottages that had stood for centuries, demolished fields and flocks.

People fled – peasants running as fast as their legs could carry them, mothers with babes in their arms and children in tow.

Their screams rose above the thunder of the reavers.

Those that ran clear of the reavers' path would live. Those who failed would never fail at anything again.

The blade-bearers at the front fed on sheep and peasants until they could stomach no more. Then they regurgitated their meals and moved on, feeding anew.

Gaborn felt numb. To the west, Langley's knights rode behind the reavers, slaughtering the laggards. The men's lances were all broken, so they resorted to horsemen's warhammers.

But to the east, peasants and wagons darkened the road. The highway through town served as a bottleneck for those who fled. People shouted in terror but could not move fast enough. At least ten thousand people still remained in the reavers' path.

One of Skalbairn's men peeled off from his ranks, came

riding up from the valley below. When he drew near, he raised the visor of his helm. It was Marshal Chondler.

'Good news!' Chondler cried. 'The reavers couldn't keep the pace. We rid ourselves of thousands in the hills!'

No one cheered. The warrior looked over his back, to see why the others stared. His smile turned to a scowl.

'Milord,' Chondler asked. 'What can we do?'

Gaborn did not answer for a moment. In the past hour, he had considered every option – archery barrages from the hillsides, charges with lances, holding fast behind the stone wall and braving the worst that the reavers could bring against them. All paths led to disaster. Only one answer sufficed.

Gaborn whispered angrily, 'Stay out of their way. Kill any that fall behind.'

A part of him refused to believe that this could ever happen. He was the Earth King, and could still hear its voice. He'd felt certain that in his hour of greatest need, the Earth would respond. Yet now he watched the slaughter, and could not stop it. Most of all, he mourned the sick and wounded still trapped beside the river. Their fate was sealed.

Now the reavers neared the heart of Feldonshire. They slowed as they pushed over cottages and shops, took a few seconds to ferret people from their hiding holes and gobble them down.

Gaborn reached out with his senses. Many of his people had fled. Some were on the far side of the river to the north. Others had gone south into the hills. The reavers' course would lead straight through Feldonshire. His people to the north and south should have been safe.

Yet Gaborn felt a rising danger, even for those who had left the reavers' path. It could mean only one thing. Once the reavers reached the pools at Stinkwater, they would swing back to hunt the people of Feldonshire.

Yet something even more profound had happened. Gaborn reached out with Earth senses. The Earth warned him that now the danger had risen tenfold. The world's peril had increased. Gaborn wondered what might have changed.

Then he felt it. Raj Ahten was gone. Gaborn could only surmise that the reavers in Kartish had killed him. With his death, everything seemed ready to fall apart.

Gaborn felt staggered.

Chondler watched the reavers spread their decimation and argued, 'Milord, I'm sworn to the Brotherhood of the Wolf. I'll not stand here idle while people die.'

Gaborn shook his head sadly, tried to make the man understand. 'You see their formation? If you attack their lines, the front ranks will retreat a few steps while those at your side move up. Then the arms of the star will swing round and close on your position, circling you. You'll die!'

'All men die,' Chondler said. 'I'm sworn to protect mankind.'

Couldn't he see? Couldn't he see that Gaborn acted in their best interests?

'Damn you, Marshal Chondler,' Gaborn shouted. 'What do you think I'm trying to do? If you go down there, the reavers will have you and destroy Feldonshire anyway.'

'I'm sworn –' Chondler began to say.

Gaborn drew his sword ringing from its sheath. 'For mankind,' he said solemnly, 'and for the Earth.' Around him, the men of the Brotherhood of the Wolf cheered.

Chondler stared at him in surprise, unsure how to take this. The king would join the Brotherhood of the Wolf? Was he renouncing his kingdom?

Gaborn knew that his deed put Chondler off balance. But in his own mind, he was only reaffirming the commitment he'd made to his people long ago.

He looked out over the crowd. 'So, good sirs, it's a fight you want?' he asked. 'I assure you, this battle has only begun.'

Chapter Fifty-eight: THREE KILLS

The most enigmatic of reavers is the 'fell mage,' the leader of an attacking horde.

Hearthmaster Magnus contended that they are a separate species from other reavers, while others suggest that powerful leaders always rise from within the ranks of sorceresses.

It is of course tempting to assume that something as malign as a reaver horde would have to have a leader. But I often wonder if even the eyewitness accounts of fell mages are not faulty. In what respect does a 'fell mage' differ from any other large sorceress?

And since the last eyewitness documentation of a fell mage leading a reaver horde is nearly 1400 years old, I wonder if it is prudent to discount the notion completely.

Rather, I suspect that reavers form a loose society that is ultimately leaderless.

– Hearthmaster Valen, of the Room of Beasts

Guildmaster Wallach's wagon rounded a corner too fast, slewed as if it would leave the road. They'd left Feldonshire, and as she topped a hill Averan spotted two disreputable warehouses on the flats below. Hides stretched on racks in the sun outside one building identified it as a tannery.

Wallachs slowed his wagon, whistled to some men loading barrels outside the tannery. 'Reavers will be here in five minutes. Get to safety!'

The men left off loading their barrels and Wallachs was off again. The horses heaved with every breath, and they frothed now. Wallachs shouted as he sent the whip whistling over their tails.

Wallachs eyed the second building as he passed. Averan could smell the pungent, greasy odor of lye soap cooking.

After that, there was no true road. No cottages bordered the Stinkwater, not even the lowest hovel. Here on the east of town, the only businesses had been those that smelled so bad that no one would want them near.

To the west of town the land had been rich and fertile, covered with cottages and gardens, orchards, vineyards, and fields of hops and barley.

But here even the ground seemed defiled. The land flattened out. During the winters, rain would swell the Stinkwater Ponds, flooding their banks. In summer the water receded, leaving a yellowish-gray crust where almost nothing could grow. Coarse grass thrust up from sandy patches along with a few black, stunted trees that were so twisted they might never have been alive.

Averan could smell the Stinkwater, a stench like rotten eggs.

The ponds, green with scum, boiled out of the ground not far ahead. A thin haze rose up from the steaming waters. A dozen wagons were there, with twenty or thirty men offloading barrels.

Wallachs drew near, shouted, 'How do you fare?'

'We've got enough lye in there to eat the flesh off your bones,' one man shouted, 'and with all the turpentine, I'd not get a flame close to it for any woman's love!'

Averan looked at Binnesman's face. He seemed unprepared for how large the ponds really were. They looked larger down here than they did from up in the sky. Each one covered several acres. Kegs of poison floated in them.

In the distance, the earth thundered as the reavers approached. Binnesman's countenance was pale.

'By the Powers,' he whispered, 'I can't heal those waters – not in an hour, not in a day!'

Wallachs grunted and nodded, as if his suspicions had been confirmed. He shouted to his men. 'You've got three minutes to clear the ponds. The reavers are coming!'

He snapped his whip over the ears of his team, and raced ahead.

'The road gives out just east of here,' Wallachs apologized to Binnesman in a worried tone. 'Not more than a mile, and you're in the woods.'

He left much unsaid. If the reavers came after them, there'd be no place to run.

'A mile should be far enough,' Binnesman said. 'Take us to yonder rise, and let's see what happens.'

Wallachs urged the horses on, and the buckboard bounced mercilessly over the bumpy trail, rattling Averan's teeth. Behind them, a cloud of dust rose from where Feldonshire had stood, and the faint screams drifted over the plain.

Averan's stomach knotted. The horses were tiring. They couldn't keep up this pace for mile after mile. Even if the road had kept going, the horses couldn't.

Now the wagon rolled up a small knoll where a few black trees thrust from the sparse grass. From there, Averan could see the hills above town and look out over the Stinkwater.

She'd seen the ponds before from the sky. Up high, they looked like three bright green gems with white edges. But she knew that it was just a trick of the light.

Now the wagons pulled away from the ponds, with men whipping their horses. Broken barrels bobbed on the water, spilling scum. The steam rising from the ponds' surface made them look like bubbling cauldrons.

Averan's heart pounded. They had barely stopped, when the reavers crowned the hill above Feldonshire, stampeding for the Stinkwater.

The horde thundered across the plain, teeth gleaming wickedly in the sunlight. For hours they had been running in the Form of War.

Now they broke ranks. The largest and greediest blade-bearers surged ahead, making for the ponds.

But even half a mile from water, most reavers sensed something wrong. Many rose up on their back legs, philia waving madly, and drew back from the stench. Others merely slowed, stalked forward cautiously.

A few thousand reavers, so crazed that their senses were gone, galloped forward and threw themselves into the ponds, dipping their heads down deep in the water, then throwing them back up as they drank in a strangely birdlike fashion. They crowded together, cheek to jowl, a solid mass of gray leathery hides and flashing teeth.

It was a horror to watch.

Behind the reaver horde, Gaborn's knights advanced over the hills.

With the breaking ranks and their loss of hope, many reavers floundered. They dropped and lay insensate, unwilling to move.

Knights on their force horses raced to take them while they were down. Their silver mail flashed as horses wheeled and turned, darting after the slowest gray reavers. Through half-closed eyes, the knights reminded Averan for all the world of silver minnows in a pool, flashing in the sunlight as they struck at a bit of food.

The knights brought down a few hundred reavers, then wheeled their chargers south to a small hill nearly a mile and a half away. They formed ranks there. Lances bristled as they aimed at the sky. Local farmers and merchant boys rode up to meet them, swelling their ranks to thousands.

Closer to hand, the reavers that had reached the Stinkwater and drunk the most began to die. Muscle spasms caused them to flip to their sides, kicking dust in the air as they spun.

Those that drank only a little drew away from the fouled water after a swallow or two, and simply heaved the contents of their stomachs onto the ground. They groped about, almost too weak to move.

By far, the vast majority of the reavers merely retreated from the ponds and stood, dazed with dehydration. Their philia drooped in exhaustion, hanging from their heads like dead vines. The rasping of their heavy breathing filled the air, becoming a dull rumble.

Dozens of reavers began to trudge in aimless circles, no longer cognizant of where they went.

From the south, a hundred force horses came charging over the plains out of the wooded hills. Gaborn led them, riding with Knights Equitable, as if to race the wind. He'd circled the reaver horde. Now he rode up toward Averan on the hillock. Skalbairn rode with him, along with Baron Waggit and many other knights.

Gaborn nodded at Averan and leapt from his horse, gazing west at the reavers. 'What's happening?' he demanded. His countenance was grim, determined.

'Their run to water has left them broken,' Binnesman answered. 'I suspect that over half of the horde has succumbed.'

'Not quite half,' Gaborn said. 'I estimate nearly forty thousand reavers left in the horde.'

'They're dying,' Averan added. 'They won't make it back to Keep Haberd.'

'I think,' Wallachs said hopefully, 'I think we've done it. I think we've won!'

Averan watched Gaborn. He licked his lips, stared hard at the reavers. Eventually they would all die, and Gaborn would lead her to the Waymaker. There she would feed, and learn the path to the One True Master.

'We haven't won,' Gaborn told Wallachs. 'They may die, but not without a fight.'

Even as he spoke, a great hissing erupted among the center of the horde.

A mage rose up high on her legs, began casting her scent far and wide. The glowing runes on her body glimmered in the sun, and her staff suddenly blazed like white lightning.

Three Kills was her name. In Averan's memory, she was young and fearsome, easily the most cunning mage in the horde. Only her relative youth and small size had kept her from leading the band before. Three more reavers rose up, faced Three Kills and began hissing in return.

'What's happening?' Gaborn demanded.

'It's an argument between lords,' Averan said. 'They often argue.'

'Which one is their leader?' Gaborn asked.

Averan was astonished by the question. It was so obvious. 'The one with her butt highest in the air. See how the others keep theirs lower? She'll kill them if they don't.'

Gaborn watched them so intently that Averan felt guilty for not being able to tell him more. He went to the lip of the hill, drew his warhammer and planted it in the ground, much as Binnesman did his staff. Then he held the handle, and peered at the reavers, as if trying to read their thoughts.

If I had the senses of a reaver, she knew, I'd be able to smell what they said. I'd know what they were arguing about.

But she only knew that an argument like this might last for an hour or more.

The sunlight seemed so bright, so painful. As the reavers held their council, Averan half closed her eyes.

Down in the valley below, Three Kills's argument ended abruptly. A rival raised her tail slightly, and Three Kills leapt, thrust her crystalline staff through the sweet triangle of her adversary. There was a dull explosion, and the sorceress's head ripped into ragged chunks.

She had had her say.

Now Three Kills snatched gobbets of her brain, while others in the horde ripped out the sweet glands below her legs.

The remaining reavers drew back, began rushing about, taking up new formations. They separated into nine camps, each led by a scarlet sorceress, each in the Form of War.

They turned and began stalking east, spreading to the north and south as they went. It was a distinctly odd maneuver for a reaver.

Reavers lived in tunnels, and tended to walk in single file through the Underworld – head to tail. That way, orders could be relayed backward easily.

Spreading their forces went against the reavers' most fundamental instincts. More than that, the horde was heading downwind. They wouldn't easily be able to smell adversaries in front of them.

'What are they doing?' Gaborn asked. 'Is this what I think?'

Averan began shaking. She could see it all so clearly. The nine armies would create a front perhaps eight miles wide. Already Gaborn's troops on the far hill recognized the danger and began to retreat. 'You're right. The reavers know they're going to die,' she said. 'But there are a lot of people in Feldonshire. They'll hunt down as many peasants as they can. After that . . .'

'They'll keep hunting,' Gaborn said. 'I can sense ripples of danger everywhere. They'll circle and head downriver, through city after city until they reach the Courts of Tide.

'Averan, how can I stop them?'

The reavers loped off to the east.

Averan thought quickly. Each time they'd killed a leader, the new mage had changed tactics. Even now, the other sorceresses questioned Three Kills's wisdom. She'd led them to water, only to find it poisoned. The reavers were on the verge of mutiny.

'You must get rid of Three Kills . . .'

'Of course!' Gaborn said. But he'd lost sight of her. 'Where is she?'

'The middle formation,' Averan answered.

His face paled. She knew that he was considering strategies, counting the potential cost. He looked grim, lost.

Chapter Fifty-nine: BROTHERHOOD

I have learned that my kingdom has no borders.

And that all men are more than mere subjects – they are my kinsmen, my brethren – and therefore deserving of my devotion.

I find that I grieve the loss of strangers as I would grieve the loss of my only child.

– Erden Geboren

Skalbairn sat on his charger as Gaborn studied the reavers. Skalbairn could see the wheels of the lad's mind turning as he considered how to best the reavers. The reavers were stalking toward Feldonshire.

The boy had no time to plot any elegant strategies. The main force of his cavalry held the hill to the west. But if Gaborn raced to them now, he would have to skirt the reavers' lines. By the time he reached his men, the reavers would be into Feldonshire, hunting.

'Gentlemen,' Gaborn said firmly. 'I believe we can stop the slaughter before it begins – but only at great cost.'

Gaborn looked up at the hundred men who had ridden with him, staring each in the eye. 'I'm for the Underworld, and cannot lead the charge. And any man who rides now must consider his life forfeit. Will you ride?'

The lad was serious. Skalbairn had never seen an expression like Gaborn wore now. There was suffering and pain in his eyes, and sorrow in his brow, and a consuming need.

Skalbairn's blood went chill. As a child he'd dreamt of being a warrior, and in his fondest dreams he'd imagined that an Earth King would arise someday, and Skalbairn would fight at his side.

But he'd never dreamt of it like this. The Earth King never asked him to die.

There was a moment of silence from the lords. Skalbairn knew that his men would ride, but none wanted to be the first to speak.

'In the world to come,' Skalbairn inquired, 'may I ride beside you in the Great Hunt?'

'Aye,' Gaborn said. 'Any man who rides now, will ride with me then.' It was an empty promise, Skalbairn knew. Not all men rose as wights.

Skalbairn spat on the ground. ''Tis a bargain, then!'

A cheer rose from the men at Skalbairn's back. Some drew their warhammers and beat them against shields, others waved their lances.

The only man who did not cheer was Baron Waggit, who sat silently on his mount, thinking. It was a capacity new to him, Skalbairn reasoned, an unfamiliar tool.

Gaborn raised a hand, warning them to silence.

'We'll need a diversion,' Gaborn said. He drew a hexagon on the ground. 'You'll break into three squadrons. We'll send fifty men on a charge here to the left, another fifty to charge to the right. As the reavers move to attack, it should thin the line here at the front. A small force of men on fast horses can race through the lines and lance the mage.'

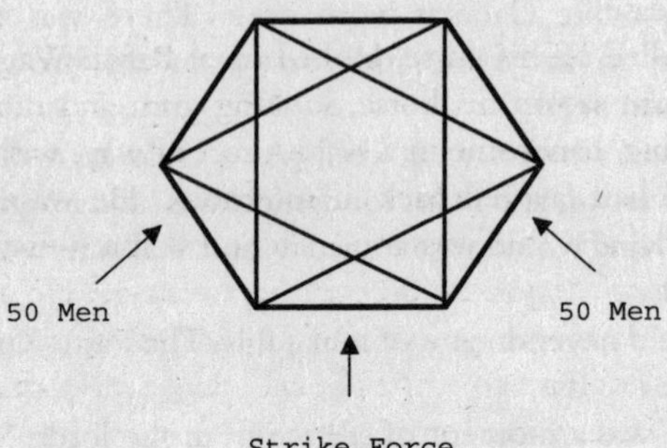

'Milord,' Skalbairn asked, 'may I volunteer to strike the blow?'

The lad's face was pale. He took a deep breath, nodded.

Skalbairn was sure then that he would die. Marshal Chondler said, 'I'll ride with him, as should any man of the Brotherhood of the Wolf.'

With that, a third man made the offer, Lord Kellish, and Gaborn nodded, and said, 'That's enough.'

Gaborn stared evenly at the hundred Knights Equitable who were going to ride into battle, said in a solemn tone, 'Thank you. I'll need each of you to fight like reavers now.'

Gaborn pulled out his warhorn and said, 'The left wing charge on my command, two blasts quickly. The right wing will go on one blast long. Skalbairn, I'll ride with you part of the way.'

Skalbairn and the knights quickly dismounted, checked their girth straps. Not every man had a lance, but every man wanted one. He quickly checked his charger's hooves. The heavy war shoes were all in place. The leather bindings for its barding were tight.

For years, Skalbairn had lived as a moral failure. For

years he had believed that only death might bring him some release.

He pulled off his purse, looked up at Baron Waggit. The young man sat on his horse, looking grim and thoughtful. He was big, handsome in a brutish sort of way, with a color of blond hair favored back in Internook. He wasn't riding into battle, and that was good. He knew that this fight was beyond him. Maybe he'd never be a warrior. He'd make a fine farmer, or perhaps someday go back to the mines. With any luck, he'd live to a ripe old age. Right now, that was all that Skalbairn wanted from the man.

Damn it, Skalbairn thought. A day ago we all thought him a fool, and now he's wiser than all the rest of us put together.

'Waggit,' Skalbairn called. The young man turned, his pale blue eyes piercing in the mid-morning sun. 'Some gold. I'd be grateful if you'd take it to my daughter, Farion. See that she's well cared for.'

Waggit considered the request.

Skalbairn felt certain that if Waggit saw the girl, he'd feel for her plight. Waggit knew better than any man the world his idiot daughter was trapped in. He'd recognize her virtues and her goodness. His daughter was as kind as she was simple, and her smile was as infectious as a plague. She'd never make another man a proper wife. She could do small chores – bring in firewood or pluck a chicken for dinner. All she needed was a good man, capable of loving her. He'd need to be a patient man to care for her, to buy goods at the market and help her rear her children – one forgiving of her weaknesses.

Skalbairn whispered to the Powers, Let him be that man.

Waggit nodded. 'I'll give it to her.'

'May the Bright Ones protect you,' Skalbairn said softly.

Skalbairn climbed on his horse, spurred the mount down the slope, leading the way. There was no more time for niceties.

In moments, Gaborn and the others all gathered around him, and the assault began without fanfare, a hundred men against more than three thousand reavers.

The reavers were running fast, heading toward Feldonshire, loping over the plains with their backs to him, each reaver like a gray hill.

Skalbairn let his huge black charger race. He dropped his lance into a couch. Beside him, a hundred men fanned out. The sulfur and alkali crusting the plains muted the sound of the horse's hooves, and went flying as they charged.

The plain was as flat and barren of stones as it could be. There were painfully few trees or bushes, hardly even any grass.

He'd never had a better surface for a cavalry charge.

Langley veered to the right, leading fifty men to the far side of the hexagon. Lord Gulliford guided another fifty left.

'Ranks three deep,' Gaborn said to Skalbairn, Marshal Chondler, and Lord Kellish. 'Make sure that you cut through the lines!'

Gaborn sounded two blasts short. Gulliford's riders gave their chargers their heads.

Gaborn sounded one blast long, and Langley's men swept to the right, driving hard.

Gaborn held his three champions back. Baron Waggit rode beside them.

Skalbairn reined his mount, watched the enemy lines.

Gulliford's men swept into the reavers, lanced dozens from behind, then veered away from the front, riding as if in a Knights' Circus. The reavers spun to face them, blade-bearers closing ranks to form a wall of flesh while sorceresses leveled their staves and hurled dire spells. Clouds of green smoke rained down on the fifty. In the mountains the reavers had thrown stones, but the sandy soil here left their artillery with nothing at hand. Only half a dozen men fell under the onslaught.

Almost immediately, Langley's men hit the reavers' right flank.

As Gaborn had predicted, the untrained reavers broke rank on both flanks, rushed to do battle.

Thus the front before Skalbairn thinned.

'Fare thee well!' Gaborn shouted.

'Till we meet in the shadowed vale!' Skalbairn roared, and spurred his mount. The ground blurred beneath his charger's feet. Skalbairn's black stallion had three endowments of metabolism, and would rank among the fastest in the world. Many better-endowed mounts could hit speeds of eighty or ninety miles an hour, but his outraced them.

To hit a reaver at that speed would surely leave him dead. To fall from his horse would break every bone in his body.

Skalbairn held his lance steady. He glanced back, saw Chondler a hundred yards behind him, followed by Lord Kellish.

He spurred his mount and shouted, 'Faster!'

Many of the blade-bearers held no weapons at all. He aimed his mount between two of them.

At two hundred yards he drew close enough so that the reavers could sense him. But with his mount racing at over a hundred miles an hour, the reavers barely had time to spin. Without a glory hammer or a blade for the reavers to defend themselves, he darted easily between the first ranks.

A hiss of warning rose from reavers all around.

Off to his right, a quick-thinking sorceress hurled a spell.

A billowing stench flowed out behind him, bowled into the lines ahead, staggering a blade-bearer.

He swerved left now, into the second rank of reavers, never slowing. These were smaller beasts, without weapons. A reaver off to his right did not even spin to meet him. It was loping along, philia dangling, dead on its feet.

He aimed his mount toward it.

He heard the clatter of armor behind him – a shattering

lance and a man shouting a war cry. A horse screamed. Reaver spells exploded in the air.

Baron Waggit's horse walked beside that of the Earth King, and he watched the Runelords charge into battle. He'd witnessed a hundred deaths in the past day, but would never grow used to it.

He felt loath to lose Skalbairn. As High Marshal of the Knights Equitable, the huge warrior had the respect of every lord in Rofehavan, and to Waggit's surprise, the man had taken him under his wing. He'd taught him a little of how to use the staff yesterday. Miraculously, he'd even sought to match him with his daughter.

In all his life, Waggit could not remember any man ever wishing him as a son-in-law. No woman had ever desired him as a lover. No man would have wanted him as a brother.

The gift of memory was such a many-faceted thing. Now, for the first time in his life, he was desired. Yet his memory was unstable.

For the past day, he'd troubled himself in idle moments, trying to recall his real name. From time to time, it had come to him in the past, but he'd never been able to hold it for more than a few minutes. He did not want to go through life called by the name Waggit, for he felt sure it had been foisted on him derisively.

Yet his real name would not come to him, and the few memories he dredged up were full of pain. He recalled his father beating him as a child, for he had put too much wood in the hearth and the whole house nearly caught fire. He recalled sitting up in a tree one night, feeling lonely as he watched a V of geese wing past the rising moon, while children taunted him below. Of his mother, he could remember nothing at all.

It seemed that the memories he was making now were all darker still. He'd watched from afar as the horde destroyed

Feldonshire. He'd heard the muted death cries on the banks of the river Donnestgree as the reavers fell among the wounded from Carris. Even now, they echoed in his memory. He suspected that they would forever.

Thus Gaborn's blessing became a curse.

'Skalbairn's going to die, isn't he?' Waggit asked Gaborn.

'Yes,' Gaborn said. 'I believe so.'

There must be an end to the dying, Waggit told himself.

'Am I going to die today?' Waggit asked.

'No.'

'Good,' Waggit said.

He spurred his mount toward the reavers' battle lines.

Skalbairn glanced back. Chondler had tried to cut past a huge blade-bearer armed with a knight gig, but it darted in front of him. The monster snagged Chondler's charger out from beneath him, ripping open the mount's belly. The horse's gut spilled to the ground, and Chondler went down with it.

Behind him, Kellish veered and slowed. A sorceress hurled a dark yellow cloud that swallowed man and horse. Lord Kellish screamed and his horse never made it from under the shadow of that foul curse.

There would be no second chance, not in this charge.

Skalbairn burst past the second rank, neared the mage's escorts – a dozen large blade-bearers. Their ranks drew tight around her. Several of the monsters shifted to meet him.

But the mage was larger than her escorts, towered over them. He could see her well, marching away from him, ass high in the air.

In the distance ahead, he heard warhorns blowing. The foothills that hid Feldonshire rose in brown humps, and suddenly two thousand Knights Equitable topped the nearest rise, not half a mile ahead.

They had heard Gaborn sound the charge, and thought that he called to them!

A blade-bearer swung his knight gig and Skalbairn knew he would never evade it.

Yet the great mage was tantalizingly close. He wouldn't get a quick-killing blow, not one to the sweet triangle.

'Farion!' he cried, as he hurled his lance over the escort's head.

It lofted up twenty feet, and began to descend in a graceful curve toward the mage's back. He never got to see it land.

His horse whinnied in terror, tried to turn. The emerald staff hit its breastplate, and searing flames erupted from it, cutting the horse in two. Skalbairn's weight bore him over as the charger stumbled, and he knew no more.

Waggit raced through the reavers' ranks. The monsters hissed in seeming astonishment as two thousand knights charged the far side of the field. Sorceress's spells welled up in dark clouds, sweeping the front ranks. Dozens of lords died under the onslaught.

Suddenly, the reavers' attention was diverted.

Waggit rode through the horde with no weapon drawn. He dodged past a huge blade-bearer that swiveled its head as if looking for other prey. He rode past a second, using its bulk to shield him from the spell of a nearby sorceress.

He'd had little time to reason it through, but suspected that without a lance, the reavers would not consider him much of a threat. And of all the men in Gaborn's retinue, he was the least able to bear a weapon here.

Desperately Gaborn sounded his warhorn, blowing retreat.

Waggit had lost track of Skalbairn, but saw the fell mage rear up and whirl about. Skalbairn's lance had skewered her through the abdomen, and now she tried to pull it out. It was a deadly blow. She'd not last an hour under normal circumstances. But among her faithless companions, she would not last fifteen seconds.

Around her, a few young sorceresses saw her grim wound

and rushed in for the harvest. Blade-bearers followed in a grotesque knot.

They tore the mage from limb to limb.

'Skalbairn!' Waggit called.

There was no answering cry. But Waggit spotted Skalbairn's remains on the field, beneath the legs of a reaver. The reavers had made doubly sure of him. There was nothing left to save, nothing he could do.

Waggit spurred his charger away from the bloodbath, and the poor mount wheezed as it set off through the horde.

He guided it swiftly through a knot of smallish reavers that all fled as if a Glory had appeared among them, and in moments he was racing away from the horde altogether, his horse's hooves blurring as it sped over the sandy soil.

He charged toward the Stinkwater for a hundred yards, then wheeled back toward Gaborn. Langley and his men raced before him in full retreat.

Waggit looked up, saw a flock of geese in a V above the hills. The sun shone on the sparse fields and the woods beyond, making them shine in shades of wheat and vermilion.

From the dim recesses of memory, he recalled a time long ago, when he watched the geese fly over his father's barn during the bleak midwinter, and his mother called out warning him to put on his cloak. The memory rose like a clear bubble, and it burst within him.

In the memory, his mother called him by a truer name.

Chapter Sixty: THE WAYMAKER

Every road will lead you to a thousand byways. The easiest path is often not the best.
– From a placard at the Partridge and Peacock Inn, a training stop in the Room of the Feet

Dust rose in the vale below Averan – the dust of reavers marching to war, the dust of men charging into battle. From her vantage, the dust obscured the details of the fight. Gaborn's men swept into the horde on their force horses, their actions a blur.

The lords pounded into the reavers on four fronts, providing the much-needed diversion. Skalbairn rode in and died as he skewered Three Kills.

When it was done, fewer men rode back.

Averan thought that she should mourn, but no tears would come. Too many friends had died already.

The reavers hissed, sending their undetectable words across the field, and at once the nine Forms of War began to merge into one. Under new leadership, the reavers marched back west toward Feldonshire.

When Gaborn's army fled to the south, the reavers did not give pursuit.

The horde was leaving, thundering across the earth in dwindling numbers, hissing like the waves of a retreating tide. The reavers were heading back for their lair, though few had the stamina to survive the arduous journey.

In the distance Gaborn's men began to cheer. They rode to the hilltops south of Feldonshire and gave a rising shout as the reavers passed. She saw men leaping, hugging each other.

In the hills and in the woods across the river Donnestgree, cheers also arose from villagers.

At Averan's back, Gaborn's Days had been studying the battle in silence. Now he whispered, 'A great victory.'

But Gaborn merely sat on his charger, his lance balanced across the pommel of his saddle, head hanging. He had lost dozens of troops in the fray.

'I've warned him,' Binnesman said. 'Erden Geboren did not die of a mortal wound, but of a broken heart. Gaborn will do the same.'

'How can we help him?' Averan asked.

But she already knew what Gaborn would want. He'd dog the reavers for the day, and have her search for the Waymaker. He'd want her to feed again.

'Listen . . .' Binnesman said. He looked off to the north and then south. Beside him, the green woman cocked an ear, as if Binnesman had given her the command to listen.

Averan could hear nothing unusual. 'What?'

'The silence is profound. It spreads for miles.'

Averan wasn't quite sure what he meant. People were still cheering. The reavers rasped and the earth seemed to groan beneath their weight.

'No birds sing, no crickets,' Binnesman whispered. 'No cattle bawl – not a sound other than man and reavers for miles and miles. What is the Earth telling you?'

Averan didn't know what he meant. To her, it felt as if . . . suffering. The earth could be suffering.

She felt tired. She wanted to end this war.

On the hills across the valley, Gaborn's knights gathered in a great circle. Now they held up their shields in unison and began to flash them, sending news of their victory in every direction as far as the eye could see.

The sunlight was too bright. Averan raised her hands to protect her eyes.

Downhill a hundred yards she noticed a black tree that thrust from the ground, a small, gnarled thing. It wasn't really a tree. It was hardly taller than a man – more of a bush, with a dozen twisted branches. Stunted, vile-looking.

Yet she sensed life within it. It had managed to survive beside the Stinkwater where no other trees could. It was noble and hardy.

She didn't think about what she was doing.

She merely leapt from the back of the wagon and walked down to the tree.

It looked at first as if it had never had leaves, but as she neared she saw that they had already fallen for the winter. They lay upon the ground, broad and brown.

Up close, the bark was shiny, a deep gray that almost seemed charcoal. A few wrinkled seedpods still clung to the limbs.

She had never seen a tree like it, could not have named it. Yet it held her spellbound, enthralled.

She reached out experimentally, grabbed the central branch, and gave it a tug.

The limb pulled away so easily she almost thought that the tree must have died long ago, and the wood had all gone to rot. But she could feel power beneath the bark, could feel its vital essence.

No, the tree had given itself to her.

It was a good staff, strong and powerful and dangerous. It was her staff. She began breathing hard with excitement, shaking.

At her back, Binnesman broke her reverie. 'Hmmm . . . black laburnum – a strange choice.'

'What is its nature?' Averan asked. 'What does it tell you about me?'

'I don't know,' Binnesman said. His tone was thick with suspicion, and he peered at her closely from beneath his bushy brow. 'No one has ever chosen it before. I have never heard of an Earth Warden who chose his staff from a poisonous tree.'

'Poisonous?'

'Every part of a laburnum is deadly – root, bark, leaf, berry, nut. The black laburnum is the most poisonous of all. In the hills of Lysle, where most of it grows, the locals call it poisonwood.'

'Poisonwood,' Averan repeated. The name had an ominous ring. Yet it seemed fitting that she should choose her staff from such wood, here, where so many of the reavers lay poisoned.

She looked into his eyes. Averan had never been good at reading people, at knowing when they lie. But she wondered about Binnesman now. He was studying her narrowly, suspiciously. He knew something about her, or guessed something from her choice of staff.

Gaborn had turned his mount, now he raced back up to the hillside. He looked distraught. He bore sad news. He called up to his Days, 'Queen Herin the Red died a few moments ago in the charge.' He shook his head wearily.

'Averan,' he begged, 'I saw a reaver with thirty-six philia, down by the pools. It has big forepaws. Will you look at it?'

Averan swallowed hard. She could not bear to feed again, not from a reaver that had knowingly drunk its own death.

She raised her staff, held it defensively as if she were Spring, ready to parry a blow. Then she realized that she really was trying to parry a blow.

She raised the staff, holding each end overhead, as Binnesman had done when blessing Carris. She did not know why she held it thus. It merely felt as if the staff needed to be held that way.

As she did, an image came to mind: the Waymaker, with his thirty-six philia and his huge paws. She could see him in her mind's eye – still running among the horde, racing toward the Underworld. He had a scar on his flank, a lance wound by the look of it. His philia drooped from fatigue. Around him, reavers marched by the weary thousands, and he could smell the scent trails of those who marched before, the whispered mutterings of pain and despair that reverberated through the horde. There were thousands of them speaking, thousands of voices that humans had never heard. The scents overwhelmed Averan.

'He's alive!' she told Gaborn. 'The Waymaker is still alive.'

Gaborn gazed at her, mouth open.

She glanced back at the wylde, eager to try something. 'Spring, come help me!' she said. The green woman came and Averan said, 'Grab my staff. Help me summon.'

Spring stood at Averan's back, so that Averan could lean back and feel her taut body against her shoulder blades. The wylde reached up, grasped each end of the staff.

Averan closed her eyes and held the reaver's image, until she found herself breathing in rhythm to the Waymaker's rasping, felt as if she ran each step with him.

He was weak, burning from thirst. The muscles in his four legs were worn. Each loping stride was a jarring blow to his knees. He knew that he was dying.

He felt too weary to keep up with the horde much longer. Yet he ran in measured terror, counting his fluttering heartbeats.

Averan felt his mind, the vast intellect. It was overpowering. She could never have reached him, could never have touched him, without the help of her staff and of the wylde.

But now shadowy fingers seemed to form in the air, and it grew cold around Averan. Tendrils snaked out through the sky, grasped the Waymaker's weary mind. She seized his consciousness, called to him desperately. 'Come to me.'

Far across the valley, a lone reaver stopped, as the others marched on. After a long moment it turned and began loping wearily toward Averan.

Gaborn's troops had all topped the hill. There was no one down on the plains seeking to slay the beast.

He was coming! Averan tried to stifle her excitement. She took the staff in hand, held the Waymaker on her own, now that he had turned.

Averan looked up to Gaborn on his mount. 'See the Waymaker coming toward us? Take me to him.'

Gaborn grabbed her arm, and swung her up before him into the saddle.

Averan held her staff high, and together they rode over the scarred plains, past Gaborn's troops, past Langley and Baron Waggit, past the sulfurous ponds and the dead reavers that lay black around them, out over the battlefield.

Sweat began to drench Averan. Holding the contact was hard work.

The Waymaker loped toward them at a sluggish pace, and stopped.

Averan could sense his consternation. He had answered her call, felt overwhelmed by her. Yet he began to panic in the presence of a human wizard. She wasn't sure that she could hold him for long.

Averan sat in the saddle, and peered into his mind.

'Show me the way,' she begged. 'For the good of both our people, show me the way.'

His consciousness unfolded to her, as gently as a flower opening, laying his thoughts and memories bare.

The Waymaker was a powerful reaver, his intellect deep, and his memories vast. He had fed upon the brains of

Waymakers before him – an endless line of them that spanned thousands of years. The knowledge came to her in a blur.

Reavers recall scents far better than men recall words or images. So the map of the Underworld that began to take shape in Averan's mind was a map of scents.

The map revealed the meanings of various warning posts that would tell how to open secret doors, or find hidden tunnels, or avoid dangerous beasts.

The Waymakers had traveled far in the Underworld, had even sailed the Idumean Sea in boats made of stone. They had followed paths that other reavers feared to tread. Averan recalled wonders and horrors and the positions of ancient duskin ruins and other historic sites.

She climbed from her saddle, stood before him.

The great reaver merely knelt, overcome by exhaustion. He was huge, towering above her, peering at her with philia that merely twitched.

She stared into his mind, sifting his thoughts.

He had come to the Overworld to begin mapping it, to study its paths and blaze new trails. It had been a grand adventure, a journey that promised danger and excitement. He knew now that it led to death.

Chapter Sixty-one: PASSAGES

We are often called upon to make our way through dim passages, never knowing whether they open into shadow or to light.

– Jas Laren Sylvarresta

Borenson stumbled upon Fenraven shortly after setting Myrrima adrift in the stream. His mind was reeling with fatigue, and his sight was blurry. He stood looking for a long moment. The dilapidated village sprawled on a small hill, open so that morning sunlight played upon the thatch roofs of its cottages. Around the village, the fog still held thick upon the moors, so that the hill rose up like an island in a sea of mist. It had a gate that stood halfway open, and beside the gate were braziers where dwindling watch fires burned. Silver mirrors behind the braziers would reflect their light, focusing it onto the road.

Borenson staggered forward, feeling as if every muscle in his body were slowly transforming into pure weariness.

The inn at Fenraven was a small affair, with nothing more than a single room. It was in the process of being vacated by a pair of gentlemen from the south.

The mistress of the inn was cooking breakfast, morning savories with mushrooms and chestnuts. Borenson was worn to the bone, and heartsick. All of his thoughts were on

Myrrima. But he had a job before him still, and he knew he had to keep focused for a little while, at least until he went to sleep. He sat on a stool, and solemn pain settled into his back, between his shoulder blades.

As he waited for breakfast he asked, 'So you've just the two boarders? No one came through in the night?' His voice felt rough, as if from disuse.

'In the night?' she asked.

'A man – a lone rider with sheepskin boots on his horse?'

'No!' she said, in exaggerated horror. 'He sounds like a highwayman, maybe, or worse! There's assassins on the road, I hear. They found the body of Braithen Towner nine miles down the road yesterday morning.'

Borenson wondered at that. Assassins on the road still. Raj Ahten's troops down here probably hadn't heard about the fall of Carris. It might only have been a random assassin. But Borenson wondered. He couldn't escape the feeling that the fellow had been searching for him.

He rubbed his gritty eyes, all done in, and ate a small bite of pastry while the other guests vacated the inn.

Afterward, he told the mistress that he would be leaving when he woke, and asked her to go about town purchasing supplies for his trip to Inkarra. Here at Fenraven, he was but a hundred miles from the mountains at the border, with few cities between.

He went to the single room and found it more than adequate. It was clean and cozy. The straw beneath the mattress was fresh, and the mistress's daughter took out the old blankets and brought in new. He didn't have to worry about fleas or lice.

The food had been good, and the stableboy knew his business. Borenson felt well provided. It was his first chance for some real rest in days, and without an endowment of stamina, he needed it sorely.

He lay down on the cot, and began trying to think about the coming journey. Tomorrow he would have to go in search of some endowments of stamina. An upwelling of sadness took him. He couldn't think about anything but Myrrima, the taste of her lips, the feel of her cold body beneath his arms as he placed her in the water.

He ached not for himself, nor even quite for her. He felt that the world had lost something beautiful and needful and glorious.

His eyes were so gritty, he closed them only to ease the pain, and fell into a deep slumber.

He woke hours later, and came awake only slowly.

He became aware that there was a guest in his bed, and that it was night already. It was common for guests at an inn to share beds when necessary.

But it wasn't common for a woman to share a man's bed, and he could tell by the smell of her hair and by the light touch of the arm that wrapped around him that a woman lay beside him.

He came full awake with a start, bolted up.

Myrrima was lying next to him.

'What?' he began to ask.

Myrrima climbed up on an elbow, stared at him. Outside, there was a slim moon, and stars filled the night, shining through an open window. No one else was in the room.

'Are you awake, finally?' Myrrima asked.

'How –!'

'You put me in the water,' Myrrima said. 'I was weak and nearly dead, and you gave me to the water.'

'I'm sorry!' he said, horrified. He'd thought her dead for sure. But she sat here looking as healthy as ever. Her clothes were dry.

'It's all right,' she said. 'I've discovered something. Averan isn't the only one around here who was wizardborn.'

Borenson was filled with a million questions.

I should have seen it before, he realized. I should have known it from her every manner, the way she's gentle when she needs to be gentle, the way she's hard when she needs to be hard, the way her touch soothed me, just as the touch of the undine soothed me after I slaughtered the Dedicates at Castle Sylvarresta.

He'd sensed something in her. But only one word came out of his mouth. 'How?'

'The water took me,' Myrrima said. 'I dreamt of it – of clouds heavy with moisture and waterfalls that misted the air, and of brooks that tumbled over clean stones. I've always loved water. I dreamt of the great wizards in the ocean depths, and the strange and wondrous things there. The water healed me, and would have taken me out to sea, out beyond the Courts of Tide. I could have let it take me.

'But I realized something,' Myrrima said. 'I realized that I love you more. So I came back, to be your wife.'

Borenson stared at her in dumb amazement. She had not truly died, he could tell. She had been near it. But she still had her endowments of glamour. Belatedly, he realized that he had put her in the water knowing that, on some level. His mind had been muddled from exhaustion, so weary that it could think no more. He'd been watching her face for some sort of transformation, for that moment when her endowments departed, but it had never come.

That's why he'd felt that placing her in the water was an act of betrayal.

More than that, he realized how truly she loved him. She didn't just want to follow him to Inkarra. She'd just given up a chance to serve the Powers, to become a wizardess and live in the sea. Few who were born to such a fate could resist the call of the oceans.

Myrrima leaned into him then, and kissed him. Borenson felt his body respond to her. Binnesman had healed him, beyond his wildest hopes or imagining.

The room was empty but for the two of them, and finally he felt ready to love her in return.

'I guess I ought to pay that wizard more than a pint of ale after all,' Borenson teased. He held her passionately for a long moment, and pulled her close.

As afternoon waned toward night, Erin and Celinor rode out of Fleeds, through southern Heredon, and into the borders of South Crowthen. As they went north, the land got drier, and the colors of autumn leaves lit up the countryside.

Erin had not slept last night, dared not sleep again. Yet all day long she considered the words of her dreams, the talk of the dangerous locus Asgaroth who had come to destroy her world. She did not speak of it to Celinor, for she considered that if she did, he might think that she was raving.

Yet the owl's words had pierced her, inscribed knowledge on her heart. She suspected that the owl had summoned her, that perhaps some part of her even now was trapped in the netherworld, awaiting further instruction.

She believed that something more than a mere Darkling Glory was on their world – that a locus had come among them. She craved to know more about it, yet dared not succumb to fatigue.

Guards met Erin and Celinor at the border, several hundred knights and minor lords who had set bright pavilions along the roadside. The borders here were hilly, and filled with bracken. A few dozen carts and horses had stopped as merchants tried to pass the roadblock.

As Erin and Celinor rode past, one old man recognized Celinor and shouted, 'Prince Celinor Anders, speak to your father for me. I've traded with him for years, eaten at his own table. This is madness!'

Celinor made to ride past the roadblock himself, but pikemen blocked the way. A young captain led them. He was dark of hair, like Celinor, and nearly as tall. His eyes had a fanatical gleam to them. 'Sorry, your lordship,' he said. 'I have orders to let no one cross.'

'Gantrell?' Celinor asked. 'Are you going blind? Or have I changed that much?'

'These be dangerous times,' Gantrell apologized. 'My orders are clear: no one in, no one out.'

'Even your crown prince?'

Gantrell gave Celinor an appraising look, said nothing. Erin could imagine the turmoil in the man's mind. If he let Celinor through, he would be violating orders. If he didn't, Celinor would hold it against him for the rest of his life – and King Anders was rapidly getting old, declining in health.

'I'll let you pass,' he said cautiously, 'with an escort.'

Celinor nodded. 'That would be appreciated.'

'But not the woman,' Gantrell said, glancing at Erin. She wore a horsesister's simple attire – a woolen tunic stained from the road over her leather armor.

'"The woman,"' Celinor said, 'is my wife, and will someday be your queen!'

Gantrell tilted his head to the side and cringed, as if he had just recognized that he'd made a mistake that would cost him a career.

'Then,' he said, 'welcome to South Crowthen, milady.'

He bowed curtly, and Erin rode into South Crowthen under heavy guard. Knights rode at every side – a dozen ahead, a dozen behind, a dozen to their left and another to their right. Gantrell rode beside them, and kept sneaking sly looks at Erin.

'Am I under arrest?' Erin demanded when she could take it no more.

'Of course not,' Gantrell replied. Yet he did not sound sure of his answer.

Sweat poured from Averan. She held the Waymaker with her mind, absorbed his knowledge. Without having tasted the brains of other reavers, she would not have been able to make sense of it all. She concentrated on building a mental image, a map of the Underworld. As she did, all other sights and sounds were gone. She was not aware of the scents of the day, or of the noises, or of the time that passed.

When Averan broke contact, she collapsed in a swoon.

In a daze she looked around her, saw that night had descended. With the sun departing, the air had cooled. She had searched the Waymaker's memory for hours.

The Waymaker lay before her, dehydrated, rasping its last. Its mouth gaped with each breath, and the philia around its armored head hung like rags. The creature would not survive the night.

Gaborn had stayed beside her all this time.

Now he picked Averan up, held her in his strong arms. 'Come,' he said, 'let's get away from this monster. It's still dangerous.'

He won't eat me, Averan wanted to tell him. But she didn't know if that was true. Besides, she could hardly work her throat. Her mouth was dry, and she felt so weary, so drained, that it wasn't worth the effort to speak.

Gaborn carried her a dozen yards, to a cart. A driver sat atop it, rubbing his eyes, fighting sleep. The team of horses stood dozing in their traces.

'What happened? Where is everyone?' Averan managed to croak. Her head was spinning.

'You've been standing over that reaver for hours, for the whole day,' Gaborn said. 'The rest of the knights are following the horde south. But Binnesman is here, and his wylde.'

'Good,' Averan said. She always felt comforted in Binnesman's presence. Overhead a fireball raced across the sky. It left a churning red trail of smoke behind. Almost immediately she saw another flash of light, and another. Everywhere in the sky, the stars were falling. Dozens came in the space of a few heartbeats.

'What's going on?' Averan asked, as Gaborn put her on a seat. He climbed up beside her. The driver cracked his whip, and the cart lurched forward.

'The One True Master has bound the Seal of Heaven to the Seal of Desolation and the Seal of the Inferno,' Gaborn answered. His jaw was tight. 'We must break those seals.'

'You mean it's already done?'

'Already,' he said. 'And there's something else. I suspect that the reavers defeated Raj Ahten at Kartish. Now the danger is . . . far more immediate, and growing by the minute. Do you know the way now to the Place of Bones?'

'Yes,' Averan said with conviction.

'Can you tell me how to get there?'

'No,' she said. 'Not if we had a month.'

'Will you lead me then? While you were busy, Iome brought some men – a facilitator and some vectors. I've already taken endowments of scent. I can smell the reavers' words here, thick on the ground. But I can't make sense of them.'

Averan shuddered. She had glimpsed the Underworld through the eyes of reavers, through the eyes of the Waymakers who knew it best. The journey would be long and perilous. Worse things than reavers lay before them.

Her thoughts seemed muddled.

The darkening skies yawned wide, and stars dropped from the firmament. What happens when they all fall down? she wondered. Will the night go dark?

She shuddered again. This is not what she'd have wanted from life.

'Take me to the vectors,' she said. 'I'll lead you the best that I can.'